friends and lovers

Also written and edited by John Preston

Fiction
Franny, the Queen of Provincetown, 1983, 1995
Mr. Benson, 1983, 1992
I Once Had a Master and Other Tales of Erotic Love, 1984 (Short Stories)
The Mission of Alex Kane Volumes I–VI
The Master Series

Edited:
Hot Living: Erotic Stories About Safer Sex, 1985
Flesh and the Word: An Erotic Anthology, 1992
Flesh and the Word 2: An Erotic Anthology, 1993
Flesh and the Word 3: An Erotic Anthology, 1995

Nonfiction
The Big Gay Book: A Man's Survival Guide for the Nineties, 1991
My Life as a Pornographer & Other Indecent Acts, 1993
Hustling: A Gentleman's Guide to the Fine Art of Male Prostitution, 1994
Winter's Light: Reflections of a Yankee Queer, 1995

Edited:
Personal Dispatches: Writers Confront AIDS, 1989
Hometowns: Gay Men Write About Where They Belong, 1991
A Member of the Family: Gay Men Write About Their Families, 1992
Sister and Brother: Lesbians and Gay Men Write About Their Lives Together, 1994
Friends and Lovers: Gay Men Write About the Families they Create, 1995

edited by john preston
with michael lowenthal

friends and lovers

gay men write

about the families

they create

A DUTTON BOOK

DUTTON

Published by the Penguin Group
Penguin Books USA Inc., 375 Hudson Street, New York, New York 10014, U.S.A.
Penguin Books Ltd, 27 Wrights Lane, London W8 5TZ, England
Penguin Books Australia Ltd, Ringwood, Victoria, Australia
Penguin Books Canada Ltd, 10 Alcorn Avenue, Toronto, Ontario, Canada M4V 3B2
Penguin Books (N.Z.) Ltd, 182–190 Wairau Road, Auckland 10, New Zealand

Penguin Books Ltd, Registered Offices:
Harmondsworth, Middlesex, England

First published by Dutton, an imprint of Dutton Signet,
a division of Penguin Books USA Inc.
Distributed in Canada by McClelland & Stewart Inc.

First Printing, April, 1995
1 3 5 7 9 10 8 6 4 2

 REGISTERED TRADEMARK—MARCA REGISTRADA

LIBRARY OF CONGRESS CATALOGING-IN-PUBLICATION DATA
Friends and lovers : gay men write about families they create / edited
by John Preston with Michael Lowenthal.
p.   cm.
ISBN 0-525-93858-3
1. Gay men—United States—Family relationships.   2. Gay
communities—United States.   I. Preston, John.   II. Lowenthal,
Michael.
HQ78.2.U5F75   1995
806.87'08'6642—dc20   94–41345
                                                        CIP

Printed in the United States of America
Set in Garamond No. 3

DESIGNED BY STEVEN N. STATHAKIS

editor's note

When John Preston became ill at the end of 1993, he asked me to work temporarily on the manuscript of *Friends and Lovers* until he was well enough to resume editing. A few months later, when it became clear that he would never be well enough to go back to work, John officially transferred the editorial duties to me. We talked in the final weeks of his life about his intentions for the collection, and I have done my best to honor those intentions in bringing the book to completion.

John placed great importance in acknowledgments and dedications, and in that spirit, I gratefully dedicate this book—his book—to the memory of John Preston. He claimed that finishing this anthology was my gift to him, but it was much more his gift to me—one of the uncountable number he gave. He will always be an inspiration.

contents

friends and lovers

introduction

It has finally come into our vocabulary that Tom is my significant other. After eight years, we have finally acknowledged what to others has probably been self-apparent all along.

Tom cares for me virtually every day, and when he cannot be with me himself, he arranges for others to help. He buys my groceries and keeps his Tupperwared lunches in my refrigerator. He knows which underwear I want to put on any given morning, and which drawer he'll find it in.

Tom's significance is more than logistical. He is my medical and legal power of attorney, the one who if and when it comes time, will decide what measures should be taken to let me live or die. He will plan my funeral. He is the sole beneficiary of my will.

These are usually roles fulfilled by a lover, but Tom is not my lover. Although he has spent many nights in my apartment, we have never had sex. There's also a big difference in our ages that kept me from bestowing a name on our relationship. I'm forty-eight and he's twenty-seven. But to call us merely best friends denies the depth of who we are to each other.

I met Tom when he was a student at Colby College, head of the gay student group, such as it was. He was also trying to set up a lesbian and gay youth group in Portland, where I live. I agreed to advise them on certain matters and donated a small amount of money to get them started.

I was intrigued with this kid, who had the outward appearance of a jock but an intellectual spark in his eyes and a voracious appetite for literature. (I eventually came to introduce him as the only set of twenty-inch biceps that can quote William Blake.) Tom kept hanging around my place, even when there was no youth group business to discuss, and that Christmas I discovered that he needed a vacation job, something to earn money when he was in Portland. I had stacks of paperwork to do and needed someone to help me with filing and getting photocopies made. It was an obvious match.

Tom reorganized my entire office. He labeled dozens upon dozens of hanging files and alphabetized them in long metal cabinets. This was the kind of detail work that he actually enjoyed. Tom continued to come back most weekends when he was home from Colby. Soon he was my official assistant.

Tom also took on the role of reading and critiquing my manuscripts, and very quickly I saw that he did a good job at it. He was unrelentingly tough on my writing, but with the kind of severe love any good editor must possess. His support of my work became a major part of our relationship. This support became especially important as I undertook projects like *The Big Gay Book*, a logistical nightmare that was quite tedious and required his organizational skills. (Which translates that he's compulsively organized and controlling.) The acknowledgments pages of my various books from that point on, through *Hometowns* and *Flesh and the Word*, right up to my most recent book, *My Life as a Pornographer*, read like a record of our evolving friendship.

Our relationship worked so well in the beginning because we each had something to give the other. I was the experienced activist, the gay rights pioneer who could provide Tom with details and perspective on our history. He was the young organizer, whose enthusiastic curiosity inspired me to continue documenting our lives. We did begin with an obvious power dynamic: I was the one paying Tom for all the office work he accomplished. But everything felt very mutual, not proprietary. His editing of my manuscripts helped maintain a balance.

I am conscious of using Tom in ways that he doesn't use me, mostly because he is so strong. I'll say, "Tom, it's time to get the fifty-pound bag of dog food," and he'll say, "Oh, okay." He moves my furniture. He constructs my bookcases. It's incredibly handy to have him around the apartment and it's also great fun to watch him lift and flex.

And Tom is wonderful to take to publishing events, since he's so young and so muscle-bound that the New Yorkers fall all over themselves. I've brought Tom and some of his ex-boyfriends (who are equally well-endowed) to various literary functions and created fantastic "buzz," as publishing types like to say. Victor Zonana once told me he only realized why he wanted to be a writer after he attended the Boston book party for *Flesh and the Word*, where Tom and his friend Mark were bartending bare-chested. "I want to have an entourage like that," Victor said.

But the unexpected dimension of my relationship with Tom, the real depth, came with my HIV diagnosis. In many ways, the progression of my disease has been the progression of our friendship.

Tom was already working for me when I was diagnosed. He was one of the first people I told, in fact. It was a Saturday and he was down from Colby and working in my apartment. What would he do if he knew that I had AIDS? I asked. He looked at me and said, "I'd hope I was brave enough to take care of you."

Tom was nineteen years old when he first told me that. I didn't *want* him to be a caretaker, I wanted him to be able to take advantage of all the options in life that the gay world had created for him. This was the time in his life when he should be most free, not burdened with responsibility. But he was the one who proved himself to be the most trustworthy and available of my friends.

I had seen too many people who were unable to have any control over their lives and their illnesses because they hadn't done the necessary background work. I was healthy enough at the time, my T-cells hanging steady, but I knew it couldn't last forever. I knew I wanted to give someone a medical power of attorney and other legal functions. It finally came down to Tom.

He wasn't there for the drawing up of the documents. Since he was going to be in charge of all my affairs, it wouldn't really have been appropriate for him to be the witness. So I went down to the attorney's office with my friend Pam and had her cosign the relevant papers.

When everything had been duly notarized, I went home. Tom was waiting. I carefully explained all the documents to him. He would have to keep them at his house, just in case they were needed.

He seemed distressed by the whole encounter, but, uncharacteristically for him, he said nothing. He just took the papers and went to work. He was a lifeguard at the time, at the local YMCA. Just a while after he had left, he called me. I could hear the sounds of the swimming pool in the background.

"John, there's just one thing I need to know."

"What?"

"Do I have to bury you?"

I thought he was asking if he would be responsible for the cremation that I'd asked for, or for setting up any ceremony, but when I began to explain that my family would probably handle those details, if he didn't want to, he interrupted me. "No. No. I mean, do I have to bury you? Do I have to put you into the ground?"

"Tom, I don't think I'm going to care," I said.

"Great. Then I'm not going to. I'm going to get a fancy urn and I'll put your ashes in it and leave it on a mantel or something like that, somewhere I can see it all the time and I can get mad at it and yell. Okay?"

"That would be fine, Tom. It'll be up to you to do what's best."

And then he hung up.

Since then, Tom has been my constant companion as I have navigated through the twisting channels of HIV and AIDS care. He made it clear early on that if he was going to be involved, he had to be *involved*. He would have to accompany me to every doctor's appointment. I was amazed during one of those first visits when Tom whipped a notebook out of his bulging backpack and began scribbling down everything the doctor said.

I have always been somewhat intimidated by the medical establishment. They've earned all those impressive credentials, and I haven't. But Tom never hesitates to interrupt the doctor and ask him to explain something again in plain language, or how to spell some complicated disease. His notebook is an up-to-date record about drug trials, blood counts, and nutrition. He's my own personal AIDS encyclopedia.

One morning in May of 1991 I woke up suddenly in excruciating pain. The slightest movement was agony. It took me minutes to reach the telephone—a foot from my bed—and call a friend. Soon I was in an ambulance and then in the emergency room of Maine Medical Center, an oxygen mask forcing breath into my lungs. I had a raging fever.

Tom arrived shortly, power of attorney in hand, and began running the show. He took care of the paperwork, called my family and closest friends, and followed the doctors through every step of their hunt for what was wrong. X rays were taken, blood was drawn for tests. I had numerous doses of morphine to relieve the pain in my chest so that I could pull more air into my lungs, but the drugs didn't touch the pain. My fever went up again to 104 degrees. I was crashing and burning.

By the end of the day, I had been seen by pulmonary specialists, critical care specialists, infectious disease specialists. They all agreed that if my breathing didn't improve soon, emergency procedures would have to be taken: an opening in my throat, a respirator, something.

Tom spent the night. He was desperate to do something and began to keep cold cloths on my forehead. They seemed to heat up and dry out as soon as they touched me. He kept rotating the compresses, using them to fight the fever, and sometime before dawn my temperature finally began to drop. Once it started, it fell rapidly, moving away from the brink just before the deadline the doctors had set for more emergency measures.

I eventually learned it had been a bizarre form of pneumonia, not Pneumocystis but a sudden and dangerous attack. If things had gone just a little differently, the hospital staff was absolutely sure I would have died. The nurses all credited Tom for pulling me through. He had literally saved my life.

After ten days I was told I could check out of the hospital. The doctors had watched Tom by my side throughout the entire process and they were convinced that I would be well cared for at home. I was convinced as well. Despite my misgivings about burdening Tom with too much responsibility, I knew I had made the right choice.

Tom's mother wasn't as lucky as I had been. Soon after my own near miss, she succumbed to cancer, a long and drawn-out process that really took it out of Tom. I saw him wrestling with questions about morality and justice and acceptance, the very same issues about my own death that I was dealing with. When his mother finally did die, Tom seemed to transfer many of his feelings for her to my own mother. Both women were strongly independent

New England matriarchs, so the connection was natural. Tom and my mother developed a relationship with each other totally independent of me. They adore each other. She told me she was very disappointed last year when he didn't show up in Medfield for Mother's Day.

As I have become sicker in these last few months, it has been gratifying to see Tom get even closer with my mother and with my sister, Betsy. When it became clear I needed somebody to stay with me every day to help cook and clean, the mundane logistics that become insurmountable hurdles for someone confined to bed, Tom arranged a weekly rotation where my mother comes up Mondays, a friend on Tuesdays, and Betsy on Wednesdays. It comforts me to no end to drift off to sleep, hearing the sound of Tom and my mother, or Tom and Betsy laughing in the next room, telling jokes and family stories.

And it's been so many years now that Tom really does feel like a part of my family, or that he *is* my family. We can fight every once in a while, but never for more than a few days. When we do bicker, we tread over and over the same old ground—the way it is with a longtime lover. I think he's a superb writer and I bug him to produce; he thinks he has nothing to write. I think his drive for monogamy is compulsive; he thinks my bachelorhood is.

Tom now has a healthy cynicism about our relationship that feels very familial. Sometimes I long for that time when Tom was nineteen and desperate for knowledge about gay life; he'd happily do my filing, organize my papers, run errands, anything to be around here. He used to put up with the animal hair and the cigarette smoke without complaint. Tom, of course, isn't impressed at all now. He never hesitates to point out all my faults. But when somebody else levels a complaint, Tom is the first one to leap to my defense.

After so many years Tom and I have developed the kind of telepathy that lovers and family have. My sickness has made it clear just how much this is the case. Tom never has to wait for me to ask for a certain kind of food. Just as I'm about to say how much I'd like a bowl of tapioca or a Carnation instant shake, he presents one to me. If I'm starting to sweat through my undershirt, he has another one on the bedtable before I've said anything. And it's always the right color.

I think it's our extraordinary level of closeness that confused me for so long about what to call Tom, because there are really no models for our relationship. I've joked about being his Daddy, but that never seems to work—he has a real father whom he loves and who lives just a few miles away. Besides, "Daddy" has all sorts of sexual implications for me, and Tom and I have never been genitally sexual. (He has told me he has fantasies about accompanying me to leather bars in a collar and no shirt, that sort of thing, and we do look at each other occasionally and wonder why we don't have sex—but we both know it's too late in the relationship for that.)

I got by for a while by explaining that he's some sort of an adopted nephew. The nephew/uncle relationship is an important one in my family. I was particularly close to a great-uncle who died when I was in high school, a gentle bachelor whom I've been told was probably gay. I remember walking with Uncle Ducknick through the forest surrounding our family's summer cottage in New Hampshire, having the kind of long, intimate conversations that can only happen when there's a generation's time between two males. I like the idea of re-creating that dynamic with Tom. Our own generation gap certainly provides much fodder for our friendship.

Maybe the nephew status would have worked for Tom at the beginning of our relationship, when our roles were more clearly distinguished. But who we are to each other has changed and evolved dramatically since then, often reversing itself. My emotional caregiving for the young college student has turned into his vigilant attention to my medical needs.

Which brings me back to the recent revelation that Tom is my significant other. I know some people don't like that term. It's too generic, sometimes even euphemistic. But for Tom and me, I think it's an accurate description. He is the most significant other person at this stage of my life, the one who knows my emotional and physical self more intimately than anybody else.

As my illness progresses, Tom's significance becomes more clear on a daily basis. What is left of my life, and my eventual death, will quite literally be in his hands. I would trust no person more to be in that position.

Gay men have historically created our own families. For some, it's a question of replacing traditional "blood" families that have denied or expelled us. For others, it's simply a natural evolution of maturity. As we seek to define our lives on our own terms we gather a chosen network of people to nurture and care for us.

Everybody has friends. Gay men have no monopoly on camaraderie.

But perhaps because we have so often been separated from the automatic kinship of our blood families, gay men seem to approach friendships with a certain self-conscious determination. Just as students of a foreign language often understand the rules and exceptions of that language better than its native speakers, gay men can see the nuances of "family" with the clarity of outsiders. We make a concerted effort to master the rules of a form most straight people take for granted.

At the same time, gay men have always been rule-breakers. The very fact of our having sex with men contradicts the basic assumptions on which our society is based. As pioneers in a new life, we have been willing—and in some senses forced—to experiment with new forms of social interaction.

The many different forms of social and intimate relationships gay men enter into are the focus of this collection. This book is a conversation among gay men about the people who are most important in our lives. The writers included here tell personal stories about their friends and their lovers, about how it feels to be a gay man living today among other gay men. Some relationships described will automatically be seen as important family-substitutes, such as long-term lovers, adopted sons and siblings. Others might seem shallow or frivolous at first—a favorite bar, a movie-making collective—but they still may perform the function of families in our lives.

Gay men are notorious joiners. Look at the events calendar of any gay newspaper and you'll see weekly meetings of the gay Alcoholics Anonymous, the gay fathers' group, the gay volleyball team, ACT UP, an s/m club. On more personal levels, gay men often enter into communal activities such as vacation time-shares, reading groups, and, in previous years, consciousness-raising groups or living collectives.

A major question posed here is what if any connection there is among these various kinds of relationships and activities. Does being a member of gay AA fulfill the same function as having a long-term lover and an adopted child, or being in a gay political-action group, or joining a gay syna-gogue, or having a gay lunch group at the office, or becoming close with a lover's parents?

Soliciting essays for this collection, I didn't establish any single ideal for what a "gay family" should look like. I left it wide open for writers to tell who their friends and lovers are and how, if at all, these relationships constitute new kinds of families.

Not everything in this book is perfect. Every relationship does not work wonderfully, and not everybody lives happily ever after. We learn as much from our failed attempts at creating families—and from those people who disagree with "family" as a goal—as we do from our most lasting bonds.

A special note must be made about the place of AIDS in this collection. There is no essay included about being an AIDS buddy, or in an HIV support group, or a chapter of ACT UP. Yet AIDS is a dominant presence throughout the book, as it is in our lives today. As my own illness has brought into sharpened focus the important role Tom plays in my life, so too have HIV and AIDS affected many of the writers represented here.

The obituaries which we have all become so accustomed to reading and writing in these past few years stand as a metaphor for the questions raised in this book. Whom do we list as our survivors? By what names do we call them? For all its devastation, the AIDS crisis has had the positive effect of demonstrating who our friends and lovers are, and reminding us just how important they are. The way a family functions together is brought into high relief during times of stress. This has been abundantly true with gay families—and the collective family of all gay people—during the AIDS epidemic.

It was hard to be gay when I was growing up. There were no models, no road maps to follow, and no guides on how to go about creating them. The series of anthologies of which this is the third—*Hometowns: Gay Men Write About Where They Belong, A Member of the Family: Gay Men Write About Their Families*, and now *Friends and Lovers: Gay Men Write About the Families They Create*—has been an attempt to create those models and road maps for the generations of young gay men who will follow.

The essays in these books are engaging stories that make for compelling reads. Many are emotional tales, some are humorous. But they also serve as documents of how we gay men lead our lives. Not that every gay man has to follow the models set forth in these collections. These are just a few examples, a few specific stories. Readers may find themselves reflected in these essays, or they may find that they have their own ways of being gay and creating gay families. Above all else, the message I hope people take away from the books is that they have options. That is what we have been fighting for all along.

m i c h a e l   l.*

gay aa
a family
of my own

For Bill P. and Michael Z., with love

Okay, I admit it: I don't know where to start. This, of course, is the Writer's Nightmare—that there are stories to be told, that *must* be told, if only the critical point of entry can be found. Most of the volitional act of writing involves trying to find the thing to say, and the voice in which to say it, that will make all the rest say itself. Sobriety is like that, too. First you're drunk, and then you're sober. You may want to be sober for years, but you

* Michael L. is a writer and a member of Alcoholics Anonymous. He omits his full name in observance of the Traditions of AA, which state: *". . . we need always maintain personal anonymity at the level of press, radio, and films"* (from *Twelve Steps and Twelve Traditions*, published by Alcoholics Anonymous, copyright © 1952).

    It is always dangerous for the program as a whole when one member of Alcoholics Anonymous undertakes to single out his or her own personal experience for the public, no matter what the reason, because the program only works if the "common welfare" of the fellowship comes first. I have set down a fraction of my experience in sobriety here—the part germane to my own family story—not as a guide to recovery in AA or any other Twelve-step recovery program, nor as an example to anyone who is working or may need to work such a program, only because it is impossible to talk about what the program has given me without identifying myself as a member. I could not bluff my way through this writing speaking of "a codified program of recovery," which is what we are encouraged to do instead of specifying membership in AA. No one should make the mistake of thinking that there is only one way to achieve sobriety, or use that fear to keep from contacting AA should he or she feel the desire to stop drinking. There are as many paths to sobriety as there are people to walk them, and AA is gentle and broad enough to accommodate them all.—*M.L.*

cannot stop drinking, until suddenly, mysteriously—some would say miraculously—you do. After that, if you're as lucky as I have been, or perhaps "exceedingly blessed" is a more accurate phrase, your sobriety stays sober for you even on those days when life becomes unbearable and a drink seems to be the only possible answer, solution, or escape.

And no matter how sober you may be, there are days . . . and successions of days . . . during which life *is* unbearable. But that's what Buddha and boys who are not yet jaded are for—respite, if not salvation.

Finding the beginning. I wanted to start with one of the well-turned family anecdotes I tell that make people gasp gleefully at what we grandiose gay artistic types had to suffer as the children of middle-class suburban grims. But humor has left me for the time being, and neither benevolence nor serenity has yet replaced it. And so I will stick to the facts, as much as I can, and hope that they are as eloquent as they are, at least, tangible.

The essentials are these: My name is Michael L. and I'm a gay alcoholic. I joined Alcoholics Anonymous in Los Angeles in August of 1976 to stop drinking. What I was given by the gay men who were sober and getting sober in the City of Angels in the late seventies has enabled me to stay both clean and sober for eighteen years, as of this writing. More than anything, I was given a sense of family as a positive and nurturing place—not the dark and dangerous island I had experienced as a child (a kind of Jurassic Park of the fledgling psyche).

The long solitude of my life was lifted for the first time when I walked through the doors of AA. I was twenty-nine years old and could not have told you the last day I had not been drunk, hungover, or craving alcohol. It had been, I can promise you, years.

Of course, you'll want to know something about the family of my genes. Otherwise, how can you understand what an extraordinary difference the universe of AA is from that of my parents' house (always *their* house, never *ours*—my presence always tentative, and by their sufferance).

Mine is not a dramatic story at all. There were no wire hangers, no movie-star harpies wailing in the night. I was not forced to eat gruel or clean the cinders from the kitchen fireplace, nothing so picturesque, nothing that implied a happy ending somewhere to the right of the final illustration. I was, simply, the only child of high-school-educated, white, Anglo-Saxon,

Protestant Republicans—one among millions born in the first bombs-bursting-in-air year of the Baby Boom, 1947.

I grew up in a clean—no, a Teutonically and obsessively *immaculate*—well-lighted tract house surrounded by African violets and relatives who ate and drank, and frequently made merry—within reasonable limits (namby-pamby moderation was always king). The long-haired Lutheran God was often quoted (or, rather, misquoted), but material possessions seemed always to be held in higher regard than human emotions (at least *my* emotions), which were allowed no place in our home. Nor were deviations of any kind. My parents are addicted to normal.

Ironically (or perhaps as a result), I was a precocious, talented, even difficult child. My parents did not want to hurt me, I am sure, but they did—not because they were evil, but because they are unenlightened and unremarkable, leading guilt-free unexamined lives with the blindered determination of their generation. Affection was tendered along with clothing, shelter, more than enough food, and plenty of toys. But I was never allowed to feel that I deserved succor. Gratitude was the required response, and I came to feel like the object of duty rather than love. And nothing I was given began to compensate for not having siblings, particularly a brother, which I deeply desired.

There was a second pregnancy, in 1949, aborted after my mother contracted German measles (probably from me). But I didn't know about that for decades afterward. It was the Family Secret. Correction: It was *one* of the family secrets. Secrets are a way of life in families, in my family at least. In AA they say, "You're as sick as your secrets." It's a sentiment as true as true gets. The Catholic Church got it right (in this one, rare instance): Confession *is* good for the soul.

What haunts me still when I see my gene donors in their unchanged native habitat is how rigorously they have insulated themselves from everything unpleasant, difficult, or even annoying, and how thoroughly they have based their lives on the essential middle-class delusion that the absence of pain is equal to pleasure. And how doggedly determined they were that I would have no identity separate from the one they imposed upon themselves.

And I find myself sadly unable to forgive them for their relentless repression of everything human or unique about me. My mother actually told me, when I was twelve or so, not only that I had no right to express an opinion, but that I had no right to *have* one. I was instructed that I was ordinary and unattractive; that my intuition was unfailingly faulty; that I would surely fail to survive without them; that the pursuit of the arts was for the truly talented only (not for me); and that I should go out and play with other boys. Who loathed me.

What my peers saw was what I saw in myself: a fat sissy who liked music, art, and learning. I spent my childhood in solitary confinement hiding who I was, and frequently wishing I were a girl, just so I could stay safely sequestered in my room to read books instead of being forced to mow lawns, weed gardens, wash cars, polish bathrooms, dust, vacuum, and clean out basements and garages every Saturday of my life until I left home at eighteen. I passed my childhood in a constant state of terror, subject to violent headaches, fits of anger, cruelty, and despair. And shame. Always— and still—a burning sense of immutable transgression.

Was it Larry Kramer who first pointed out that we queers are the only minority people born into the enemy camp? Without a sibling, there was no ally in the face of injustice. I felt like a song bird in the company of lobsters; to the outside world, I was a rhinoceros rampaging through a well-managed Serengeti of impalas.

All right, then, some family stories.

My father recalls my first night home from the hospital after my birth. Apparently I had the infantile temerity to cry. Mr. Y-Chromosome woke up, came into my room, and bellowed into my crib that I should be quiet. I did not cry again. I did, however, dream of Daddy as a razor-fanged monster, and expression became as necessary as air.

The year I was eight, I used my allowance to buy candy for myself instead of a Mother's Day gift. My mother did not speak to me all day. I was in tears, frantic to know what I had done to so grieve her. She finally said she was deeply disappointed with me, that my thoughtlessness and selfishness had hurt her, because being a mother was the most important thing in her life. Many things became clear to me in an instant: that I was a selfish wretch; that my purpose in life was to fill her needs; that the rituals and outward shows of love were more important than the fact of love; and that my mother's affection was not a given. Rather, it had to be wooed and won, pandered, catered, and sacrificed to—or it would be withdrawn.

That year, conscious even then of my own loneliness, I asked for a dog for my birthday. I got, instead, another character defect: I was too *irresponsible* for a dog. And so I got a parakeet instead (a creature within my mother's tolerable limits of biology). The day we brought this booby prize home it bit me, and I washed my hands of it (thereby proving my irresponsibility for all time). I began to drink—truly—that melon-ball-salad afternoon, draining the cut-glass highball glasses of each of my adult relatives at my backyard birthday barbecue.

For my senior prom, my parents gave me insanity. "You must be crazy," they told me when I mumbled over one of our interminable family dinners (attendance required) that my intended date was one of the half-dozen African-American students at my school. I was dumbfounded, and told these Christian racists at the kitchen table that I saw no difference between black people and anyone else. "You don't even believe that," my mother said, as she had said so many countless times before. "You just say these things to upset me." I went to my prom with a white, Anglo-Saxon, Protestant girl whose name I no longer remember, and whose loopy whey-faced expression in the photo that was taken of us that night is now repulsive to me, so symbolic it has become of my cowardice.

And so when I hear the awful words "traditional family values," I think of repression and hypocrisy, of narrow-mindedness, bigotry and lies, of bartered affection and the crushing of spirits, of indifference to real needs, of claustrophobia, castration, asphyxiation—of always being wrong. No wonder I came to find more authenticity, more honesty, in the hustle of Times Square than I ever experienced in the living room of my parents' house on Long Island. At least on Forty-second Street the bargaining was not covert. As addled in my thinking by drugs and alcohol as I was, there was ample reason for my predilection for life lived without apology or sham, in the raw survival state, without the Early American trappings and Hummel figurines.

When I hear the words "traditional family values," I picture myself as a child so lonely I stayed home from school one day to search for adoption papers; as a junior high school outcast who put pinholes in my father's condoms because I could no longer go on being alone with these creatures who claimed they loved me and kept telling me I was crazy; as a teenager who felt I had no one to talk to and nowhere to turn to unburden myself of my horrible, increasingly sexual secrets; as an adolescent who spent week-end evenings drinking alone in strip-mall gin mills with the disreputable fathers of my boyhood friends.

Abuse? I don't know. But it was bad enough. I find I identify fully and absolutely with the emotions recounted by victims of full-blown child abuse. When I hear of the children who are beaten, tormented, flayed by their parents, maimed, mangled, stuffed down drainpipes and crushed in trash compactors, I want to murder. These real crimes against nature seem different from my childhood only in degree. Power, and the abuse of power— How can traditional family structure be about anything else when heterosexual men (these predators in the nest) are at the apex of the social pyramid, from families and churches to armies and nations?

And so when one fine night at a gay AA meeting in the early years of my sobriety, when someone referred to our sober band of merry men as his family, I stepped to the podium shaking and said, with venom dripping from my voice, that "I would not demean the gay men of Alcoholics Anonymous by likening them to my family."

But I have skipped over the colorful part of my story, the drinking days. And they were a kaleidoscope, though the rainbow was far from benign, the ribbons not sweetly pastel but livid, lurid, tawdry—all of them tinged with bile and, occasionally, blood.

I was on the lam from my family as soon as I left for college. (I was, of course, forbidden to apply to my college of choice—the University of Hawaii, the most distant American campus I could find.) And I drank, prodigiously, while coming out awkwardly in the every-fag-for-himself days before Stonewall. I drank to shut out pain and confusion. I drank so I could feel a part of the world. I drank to loosen inhibitions. I drank because a boy I loved did not return my love. I drank because a woman I did not love was pursuing me with a sexual agenda as draconian and surreptitious as my mother's. I drank over insights such as these.

I drank at the opera and in porn theaters. I drank at home and in bars. I drank secretly and hid alcohol. I drank openly and brazenly. I drank one drink and lost control; I drank a dozen and felt nothing. I stole alcohol. I stole money to buy alcohol. I stole money, period. I lied. I maligned people who were kind to me, people I cared about and needed for support. I was a self-centered, self-righteous, self-obsessed opportunist. At one party I had sex with a man in a shower while his wife and assembled guests pounded on the bathroom door begging him not to submit (though he had been more than encouraging). I drank in the morning. I drank through every rule I had about not drinking.

Once I had to be restrained from throwing a garbage can through a liquor store window because I wanted a drink in Connecticut on some holiday when no alcohol was sold. I used drugs, naturally—grass, poppers, pills, LSD, mescaline. At a party in London with actors from the National Theater I got so sick on a combination of scotch, brandy, and hashish (hallucinating on the patterns the vomit made as it slid down the sides of the toilet bowl) that they trundled me into a cab, afraid of the scandal it would cause if I died at their soigné Knightsbridge soiree.

But vomiting was not unusual for me. I threw up often. Sometimes I passed out or blacked out. I came to not knowing where I was or *who* I was. I was analyzed, evaluated, and cleared for commitment at a mental health facility. I was arrested and jailed. I was an animal, wounded and panicked. I was in a state of constant humiliation over my behavior. I was depressed, destructive, and suicidal, of course. A braggart and a coward. A snake and a babe in the woods. I walked the streets of New York, Los Angeles, San Francisco, London, Vienna, Berlin . . . alone, seeking love desperately and finding, at best and only occasionally, sex.

I have the following image of myself from the last days of my drinking: After a night at a gay bar in which I do not speak to a soul, but lust after many a body, I walk slowly through the cruisy part of town. Unsuccessful, as always, I careen home, where I strip, pour a water tumbler of Johnny Walker, and make a peanut butter and jelly sandwich. I am already so drunk I can't really eat or drink. I stumble around the apartment in the dark, bouncing off walls, splashing the booze over my now-enormous girth, dripping jelly onto the bare wooden floors, slipping in the candied fruit, spilling the liquor trying to get up. Finally I navigate to a seat by the window, where I sit, teary-eyed, watching my neighbors make love until I manage, somehow, to fall into bed. Alone. Always, always alone.

By the time I entered AA I was introducing myself as the "fat fairy nobody loves" and referring to myself as "God's little irony," the "little" being ironically applied, since I had the measurements of a sow—the very nickname my school chums had given me back home on the idyllic Long Island of my graceless youth.

Suffice it to say that the first time I heard the term "low self-esteem" at an AA meeting, I thought it was something to aspire to. I had passed low self-esteem so many years before 1976 that even "self-loathing" didn't seem adequate to express my contempt for who I was, or who I had become. Everyone pays a price for alcoholism, and this was the price I paid. It didn't seem unreasonable at first, but, like the disease, the price one pays is progressive, the inflation rate geometric. The more one runs away from the feelings that cause self-destructive drinking, the more alcohol it takes and the higher the cost to mind, body, and that most elusive but sensitive entity, the soul.

I moved to Los Angeles on July 28, mentally exhausted after a tempestuous three-year relationship with a spitfire named Roberto. (In a classic exertion of self-will, I picked him up in a bar on St. Patrick's Day in 1973 after deciding earlier in the day that what I needed was a long-term lover.) I was bankrupt in every area of my life.

It was raining the day I arrived at LAX, which was not a good sign at all. I moved into borrowed quarters in a town about thirty miles north of the misnamed City of Angels, where I would be teaching come September. I started drinking at the discos of West Hollywood, where I was being, as usual, completely ignored by the bronzed and muscled beauties who seemed to find both happiness and gay life so effortless. The traffic bumps between the lanes of the California freeway system kept me alive: They jolt you awake when you nod off at eighty or ninety miles an hour. I was on a crash course with disaster. I called it, in my charmlessly elitist neoclassical way, fate (translated, of course, from the Greek).

Now, it's difficult to explain why an alcoholic suddenly believes that sobriety is desirable, necessary, or possible. And yet, after all those years of drinking, and without even consciously *wanting* to be sober, I took my last drink at the Biltmore Hotel in downtown L.A. on the eleventh of August, 1976, between my first gin and tonic of the day (shortly before noon) and my anticipated next nightly binge.

I was at a professional convention with my old friend Leda, a lively and unpredictable African-American woman who was a drinking buddy left over from drama-school days. She wasn't drinking, and I wanted to know why. She looked me in the eye—right there on that Spanish rococo Biltmore Hotel staircase that has appeared in a thousand films I have seen since—

and told me she'd joined AA. I was shocked, since I'd never thought her drinking was excessive. It was certainly not nearly as out of control as mine, and maybe that was the trigger. I agreed to go with Leda to that first meeting—to see what it was like for those I knew who needed it, I believe I said. But go I did. It was the turning point of my life.

The Wednesday night Los Feliz Group meeting of Alcoholics Anonymous is held in the low-slung basement of a Lutheran church in unfashionable eastern Hollywood. I hated the venue, the Lutheran church I grew up in having become to me the living symbol of revolting two-faced, backbiting racist bullshit (about which I have not changed my mind a bit).

But the meeting was a lesson. In this room, which seemed at the time the size of a football stadium, was every kind of person Central Casting could muster, from well-known actors to street people, people of every color and social, ethnic, sexual stripe. They were all sober and they were all laughing. Strangers smiled and extended their hands to me. They gave me phone numbers. They said, "Keep coming back." They said, "Sit in the front row," and, unused to taking direction as I was, I sat, smoking ceaselessly, between Leda and a man named Roy.

Although I do not remember all the details of that first meeting, I do remember that I heard a man named Peter speak from a podium about telling lies—and about one lie in particular. As a cover for his gayness, he said, he had created an imaginary child, only he could never remember how old the child was getting to be or what his name was, and so he was constantly caught in his lie, though this did not stop him from perpetuating it. Hundreds of people laughed aloud at the story. This was not the kind of thing that ever happened in my family. If you made a mistake, you suffered for it inwardly or were ridiculed in public from time to time, but there was no opportunity to air the error of your ways. ("I'll forgive you," my mother once said after I was caught stealing large amounts of cash, "but I'll never, ever forget.")

When I told my parents I was queer, in a fit of pique at the age of twenty-four, they said they were not surprised (my sixth-grade teacher had taken the unenlightened liberty of predicting as much), but we would not speak of it to anyone else in the family. Unfortunately, alcohol—the social lubricant—also had a liberating effect on my tongue, and I couldn't refrain from veiled references to my homosexuality in the presence of dozens of relentlessly heterosexual cousins—all of whom either knew or suspected I was . . . special.

After making a sobbing spectacle of myself at one cousin's wedding, I did not speak to a blood relative for fifteen years. In AA there is no silent treatment, no deafening silence; in AA I heard a healing cacophony of supportive human noise.

I was transported—not just by the ambience, but by the specifics of the first story I heard from an AA podium that first night, from a man I still admire and respect. I, too, had become a notorious and inefficient liar. Starved as I was for real family affection, I, too, had created a child, and had been caught in the web of my own lies over and over again. I felt the old shame, but the laughter that came from that group of recovering alcoholics dissolved my self-disgust. It said, in effect, that there was hope for a new life. You can become your better self, it said. Your problem is not that you are evil; your problem is that alcohol has led you away from your truth and has caused you to act in ways so alien to your essence that you feel abandoned and without hope.

"Pitiless and incomprehensible demoralization" is the phrase from *Alcoholics Anonymous*, the so-called "Big Book" of AA, the repository of the nuts and bolts of sobriety, and the basic text of the program. These people did not say, "Toe the line and we will tolerate your presence," as my parents said. The men and women of AA said, "We welcome you whatever and whoever you are. We embrace you *no matter how far down the scale you have gone.* You can find sobriety here and peace. You never have to drink again."

And I never have.

I met people at my first AA meeting in 1976 who are still friends. Roy became my first real sponsor. He lives on the other side of the country now, but has watched the arc of my growth (as I have watched his) and is, unquestionably, a brother to me—or at least is the best kind of brother I can imagine. It was he who listened to the fearsome inventory of past wrongs the AA program offers as its fourth of twelve steps of recovery.

A written record of the harm we have done to others, my "fourth step" was also a kind of massive, instant confession, cutting through my isolating, larger-than-life secrets like an obstetrician's scalpel severing a cancerous umbilical cord. I was, from the moment I read that rambling, confused, mortifying document to Roy, gradually released from guilt, self-abasement, regret, and the power of the past. Or perhaps my emancipation dates from the symbolic burning of the dreaded manuscript in the barbecue on Roy's West Hollywood patio.

One of the basic principles of AA is that you cannot keep your sobriety unless you give it away, and so the spirit of selfless generosity predominates. As newcomers arrive, with that same look of dejection (or proud hauteur), the sober members put out their hands in welcome. There was no self-congratulatory nobility about this. We did it for ourselves, so that we could stay sober. But the result was that more and more people came in, cleaned up, and prospered. No one required a Mother's Day card or outward shows of gratitude. They only suggested we each treat the newcomer behind us as we had been treated, and it was very little effort at all.

As a gay man, meeting people had always been difficult for me, homophobic rejection being implicit in every encounter. One of the first questions I ever asked in an AA discussion meeting was, "How do I get rid of the enormous resentment I feel to heterosexuals?" And so it was to the gay men of AA that I adhered, in fact, bonded. For a year, I went almost exclusively to gay and mixed gay/lesbian meetings at a center devoted to our recovering community. And our need is great.

Among minority groups only Native Americans are more devastated by alcohol than homosexuals. We queers smoke and drink too much. It is as if the rate of alcoholism is directly related to the extent of social alienation. The Coors people know this, which is why they are so irritated by the gay and lesbian community's organized boycott of their beer (a reaction to the homophobic policies of Coors family members and the right-wing political action groups these profit-participants support). In the world of alcohol advertising, we are a disproportionately high market share.

The ad-placement folk at ultra-hip Absolut vodka know this, too: Why else would they plaster their product on the back pages of *Out* and *The Advocate*? Because they support our political agenda? They buy our attention and good will not just because they know we have disposable income, but because they know we too often internalize homophobia and treat ourselves as disposable people, squandering that income on better-than-average, higher-than-healthy quantities of hooch.

But this is all personal rant. Alcoholics Anonymous itself takes no position on sociopolitical matters—or on anything at all. In all things, what

I write here is the opinion of one cantankerous gay member of AA. But it is clear to me that it is precisely *because* alcohol, drugs, and tobacco are self-destructive that they appeal to the insecurities of a community consciously singled out to be rendered insecure by a majority culture. And because this low self-esteem is imposed by the majority culture on *purpose*, the high rate of alcoholism in the gay and lesbian community may be said in some serious measure to be an effect of homophobia, the same genocidal hatred that causes such a sadly large number of our adolescents to commit suicide.

This, too, is why the Twelve-step recovery process has become almost a "movement" in our community, so clearly is self-destructive behavior linked to exactly the kind of low self-regard produced both by racism and homophobia. And why being clean and sober has repercussions in the community (and why the Sober contingent in New York's annual Heritage of Pride parade is the biggest and most supportively received). Unfortunately, the very fervor—perhaps even self-righteousness or *over-zealousness* of some recovered gay men and lesbians—turns off some addicted men and women who could benefit from recovery. The point of recovery is not social justice, but individual growth in the context of a support group with common experience.

The bottom line is that Alcoholics Anonymous is not for people who need it, but for people who want it. As for explaining the program to nonmembers . . . Well, said a Greenwich Village wag recently, it's like trying to blow out a lightbulb.

Abstractions aside, my *experience* is that the lesbians and gay men of AA opened their arms and their hearts to me. There was always someone to listen to everything I had to say, no matter how "incorrect," naive, or hostile. I was no easy baby in AA, either. I was, at twenty-nine, angry and resentful of everyone and everything. I was pigheaded, contrary, defiant. I even threw the Big Book at a meeting secretary once because he gave me an answer I didn't want to hear. He didn't strike out or punish me. In fact, he laughed and said, "Keep coming back."

No one ever told me to leave or threatened me with banishment. No one ever suggested there was any line over which I could step that would be cause for my exclusion. This was a club with an open membership policy, and everyone was equal ("Our leaders are but trusted servants; they do not govern"). As I began to believe it, I began to trust. You can be disinherited by your family, cut off, written off, ignored. But the only requirement for membership in Alcoholics Anonymous is the desire to stop drinking.

Because I was using being gay as an excuse to drink, it was necessary to find sobriety in the presence of sober gay men and women. On the first anniversary of my sobriety, I was given a party by my sober gay friends. The next day I celebrated at a "regular" AA meeting, and said that I was a sober gay alcoholic who had not taken a drink or drug for 365 days. And that I was unknown to most of the people in the room because I knew that if I were to regain sanity along with sobriety, I had to find my roots with my family of queers. I was welcomed with applause, with hugs and kisses, and invitations to share my story at other meetings.

The acceptance touches me to this day. After all the hatred I had felt in the world, I felt little or none in AA (except from some of the older queens who seemed threatened by all the public affection among the whippersnappers). I found the courage in AA to stand up to homophobia, and when I found it, I confronted it. People listened, apologized. Some, looking for the first time at the real and potential consequences of their bigotry, actually changed their behavior. AA was a family in which each member is, by design, as much concerned about the welfare of others as about his own. In that respect, AA is the idealized "good parent" of us all.

Despite the ease at which gay and lesbian members of AA move among their heterosexual fellow drunks, I am never more comfortable than when I am with my clan: those gay men who took me in without knowing a thing about me and included me in their busy lives. I was within days a member of the inner circle of young, energetic, healthy, attractive, sober and positively gay men. I had spent a lifetime trying to find acceptance in peer groups to make up for the rejection I felt at home. Nothing I did ever seemed to win me the approval I craved as passionately as I longed for a brother, a soul mate, a lover, or a second drink after a first. Here was a group as wonderful as I could imagine, and they were welcoming me in, enthusiastically, not because of who I was or what I had achieved, but because of what I was no longer doing—drinking—and because of who I would, they already knew, become.

It was in AA that I heard an extremely funny and extremely bright woman named Anne talk about a paper she was writing. She had been an unwitting fence for a Mexican mob in her drinking days and won a hearty round of applause when she said she liked her men mean-looking: "I liked 'em to look like you didn't know if they wanted to fuck you or kill you," she said, unabashedly in that same Lutheran church basement. Now she was a graduate student at UCLA writing about AA as a tribe, in the tradition of Native Americans.

There are suggested rules of behavior, she explained, that exist for the common good as well as the good of the individual. All persons in the tribe have equal status. There are no classes or castes. There is no sin. There is no judgment. There is no punishment. There is no ostracism. "Transgressors" are brought back into "grace" by the love of their peers, not by the verdict of their "betters." Anne has long since died, but her message is still with me.

My first boyfriend in sobriety was also sober under a year. His name was Andy and we were trying not to fall into the sack because of the unwritten but often repeated caveat that it was better in one's first year of sobriety not to enter a romantic relationship. Had we tried harder, we might have made it, but we fell in love before our first anniversaries, and for a while it was bliss. We were both teachers. We were both sober and idealistic. We told the truth and wore each other's clothes. We were not jealous or possessive.

When it was clear that it was ending, we let it be over. It was the first relationship in my life that caused no scars and in which I did not feel in some way responsible for inflicting damage. It was, in short, a perfect relationship. That it did not last forever did not diminish it. I had learned how to be an adult gay male in love with another adult gay male supported by the love of a gay male peer group. We held hands at meetings and older men sighed at the way we looked into each other's eyes. And that felt very sober and very good, indeed. And it still feels good whenever I think back on Andy and those mad days, because I love him still and wish him better than life has, alas, given him.

Always, no matter what happened in my life, and no matter what time of day or night, there were allies: people to talk to, people to allay guilt and assuage fear, to offer direction. Sometimes it was straight women or even straight men, but most of the time, for me, it was gay men, my warrior brothers, the boys who were never there when I was a boy. My wounds, I felt, were healing. When I was in trouble, I did not even need to pick up the phone. It was as if some telepathic message would go out to the world, and a program friend would call up to find out how I was. If I said I felt like I needed to cry, tall tan Marty said "cry," and I cried. I learned from these men to have emotions, to trust and respect my emotions, to express and even to love them, not to shrink from or hide them, as I had been ill-taught as a child. "You're too sensitive," my mother had drilled into my head. "Your vulnerability is your strength," my sober compatriots told me.

Recovery, after all, is about learning to feel, and then learning to live with, emotions we drank to suppress. It is not about etiquette or social niceties, although we socialized like demons, and tore up the dance floor at Studio One. We were determined that sobriety would be a means to a life, not a life in and of itself. After a year, I had lost an enormous amount of weight, looked good, felt good, and was acting like my own definition of a decent human being for the first time in my life. My emotional needs were being met. I felt safe.

Of course, I bitched about being single. "Your time will come," they said. It came. I met Ben, a man who would be my lover for ten years. I became part of his family in San Diego: a gay brother, a father, and a stepmother who called at six o'clock on Sunday mornings, but was, at least, supportive. Ben and I went to dinner and to parties and movies with sober gay couples, many of them, like ourselves, interracial couples. Our holidays were rich with love and without anxiety. They became celebrations for me, not tests of loyalty, as they had been in my childhood.

When my first book was published in 1985, I showed it to my parents. It shocked them of course, since it told the truth, and told it from the perspective of an urban gay male who had come of age unhappily while drinking and using in the late sixties and seventies. They dealt with it as they deal with anything unpleasant to them: They never mentioned it. It became a non-thing, my first precious volume, another dirty family secret.

My sober gay friends crowded into steamy bookstores just to hear me read a few pages. They bought copies and asked me to sign them. They gave the book as gifts to friends. I was the guest of honor at parties. And so my sober family got to hear about my second book. My parents still don't know it exists.

I am sure, theoretically, that it is better not to live in a ghetto, that the broader one's circle, the richer one's life. And I have known some wonderful heterosexuals, both in AA and out. But the company of sober gay men—even in the writing world I live in—feels more like family to me than any group of relatives I have ever met.

The strength of family, of course, is the extent to which it copes with crisis. And my gay AA family has done that, as diminished as it now is. When dear Joey slipped back to drinking—as he frequently did—we'd haul ourselves out to find him and drag him back to meetings. This was the bottom line: You had to be sober for anything to work. Beyond that, support came on *your* terms. If you wanted to give up your law career and become a surf bum, you were loved. If you wanted to go straight and marry a woman, you were loved. If you wanted to move to Texas or Montana or New York or sleep with your mother or your sponsor or spend your life in a bathhouse or write thinly disguised autobiographical erotica, you were loved. It was unconditional, and I was not used to it at all. I require it now, and that's why I find it still difficult to visit my biological family. I leave their home on my rare visits feeling stiff and sore, as if I've been subjected to an overstrenuous and nonconsensual evening of spiritual bondage.

Soon, of course, everything in this world of love changed. Death would come to the tribe in the form of AIDS, just as the U.S. cavalry came to destroy the people of the Great Plains (armies do not like tribes). I don't remember who was first—was it Joey, whose vanity finally got the better of him, or irascible Charlie, whose anger, we thought, could easily kill a virus? It doesn't matter, of course. What I remember is the mourning, the depth of it, the authenticity. I remember us all together in groups, hugging, weeping, holding on to each other for survival.

I can remember, too, when I was eighteen years old and my Aunt Helen, my angel of a godmother, died. She was the only adult I'd ever known to love me *because* of who I was, not in spite of it. I remember standing in that damp and gloomy Catholic church in Westbury at her solemn high requiem mass (purchased along with a reversal of her excommunication for having married outside the faith). I remember sobbing uncontrollably, and being told by my mother to stop crying, that I had to think of my Uncle Jack, whose loss was greater than my own.

When one of our tribe fell, no one ranked our right to mourn in our own way. No one catalogued the need to weep.

Soon the deaths were closer and more devastating. Beloved Lee, who smiled so hugely while he played the piano, and who welcomed me to my very first gay AA meeting with a plate of cookies and a grin, moved to San Francisco, started using drugs again, then died, just hours before I managed to reach the hospital by phone.

Then came the hardest death of all. Kenny became my sponsor in 1979 or '80, when Roy moved out of town to pursue his career. I had never and have never met a man so unlike me and so like me at the same time. We met at my first meeting. In time, I came to speak to him every day, to see him nearly every day, to confide in him absolutely, to trust him more like another aspect of myself than the soul mate he surely was. Our one fight was over a man (Kenny scored—and got crabs!), but we worked it through, vowing never to let anything come between our friendship again.

It was Kenny who drove me to the hospital the day I thought I was dying (it turned out to be kidney stones). Kenny who threw me a fifth anniversary party on his front lawn. Kenny who opened the universe to me. Who gave me what it took to believe in God in the days God still seemed like a real possibility. Who even told me I could sleep with his lover if we both wanted to. Kenny was . . . my Kenny.

Before he told me he had AIDS, we spent a day driving up the rainy California coast, stopping at Muir Woods, alone with the giant Sequoias, the wet silence, and our own mutual unromantic and nonsexual love. I felt as peaceful and complete as I have ever been.

Kenny died in the dark silence of a Lake Tahoe dawn just three days after I managed to get in a final visit, on Columbus Day of 1987. A photo I had taken of him, along with another of the stunning seaside sunset we found the day of our long drive, hung on the wall of his room. His sister was there. The rest of his family had been expelled for sniping over the terms of his will (he left the money to his lover). He wanted to know all about my trip to Spain, from which I'd just returned. He looked at all the pictures. Finally, when we were alone, he asked me how I was doing.

"I'm fine now," I said. "Whenever we're together, I know everything will be all right."

"I'm glad," he said. "I thought you might be having trouble with this."

I looked around the room at the oxygen tanks, the jumble of medication, all the evidence of his imminent departure. "I'm sure I will," I said, "after you're gone. But as long as I'm with you in the here and now, I'm actually fine."

"I wanted to make sure you'd be all right," he said.

"I don't think I will be," I said. "I need you."

"You know everything I know," he said calmly, in that special way of his that reassured me every time. But he was, it turned out, mistaken. And I have not yet learned to feel joy without him in this life.

"I think it will be this weekend," he said when I didn't respond. "Now that I've seen you, I've done everything I need to do."

The call came that Sunday morning. I walked out onto the deck of the apartment, not even crying, and looked down to the street. And there, as if in double image over a car parked there, I could see—actually *see* Kenny—as I had many times, sitting in the driver's seat of the convertible he loved so much. He was wearing a rainbow-colored shirt and was smiling. He waved, put the Caddy in gear, and drove off down the street. Then he made a left turn, smiling and waving at me as he disappeared behind the Hassidic kindergarten at the corner. And this "vision"—this unexplainable thing that replays in my mind to this day—has been a secret until now.

There are deaths that become as much a part of you as the lives before them. This was one, and I am not yet over it, by any means. There are days, like today, that I cannot even look at the picture of Kenny on my wall without missing our San Francisco brunches so much I sob. At the time, I was destroyed. I called everyone I knew who knew him. We spoke endlessly. We wept together. We raged. We even managed to laugh, to joke, to keep that gay humor pumping. We were helping each other heal.

The sadness continues. Dear Bill, the beach and bathhouse buddy of my early endless summers, is HIV-positive. His Michael, who cooked such a magnificent turkey one blissful Christmas Day at Kenny's house. They fight it together—and bravely. Sweet William, the first man I sponsored to celebrate a year of sobriety, and who has just celebrated fifteen, is HIV-positive, too, but is healthy, works hard, has a new lover, is optimistic. Roy, who has buried two lovers now, calls when times are hard for me to make sure I'm hanging on. We talk and laugh, despite it all. We look out for each other, even when we are dying. And despite the pain of death, we keep putting out our hand to the new ones limping through the door on self-hatred and a beer.

At the March on Washington in April of 1993, I wandered dazed through a flood of people—how many hundreds of thousands of our people? For a man who becomes claustrophobic in even small crowds, my comfort was astonishing to me. But these were my people, and I felt no danger from them. At one point, waiting to step into the line of the march, I saw a familiar face, the third of the three Bills who has been so important in my recovery life, a sober gay man from Los Angeles I hadn't seen for years. His face lit up and he threw his arms around me. Then wheeled me around into the arms of Art, another program friend.

I met Art, a self-proclaimed "overassimilated Mexican," at my first AA meeting, Bill at his first. Bill, who is elegantly black, was clearly nervous. He was, bless his heart, wearing a suit, as I was at my first meeting—as sure a sign of a newcomer in L.A. as sweats and shakes. I sat down next to him, introduced myself, and explained everything that happened, emphasizing over and over that there are no rules in AA—only suggestions. And no timetable.

Over the next few weeks, we met for meetings, went out for coffee. He asked questions, I offered what experience, strength, and hope I had to muster by way of answer. That was a decade ago. He's still sober and, although it's not true, he credits me with getting him that way, just because I took him by the hand and talked him through his first week (as Roy and Kenny and Art and Lee and so many others had done for me). I was only a guide through unfamiliar territory.

So there we stood, three old sober friends in the middle of a multitude, just for a moment, basking in our own history, having passed down the "generations" of sobriety, blood-brothers in our special way.

When I am with my biological family at holidays—at Christmas, for example, at my cousin Lory's—and I watch my Aunt Rose surrounded by her children and grandchildren, and my mother gushes over and over about how wonderful it is to watch, and I suffer the pangs of a gay only-child whose parents yearn for grandchildren, and I am tempted to feel the loneliness of being a single, middle-aged, disaffected American queer in the middle of a widening plague, I think of my tribe of sober gay men, those still with me and those who have already gone, and I feel them in my heart. I know that I am a twig in the forest of sobriety. And I feel peace.

Home, Robert Frost wrote in "The Death of the Hired Hand," is "the place where, when you have to go there,/They have to take you in." And, in my experience, he is right. My parents will always take me back into their home no matter what happens between us. But Frost wrote, too, the next, less frequently quoted lines: "I should have called it/Something you somehow haven't to deserve." The family home I found in AA is the place you don't need to earn, yet nothing is begrudged. There is no accountant at the table. They rejoice to take you in, even if you are once again drunk as a bishop—as the father of the prodigal son rejoiced to take back his beaten-down child. They don't even have to know your name.

It saddens me to watch the witnesses of my life slipping out of this world so soon, so incomplete—my wild first lover, Roberto, my best college friend, three of my student puppies at least, the boys of summer who were my companions in the salad days of sobriety. But the family of AA is about "the common welfare" as much as it is about the people we are given to love along the road, the "principles *before* personalities," we are told. And the limitless love I have received from men I have loved is always as near to me as the next meeting, as near as a telephone.

And still, they keep coming, and their need continues to be as great as mine was when I first walked through the door. And when Kenny died, I met Eric, another sober gay writer. And when my Ben and I broke up, I met Michael. And after Clark died, there were David, Ira, and Jim. And on and on it goes in the widening gyre. Sober gay men who are my world and my strength as I stumble and "trudge the road of happy destiny."

I was promised many things when I first walked into AA. The old-timers said that alcoholism was a disease of isolation, and that I would never have to take a drink or be lonely again. I didn't know what they were talking about, and I certainly had no reason to believe them. But they didn't lie. They have never lied.

andrew holleran

friends

A Sentimental Education (Flaubert's novel) begins with two men we first meet mustering the courage to enter a brothel on the outskirts of a provincial town in France. Years later, at the novel's end, we see them again on the same spot, back home, reflecting on all that has changed them since that day. For a book with such a solid frame—two scenes as solid as bookends —the bulk of the novel is made up of the most unsolid, trivial, flimsy of material: the ordinary, minor incidents of friendship. Nothing momentous happens. The two friends go to Paris, borrow money from each other, start a magazine, acquire mistresses, drink and eat out; when something History would regard as significant, the Revolution of 18__, occurs, our protagonist leaves Paris for the Forest of Fontainebleau with his girlfriend to sit it out. Considered Flaubert's masterpiece by many critics, reading it one would be hard put to say anything was going on except the bland, mundane passage of Time—the tiny incidents involving friends that seem insubstantial to everyone but them.

Yet novels about friendship keep drawing writers and readers over and over again: From Rona Jaffee to Mary McCarthy, the shelves are filled with fat paperbacks on this theme—I suppose because most of us have friends, and nothing seems more interesting to us than the way we go through life together. That is, we measure not only time, and life, but ourselves against our friends, even more, perhaps, than against our family, since only our friends are comparable to us in age and ambitions.

At the same time, nothing is so difficult to write as a novel about friends, simply because what happens to friends, the high and low points of a friendship, is so mundane—summers at the beach, school, trips, jobs, telephone calls, nightclubs, dinners, love affairs (experienced or witnessed), the problem of how to support oneself solved or not solved. None of it is earth-shattering. There is hardly a scene in all of *A Sentimental Education*, for instance, I can remember, except the first and last; the rest is the soap opera of friendship. If, before the plague, a writer had been trying to compose a novel about a group of gay men in New York—based, of course, on the lives of his friends over the years: how they met, changed, grew closer or farther apart—he may well have been stopped by the sheer lack of dramatic content. Who, really, finds our friends interesting except ourselves? Yet, in real life, one devotes quite a bit of time and attention to them. A man who doesn't marry spends more of his time and energy, no doubt, on friends than one who does marry; they become for him, it's been said so often (at least on every other episode of "Golden Girls"), or for anyone without immediate relatives, a family. Our late-twentieth-century American version of a family, at least.

But what really are friends?

For something considered as sentimental as friendship, the few authors whose remarks on the subject I remember are all very unsentimental indeed. Aristotle said friendship can exist only between equals, and that when this equality no longer exists, the friendship cannot be expected to exist (that it is therefore subject to circumstance). Emerson, on the other hand, said the only friendship that made sense was a friendship with a person better than yourself, someone who would improve you. Proust—who formed passionate attachments to contemporaries who inevitably failed to meet his own exalted conception of their bond—hardly let one chance go by in his great novel to point out the superficiality, disappointments, and emptiness of friendship. Which leaves us to wonder why modern Americans on talk shows often say, "My wife (husband) is my best friend," as if that—friendship—is what makes the marriage last, as if that—friendship—is far superior to sex.

Superior it may or may not be, but gay men, I suspect, at least know it's different. There is a strange and powerful taboo that prevents us from mixing friendship and sex, in the vast majority of cases. On the other hand, it always seemed to me that homosexuals were gifted with friends in a way straight men were not. In the town my family lived in, men seemed to live like lions in a pride—surrounded, as Aristotle said they wanted to be, by their wives, children and dogs. It's not that they weren't friendly—they played poker, golf, went fishing together—but once a man married, his primary emotional commitment belonged to his wife and children. Married men spent most of their time alone doing the same things (mowing the lawn, reading the paper, fixing the car) in separate yards and households. The wives had friends. The men ruled separate turfs. Often I would see my father in his chair alone reading the paper and think: Why are straight men so isolated from one another?

Of course part of this was my father's age, and when my friends in New York entered middle age, I began to see traces of the same sort of male isolation in our behavior—notwithstanding the fact that we had spent decades together in the city. The demands of a career, the solidification of individual likes and dislikes, habits, the evaporation of that adolescent desire to run with a pack, all contributed to a certain growing isolation. Each one of us had his preferences, his tastes, most of which could be satisfied on our own. And I began to think that we, too, would end up with that structural curse of men—solitary lions, with or without a pride of their own. That our emotional commitment was not so much to the other particular friends, as to other homosexuals, in general: The sea of men that could toss up, at any moment, for whatever length of time, a sexual antidote to loneliness.

On the other hand, there was always something heightened about the friendship of homosexual men—especially in a city like New York, with the sort of camaraderie trench-warfare creates. (I've always thought, despite the superficial rudeness, New Yorkers made the truest friends.) If friends are what root us, in lieu of family—if friends are the only family we have, so that in middle age, we do not abandon one another—there was always something complex and communal about the band of men who wandered the city forming erotic attachments with one another. If, when I got off an airplane, I was always conscious of the fact that none of the families crowded against the velvet rope was waiting for me, I knew that I had another sort of family waiting for me beyond the arrival gate, walking down a corridor, or someplace in the city itself, an encounter that might turn into a friend or might not. After a while, it tended to less and less—perhaps because I

already had my friends (often met this way) and they were enough. (Kier-
kegaard said marriage is an investment in Time—the years two people
spend together. So is friendship.) There is simply no substitute for permanence.

That's what families offered, and what we tried to approximate by
remaining loyal to our friends. Of course, as a friend of mine liked to say
(quoting some character in a play by Tennessee Williams), "People change
. . . and forget to tell other people." But that was all right—the point was
to change together. If one didn't have someone there to note the changes,
even change was meaningless. Part of friendship was growing up together;
and growing older. And so we put up with our friends' lovers and job
changes, and apartment crises, and depressions and new motorbikes, and
(most painful) new friends, because they were—our friends. The people
you'd be checking in with, in some way, for the rest of your life.

The rest of your life, of course, never included what eventually happened to these friendships, and these friends. If it sometimes seems everything has ended up like *Valley of the Dolls*, even without the plague, at the
beginning our friendships were full of mutual support. In New York in the
early seventies, it became apparent to a newcomer that the huge mass of
gay men one saw in the nightclubs and at the beach had divided themselves
into groups—groups that shared houses together, or danced with one another, or merely got into the same car after crossing the bay from Fire Island;
and eventually you learned that everyone had his little circle of friends, and
every circle its central figure. You acquired these units without even trying
to, consciously; they accreted, adhered, and one day you realized, without a
word having been spoken, that you belonged to X, and Y. In a big city,
you might have several of these units, corresponding to different aspects of
your life, and almost everyone belonged to more than one; but at some
point, oddly, imperceptibly, you realized your home, your fraternity, your
familial pod, was X, Y, and Z. As a friend of mine used to ask about
someone he'd not met: "Who are his people?"

Exactly. Your people, of course, had no formal, legal status; long before
AIDS, I was always discomfited whenever I accompanied friends to hospi-
tals, or emergency rooms, at having to answer the question of the doctor,
"Who are you?" with the words, "A friend." It sounded so flimsy—so
infinitely weaker than, "His brother," "His cousin," "His brother-in-law."
It sounded like a euphemism; a word that did not, could not, convey what

our bond really was. It sounded as if I'd said, "I'm gay and single in the city." It said in my imagination: "We're all each other has, at this moment." Though honored in Greek legend, the lack of legal, moral, social status our society gave to this relationship seemed obvious walking down the long, fluorescent hallways of Bellevue, teeming with families and relatives chattering in Spanish. Friends seemed at that moment a sort of failure; a poignant result of not having married; a depressing badge of infertility; a pale substitute for family.

Friendship is, in a way, all that—it's both a relief from, and an inferior version of, the bonds of family life. And because it's not as clearly demarcated as family life, its reciprocal duties are much less formal. Friends, after all, can disappoint. Friends, at the very least, come and go. Friends are not children; a man has no control over them; they don't follow him wherever he goes, a traveling circus that can strike its tent and set it up again elsewhere, a portable form of permanence. When friends of mine wanted to leave New York in the mid-seventies and move to California, I could not, though I felt deserted, tell them not to go. Yet we visited each other after our geographical split and, more importantly, wrote letters for years afterward; and the letters made us closer, as letters often do. We had been young together in Manhattan; that formed a bond that lasted; and though the letters varied in frequency, our friendship was intact, frozen in time by the very separation. The point is they were people whose lives I realized at some point I would always follow; because on those lonely, cold, quiet Thanksgiving days in New York years ago, when one felt most keenly the not-having a family (holidays are mean), we had walked across town to an apartment and gathered around the table to eat the turkey and stuffing one of us had cooked. Perhaps custom, as much as blood, makes a family.

On those days it was possible to be sentimental about friendship—but eventually one sees its limits and reality, as years go by. (Which is why Proust turned against it so, one suspects; his conception of friendship when young was so idealistic.) Having seen the way close friendships ended in New York, I began to think of some friendships as a rope bridge stretched across a chasm—one incident, one remark, could snap the whole thing and send you tumbling into the ravine. Friendship had its limits; its organic growth and decay. Sometimes it lasted longer than it should, because people were accustomed to it, or lonely, or polite, and when the final severance came, it came with the violence of its overdue end. Other times, circumstances didn't allow it to mature fully, and one spent years caring for someone you always wished you could have known much better, had you been able to spend more time together. Still others, whom you haven't seen in years, you consider very important—because friendship, like love, has to do with psychological affinities, not only circumstance. Or rather, with a circumstance you will always treasure—first love, or college, or some happy years of youth. One never quite knows why some friends mean most to you—one only gets a glimpse of the reason when the circumstances in which you've been friends change, like seeing someone in a place, or activity, you've never seen them in before.

And that's partly what the epidemic did to friendship: It changed the circumstances, utterly. And when it did, "Who are his people?" ceased to be one of my friend's favorite arch lines—an invitation to gossip—and became a very practical inquiry, the one I'd disliked answering years before at Bellevue. The plague called everything—including friendship—into question. At first, the people who died were of several categories: Men you knew of, but had never met; men you knew and liked, but did not know socially; men who were your friends, and your familial pod. There were concentric circles. And depending on how far from the center the person was, the news that he had AIDS, or was in the hospital, or had died, created different feelings and obligations. Obligations, of course, were at the heart of all this; obligations that had never been defined, or had never even been imagined, much less experienced. It was hard to say, those first few years, what motivated the men who helped in so many different ways people who were and were not friends. What surprised initially was how friendship was only one of the factors involved. What surprised was how people we did not even consider "close" friends ended up helping a particular person much more, in practical ways, than those who were. Just as the most frivolous people—the ones who seemed to care only about gossip and nightclubs—ended up the most stoic and gallant when facing death; sometimes the most brazen and nervy turned out to be terrified of illness, useless. And the shyest and most withdrawn ended up taking much of the load on their unexpected shoulders. While the close friends were so undone by the turn of events, they withdrew. And the question that everyone harbors somewhere—Who would care for me if I got sick?—was answered in unforeseen ways.

However, this was really no surprise—as the plague went on, one grew used to the idiosyncratic, unpredictable ways in which people responded to it. People did what they could, or rather, what they did. There's little more to say about it. Some friendships faded, some were deepened, some remained the same. Some kept their illness from their friends. Others did not, or made new friends, and illustrated the remark: "I don't know anyone who has the same friends after going through AIDS that he did before."

The plague is not over, and there will be many more friendships made, broken, or strengthened because of it. The strangest part of friendship may have nothing to do with the living, however. That is the realization that some friendships do not really die till both parties do. The oddest *proof*, if that's the word, of friendship is the daily thought of someone years after they've vanished; the conversations one still holds with them, the things one wishes one had said, the hope that they forgave, or understood, your weaknesses and failures during their struggle. You'll never know. Instead you find things in the newspaper you'd ordinarily clip and send them, or hear some gossip that makes you want to call them up, or learn something about a mutual friend's career you know only they'd fully appreciate. Which leads you to the oddest moment: wanting to dial someone at three in the afternoon to discuss something with a friend who isn't there. To a remarkable degree we are our friends, and as they diminish, so do we.

Years ago I saw a movie in college called *LeBonheur* (Happiness), in which, after a handsome young man's wife dies, he goes on, after what seemed to me a much too brief interval, to fall in love and marry again. The cheerful movie made me furious—implying, I thought, that people are replaceable, interchangeable. Now I see, years later, that, indeed, you do make new friends after losing old ones—you have to, if you are to enjoy life at all; because friendship is so central to life. Yet I also know that my adolescent anger with that film was correct, too—that despite the acquisition of new friends, you never, ever replace the ones you've lost; because people are *not* interchangeable. They're unique. And so is the particular friendship we had with them. That's one interpretation, anyway, of the well-known line: Ask not for whom the bell tolls, it tolls for thee.

m i c h a e l
b r o n s k i

---

i'll cry tomorrow

susan hayward,

summer nights, and the

scent of memory

dedicated to Walta Borawski 1947–1994

1994

It was a cool, moonlit night in April when I went back into Sporters. My lover, Walta, had died just over two months before and a friend had decided that it would do me good to get out. Not that I was against it—I had always loved going to bars—but stirring myself out of the house at 11:00 P.M. on a Saturday night felt not hard, simply too much trouble. We entered Sporters through its legendary unmarked doors on Cambridge Street exchanging the fragrant spring night air for the scent of smoke and hops, sex and hope. As I walked around the circular bar that dominates Sporters it was as though I was walking back through history. The history of Sporters and all of the architectural and identity changes it has been through. The evolution and history of Boston's gay male community and how our bar habits changed as we dealt with age, career changes, and AIDS. And, of course, my own history. Sporters seemed to embody, at least on this night, a living, breathing history in which memory and time hung, suspended together: the past portending the future, the future overcome by the past.

Sporters was the first gay bar I ever entered. It was 1971 and the joys of gay life were manifest, exciting, and ever-so-slightly dangerous. As I walked through the bar now the music—some pre-disco/post-disco rock beat that had an R&B flavor; Martha and the Vandellas in a time warp— seemed to be eerily reminiscent of twenty-three years ago. I felt a little unsteady socially and emotionally; Walta had been sick on and off for almost two years and my bar socializing was off-time, unsyncopated to what was happening about me. I walked to the back of the bar and remembered that in 1971 there had been a pool table there, and sometime in 1975 a cut-away serving entrance to a now-long-gone pizza parlor that would supply hungry queens with slices and subs during the late afternoons and early evenings. The coat-check room was still there, augmented by a small leather-goods shop. In the 1970s the coat-checker was a tiny, bubbly, elderly woman—she must have been in her late seventies—named Mary Brown. Standing behind the battered, wooden Dutch door she would camp with the queens, exchanging gossip and dish. So much of a fixture was she that a hand-painted sign above the door proclaimed MARY BROWN'S COAT CHECK—and most men tipped her a dollar, a queenly sum in 1971 when beers cost less than that. Mary was reputed to be an ex-Floradora Girl, but this seemed unlikely given her short stature and the leggy gracefulness of those just-past-the-turn-of-the-century showgirls.

I rounded the corner of the bar to see the disco room—an addition that came sometime in the mid-1980s—and remembered how that change seemed to signal the end of an earlier time when Sporters was a heavy cruise bar, and dancing was forbidden by licensing law as well as the staunch rules of gay male social behavior. Looking across the bar into the mirrors that line the wall I remembered the nights here when I would come to visit Gerry Sawyer, one of Sporters' most popular bartenders and a friend and sometimes trick; one of the first friends to die of AIDS. Gerry, at fifty-four, was one of the handsomest men in town, his five-foot-four frame perfectly proportioned, his rugged bearded face a model of post-Stonewall masculinity. Gerry was almost always in Sporters—if not working, then cruising— and lived around the corner on Garden Street. When he died the city placed a plaque to commemorate him on the corner, but they misspelled his first name. His loss to the bar, the community, the neighborhood was so deep that the misspelling seemed not to matter at all.

As I completed my walk around the bar, passing by the doors we had entered through only minutes before, I felt as though I had returned to some sort of home after a long absence. It wasn't Sporters itself, per se, but the *idea* of a gay bar to which I had returned. The gay bars of my younger days, the early years of gay liberation, were not simply drinking holes or cruising places; they were community centers, queer cultural oases in a straight desert, places to exchange information, to gossip, to discuss community matters and politics, to compare notes about life and art, to seek shelter from the storms of life; havens in a heartless world: in short, the essence and the reality of community. Is it any wonder that feeling set adrift after losing my lover of nineteen years I would find Sporters, as changed and as imperfect it was, a comfort and a retreat?

1972

I have, for years, told people that in the summer of 1972 I went to Sporters ninety consecutive nights. I'm not sure that is the exact number but it is close. Beginning some time in the middle of May and stopping weeks before Labor Day I hung out, with friends, in what we called "the bar" for several hours a night. When I mention this now people seem amazed, not because I was at a bar so often, but because Sporters now seems rather dilapidated, second-hand, and unexciting. But in the early 1970s Sporters was *the* bar in Boston. It was mentioned in John Reid's autobiography *The Best Little Boy in the World* and was known throughout the country as the most popular bar in Boston, probably in all of New England. Boston was a clearinghouse of students, and Sporters attracted the collegiate crowd. Not just those in college (the drinking age was eighteen then) but the postcollege crowd as well. After they graduated from Boston University or Boston College, Harvard or MIT, the boys always stayed with Sporters. Beacon Hill was not yet gentrified and there was plenty of cheap housing available: from tiny, studio apartments to rooming houses to cheap-share flats, Beacon Hill was the gay male neighborhood years before the South End took its place in Boston gay male life. (This was true of the Cambridge Street side of the Hill; the State House side was grander and pissier: Louisburg Square had its share of queens to be sure, but they went to the Napoleon Club in Bay Village, a piano bar that demanded a jacket and tie until sometime in the early 1980s.) Sporters was a young bar—and it was the heartbeat, the pulse of the younger gay male community.

I did not live on Beacon Hill at the time. With my leftist, SDS background, my gay liberation activist bent, my long hair, and my tendency toward social experimentation, I had lived, since 1971, in a commune in Watertown. Only two towns away—Cambridge was in between—my home life was a model of counterculture efficiency and pragmatism. We had seventeen rooms in a huge, rambling antebellum house. At any given time there were somewhere between five to eight adults and four to six children. We shared all of the cooking, cleaning, and child-care. Thursdays were my day with kids and I got them up, dressed, off to school, back from school, occupied for the afternoon, gave them dinner, and put them to bed. Besides being a seriously rewarding experience it exhausted me weekly and made me enormously more able to empathize with my mother. We shared a common bedroom and common political sympathies, we helped run a food co-op and helped arrange child care for stressed mothers. My life was a cross between Herbert Marcuse and *The Whole Earth Catalogue*, between Shulamith Firestone's *The Dialectic of Sex* and Brook Farm. Hell, we were so with it that three of our housemates were Abbie Hoffman's first wife and kids (although they didn't stay long).

I was in graduate school then, getting an MFA in playwriting and my time was my own. I cooked, I wrote, I drove kids to an alternative day-care center, and I cruised. I was living the life of which I had always dreamed: chosen family, healthy food, creative urges, and sex. The commune was mixed—women, men, straight, gay—and everyone was supportive and honest, intrigued at our differences and willing to learn from them. But what my life lacked—what I missed—was a solidly gay, completely male community. Although I had been active in a variety of leftist, progressive causes, completely supportive of women's liberation (especially after caring for six kids all day on Thursday), and totally understanding of how lesbians were excluded and oppressed by so much of gay culture, I also intuitively understood that I needed a gay male space to which I could retire when I needed. I was working on *Fag Rag*—the first national gay male literary/cultural newspaper which continues to publish, if only occasionally, today—and attended Gay Male Liberation meetings, but this wasn't enough.

Although I was friendly with all of the men in these groups (and remain so today with several) the political work in these early days felt isolating; gay liberation was a new idea, we were committed, but not really connected to a broader range, the real diversity of how men lived as homosexuals. I needed to get out and be with gay men, hang out with them, look at them, feel as though I was part of a community. Although my queerness was completely accepted in my home, I got something different, something unique and—dare I bring up such a mid-eighties word here—empowering from being in an all gay male environment. Sporters became my gay home.

Once at the bar there were always people to talk to, gossip to catch up on, and new people to meet. But most of the time we simply hung out. Sporters was our community center, our town hall, our clubhouse, and our town square. It was where we met and kibitzed, acted out and acted up (in the older sense of the phrase); we were there to see and be seen, to cruise and be cruised. If sex happened—and it did often—that was fine; if not, no big deal.

I always like to think of Sporters, at least at that time, as a logical extension of people's lives. It was not someplace that gay men snuck into, or dreaded entering, but the obvious option for socializing. My friend Jimmy Griffith, who lived in a cramped, tiny studio high on the Hill, always referred to Sporters as his living room. His apartment, barely big enough for a bed, desk, and bureau, would not have withstood visitors, so Jimmy would invite friends to meet him at Sporters. Others did as well. On any given weeknight you could find fifteen or twenty regulars standing around, visiting with friends, meeting new people, or just watching the television that was occasionally playing. There was a free buffet late every afternoon—usually cold sandwiches and chips—and a hot dinner mid-afternoon on Sundays. This mostly consisted of meatloaf, macaroni and cheese, or, for special occasions, shepherd's pie. I don't think that any of us really depended upon these meals for sustenance—although there were some older gay men (in their thirties and forties) whom I suspect lived close to the economic edge—but they created an atmosphere of common, everyday shared life. Of course you would cruise the bar—sex, as usual, was always on our minds—but that was more often than not a by-product, not a primary intention of hanging out in Sporters.

For those of us who attended Sporters regularly the bar became second nature. Bartenders knew you, friends would stop in, if only for a few moments to chat, gossip was exchanged and the ongoing soap opera of people's lives could unfold. There was always some new information of who had gone home with whom, who had broken up, who had lost his job, who was arrested in the toilets at Filene's, who was moving out of town, and who was seen spending the *entire* day in the public bathrooms on the Esplanade. Half *Stella Dallas*, half *One Life to Live*, the entangled lives of Sporters habitués were an endless stream of the boring and the cool, the fascinating and the irrelevant. We would hear stories about men we had never met, but only glimpsed across the bar, garner details about men we might trick with in two months. The tendency of queens to gossip has long been derided, but the gossip in Sporters was not petty or mean-spirited (although some queens might be), it was honest, clear, everyday communication and storytelling: contemporary oral histories that allowed us to understand and evaluate our own lives, emotions, and experiences in the light of the gay experiences of our peers and extended families.

The cohesiveness and functionality of this insular-yet-extraordinarily real world was, to me, always highlighted with the Monday afternoon weekly film series. In those prevideo days the afternoon bartender would set up the 8-mm projector and a rickety screen in the back of the bar and unreel, for several hours, some early 1940s-to-late-50s Hollywood film that usually featured some gay icon. I can remember seeing Bette Davis in *Dark Victory*, Joan Crawford in the truly-bizarre-even-for-Joan *Torch Song*, and Susan Hayward in the Lillian Roth biopic *I'll Cry Tomorrow*. I have vivid memories of watching this film and of a drunken Hayward in a confrontational exchange with her fame-stricken, greedy mother: "Lillian Roth, Lillian Roth, it's always Lillian Roth to you, Mother. Well, I'll live my life the way I want to and maybe I'll cry tomorrow. But it will be my life. My life." Later in the film, when Hayward finally goes to her first AA meeting and stands up with quiet dignity and says, "My name is Lillian Roth and I am an alcoholic," the queens watching the movie—many of whom were on their third drink of the afternoon—cheered Roth's bravery and Hayward's performance. Later, as the evening wore on, there would ripple throughout the bar some queen intoning with Hayward's haughty tremor, "Lillian Roth, Lillian Roth, it's always Lillian Roth to you, Mother. Well, I'll live my life the way I want to and maybe I'll cry tomorrow. But it will be my life. My life." It was camp, it was a joke, it was a sly perversion of life-imitating-Hollywood-schlock-imitating-real-life, but it was authentic. To whom were these men speaking, I wondered, even then: their mothers, families, parish priests, straight friends, punks on the street who would sometimes sneer at the queens entering the bar, purveyors of public morals, or maybe even some hidden side of themselves? The catharsis of *I'll Cry Tomorrow* in a darkened theater may have been personal—but in a darkened Sporters on a sunny Monday afternoon, with an audience of gay men, in the early 1970s, it was revelatory and joyful: an affirmation of the personal and the political, of community and *communitas*.

The spring/summer that I attended Sporters—the verb is specific: like Mass or the opera each appearance was an occasion—those ninety consecutive nights were bounded by very clear circumstances. Most of the parents and children I lived with in my communal home had gone on various vacations, leaving only us single people. We had a collection of part-time jobs, miscellaneous political work, books to read, and the use of a Jeep. With the children gone the strict everyday routines broke down; our responsibilities altered and adjusted, and we began to take care of our own needs. After leisurely summer dinners we would hang out, play Scrabble, and on toward eleven o'clock the gay men—myself, our housemate Dennis, perhaps Ken and Stephen from a neighboring commune—would drive off to Sporters. It was a quick fifteen minutes along Storrow Drive and the night air would invigorate us.

Besides the cruising, chatting, and schmoozing, being at Sporters was in many ways pedagogical as well. It was a space that allowed me to understand how complicated the realities of living as an openly gay man in a straight world were: What were my responsibilities to my housemates, my writing, my straight friends. How might I nourish my gay identity, create a safe space for it, and have energy left over to enjoy myself. It was here that I also realized how intricately woven the tapestry of gay life was, how boundless and how complicated the lives of gay men were. Although many of these men were not "political" in the same sense that I lived my life, they embodied the ideas of "community" and "identity" about which my fellow politicos and friends constantly argued. Carl Wittman, one of the founders of SDS, as well as Gay Liberation, once wrote in a position paper on organizing Southern factory workers, "we are people and we work with people." It is an admonishment that many political activists and thinkers do not keep in mind nearly enough. Sporters reinforced for me—no, embodied—the sense of community and political family that is the building ground, the essence of politics: its affirmation as well as its reason for being.

1994

My ninety evenings at Sporters seem like a dream now. I have new senses and spaces of community. Gay Liberation has changed the world, and my life over the last twenty-two years has changed as well. A career as a cultural critic and free-lance writer, community work, political activism, a nearly twenty-year-long relationship have all made me who and what I am today.

Going back into Sporters on that April night, two months after Walta's death, was a glimpse into the past. Life has changed since 1972; in some ways AIDS is only the obvious marker. We have had an entire generation grow up since the Stonewall riots. Disco and bathhouses are come and gone, the glittering gay seventies and the more acquisitive eighties have appeared and left their mark. Most of the gay men who lived on Beacon Hill moved to the South End in the 1980s and made Chaps *the* bar to frequent. Gay news now appears in the *Globe* and the *Times* and we have gay newspapers and gay magazines. Maybe the town-square approach to gay bars is no longer needed. We are both far more sophisticated and, in some ways, far less empathetic with one another now. Our community is so large, so open, we now rightfully refer to *communities*. Do I long for the old days? The Sporters of 1972 when community and politics seemed easier, simpler? No. First of all, time moves on—no matter what. History, age, change, and—as it has now become increasingly palpable in all of our lives—death are simply inevitable. Sometimes I think about those nights at Sporters and wonder what I had in common with all those men; what it was that made it so important for me to be there. Although I had my own clique, there were hundreds of men with whom I never spoke, whose names I didn't know, whose bodies I never touched. Men whom I'm sure I would not have even liked.

Several years ago when I viewed the Names Project AIDS Memorial Quilt for the first time I had a revelation. Immensely moved as I wandered through the patchwork of names, faces, memorials, and remembrances I began to realize that I would not have been friends with—or even liked—

many of these men. But this never meant that I did not view them as part of my community, of a common shared experience. The same is true of Sporters in the 1970s: Of course we all had nothing in common, but at the same time we had everything. In some mysterious way this is the essence, the primordial basis of our community. And the community that I had then was the basis for the community I have now. Change is inevitable, but change does not happen without continuation and constancy, without pain, and hopefully not without progress.

Walking around Sporters now I look at the gay-themed comedy on the closed-circuit television sets. Susan Hayward, dead of brain cancer in 1975, is no longer featured here but instead is relegated to the back shelves of video stores. Other ghosts flicker across the Sporters-in-my-mind: Gerry Sawyer who died in 1985 pulling the IV tubing out of his veins at Mass General when he became simply too sick and tired to live; Allyn Admundson, a Sporters regular, into heavy s/m before almost anybody else was, who jumped out of a window on Blossom Street—right across from Sporters—in 1975, taking the entire window frame with him; Bob, whose last name I never knew, who I heard died in San Francisco in 1986, although my friend George who told me said he didn't *think* it was AIDS; Douglas Bassett, who did artwork for *Fag Rag* and with whom I worked as a pastry chef for a while, whose death I first learned about when I found his quilt panel four years after the fact; Walta, who never liked Sporters (except for visiting Gerry) but who loved Susan Hayward, but never as much as Barbara Stanwyck, Greta Garbo, or Barbra Streisand.

"I'll cry tomorrow," shouts Susan Hayward in my mind. But in so many ways I am crying today. For Walta and Gerry, Douglas, Allyn, and Bob whose last name I never knew. And for the past and for the future. For how much simpler life was in 1972 and how infinitely more complicated, fuller it is now. My friends and my family live on in life, in memory, in my mind. I'll probably cry tomorrow as well. But I will have my life— richer and more complicated than anything I might have imagined on those spring evenings, the air smelling of newly blossomed trees and untried experiences, as I entered Sporters knowing that I had found a family, a community, a home.

historical notes

the collective

My years in the Gay Men's Collective of the Berkeley Free Clinic (hereafter, "the Collective") represent my first success in finding friends and lovers among other gay men. "Success" is probably not the ideal term for a period that ended in death and several kinds of dissolution, but it seems as close as anything.

The era is easy, from here, to mark off: It began in fall 1972, when I first went to the Friday night raps, and ended in early 1977, at Michael's grave. It featured a political and sexual awakening, countless groups and meetings and events, an ill-starred romance, a loss of faith, and retreat into private survival. At the start, it seemed like "the sixties" might still come to something; the end foreshadowed Reagan, and AIDS.

Lives of the forebears: an epic of sorts, untold. A few notes here, in memory.

snapshots (1)

Berkeley, summer 1972. Nixon is president, the Vietnam war goes on. Though antiwar activities have fallen off, the counterculture flourishes. On offer, among other things, are paths to enlightenment and varieties of "liberation" (connoted by bells, feathers, bare feet, incense, tea, grass, Rock, headbands, hair, living and crashing arrangements of every description). Feminists, among others, hold "consciousness-raising" groups: experience shared, oppression recognized, shame cast off. Personal as political.

Stonewall is three years past, but gay consciousness isn't high. The boys in the band persist, buying into stereotypes, "discretion," life as cabaret: happy homosexuals/gay corpses, etc. A lot of crude stuff goes uncontested. Entry-level gay culture is bars, baths, tearooms; some adapt to the system, go on to lovers, parties, brunches (with varying degrees of satisfaction). Many, however, don't.

I'm twenty-seven, with shoulder-length hair and a beard, have just quit after four years as an Oakland mailman. I've been in a quiet, post-crash phase, after a lot of sixties running-around (draft problems, quitting grad school, dope-dealer's flat in the Haight, etc.). Though I've mostly been a loner, I'm living with Bonnie in a one-bedroom near campus; our (dismal) sex life has ended, I've gone to gay baths a few times. That's been dismal too, like my previous sporadic contacts; I'm tortured and inept, scared of men and sex, usually unable to get it up or keep it up. The gay men I've known have more or less confirmed the worst: I think faggots are dumb, shallow, sex-crazed, doomed to lonely trashy lives.

The term "collective" was fashionably vague. The dictionary definitions include:

1. "Characteristic of or relating to a group as an aggregate of individuals; as, the *collective* interests of a community," and

2. "A collectivistic organization or unit in a socialistic regime."

The Collective aspired to something of both—an early, modest attempt at creating an institution for a "gay community" (among other such attempts that proliferated to produce those contingents that go by for hours at the big gay parades); and something more radical, of its historical moment, equating personal and political. The founding members belonged to an ongoing encounter group, had in common to differing degrees the Free Clinic, leftist politics, gay lib (and alienation from existing gay culture), and Gestalt therapy. A sixties mix.

On the level of plot, the Collective was, at any given time, ten or twelve men who organized weekly drop-in rap groups for gay men, oriented toward consciousness-raising, and held weekly meetings (more business than consciousness) for Collective members. There was a series of houses, inhabited by various Collective members, there were some adjunct groups (more consciousness than business).

The rap groups were a therapeutic artifice: a large group breaking into smaller ones, a circle, a time span, a "facilitator" from the Collective, usually some structure based on simple group exercises. They were intended to set men in unfamiliar relations to each other, so they might behave in new, "authentic" ways. Since nobody knew exactly how to get there, or what "there" would look like, groups were hit-and-miss, dependent on who led them and who was in them, what everybody's mood was, what private agendas were pursued (there was always cruising, on some level). Sometimes they produced random chatter, sometimes provocations, disasters, epiphanies. You never knew. The Collective lasted three or four years; the raps began at the Free Clinic in July '72; soon after, I went to my first gay group there.

snapshots (2)

The first night, I wind up in a small group in a side room: There's an exercise, maybe just saying what we're feeling or what's brought us there; I talk about Bonnie, my isolation and failure at gay life: I say, "If this doesn't work out, I don't know what I'll do." At the end we form a tight circle, and in turn lean and let others catch us, so the whole group holds you up.

Afterward, a cute young guy from the group, with dark curly hair, picks me up; I go to his place and get fucked, which I can do without having to get hard. (I like some of the before-and-after, anyway.) The next afternoon we fuck again, then he doesn't answer calls, and vanishes.

My group consciousness, at this stage, is minimal: I think meeting men for sex is the only real point. The raps are a venue, at least; I go every Friday, but beginner's luck fades. Before long, I'm invited to a Collective meeting. I have no idea what I'm getting into, but it seems a way to hang out at the raps.

At the first meeting, it turns out everybody else is a founding member. There's a lot of Gestalt jargon ("I hear you"; "I'm feeling . . ."), a lot of scraggly beards and sloppy looks, even beyond the Berkeley standard. In

some ways I don't fit: I'm the only WASP, more into cheeseburgers than
vegetarian potlucks, think therapy's silly (since a few sessions with a pipe-
smoking psychoanalyst, in college). But these guys aren't scary: They're
misfits, like me, with sixties values. (The Collective will at various points
include a pre-op transsexual, a drag queen, a warlock, an English professor,
a computer programmer, a travel agent, a nurse, and so on; but the observation mostly holds. Nobody, for example, has a "career" or thinks money
measures anything that matters.) And they're trying, however awkwardly,
to connect.

Somewhere in here Bonnie and I have a last fight; she kicks me hard,
in cowboy boots, and moves out. (I limp for a week.) So meetings, and guys,
can come to my place.

Excerpts from a handout for Collective members, titled "Exercises":

A. Openings
    1. Have each member say his name and:
        a. say how he's feeling
        b. say why he came
        c. say what his expectations are
        d. say what he wants from the group. . . .
C. Encouraging Risky Statements . . .
    3. Have everybody write something they are afraid to say.
    Put the slips in a hat. Each member draws one and reads
    it aloud. The group should discuss (positively) the risky
    things. (Attempts to guess who wrote what should be
    discouraged.)
D. Role Playing . . .
    4. Have the group role-play being in a bar.

Of several exercises it's noted that they "may evoke strong feelings."
The handout was put together over several Collective meetings. (The "risky
statements" on slips of paper usually included a stockpile of pills, a shameful
sexual practice, and so on.)

Slowly I got addicted to groups, started facilitating. Mostly it was just
that, as always, the guys I had sex with weren't adding up to much, and
you could get a kind of intimacy in groups, with their inverted values

(chatty was bad, real was good) and structural limits, that was hard to carry over to real life. And, as a by-product, my consciousness was in fact getting raised: so many different guys, with the same pain.

Groups were the context. At its height, I was going to Collective meetings, raps, an ongoing C-R group recruited from the raps, and the occasional week-end encounter group (where emotions escalated under pressure: tears, fights, sex, etc.). There were such crowds of people around, one way or another, that it was hard to see the significance of individuals. In retrospect, there were two, without whom it would have been a blur, ultimately not-much.

Michael was the one who asked me to join the Collective. Once, for an article, I asked him what I'd probably get wrong about him. He said I'd make him into an exemplar of political activism, high-minded and abstract, when he actually did everything for selfish reasons.

Michael's selfishness was of a particular kind. After twenty-nine years of sexless existence, getting his Ph.D., running to psychiatrists to "cure" him, he finally exploded out in the turmoil of the late sixties, buying into not just gay liberation but the sixties analysis—racism, sexism, imperialism, false values—and the sixties dream—some way of living differently, past all that. By the time I met him, he'd been fired from two colleges, was scrambling for money, living in a little Collective house in Oakland (where, as it happened, A loved B loved C loved D—Michael was A), going to meetings and rallies and organizing committees for gay and lefty causes. What was selfish was he'd always been a misfit and he wanted a life, a world to belong in, or he'd die (he'd already tried suicide, and accidentally sur-vived). He described us as "all these people without a way of life, skittering around trying to find something that works," and imagined "a revolutionary community in which love is possible, trust is possible, a community without winners and losers."

Which is getting it wrong, making him bloodless: Michael was plump, dowdy, considered himself a "social idiot," had a history of falling for ill-chosen young men (what he wanted, he said, was a "sugar son"), talked loudly in restaurants, and made people nervous. Classic loser. On the other hand, he was funny: e.g., about his unpleasant jolts from boys he said, "If aversion therapy worked, there wouldn't be a faggot left anywhere."

He saw the sixties as "when people saw the world was breaking up and would have to be remade," and the seventies as "when they realized it

wasn't going to be fun." I was confused, not doing much except going to
bars, baths, and gay groups; but there was Michael, farther out, waving or
drowning, dragging me to rallies for grape pickers and persecuted Chip-
pewas, making it seem that gay lib and women's lib and the other libs were
the natural extension of the sixties, that it was all still somehow on track.
We'd speak at schools, churches; the raps were always bringing in recruits;
a lot was happening. There was always great stuff, like hairy political types
earnestly bopping around in nail polish and net stockings, to atone for their
"male privilege." I told Michael it was like living in a Dostoevsky novel,
all ferment and chaos; he said that that living-in-a-novel attitude was part
of the problem.

snapshots (3)

June 1974, with my lover John at the San Francisco gay parade (much
smaller and seedier than in later years, mostly bar floats and drag queens,
a turnout in the low tens of thousands). After meeting at the raps, we've
been together, off and on, about a year. By this time, my hair's cut and the
beard's shaved off and I can appeal to a more conventional sort—John's a
teacher, just coming out, secretive and conflicted, not Collective material
(he found the raps through a flyer he saw on a pole, didn't know how to
find a bar). With John's help, I've gotten better, though not great, at sex.
I've never, before him, slept better with anyone than without him, or thrown
a plate, or traded clothes, or cried to stupid love songs, or . . . whatever.
Momentous and commonplace. At the parade, John and I are honeymooning
after a breakup and patch-up (on our way to an eventual bad end).

My journal in these years mostly frets about not having a boyfriend,
or not wanting the boyfriend I've got, or what to do when I grow up (my
parents are supporting me, a nervous arrangement in every way); in the gay-
lib pieces I do for the *Berkeley Barb*, by contrast, you can hear the Collective
effect. From the first one: "I am so tired of all this. It is such a phony issue.
Gay men are no better or worse than anybody else, and if they are maybe
more unhappy than they ought to be it is because they have had to put up
with so much for so long." And: "We can all imagine that terrible day
when the revolution is won and gay people can be *exactly as happy as everybody*

else, but we are not even *there* yet, not even close. There are still laws against us, if you can believe that."

Of John in particular: "I know that things happen between us that have more intensity than anything else in my life. It sometimes occurs to me, with a sense of dislocation, that John and I are 'gay.' Does it ever occur to husbands and wives, male/female lovers, that they are in fact 'straight'? It would be insane, and I could only wish for a world in which no two people would ever have to categorize (or be categorized in) their love for each other."

Having John at the parade I feel lucky in love, and high: "Marching down the middle of the street arm in arm, crowds of gays in the windows, on the sidewalk, smiling, waving, we goddamn owned the town. Just sensationally together. And there are times, there have to be times, when straight people just don't matter. Who CARES how they react? It's our day, our space, our street, our time. OURS.

"They can't take that away.

"And so we all piled into Civic Center and there was a Gay Fair with booths and a rock band and people stripping in the reflecting pool and everybody milled around and that was pretty awful. The weather was foul and it's an ugly concrete cheerless place to start with, so no conclusions really need to be drawn. It's hard to imagine any fitting end to the parade, any climax adequate to that peculiar rush of solidarity. Gays are only human, and human solidarity is a rare bubble, floating to earth."

(Two notes: There is nothing special anymore about gays seeming to own a part of San Francisco; we became a power-bloc long ago. And it's hard to imagine, in the multifarious and specific parade contingents that have become the norm, a group of gay strangers walking down the street arm in arm and that being, or seeming to be, an expression of gay unity or a statement of anything.)

Pages fall off calendar. Transitions.

Early on, people wondered if the Collective would lead to anything. Once, a sociologist got us together to fantasize into a tape recorder—about all living together in networks of houses, organizing social and political clubs, radical therapy for everybody, etc. There was always at least one Collective house (never with me), with house meetings and house study groups and house rules and messy, unintended emotional complications (Mi-

chael went from one to another, always with different roommates). The more
political types got involved in Black Panther Bobby Seale's run for mayor
of Oakland. (At a gay party, Michael brought Bobby through, shaking
hands. I said, "I don't know what to say." Bobby said, "Just say Power to
the People." The black kids outside yelled, "Hey Bobby, that's a faggot
party.") This was early "coalition-building," the sort of thing that led to
other alliances, later on. At a big meeting for Bay Area gay groups, Michael
introduced me to (then-obscure) Harvey Milk, who had a long ponytail.

But mostly the Collective just did what it did, meetings and raps.
There had always been a rift of sorts between the Collective, with its politics,
and a lot of the guys who attended and just wanted a little socializing and
light, nonalcoholic cruising. The raps concept was too broad, the original
ideals were diluted, the exercises got stale, Collective members left to follow
specific interests. By the time it ended (1976 or so), all the founders were
gone. In the meantime, a professional gay group had gotten some grants
and established more genteel raps at its own community center (our raps
had used space in different churches, after the Free Clinic), a forerunner of
other groups that would provide varieties of counseling to gay men. Careers
were beginning to be made.

snapshots (4)

By 1977, Michael's working as a gay counselor at Stanford (of all places).
He's exercised, lost weight, started scoring at the baths, but more tricking
hasn't cheered him much—rather the opposite. He's in another group house,
in San Francisco, this one very Marxist-Leninist, where, despite a lot of
criticism and "self-criticism," he isn't fitting in. He's just been dumped by
a Marxist twinkie, who finds him "too intense."

I'm still in Berkeley, for no good reason, hacking morosely through a
doomed book on gay relationships (I don't understand gay relationships,
and the mountain of theory I digest doesn't help) and considering going to
computer school. John is long gone, having bought a house with a new
lover.

Michael and I see each other mostly after tai chi class, at a bar overlooking the bay. We bitch, moan, and riff. He compares the latest ideological "line" from his housemates to new "lines" in fashion—raise the hem,

change the terminology. (He does an "ideological fashion show," featuring "Asian" replacing "Oriental," etc.) Neither of us goes to raps anymore: He's cruising more, I'm hiding out in celibacy, pretending to channel my gay idealism into the book. Actually, I don't have any gay idealism left; neither does Michael, now that he's realized most gays aren't radical in any sense that would do him any good. It's not a misfit's world, and isn't going to be. The sixties faith has pretty much dissipated.

Still, I was shocked when I got the call, saying Michael had been gone two nights, without explanation. With his history, everybody knew what to expect; Bonnie and I (we'd become friends, eventually) went to a bar and in Michael's honor lit a brandy glass, which I'd seen in a Polish movie. (It was harder to light than in the movie, and the glass broke.) He turned up dead in his car in a state park, after I got the note he'd mailed, in which he said he was "*tired.*" The family arranged a traditional Jewish service; our tai chi master sent a paper with Chinese writing, to be burned at the grave, which I did.

Ahead lay computer school, and Reagan, and nearly ten years before I'd find another cause, another connection with gay men. And by 1977, though nobody knew, people were already being infected. It seemed that the worst of the sixties lived on as New Age or Political Correctness, the best was largely interred with its bones.

I lost touch with almost everyone who'd been in the Collective. One, I read, was elected to a community college board in Oakland, two died of AIDS, one I ran into at a training for an AIDS hotline, one died of a hereditary disease, one practices psychotherapy, one moved to Texas, one left a message on my machine last fall, which I never answered. The others could be any-where, though some additional number are probably dead.

Vince, who recently died, looked back on the Collective as "a golden age." Well, yes, in some ways, but there are my diaries, with their endless whining and fretting, to bring a little reality to the reminiscence. Not knowing what you're doing wears you down; you just want something easier.

In the Collective era, we saw how prejudice against gay people had warped our minds and made us unhappy in ways we didn't need to be. And in the years since Michael died, further developments have made it easier for others to see what we saw. Coming off the millennial sixties, nobody knew what the limits of our liberation might be—all kinds of misfits, all kinds of sadness, might come to a good end. As it turned out, of course, there was no remission from individual fates: Winners won, losers lost. But gay people have got steadily closer to being exactly as happy as everybody else—which is, on the whole, another success.

john gilgun

home alone
a lifelong
search for an
alternative family

Toward the end of his life Basho cautioned fellow haiku poets to rid their minds of superficiality by means of what he called *karuma* (lightness). This quality, so important to all arts linked to Zen (Basho had become a monk), is the artistic expression of non-attachment, the result of calm realization of profoundly felt truths. . . . Basho's mature haiku style, *Shofu*, is known not only for *karuma* but also for two other Zen-inspired aesthetic ideals: *sabi* and *wabi*. *Sabi* implies contented solitariness and in Zen is associated with early monastic solitariness.

—*On Love and Barley: Haiku of Basho*, translated by Lucien Stryk

Sabi, contented solitariness. There is no equivalent word in English. But I have experienced it here in my workroom in this house in Missouri. *Sabi* feels like being totally in touch with myself, in tune with my thoughts, unaware of the passage of time, immersed in my writing or in reading. *Sabi* is peace of mind, a feeling of being integrated, a consistent sensation of wholeness. Of course, I have a vocation. I am a writer.

When I was twenty-five, during the period of my traumatic breakup with my first lover, the poet Raeburn Miller told me, prophetically, "The problem with human beings is they cannot sit quietly in silence in a room by themselves doing absolutely nothing. You will never even begin to be happy until you find yourself sitting alone in total silence in your room doing your writing."

I rejected that idea. I had to be with someone. I had to be in love. I had to be in the process of creating an alternative family. I could not bear to be alone.

I was alone a lot as a child. My parents were alcoholics and they had their enclaves—taverns, roadhouses, the homes of friends into which they would disappear to drink and party for days at a time, particularly on holiday weekends. From the age of seven, I learned to take care of myself. I was also responsible for feeding, clothing, and "minding" my younger brother and sister. From an early age, I learned that it was often better when my parents were away. The house was quiet. There was no violence. I could keep things orderly. But one Labor Day weekend, when I was eleven, something snapped in me and I made a vow to myself that never again would I find myself in this position.

My parents had disappeared on Friday afternoon and they would not appear again until Monday evening. On that particular Labor Day weekend, my sneakers rotted on my feet. I had been aware, as I drifted around the neighborhood, sat on the front porch, or stared out the window, that there was a peculiar smell in the air. It was everywhere. I was so out of touch with my surroundings and with my own body that it took me a long time to figure out that the cheap sneakers they'd bought for me in June had decomposed on my feet and that that's where the smell was coming from. I peeled them off my feet and put them in the trash can. I remember weeping out of anger, frustration, and loneliness. Then I vowed that I would never suffer through another Labor Day weekend alone. A year from that date, I told myself, I would have a boyfriend. And once I had a boyfriend, I would adopt his family.

It was a working-class, Irish and Italian, Catholic culture in Malden, Massachusetts, in the late forties. As a boy, I was expected to spend all my time with other boys. Boys were not supposed to have anything to do with girls. That I thought of my friends as boyfriends and was actually in love with some of them was either something that was deliberately overlooked, was not understood, or was even half acceptable. Since nothing was ever put into words, I never really knew.

We boys traveled in packs, spending all our time together, in the parks, in the woods, at the ponds or lakes. Part of the mystique was in the joy we took in the fact that parents never knew what we were doing, including, of course, the fumbling, groping sex-play we indulged in. Joey Martello's mother, for instance, seeing us troop into her immaculate kitchen covered with dirt and grass stains, said, "Have you boys been fighting again?" No, in fact we'd been in the orchard, rolling around in the grass, groping each other. Our response to the innocence of parents, particularly mothers, was a knowing smirk. We lived in our own world and there was sufficient space in it—suburban sprawl was just beginning and Malden still had woods, fields, orchards, abandoned granite quarries, even a pond—to live freely as boys.

Joey Martello was a year younger than I was, which would make him fourteen years old in 1950. His father was Italian but he had married a woman from an Irish family and Joey had inherited a genetic combination which gave him the best of both gene pools. He was beautiful. There's no other word for it. The Martello family lived on one of the newer streets with a romantic name—Avalon Road. There was even a song connected with that name: "In Avalon, my Avalon, beyond the sea. . . . I dream about my Avalon, from dusk to dawn. And so I guess I'll travel on to Avalon." I've been traveling there in my mind all of my adult life.

The Martello house was a white Cape Cod colonial. That spring Joey and his father and I mixed up concrete and poured a patio. The idea was to sit out there on summer evenings at a picnic table. It was like something you saw in ads in *The Saturday Evening Post* or *Life* or *Coronet*.

The interior of the Martello house was always spotless and always smelled of good food. Mr. Martello drove a black Buick Roadmaster. My parents lived many blocks from Avalon Road in a two-family house. They rented. They did not own. My father drove a Ford and would have been scornful of patios and picnic tables, if he'd ever given them a thought. The backyard was where you kept the trash can. My mother said to me once, "How do those Martellos live so well? After all, he only works for a produce company!" I answered, "Well, they don't drink, so that gives them extra money to spend."

Joey never entered my house. I never allowed any of my friends to enter my house. He would stand on the sidewalk and shout my name if he wanted me. One night he wanted me to go to a Boy Scout meeting with him. It happened to be one of the nights my father went berserk and attacked me. When I came out onto the street, it was obvious that I'd been beaten up and I was sobbing violently. "I hate my father!" I told my friend. And he replied, "I love mine."

That was a new idea to me, that anyone could love his father. It also surprised me that Joey would use the word *love*. I had begun to write. I filled the notebooks I bought at the five-and-ten with daily entries describing my adventures with Joey. There wasn't any privacy in my home and, though I found hiding places for my notebooks in corners of the cellar, they did get found and they did get read. So I never wrote the word *love* in connection with Joey.

But I knew that love was what I felt. I never lied to myself about it. I was *in love with him* and that was that. I was also in love with the act of writing. Both loves had to be hidden from the adult world. I remember writing, over and over again, "I never want to grow up. I never want to be an adult. I hate grown-ups." Loving Joey was my defense against emptiness. But so was my writing. So when I wrote about Joey, which meant every day, since I was compulsive about detailing everything we did together, I thought I was as close to heaven as I had ever been.

One Saturday morning, Joey invited me to spend the summer with them at the "camp" they rented at Island Pond near Hampstead, New Hampshire. At fourteen, he could still be tender and loving. He could say things like, "I want *you* to be with me this summer." We sat in the kitchen in that Cape Cod colonial house eating gingersnap cookies his mother had baked, and he said, "So, please, ask your mother and father if you can spend a month with me."

His father came in and said, "Hey, you two ought to get married!" It would not have occurred to me at that time that there was even a hint of anything pejorative in this. Boys were supposed to like each other. We were being complimented. I hadn't a clue. But something was brewing and it was on the immediate horizon. I was about to turn fifteen and I "didn't like girls."

Do parents still put boys together in the same bed? At the camp, I was expected to share a bed on the screened-in porch with Joey. After a couple of nights of this, I had a wet dream. I woke up with Joey sleeping beside me and I'd made a mess in the sheets. In my dream, I'd been holding and fondling him. Awake, I couldn't do much more than place the palm of my hand lightly on his shoulder. In the morning, the mess was still there in the sheets. We never spoke about it. But he asked his mother if he could sleep on the couch in another room. I said I didn't want that and we continued to sleep in the same bed. Then one morning I woke up to find that he'd moved to the couch in the other room anyway. He never came back to the bed on the screened-in porch.

Relatives arrived, some of them more savvy than Joey's mother. One afternoon, lying deep in the hammock out of sight, I heard Joey's uncle talking to Joey's mother on the screened-in porch a few feet from where I was lying. "He'll do it with girls. He'll do it with boys. He'll do it in the woods. He'll do it in the fields. You can't stop him."

I knew I shouldn't have been listening. I coughed so that they'd know I was there. The conversation stopped abruptly. About twenty minutes later, the uncle came out and took a paperback book away from me in an angry, contemptuous manner, almost slapping it out of my hand. I remember the title of the book—*The Big Sky* by A. B. Guthrie, Jr. So I had nothing to read. And, of course, it wasn't possible for me to write in a notebook while living with the Martello family at their camp. There was nowhere to conceal a notebook. I spent a lot of time sitting on a rock staring at the ripples the bugs made on the surface of the water of the pond.

Joey had more or less stopped speaking to me and spent most of his time on a diving platform on the pond with other boys. It was clear that I wasn't welcome out there. If I swam out to them, they swam away. Finally, after two weeks of hurt feelings and confusion, Joey's father put me into the Buick Roadmaster, drove me back to Malden, and dropped me off at my house. I had failed miserably with my adopted family. But worse was to come.

My mother said, "I thought of calling the Martellos and asking them what went wrong up there, but . . ." But she was in denial. My mother, who worked all her life as a waitress and a barmaid, knew gay men. Some of the waiters she worked with were gay men. And she knew exactly what "not liking girls" meant in connection with her oldest son. But she never put it into words. A knowing look was all she could manage and even that look threatened something in her, something she definitely did not want to put into words. However, since her denial also protected my privacy—tenuous as that privacy was in our house—I was grateful for it.

My "problem" was working its way into language, however. That summer, I was told by an older boy that I had "a complex." That meant, "You don't like girls." There were specific girls—a Claire, a Jackie, a Ginger—that you could prove yourself with by "feeling them up." But I was vocal about wanting to do no such thing.

A distant cousin "knocked up a girl" and I said, in all innocence, "I'm surprised. I thought you were like me. I thought you didn't like girls." This passed through all levels of my father's large family almost instantaneously. What I had said was repeated over and over again. There was a lot of snickering but no one let me in on the joke. The "problem" could be acknowledged up to a certain point. But beyond that point there was silence. Sometimes I got an ironic and very Irish-American smile, but beyond that —nothing.

However, I had read *King's Row*. In that novel, a boy kisses another boy. I mentioned this to a friend who expressed his disgust. Still, there it was—a kiss, right there on the page of a book. But, if disgust was the proper reaction, I'd go along with that. "Yeah. Disgusting." Anything to get along.

Joey, in desperate haste, began to like girls intensely. I think he was genuinely attracted to them and they made a great fuss over him. He was so attractive. He later married the first girl he ever dated, a girl he met in his eighth grade class, Theresa. I met her, of course, that terrible summer, hanging out on the corner, but we never had anything to say to each other. It was clear that we were rivals and I was the one who was going to lose. I wished she'd go away. But in the end, I was the one who went away.

The day after my fifteenth birthday, Joey told me to leave and never come back. We were standing on Avalon Road, confronting each other. His mother came out of the house, dressed to "go shopping in town." She knew what was going to happen. She drew him aside and said, in a firm voice, "Don't fight. I don't want you to fight. Don't fight with him."

As soon as she'd turned the corner and passed out of sight, he asked me again if I intended to leave. I refused again and he fell on me and beat me half senseless, banging the back of my head against the sidewalk until blood spurted from my nose. Even so, I wouldn't agree to stay away. I even said, "Tomorrow we'll be friends again!" as I lay there under him being beaten. But he shouted, "Naw!"

We never spoke to each other again. Nor did I ever have another friend in Malden during the time I lived there. He saw to that. He also said, as he lay on top of me, hitting me in the face, "I'll tell everyone about you!" And I shouted back, "Tell them *what*!" But I got no answer because there were no words for what was supposed to be wrong with me. It was something you just knew. Whatever this thing was, I was "it." No one was to have anything to do with me ever again and I was supposed to spend the rest of my life alone.

After a terrible sophomore year in high school, I elected to leave Malden the following summer to work at a caddy camp in Sunapee, New Hampshire. After an even more terrible junior year, I took a job in a hotel in Boothbay Harbor, Maine. Being ostracized in Malden meant that I had to move out into the world. But while I was in Malden during the fall, winter, and spring months, I lived entirely in books, reading Elliot Paul, Steinbeck, Salinger, Fitzgerald, Orwell, Hemingway, Faulkner, Joyce, Sherwood Anderson, Thomas Wolfe. I had the ability to zero in immediately on the modernist canon, ignoring the thousands of other books in the Malden Public Library. I knew what I needed. In some ways, it was uncanny, as if I had a destiny, a notion the biographies of these writers promoted.

And I would translate everything I read immediately into the written word. The first thing I purchased with the first money I ever made working as a busboy with my mother was a secondhand typewriter. It cost $13.00. And the first thing I did with that typewriter was to imitate James T. Farrell's *Studs Lonigan Trilogy*. At the same time, my mother went to the woman who lived in the flat upstairs and told her, "If the noise he makes typing bothers you, I'll make him get rid of that machine." The noise of the drunken fights which took place in our flat every weekend were just something the people upstairs—who actually owned the house—had to put up with. It was the sound of my typewriter which my mother was more than willing to silence.

To be immersed in books in working-class Irish-Catholic Malden, Massachusetts, in the early fifties was to be so far beyond the pale as to be hardly recognizable by the populace as a human being. But books and my writing were all I had. And since they were all I had, they stood in for everything I didn't have.

But I never lost my need "to be in love." And I never stopped "being in love" with Joey. I remember standing outside that Cape Cod colonial house on Avalon Road several times during my high school years, staring up at the kitchen window with intense longing and regret. It was always at night and usually after my father had thrown me out into the street. What would the Martellos have said if they had looked out a window and seen me standing there? In my fantasies, they always said, "Come on in." I have had one consistent dream since 1950. I return to Avalon Road and am welcomed back into that house by his mother, his father, and Joey himself, in that order. I always wake from this dream happy.

In 1982, I returned to Malden, borrowed my sister's car, drove to Avalon Road and parked across from the Martello house. I had checked the City Directory and, amazingly, Joey was listed as living there with his wife Theresa. His parents must have sold or deeded the house to him. I didn't believe they were all living in there together. But it was possible. I sat in the car and stared at the house. It was still painted white and was still fulfilling its Eisenhower-era cultural imperative by being benignly and beautifully Cape Cod colonial.

I did not get out of the car and walk around to the back. But surely the patio was still there. Perhaps there was even a picnic table on it. What if Joey had come out? He'd have been a middle-aged man. Would he recognize me? What could I have said to him? "In ruining my life, you actually gave me a life. Because I got out of Malden. But you're still here."? Forty years after the event, no reconciliation was possible. What else could I do except drive away?

The experience with the Martellos left me with a distrust of adopted families. But it's a lonely life and for years I kept experimenting. In the early sixties, after I began to get jobs teaching at colleges, I tried twice to make friends with straight couples on the faculty. I always found something which my American culture approved of and was busily promoting at that moment. Both couples were white, Protestant, Middle Western and middle class. Both had the requisite number of children—two, one male, one female. Both lived in suburban tract houses with patios and charcoal grills.

And in both cases, the wives eventually threw themselves into my arms at parties, declared that they had fallen in love with me, and looked up at me as if they expected to be kissed. After coming out to two saddened wives and two angry husbands, I concluded that this kind of alternative family was not for me either.

My first real lover, Jerry, was from a town of three hundred people in northeastern Iowa. (I had left Massachusetts for good by the time I was twenty-four.) I was a graduate student. He was a sophomore but was older, having been in the navy. We shared a tiny apartment in Iowa City for nine months before he threw me out saying we were "incompatible." But while we lived together, we spent each Sunday at the family farm. I was taken in immediately "as part of the family." His father was a pig farmer. His mother adopted me "as one of the boys" immediately. (Jerry had an identical twin, Gene, also gay, who lived in the same house with us in Iowa City.) I remember the groaning dining room table in the center of the farmhouse dining room, the dozens of relatives, each bringing a covered dish—macaroni and cheese, shepherd's pie, apple pan dowdy, tuna casserole. From the street where Jerry eventually tossed me, however, I vowed never to fall in love like that again and never to adopt or to be adopted by another family. I would commit myself to my writing and to my teaching. I had a vocation. I'd give everything to that vocation.

I failed at this. There is a cultural imperative and, of course, gay men, as part of the culture, feel it. "Get married! Settle down." There is also a biological imperative, though I have always been able to satisfy myself sexually. And there's what I call "the politics of loneliness." Loneliness propels us into relationships. And there is a clear political reason for that—if you are straight! The culture expects you to create a nest in which you can nurture children. Come in out of the cold. Have babies. And since the culture I grew up in presented only this model—heterosexual coupling in the suburbs—I had to create a "home."

In 1964, I moved into a vine-covered cottage in Des Moines with my lover, Larry, and we shared a more or less monogamous life together, following our understanding of the heterosexual model, for four years. He is intensely blond, blue-eyed, Middle Western, Protestant. In other words, he fulfills all the cultural imperatives. I adopted and was adopted by his mother, father, and sister. To this day, his mother, who is ninety-seven, calls us "her boys." Though we have not lived in the same house together since 1968, when I left to go back to graduate school, I maintain "my room" in his present home. It's there for me when I come to visit. Ours is a "committed relationship" in that when we talk, he can complete my sentences and I can complete his. I have had experiences in which I wake from dreams and know that my spirit is connected with his. We have, after all, known each other for thirty-five years.

And yet it was never enough. I was never at ease in my soul unless I had a book open in front of me, a pen in my hand, and a kind of light in my mind. "Why are you in the other room with your books and not out here with me watching television?" "Because I'm a college teacher and I need to prepare my lectures for tomorrow. Besides, I'm studying for the GRE exam." Nothing that I have found in American culture honestly promotes "the life of the mind." But without "a life of the mind," I cannot really live.

My first lover came in once from a movie called *Some Come Running* and burst into tears. "It's about a writer. He tells his girlfriend she'll never understand him. You're a writer. You can never really love me." I loved him. But I also loved whatever happened to be manifesting itself creatively in my own mind.

A few weeks ago, I had coffee with Larry in Des Moines. I introduced the topic of "Mind." He listened patiently and replied, "Catholic. I associate it with being Catholic." I looked into the logical, Protestant, emphatically blond and blue-eyed geometrics of his face and knew that he was right.

At a different time, in a different culture, I might have been a monk or some kind of mystic. My American culture gave me, in my lifetime, instead of "a life of the mind," the image of a Cape Cod colonial house, a patio, a picnic table, and the gleaming chrome grille of a Buick Roadmaster. But what my spirit demands is silence, contemplation, meditation, the written word, peace of mind, and at best a few compatible students. It took me fifty-seven years to come to this realization. For what it's worth, I want to share my insight with other gay men. My view of the world might have been through the window of Basho's shack. His window wasn't a picture window and he didn't drive a Buick and there were no patios on the mountainside. But when a heron flew over he knew the wild blue color of its wings in his mind.

william
haywood
henderson

---

three friends,
sunday morning,
late coffee
and oranges

1

The room was tall, with seamless sheets of glass rising twenty feet, huge banks of curtains drawn open. Outside, ranks of trees had been trimmed and trimmed until their branches gnarled into snaking nubs, and there was the marble and wrought-iron of Sather Gate. Beyond the redwoods rose the white pillars of Wheeler Hall, a monument to all I would soon learn and eventually forget. It was 1979, the University of California at Berkeley, a meeting of the Gay People's Union. I was a boy from Colorado, a transfer to this fringe of the continent.

"This is my first meeting of this kind—ever," I said to the man beside me on the couch.

"Congratulations."

I was waiting to be called to order, waiting for bits of unimaginable business. And then, at the door, some serious action finally stirred—a man strode in, followed by two others carrying a coffee urn, a plate of cookies. The man dropped his papers on the long table against the wall and turned to survey the room. He smiled, nodded here and there, tossed out a name, stepped forward and took a kiss, another, set a knot of men into fits of laughter, moved on.

What is he, I thought. He was square, solid, with black hair, a reddish moustache drooping, and lips as full and carved as—I couldn't be sure— some idol in a temple to fleshy rites. He was soft, dark, his eyes black. Native American, I would learn—California coastal tribe. He saw me sitting hip-to-hip in the crowding of men on the couch, he came across the room, stood at my toes, and said in a deep, honeyed voice, "We haven't met. I'm Ken. Let me sit." I couldn't struggle to one side or the other before he'd landed himself on my knees. I felt the full weight of him right down through me, watched his smooth arms, thick hands. I introduced myself.

"Beautiful," he said, turning away to watch a youth with gold curls pause at the elbow of a smaller, balding man. The youth tilted his head, leaned without hesitation, and kissed the man on the lips. They embraced and leaned back a bit and started to talk, arms linked. Beautiful was not a word I would have chosen for men—a new word.

Ken said he was going to San Diego for spring break. I was going to L.A. We would go together. He stood up and clapped the meeting to order.

On our way toward Los Angeles, we headed down Interstate 5—the long straight stretches through almond groves, peaches, open range, with the dry hills to the west, the Sierras swallowed in moist haze to the east. My VW sputtered along.

A Porsche pulled up, slowly passed us, and Ken looked across me, smiled at the driver. Embarrassed, I watched the dotted line. "Speed up," Ken said. I pressed on the gas. We rushed along, that sharp profile in the Porsche inching away. "Don't worry. He'll wait for me at the next rest stop," Ken said. I imagined following that red waxed blur onto the slow curve of an off-ramp, into an area of shade and picnic tables, and there would be an opening of doors, a casual greeting, a blanket spread on the dense, well-watered lawn. What would Ken do with a man like that?

Mile after mile, Ken talked of the men he'd laid, the men he'd fought, the bones he'd broken. He listed sizes and shapes, placed himself on top or beneath. At every corner, it seemed, behind every door, men waited for him.

In a bookstore, a glance would take him into an hour of dark heat. On the subway, a casual bumping of knees would lead to a long foray into conversation, an exit and fast walk to the most convenient enclosure, a grinding encounter that was the best yet, to be supplanted by the next story, and the next. A breakup started with a wild screw and devolved into a fistfight on a narrow balcony. He engaged a lover in the shadow of eucalyptus. There was no way that I could hope to learn this language—too blunt, too rich—but I wanted him to keep talking, to continue until the heat-charged static of his stories filled completely the space between us. He poked at my shoulder to emphasize his laughter.

And there I was, closed in with a man I couldn't have imagined a few weeks before. What would people think if they saw us together? I suppose I would have looked vaguely frightened—wide-eyed and listening, a half-beat off the rhythm. Or maybe I would have seemed nearly as exotic as Ken, the mere fact that I was near him lending me a certain unusual charm, an indecipherable, dangerous edge.

"Once," Ken said, "driving down this highway with a friend, I was bored, so I opened his glove box, and inside was a dildo and a tube of K-Y. I shut the glove box. We drove on in silence for an hour or two." He reached forward and opened my glove box, peered inside, shut it.

We danced at Studio One with Ken's friends—a tall, quiet blond of slender build and his flighty, sparkling little lover. A huge place, that club, alive with the most surprising men, the raw maleness of them. Ken churned us out onto the floor, swung his hips behind this man and that, gave me a serious scowl cut only occasionally by the flash of a smile. I tried to catch his moves, tried to look as he looked, boldly down the line of each body.

We spent the night at his friends' apartment, in a bedroom with two double beds—just "roommates" in case a parent dropped by. Ken and I took one bed, and the others curled in the bed across the room. In the darkness, they all joked and tossed pillows and kicked about, and I laughed and flinched and felt naked in my boxer shorts. To think that those two, Ken's friends—both beautiful men—slept together every night in that room, in that bed.

We settled down, no sheet across us—the heat. I rolled toward the wall. Ken placed his hand on my back for a moment, placed a kiss on my shoulder.

I lay wide awake for hours, afraid to move, afraid that Ken, as he hovered behind me, as he placed his hand again on my back, removed it, would guess at my fear, my shyness, my excitement. I wouldn't turn toward him, wouldn't face him. He was close to me, his breath on my shoulder, and I lay there wondering if or why a man like him would want to be with me, with a boy so spectacularly unschooled in the ways of men, and I concluded that he wouldn't, that he was only a friendly sort, a man with pity, a teacher.

Over the Hollywood hills I heard a helicopter passing through the darkness. It seemed to come close, to hover, to swoop around and search again.

Early summer I stayed with Ken for a few weeks as I looked for a new apartment. He took me shopping at the Berkeley Bowl, and we returned with strange substances—smooth white blocks of tofu, huge dried mushrooms, cellophane packages of finely folded noodles. "You wrap it in foil," he said, "you douse it with pepper, you dash it with sesame oil."

At night I slept in his bed with him—no question, he just placed me there. Who would place a houseguest in his own bed? From the headboard a fern, an ivy, a lacy pine reached down. I brushed a frond from my face. Against the window, against the glow of the city and the world beyond, there were more plants—bromeliads with their waxy flowered spikes, cacti snaking, fig trees.

We went up onto the broad flat roof to eat lunch. On our blanket on the gravel, we sat and looked west to the long purple gap of the bay, the bridge golden against the fog, the hills of crowded white buildings.

We were above the streets, cars, sirens, we were up among the peaked roofs, palm trees, spikes of redwood, we were up into the open sky. North from Oakland, south from El Cerrito, seagulls flew. "They see what we're eating," Ken said. "They want some." The birds, in long gray-white strokes of their sharp wings, approached from all sides, swirled overhead, silent, found us stationary, unready to move just yet, and they scattered toward the bay, toward the richer pickings elsewhere.

2

I graduated, lived in the mountains of Wyoming for a year, returned west to take a job at a publishing company in San Francisco. In a windowless office barely larger than my desk, I stacked green manuscript —chapters on taxes, bankruptcy, wills, and trusts. I kept my office door open, watched the passage of each body through the gap of fluorescent light, against the bookcases heavy with reference volumes. Through the wall I heard Terri typing at her computer, humming "You're No Good," telephoning her soon-to-be-dumped boyfriend. I licked a yellow tag and attached it to a manuscript, and I carefully penciled "Tense. Consider rephrasing?"

A new body passed, a beautiful man with a sharp, innocent face, curls of dark hair, a serious moustache. John. He entered the office across the gap, switched on the light, squeezed around behind the desk, and sat down. He reached for a box of supplies and began filing them away. I watched. He looked up, saw me, smiled a sweet smile, and went back to his paper clips.

Months later, John and I met at a subway station and started walking. We climbed the hills until the bay spread below us, the water frothed with whitecaps and the scud of ballooning spinnakers. Through that long Saturday we wandered the canyons of filigreed facades, took a browse through City Lights, rested together at the base of Coit Tower. Fog crept in and burned away. At dusk we lit a joint in the lee of a bus shelter and dragged ourselves into sleepy sunburned warmth.

In a restaurant I looked down into my white bowl of bouillabaisse. The black shells lay open, baring their fleshy tangles. The red watery soup might hide something more appealing—I stirred around and found nothing. I attacked a shell with a spoon and fork, and the red splattered my white shirt.

An hour later, I stood at the edge of the fountain in front of City Hall. Water cascaded from one pool to the next, lights shone up into the trees, a car cruised past the bronze heroic man on horseback. John climbed onto the edge of the fountain with me. "You're cute," he said. The lights moved around the edges of the square. He hugged me and took me home.

He lived in the upstairs flat of a Queen Anne on a hillside—the high ceilings, ornate trim. In his bed, we listened to the couple downstairs groan toward a wail, and then silence. John hugged me so tight I thought my back would break.

I caught him in the stairwell at work, and we kissed. He was a lovely man—smart, small-town boy, with large ears, a silly laugh almost a gurgle. I imagined the trips we'd take, the journeys alone through the mountains, along the rocky shore of a lake, on down into the desert and the sharp brown ranges and the dusty wind and sage. With my grandmother's gray wool blanket pulled from the trunk of the car, we would wander out onto the flats, lie beneath the tiny hot sun, listen, and hear only the sound of the wind buzzing the dry grass. Perhaps our fingers would slowly intertwine.

I arrived at his door at the appointed hour, carrying a shopping sack. He answered the door wearing only a pair of blue nylon shorts, and I followed him upstairs, into his room. He lay back down on his weight bench and began hefting the bar. "I can almost lift my own weight," he said between gasps. He had a nice body—a man's body—muscle blue beneath the plain white skin.

"Look what I brought," I said, pulling a baguette, cheese, fruit from my shopping bag. "For a picnic."

"I'm not hungry," he said, and he hefted again.

Barely two weeks old, our relationship was over. He was still a sweet man, and I tried to imagine what he might desire.

John's roommate moved out, and I offered to fill the vacancy. Who knew what might happen in close quarters? I took John's old room, and John took the front room. I bought a huge bed, an antique dresser, a table, and placed them in the tall, cold, peach-tinted space. We cooked dinner together, set mousetraps (he swept away the corpses before I had to see them), entertained friends, and we each dated a variety of the savory and the unsavory, the short time and the slightly longer. But, really, I didn't date much, and soon, out of mortal fear, I barely dated men at all—instead, I spent my time with my girlfriend from work, Terri, seeing movies, taking in a nice meal, walking her home toward her apartment. Sometimes I'd see John out and about, at a bar or moving through a late-evening subway station with a friend and a bottle of wine, but our meetings outside the apartment, in the weekend nighttime, were rare.

On an unusually hot night, when the windows facing windows all stood open, house against house, I lay in bed, heard the couple downstairs working themselves into a froth, but this time the voices rose clearly. They finished with a great roaring groan, and laughter spilled and echoed from the windows, all around.

3

And so I lived with John, an elegant domestic arrangement in the cool spaces of our flat. I took to writing stories, locked into my room in the evenings after dinner. Stories of Wyoming, set in the town where I'd spent a year on a ranch after Berkeley, before San Francisco. John floated in the tub, and he invited me into the steamy room, asked me to read to him. The water was clear, solid, still around his body, his arms up on the edge of the tub, head back, eyes closed. I saw age in the heft of his chest, beautiful. I unfolded a wooden chair, sat at the foot of the tub, began to read my story of Kirsten, a young woman whose car breaks down in a Wyoming mountain town, who stays, who loves the place. *She dipped below the surface of the geyser pool and the water disappeared, leaving only a warmth surrounding her. Moving her limbs, she drifted into deeper water. She thought of the distance below her, of the passages that allowed this water to rise so calmly from the fissures and faults, the base of the mountain. She thought she could hear a familiar sound, like blood pulsing through her veins or water pulsing in deep darkness.*

Ken took me to one place and another. At the American Indian Center, we watched a drag Dolly Parton lip-sync for hours, working her way through each and every album Dolly had ever recorded. Her leather backup boys emerged occasionally and snapped open fans, carved the air. The audience gradually fell into a drunken, lolling stupor, unable to appreciate the finer details of costume number twelve.

At a party in Noe Valley, Ken told me that the charming little man I had spoken to for half an hour enjoyed using his charming little fists. "You saw his bandana, didn't you?"

On Halloween, Ken arrived at my door with a paper bag of goodies from the Salvation Army, and said, "Put these on." After I'd dressed, he applied my makeup, and we headed out into the night. I was a giantess in clogs and blue knee-highs, a jacket and skirt five sizes too small, hard little breasts. As I approached, men on the street fell back in horror at the looming shadow of my frizzed blond explosion of hair, or they moved into my path, reached up under my skirt. I returned home with a nice prize—a plaque engraved "Ugliest Woman."

We danced in a club—a tangle of men, a maze of chain-link fences.

Ken met John. John took to Ken's jokes. Ken and John soon had their own telephone conversations, own connections. I didn't know where to place my jealousies—they were both close, both mine, and now they were also each other's.

4

Six years passed since I first met Ken, two years since I first met John. John and I moved together to a new flat.

On a Saturday evening, Ken and I wandered through clubs, danced for hours, silent and sweating and moving into an occasional shared choreography, sparring like boxers. We returned home late and sat together on the edge of my claw-foot tub, soaking our feet, and John found us there and called us "old ladies," and Ken said, "Where have *you* been this evening, hon?" and accused him with a list of wonderfully lurid possibilities. John laughed and waved us off and headed for bed, and Ken and I dried our feet. I put on my bathrobe and Ken his pajamas, and we sat at the window in the darkened living room and watched as the streetlight slowly illuminated the 3:00 A.M. movement below. Around the corner of the park, down the hill, men wandered and paused, and a few seemed to speak a line or two. A car pulled up, someone stepped forward, and everyone shifted a few paces left or right.

Directly across the street, a doorway at the back of a dark room illuminated, and a shape came out from that bright square, and we saw a man naked, pinching a telephone receiver against his shoulder, smoking a cigarette, the red dot of fire following his wander through the room, intensifying as he inhaled. Lit blue with the night, he stood at the front window and yammered and nodded into the phone, dragged on the cigarette, and slowly his prick lengthened, arced out a bit, shrank away again.

John was sleeping at the back of the house. Ken understood, he said, why I loved John, he loved him too. It was surprising to find that Ken could love a man who seemed so much like me, who seemed to move so softly through his days and nights. But I'm sure I knew that John was not so soft—he would go out into the night alone. I truly was another case entirely, a boy who looked and looked and never quite seemed to see— before that night I'd never even guessed at the volume of dark traffic that moved just beyond our windows, down at the corner, the parlay and barter and quick words.

Sunday morning. I wake to the potted palm's dark, elegant shadow against the stark white paper blinds. I'm too tired yet to rise, but I smell coffee.

John and Ken are talking—I hear the voices from the living room, through the wall. Eventually I emerge from my room to join them, and I land myself on the sofa at the bay window, where Ken has spent the night with a blanket and pillow. The sun is full and hot, and we have our usual coffee in large mugs, three oranges on a plate. We dig at the rinds, tear them away, eat the sweet sections. The peels turn their white insides up, their orange edges jagged and obscure. We are sticky, and John walks down the hall and returns with a sponge and a stack of napkins. We pour more coffee. I tighten my robe and go downstairs to the street, bring up the newspaper. We divide the sections and start to read, hold up the Macy's ads for everyone to enjoy.

We are together in that sunny room, with the blue sky outside the window, the Bay Bridge distant beyond the jut of downtown. The cars strain on the steepness of the hill. Men move along the sidewalk toward brunch. An old woman makes her way home with an opaque plastic bag of groceries—eggs, fruit—and she pauses every few steps and rests the bag on the concrete, adjusts the scarf that holds her stiff puff of gray hair.

This is where I live, and Ken is here, and John has come forward from his room at the back of the flat. Ken harasses John with a blossoming barrage of innuendo, and John laughs and allows himself to be mocked, occasionally adding his own details to the joke. We make a bowl of com-pote—strawberries, cantaloupe, blueberries, apple. I read to them from a book of poetry, and they seem barely amused, barely awake. I watch as Ken moves close to John, jokes with him, entertains him there on the sofa against the morning light, and I feel alone and angry and I want to show Ken the door. But then Ken lightens everything with an unusually delightful string of sexual barbs, and it seems that we are floating in the sunlight, in the warm morning, and the world is one big naked embrace.

One weekend, and the next, and the next, we went through the same routine. Saturdays, Ken and I would spend the evening wandering, and then we'd return to my flat, and Ken would pull his pajamas from his backpack, brush his teeth, find the blanket and pillow in the closet, and settle onto the sofa in the living room.

And then Sunday morning arrived—it was peaceful, came to be expected. John and I knew that Ken would be there, that we would share the morning, that we would laugh. It seems that this was my life for year upon year.

On Sunday morning, as on no other morning, I could sit long enough at the window for distance to come clear, for my life to circle around. Down across that jumbled white city, east across the bay, the far hills rested dark and sharp, and the buildings rose through the trees, and the bell tower spiked clearly above the Berkeley campus. And there was Ken again, as I remembered him from our first meeting, that exotic strange darkness approaching, sitting on my lap. And there was my apartment on the Berkeley hills, my terrible broken bed where I slept through a winter and thought that John would be with me, would take me with him, we would be together, and then I left that apartment and moved to the city, moved in with John, a friend.

The distance across the bay seemed immense—the freighters carving that purple expanse were flecks, nothing of their bulk evident, nothing of the tremendous weight of iron, the throb of engine, corkscrew tearing at the surface of the water, moving some unknown cargo out through the gap, west toward something vastly exotic. That view was silent. Light sparkled from every moving object—endless, circling, cloudless.

I loved those men—beautiful men. I had spent nights in bed with each of them. Now we joked about each others' bodies, as if we'd never been together for anything more than comparison, fodder for humor.

Sometimes I saw John coming up from the dim stairway and I wondered for a brief moment who he was—brother, father?—why was he so familiar, why did I feel that I had always known him?

Sometimes I caught Ken for a flash on the street before I'd fully recognized him, and I saw that odd slinky boldness to his moves, saw it as others must have seen it, and I wondered why he spent his hours with me, wondered if we were really different at all, wondered if any of the stories he'd told me were true.

Sunday morning. Now I count back through the years, add and subtract, and realize that our Sundays together could not have been many. Perhaps they stretched over a few months, maybe a year.

5

Before I left San Francisco to attend graduate school in Providence, Rhode Island, Ken gave me a painting he'd created for me. It was the story of two men, he said, and he'd started writing the story on the back of the canvas in pencil, but he'd forgotten how it went and the words were smeared, they trailed off. Ken's paintings had always been complex, cleanly precise, nearly architectural constructions of squares and arcs and perfect dots—a refined geometry of native memory. The painting he'd created for me was something else.

Through the gaps in billowing layers of purple-gray clouds, bits of orange light leaked, and stars strung along in lines, formed into circles, angled away again, drawing grids, a map, seeming to go someplace, to pause and circle around, to continue, directions blurred by that exotic overcast. Through the clouds figures fell, danced, clung to each other. A skinny man crouched, kicked a leg out, his genitals a graphic dangle, weighty. A boxy rock man held out his stubby limbs, seemed solid, though his form was nothing but oil-pencil sketch, cloud shining through. Spiky waterbugs copulated. Men and men and men, men bleeding into the shapes of animals, always the dangling organs.

The phone rang in my low-ceilinged apartment in Rhode Island. Ken had been to see John in the hospital. "John is nearly gone," he said. "I won't be going back to visit him again."

I called the hospital. John's mother answered the phone. "He's tired," she said, her own voice wavering, elderly. She put him on. His voice seemed as strong, as young as I'd ever known it, and I hung up thinking that they were all mistaken, that he would climb up out of this depth, continue along the trail.

I circled through Kennedy Park in downtown Providence. I was sure I'd seen John sitting on a bench, beneath a tree. Ridiculous, my lurking, my approach toward a better vantage. But it *was* John, exactly, it had to be.

I began writing a novel about three men in Wyoming: Blue, a man who belonged to the mountains, the West; Gilbert, a Native American who had lost his past; Sam, a young man who drifted from one dark affair to another before landing in that pure high country. Blue's voice—*I thought of winter. I thought of the fall of snow that would take the strata from the mountains and leave only bare light and shadow, blank depth. . . . Sam and I would walk on snowshoes bent from willow and secured with gut. Through woods where the snow had filtered down in an even layer. Across open ground, wary of a stream that melted the crust thin, out in the center where the land seemed to dip. Toward the Ramshorn, which lifted into the low clouds. A full-day hike until we saw Gilbert's camp—a fleck in a white valley. Scattered groves of aspen like crowdings of marble posts. Gilbert had robes to warm us. He settled us down in the structure. The gray evening light reflected through the east door. A storm had begun—Gilbert shut it away. The small fire at the center of the room gave enough light, and the smoke rose straight into the spot of bleached sky in the ceiling, directly above.*

    And when I finished the novel, years later, I dedicated it to Ken and the memory of John. In those pages, the three of us wander the West, follow a trail into the gray granite canyons of the Wind River Range.

6

Over the past few years I've lived in many places—Rhode Island, Palo Alto, Mississippi, Wyoming, Denver—and I've stayed put for anywhere from a few months to a year. I've cared for my sister's children, bunked in my brother's condo, luxuriated in a mansion, listened to roof-rats take hold in my cottage. Each night lately, as I close my eyes, there is a moment, a ritual almost, during which I wonder where I am—what state, what age— where do I live, who do I know.

In my memory, the city is almost an island, jutting into cold water. How many years till I find family again, another Sunday morning?

a eulogy
for george

We first met in Minnesota when we were in our early twenties. I had moved there to be a gay activist. George was in the Air Force and was home on leave. We were attracted to each other by our hair. Mine was long, it flowed over my shoulders. It was, my mother says, my "Jesus hair." George's was buzz cut in the required military fashion. The first night we met and made love our hands seemed to be on one another's head as much as any other part of our bodies. George was taken by the rebellion my hair represented, a rebellion he felt he'd never take part in, but was obviously fascinated with. I was responding to more base impressions—he was a man in a uniform.

Even with the difference in our haircuts, we looked very much alike. We were both over six feet tall, we had long, angular faces and the same northern European coloring. People were always commenting on our similar appearances. "You must be brothers," was something we heard so often that we didn't even respond to it after the first few years.

Our affair was short-lived. I was, he informed me, not the marriage material that he wanted. There was someone back in Denver, where George had gone to college and where he was going to return for graduate school, who offered more stability, and that was what he needed.

Yet, I insisted, we got along so well, enjoyed one another's company so much, we should keep something of this. He agreed. We would be friends.

George became a constant in my life. Our meetings would be erratic, but we kept up by telephone and letters. We were strangers to one another in many ways—certainly anyone looking at our lives would think so. I continued my political work; George and his chosen lover saved money. I saw him whenever he came to Minnesota to see his family. I would visit George and his lover in Denver often, wondering at their lifestyle—they were members of a subdued middle class, who indulged in middle brow entertainment at best, I thought. They would be shocked or titillated by mine—I was outrageously open about my sexuality and pushed too many people too far, they both insisted. But no matter how far the poles of our points of view would separate, the fabric of our relationship never did.

The most dramatic incident happened when George and I were in our late twenties. I was in Denver as a spokesman for the gay movement during conventions for two protestant denominations; their meetings were being held back to back. I had worked with many of the national staffs of the two churches over the years. To George's—and almost everyone else's—astonishment the denominations had provided most of the funding for my work. It was a time when "alternative lifestyles" were the fad as were alternative forms of ministry. I was a standard bearer for both in the minds of the liberal church people.

The first night of the first convention George and I went out with some of the people I knew. We were in a bar in the Denver Hilton. My friends encouraged us to dance with one another. It was a new time! Old forms had to go. Men could dance together, they insisted. We did. The staff of the bar didn't think things had changed all that much. There were some mean-spirited confrontations and the police were called. My friends were leading us out of one entrance just as the cops were coming in the other.

I was furious, and George was terrified of what I would do in my anger. We agreed to sleep on the incident and talk the next day. I told him then that I couldn't be silent. He had calmed down and had realized that would be my answer. He was in graduate school and aiming at a job in the federal bureaucracy; he'd have nothing to do with my public protests, but I could use his house and his telephone and do what I had to.

I did a lot. I challenged the leaders of the second convention. They were scheduled to use the same hotel from which two men dancing had been ejected and threatened with arrest, yet they funded gay community work. Which side were they really on? There was a small activist community in Denver. It seemed shocked that anyone would take on the national hotel chain, but they were willing to put up informational picket lines. The press ate it up—the religious angle, the first public display of activism from Denver, all of it.

I fed all this with endless telegrams and press releases. The phone in George's house rang off the hook for the next week. Negotiations were a little easier than might be expected because, while the local management of the hotel was inflexible, I was in contact with the company's national headquarters. There was a notorious gay bar in the basement of one of their Chicago hotels. How much publicity did they want about that operation? I asked.

In the end, we won a symbolic victory. The wording was straightforward. The management of the hotel apologized publicly to me and to my unnamed companion and vowed to Denver activists that people of the same sex were welcome to dance anywhere there was dancing in the Denver Hilton.

The second convention was still going on when the agreement was formalized. George and I went back to the bar to celebrate. When we went in we discovered the final irony. For the next many years there were no public spaces where anyone could dance in the hotel; the dance floors had been taken up, the bands had been fired. We had a drink at the bar and I laughed at it all while George fumed at the way the corporation could destroy our victory.

Holidays were big in our lives together. At first that was because we would most often see one another when George came home to his family, and those events were usually built around the holidays. In time, we just assumed we'd be together at Thanksgiving, Christmas, Easter, and many other celebrations.

We didn't have the same image of those holidays, though. George wanted small, tasteful observances; I thought a party was better the more people there were. We used to fight all the time about that— No, he would insist, I could not bring "a few more friends" to his house for Thanksgiving. There weren't enough place settings of the right kind of china. Who cared about that, I would retort, and besides, I had already invited them. Somehow it all worked out, which often meant that I won. I think that was usually because I became the Prodigal Son in George's world. I was still the rebel he always took in.

George thought that was all past when I got the job as the editor of *The Advocate*. Now I would become someone he could introduce his friends to with some pride; I wasn't just a rabble-rouser anymore. I had an apartment he approved of and a car he wasn't embarrassed to be seen riding in.

George and his lover were working on their own lives. George had gotten his job in the Veterans' Administration as a social worker. His lover had a good position with a food distribution company. To many other people that might mean great security and a chance to enjoy life. To George it meant a chance to parlay two full-time incomes into investments. I was awed when I visited them in Denver and discovered that these two professional men were existing on peanut butter sandwiches for dinner. What was going on?

They were saving for rental property. Over the next few years they would buy rundown real estate. They would work evenings and weekends refurbishing the buildings. They were perfectionists. Every floor had to be refinished to a gloss that would have done a ballroom proud. The plumbing had to be replaced, so did the wiring. City codes weren't exacting enough to get the buildings into shape for them; they would far exceed them.

George and his lover were part of an army of gay men who used their sweat equity to become independent and who left behind them blocks of improved neighborhoods. There was no single step in the process; as soon as one building was in shape to pass their inspection, George and his lover would sell it, invest the equity in another invariably larger and even more decrepit property. They never seemed to take any money out of their investments. In fact, they were constantly stretching, risking more to increase their potential.

Part of this was George's relentless drive to be financially self-reliant. He had carefully chosen a federal job because he hoped there would be more protection for him in the civil service than in any other part of the employment world. He corresponded with anyone he would find who was researching how a gay man could be defended against witch-hunts and, equally important, what were the ways the rules could be broken by the bureaucracy to trespass on individual rights.

My role at *The Advocate* was especially important to George because I had access to names and addresses and could supply him with contacts and information. He reciprocated by showing me the depth of job discrimination people felt and the importance of the issue to my readership.

No matter how strong the rules were, no matter how often people were able to keep their jobs, George was not satisfied. "This is no way for a person to live," he told me when he announced he was going for yet another graduate degree (he would eventually have two more beyond his M.S.W.). He was spending all his time building up extra credentials so he could escape the capriciousness of bigotry, and he deeply resented the need he felt to be even more qualified than other employees, but he knew that was the cost of discrimination.

My tenure at *The Advocate* was short-lived. I was left unemployed and depressed in San Francisco, never a favorite place of mine, too far from New England. "The ocean's on the wrong side," I complained to George.

I became sick. I had a terrible case of hepatitis. As soon as he found out, George was on a plane. He talked to the landlord and paid my back rent and promised to cover any future shortfalls. He took care of me as long as he felt he could afford to and then left me with a check to make sure I wouldn't have to apply for welfare. "You must never become dependent on a bureaucracy," he insisted. "I know. I work for one."

When he was ready to leave San Francisco for Denver, he ran his hand through my hair, now much shorter, beginning to show its retreat up my forehead. He was concerned, not just with this crisis, but with the way my life was going. "You know, you could at least write about this." He wasn't the first person to tell me; his wasn't even the loudest voice that told me to write; but he said it, and I never forgot that he did.

Wherever I lived, George would visit, sometimes alone, sometimes with his lover. I saved up for each trip. Not because I'd need extra money, I wasn't saving cash. It was just that I knew there were certain things that George would do—that he would enjoy doing—that I could never do so well.

George was the foremost consumer advocate in America. When a good or service was not up to standards, George would go to war. It was his kind of vacation.

Whenever George arrived in my house, I would have a box of items and sales slips waiting for him. "Perfect," he'd say as he sifted through the

evidence. "I'll get the bastards." He invariably did. I once had bought a set
of stainless steel flatware from Macy's. It rusted in the first wash. This was
George's territory. When George came to see me a few months later, he
marched to battle against the retailer. He came back flush-faced and vic-
torious. Not only had he gotten my money back, he had somehow gotten
the store to give me yet another set of flatware, one that was even more
expensive than the original. "How?" was all I could ask. "Stainless that
rusts! It was an outrage!" was all he would answer.

Plumbers and car repair services fell when he faced them down. Insurance companies revised claims, credit bureaus altered their records, realty
management companies wept for mercy.

No matter how successful George became, I always knew that there was
part of my life that he wanted, the freedom he perceived, the willingness
to create an alternative to the middle class he was deeply entrenched in.
(And there was a part of me that craved his stability; we both knew that
as well.) As time went on, his visits were always alone, without his lover.
He wanted to see the clubs I went to in San Francisco and New York. He
wanted to experience the restaurants I went to and read my magazines.

He called once to announce a social coup. I was living in New York
at the time. George had an invitation to go to Fire Island, to the Pines.
Some friend in Washington had a house there—one of *the* houses, George
assured me—and he was going to spend the Fourth of July. I couldn't have
cared less about Fire Island, it never appealed to me, but I was excited that
George would be coming through the city on his way to the resort, even if
only for one day.

The night he arrived we went on a tour of the underside of Manhattan,
to places George wanted to see. We had a marvelous time and didn't even
notice when he slipped and fell on one of the club's uneven floors.

I had a small apartment in the East Village then; just two rooms.
George was sleeping in one, I was in the other. At dawn he crawled into
my room and shook me awake. His ankle had swollen to at least twice its
normal size; he couldn't walk or even put any weight on it. Somehow I got
us both dressed and into a cab and took him to St. Vincent's Hospital. He
had sprained the ankle when he'd fallen, the doctor finally told him. (George
had to wait hours to see one, sharing the corridor with a couple gun-shot
wounds and stabbing victims. He was mortified.)

Now George was faced with a dilemma. How was he going to get to Fire Island for his long-awaited debut? I offered to do anything to help him, but it was a holiday weekend and we both knew that the trains would be crowded and there'd be a rush to get to the jitneys that took passengers to the ferries—he obviously couldn't handle that. He investigated every possibility. He was even willing to rent a private seaplane to take him to the Pines, but it proved hopeless. There were no piers that could accommodate seaplanes on Fire Island back then. He could never have walked through the bay water up to the shore with his aching ankle.

There was no option. He had to cancel and spend the weekend with me, in my East Village apartment with my cats climbing over him and me bringing in Chinese takeout. I had a great time; George never forgot it either.

For a while afterward George insisted that we visit in neutral places. I had talked to him for years about Provincetown. He hadn't been intrigued; he was more drawn to the stylishness that Fire Island represented to him. I finally talked him into going to Cape Cod. We stayed in a wonderful guest house on Commercial Street, the kind of place where the hosts provided mixers and everyone brought his own alcohol and a cocktail party was held every night.

The men at the Ranch were men much closer to George's image of what gay men might be than were my activist and artist friends. They were solidly employed, friendly and gregarious, from all over the country. They were gay men who were like him. I could sense from the first evening that George felt at home with them more than I'd ever seen him be with the very few gay friends he had back in Denver, most of them desperately closeted. He loved the Ranch.

He loved Provincetown even more. After the first full day there, most of it spent on the beach, we sat in a restaurant with our skin toasted pink, but not painfully so, and he looked out over the harbor and said, "This is the first place I've ever been where the postcards didn't lie. I have to live here."

He got up from the table and went to the pay phone without explaining anything to me. When he came back he said, "We're selling all our property. We're going to move here and buy a guest house."

The decision was made and there was no turning back. By the next summer, they'd found their place, liquidated their Colorado real estate, and entered into the self-employment they had both longed for.

Owning his own business was the ultimate goal for George. He was suddenly beyond the reach of bosses and rules and prejudice. He was the master of his own destiny. It was the same year I moved to Maine.

We were both consumed by our new homes and, even though we were geographically closer than we ever had been in our lives, we actually visited less often. George finally called me, distressed, "It's been over a year since we've seen each other!" I couldn't believe it and insisted on checking calendars. We were shocked by the proof.

"I'm coming up next weekend," he insisted. It's a five-hour drive from Provincetown to Portland on a boring interstate. We each made it a regular trip over the next ten years.

He usually came here, mainly because he would feel cramped by the small resort town after a pressured summer season, and mainly because, as we grew older, we were more interested in conversation than we were in adventures. Portland was easier for that.

Most of the people I knew were younger than George and I. I was not known for suffering people who weren't very smart or very political—the two aren't always the same thing. George would arrive with some new car-as-toy and spend his time at a meal complaining about a five-percent drop in occupancy for the fourth week of September. Or worse, he'd obsess about what kind of computer he should buy. It offended him that there was no clear-cut choice among various machines. Each one had an advantage. The investment would be thousands of dollars. He argued for hours about what he should do. When he finally did choose a hardware system, there was still the question of software. He drove everyone to distraction as he equivocated among the options.

"Why him?" the young people would ask after one of those dinner conversations. "Because he's my witness," I finally said, when I understood myself. "Because he's the person who has followed me through all the changes and all the emotions and who has stood by me no matter what happened." And I knew I was the same for George.

We always shared a bed when George visited Portland. We'd strip to our underwear and climb under the covers and continue our gossip late into the night. Sometimes, not often, rarely in fact, and never with any premeditation and only in Maine, we would have sex. It was innocent sex, the kind that boys might have during a sleep-over in junior high school. I'd feel an unexpected hand tugging at the elastic of my shorts when the lights were turned off and I'd roll over. There were never any passionate kisses, but there was a feeling of great familiarity. Our bodies fit together. They always had. And we would always rub one another's head, even though we had both gone nearly bald.

I don't think George was very happy in those years, actually. There had been a large nest egg left over after he and his lover had bought their guest house; there was no real financial pressure anymore, especially because they had bought their Provincetown property at a highly propitious time, when the costs were at a nearly all-time low, just before a bubble blew up the value of their investment. Of course they had to renovate the house to perfection, and document its hundred-and-fifty-year-old history, and make themselves valued members of the community (George sat on the board of the old peoples' home for years and he attended every town meeting and every meeting of the Board of Selectmen). But when it was all done, and that all only took five years or so at the most, there was only vacuuming and changing the sheets during the summer and a life with a bit of extravagance the rest of the year.

Without the smell of a battle, without the quest for independence and security, George's life seemed to lose its zest. He traveled extensively, but didn't seem to get a charge out of it, even when he went to China or Europe.

Eventually he and his lover bought a condo in Florida where they spent half of the year, but George, even as he claimed to love the serenity of the beach there and the calmness of his life without any need to work, seemed unhappy with the blandness of where they chose to settle down, the bourgeois resort of Naples, even as he was unwilling to live in Miami or Miami Beach—too dangerous he said, but with some longing.

When I finally told George about my HIV diagnosis, he went into a tailspin. It was the kind of response that I would learn reflected the other person's fear for himself as much as mine. I had expected George to fall apart, and I wasn't surprised that his response took this form. He had been haunted by AIDS and had been convinced for years that I would fall to it; San Francisco and New York were no longer exotic to him, they were vectors of disease.

It took George a few years to be tested himself. He worried about the decision all the time. We had endless phone conversations about it. Should he? Would there be any worthwhile treatment if he did have the virus? How was I?

When George finally did get tested, the news was awful. The virus was marching through his body much more quickly than it was meandering through mine. The phone calls from Florida became more frequent and more frightening. There were constantly new infections, new fears. George was sick almost always. Every conversation would reveal some new problem.

When he had been a social worker, George created a specialty of working with people who were dying. He confessed to me that he had always felt inadequate. He could never find the emotions to match the situation, he felt. But he worked the systems for his clients. There was no reason for physicians not to be kind and responsive; he tracked down the doctors and demanded they attend to the patients' questions. There was no reason for families to be left alone with what was going on; he formed support groups for them. There was no reason that someone who was dying should be worried about anyone else's trivia, he explained. He maneuvered the VA bureaucracies and advocated his clients' concerns. He would build a cocoon for the people he felt he couldn't touch himself, a shelter where the minutiae wouldn't interfere with the real issue at hand, the approach of death. No matter how much George would complain about his insufficiencies, I was sure those people thought he was an angel when he appeared in the concrete corridors of the VA.

As he got more sick, George wasn't really able to do that for himself. He worried too much about other people. His family had managed to ignore the evidence of his sexuality; now they not only had to deal with it, there was the added revelation of his AIDS that had to be addressed. His lover had to be taught how to use the computer and all the other things that George had handled that went into running the guest house. It didn't matter that he was obviously more ill than I was, he had to worry about my infection as well.

There was also the same old feistiness. Insurance companies were the focus of most of George's rage. Every late reimbursement, every questioned medical expense was another part of the corporate conspiracy to get gay men. George would have none of it. He fired off letters to the Commonwealth and to Washington. He filed official complaints. He argued with everyone he could reach on the phone.

There was also the question of medical care. Where was the best? We both sought out specialists from Harvard Medical School, mine were at Massachusetts General, his were at New England Deaconess. Every visit each of us made to his doctor had to be followed up with a phone conversation. What were they saying differently? Was there some experimental drug that one had and the other didn't? George's interrogations were grueling.

But the fight left him, and he knew it. There wasn't the energy. I visited Provincetown a few times when he could no longer make the drive to Portland. We talked and we held hands. In 1992, the week before Christmas, George called from the hospital and I heard the all-too-familiar death rattle in his voice. His lover asked that I come down for the holiday. It was time.

An intensive-care hospital like New England Deaconess is eerily empty on Christmas. It seemed that George was the only person on his floor. I sat with him for a while and I ran my hand over his hair. The chemotherapy he'd gone through had taken it almost all away and only wispy patches were left. It didn't matter. I remembered the buzz cut I had touched the first night we'd met; I remembered the way George later had tortured the thin strands to try to cover up his bald spot; I remembered it all.

His lover called a couple days later and said George had passed on. George was forty-five when he died.

I hate memorial services. They're for the survivors who indulge themselves in a shallow emotion and a sense of caring that they seldom showed when the dead person had been alive. But of course I had to go to George's that next spring.

"I'm going to write about it," I explained to people who were surprised that I was going to give up my policy of not attending these rituals. No one believed the cynical spin.

It was a beautiful day. As he had requested, George had been cremated. His lover and his family carried his ashes to the dunes overlooking the Atlantic, George's favorite place in the world. There was a strong wind blowing off-shore. When the ashes were thrown into the air, they flew out to the sea. This was the place that had convinced George that the postcards of Provincetown hadn't lied, they had told the truth.

I wept in a way I never had before. I had lost my witness. There were hardly any gay men of my generation left, none who had known me for as long and as well as George had. I was alone in a way I had never been before. As I watched the specks of George's life disappear over the Atlantic, I knew that part of myself went with them.

In the end, it all comes down to this: George was a good man. He was my friend. It was a goddamn shame that he died so young.

a marriage manual

As I write these words, Rick and I have just completed our seventeenth year of living together.

The length of our marriage usually surprises people, I suppose because neither of us looks quite old enough to have been married for seventeen years. That's the way it goes when you get your partner young. I met Rick when I was nineteen. Now I've just turned thirty-seven.

A bit of nomenclature: Yes, please, let me call it a marriage. No other word really suits. When we were in our twenties, we called ourselves lovers, and I thought that would always do, but somewhere along the line I stopped thinking of Rick as my lover and started thinking of him as something else. My husband? I always cringe when I hear gay men use that word, because it implies a wife, and thus a simulation of heterosexual marriage, which is never quite the case. Domestic Partner is the legal term, and as such we're registered in the city of San Francisco, where we used to live and where Rick still works. The words are a bit cumbersome, but I think I might get used to calling Rick my DP. Partner isn't bad, and neither is spouse, though I most often tell people that Rick is My Other Half, which seems to sum up the psychological and metaphysical aspects rather nicely.

Whatever the terms, ours is most definitely a marriage. Everything we own, we own jointly—the car, the house, the savings account. Virtually everything we do, we do together (including going to the baths together in the old days and nowadays going to sex clubs, though we do wander off by ourselves and meet up again later). Everything that interests us individually is to some degree of mutual interest, from television shows to what we do for a living, from the birth of my sister's baby to trying to get the city to repaint a nearby crosswalk. We take our vacations together. All big decisions (and most small ones) are made jointly, not always without agonizing, but always, ultimately, with consensus. The jobs of living which are not shared are divided: *If you'll take care of that, I'll take care of this—no,* you *make that phone call, I'm sick of dealing with those people—would you carry out the garbage tonight, I'm just too tired—no, don't worry, I'll take him to the vet, I need to run some errands tomorrow, anyway—*and so on.

I've never seen the movie *We Were One Man,* but I often think of that title in relation to our marriage. Individually, each of us is most definitely his own man, but together we are a smarter, bigger, stronger man.

Many of our friends are not married, and I begin to think they never will be. I wonder if coupling up is something amenable, even inevitable, for certain personality types, and not amenable, even impossible, for others, for whom being single is simply more natural. If so, then there's little point in giving people advice on how to have a successful marriage. But because I've been asked more than once about the secret of my marital success, it's something I've consciously thought about, and I've come up with a few ideas.

meet memorably

An anecdote to go with your first encounter is a treasure forever.

Rick and I met through twins. I was a nineteen-year-old college freshman in the middle of a torrid affair with Michael, a twenty-seven-year-old painter; Rick came home from the bar one night with Michael's twin brother, Monty, the math teacher. We saw each other for the first time in the darkened hall, passing on the way to the bathroom. The next morning all four of us went to a friend's house for brunch, where Rick, by daylight a good-looking East Coast Jew and rather exotic to my small-town Texas eyes and ears, made an unforgettable impression on me by reading aloud to everyone from Dear Abby. "How gauche!" I thought, with my pretentious little someday-I'll-be-a-novelist nose in the air.

Then, as now, Austin, Texas, had a fairly small gay community, and after meeting him I inevitably started seeing Rick around. We ended up being part of the same crowd at the old Pearl Street Warehouse, a group of randy young students who slept with each other one by one that year. One Friday at the bar, I thought: Tonight I hope it'll be Rick. He was thinking the same thing, apparently, and that was that. Something clicked: We hardly spent a night apart from that point on, and a few months later we moved in together.

(The sex! Every day, at least once, and all over the place—straddling the coffee table, standing up in the shower, rutting on the living room carpet, bending over in the breakfast nook . . .)

As for the twins, Michael the artist, one of the sweetest and deepest men I've ever known, was murdered a few years later by a no-good piece of trash he picked up in a bookstore. Monty got into channeling and, so I am given to understand, speaks with Michael on a regular basis. You see, a really good first-meeting anecdote never quite ends.

share everything

This means money. I'm always skeptical of couples starting out who keep their finances strictly separate, and I've never known of a long-term marriage where such an arrangement is workable. It's all or nothing, and it doesn't matter who makes more money; the money is there to help you enjoy life together. John Giorno once wrote a poem titled, "You're the Guy I Want to Share My Money With." That just about says it all.

seek guidance

We could never have done it without counseling. Well, maybe, but then I could probably walk twenty miles barefoot on a rocky road if I had to. I'd rather invest in a good pair of shoes.

I have friends who refuse to even consider seeing a shrink, probably because their idea of what a shrink does comes from the unreal world of movies or sitcoms. "How can a shrink know me better than I know myself? Where does he get off telling me what's wrong with me or what I should do?" Not the point. The skilled counselor merely assists you to see things you haven't been looking at; once your eyes are open, the work is up to you. This is especially true in couples counseling, because couples get into all sorts of repetitive behaviors which they can't find their way out of, because they're too close to the situation to see what they're doing.

Rick and I have hit some rough patches over the years, and I credit good counseling for helping us see it through. Bad counseling is another matter, but you'll be able to tell if he or she is a bad counselor pretty quickly. If you don't leave the session with a feeling of illumination or a renewed sense of hope, if you don't feel that the lines of communication between you and your partner are being reopened, however painfully, then find another counselor.

The biggest, hardest lesson I learned in couples counseling was this: The responsibility for every problem is absolutely and without exception *equal*. This was not an easy proposition for Mother's Perfect Little Boy to accept, especially when his partner came equipped with built-in, ready-to-exploit Jewish Guilt. Intellectually and emotionally, I could always come up with a dozen indisputable reasons why it was Rick's fault, not mine, proving that responsibility couldn't possibly be equal; but, like a Catholic facing a religious mystery or a Zen Buddhist contemplating a conundrum, I simply learned to submit to the doctrine of equal responsibility and to proceed from there. Try it: Arbitrarily acknowledge your half of the blame and you may be amazed at the results. It takes two people to make an argument, or a reconciliation, or a marriage.

travel together

Especially if you're young, or if neither of you has traveled much before. All your senses are heightened when you're in a foreign place; the simplest memories become indelibly etched. To have someone with whom to share those memories is a treasure beyond counting.

Travel disrupts any monotony that's begun to creep into your daily marriage routine. Travel gives you a chance to get back in touch with each other in a fun, happy way. If this sounds hopelessly banal, it's only because I haven't yet mentioned the shared agonies of travel.

Misery loves company, which is why people on battlefields or in horrible jobs find camaraderie with even the most unlikely companions-in-suffering. How much more intimate is the bond that's forged between two spouses enduring the miseries of travel? For their honeymoon, my sister and her husband went on a long trip to the South Pacific and parts of Southeast Asia. They tell of wretched sea crossings on crowded cargo boats and a night spent on a rat-infested waterfront—shared memories that will link them forever. How I envy them those ordeals, and their mutual triumphs over them!

Fortunately, Rick and I have such experiences of our own. The incident at the Franco-Swiss border, when we were thrown off the train in the middle of the night for not having visas, lingers particularly vividly in my mind. The cold, the confusion, the arrogance of the young porter who demanded: "You are in France now, speak French!"

Travel lets you see the worst in each other, but also the best, and some trips have left only fond memories. Like our trek down to Baja, rattling over roads that never appeared on any map and hiking through a Dr. Seuss landscape of mad ocotillos and skyscraper cacti. Like our adventures in the deserts of Utah and Arizona, especially in the Grand Canyon, Rick's favorite place on earth—rafting down the Colorado River, sleeping under the stars, getting up before dawn to take a rope-climbing trek through frigid spring water, hiking from the rim down to the river and back in a single day. Before I met Rick I had never so much as camped out overnight.

But I'd better stop now, or I'll be asking you to look through my photo albums next. You'd be bored stiff, no doubt. Ah, but how Rick and I love to remember those trips together. . . .

buy a house

A few years ago, I got the house bug, *bad*. We couldn't afford a place in San Francisco, but we could, using our savings and my inheritance money and a big capital infusion from what Rick calls the Bank of Dad, afford a little bungalow across the bay in Berkeley.

At some point during all the running back and forth and signing papers till our hands cramped, Rick said the most astonishing thing: "I guess this means you really want to stay with me." This, after sixteen years! I felt like Tevye (or is it Tevye's wife?) when confronted with that absurd question: "Do you love me?" But some people, I suppose, need a great deal of reassurance, and if you really love them, you'll give it to them.

The house has been a wonderful thing. Well into our thirties we were still living in what I called "student digs," amid an accumulation of cast-off furniture and makeshift office equipment. The house has allowed us to scrap all that and start over, spending money we've saved for years on material objects of quality, durability, and beauty—a novel experience. The stifled anarchist and eternal child in Rick sometimes questions these grown-up concerns and this creeping bourgeois sensibility, even as he's developed a wholly unexpected acumen for picking out the perfect piece of furniture for a given space.

Most of all, the house has given us something to do together. All decisions are made together, from where to hang a picture, to how much to spend on a sofa, to where to replant the bird of paradise. At first, all the decision-making required intense negotiations and no small amount of hair-tearing, but as we went on things became easier and easier. Together, as a couple, we've defined our tastes, set our budgets, determined our priorities, and gone about creating a home in which we can comfortably live. The day-to-day intimacy of this collaboration has given us a whole new world to explore, together.

have pets

My brother and his first wife once told us, by way of demonstrating their "acceptance," that they had some gay neighbors who were *just like a married couple;* why, these two men had a cat and they treated it "just like a baby."

This comment struck me as rather patronizing in a typically condescending, heterosexual way, and all the more wrongheaded for comparing a baby to a cat. Any fool can make a baby, but to achieve kinship with an animal is the act of a demiurge, a feat of magic such as the Ents performed by communing with trees, the heady, mythic stuff of Tolkien, Tarzan, and Dr. Doolittle.

Basil, a male tabby, is almost as old as our marriage. We raised him from a kitten, and the tale of his upbringing is indistinguishably a part of the tale of our marriage. When he was small, he would jump on command all the way from the floor up into my arms, which earned him the nickname Flying Kitty. My love for him was cinched on the wintry night many years ago when he was trapped on our steep roof by a patch of ice; every time he stepped onto the glassy surface he began to slip and slide and would hurriedly draw back in fear. After much coaxing from me, Basil finally put out his claws, stepped onto the ice and slid out of control, as if on wobbly skates, down the roof, over the edge, and into my waiting arms. A creature of another species put his trust in me; after that, how could I ever let him down? Now Basil is an old cat, slowed down by arthritis and currently recovering from a bout with congestive heart failure. Still, he perseveres and grows more demanding of warm laps and special treats every day—a role model for my own hopefully crotchety old age.

The really special thing is this: Basil's complete history and his many irritating and endearing habits are intimately known to only two human beings, Rick and myself.

Then there was Zoë, a plump and precious calico. Rick has always been more sensitive to the cats' illnesses than I am, and so it was Rick who first noticed when Zoë stopped eating. Our fat cat became skinnier and skinnier. The vet, a gruff lesbian, diagnosed a liver disorder, and bluntly informed us, "A cat with a bad liver is usually a dead cat." We rescued Zoë from the hospital, where the vet was trying to feed her intravenously and where I have no doubt that Zoë would have died in short order, and took her home. We put her in a quiet room; she found a spot on some towels and more or less collapsed. We fed her liquid food from a plastic hypodermic for days and days. She was so weak that she never budged from her spot. She stayed alive, I think, chiefly because she could tell that we wanted her to. Finally, one day I came home to find that Zoë had moved—only a few feet, to the opposite corner of the room, but she had moved! Shortly after that she began drinking a little milk on her own, and then to eat solid food, and in a few weeks she was as fat as she had ever been.

Zoë had several more happy years, but eventually she fell ill again. This time it was an inoperable scattering of tumors in her gut. When she was put to sleep, Rick and I stood over her, touching her together. As she died, her body went limp, and for the first time since the onset of her illness she felt as she normally felt to my touch, relaxed and soft; I realized how much discomfort she must have been in to have held herself so tense for so long, and I knew that her death was a release. Rick and I said good-bye to Zoë together.

Now Hildegarde, a rambunctious black and white, has joined the household. When we walked in front of her cage at the animal shelter, she looked me straight in the eye, walked up to the bars, and said: "Finally! What took you so long? Get me out of here!" Or something to that effect; she is quite a talkative cat. When she was little she was quite a magpie, stealing and hiding any small object, like the Gorbachev pin I bought in Amsterdam which kept turning up under the sofa, or the pecans that she would somehow pluck out of a hanging wire basket and hide in our shoes.

Hildegarde loves the new house, and especially the backyard, of which she is the undisputed queen. The squirrels tease her mercilessly, allowing her to stalk within a few feet of them and even to pounce, only to discover that their bushy tails are forever just out of reach. We laugh at her, and she sulks a bit; but in time she extracts her revenge, sinking her teeth in just a little harder the next time she seduces us to play rough with her on the little grassy hill consecrated for such games.

Oh, the stories I could tell! Of course, they would quickly bore you. But Rick and I can talk about Hildegarde for hours. . . .

jealousy

Rick and I started our marriage accepting certain premises, namely that promiscuity was biologically natural for men and, in 1976, almost a political duty for gay men. Realistically, we agreed, sleeping around was simply unavoidable in a marriage between gay men, so after the first year or so we began to try to work out practical ways of accommodating each other. (It seems to me that couples who begin a relationship on the assumption that there will never be any outside sex are just asking for trouble.)

Over the last seventeen years our rules for outside sex have gone through numerous changes. At various times it's been okay only when one of us was out of town, or only at the baths, or only when we both felt like going out. Finding rules to suit both of us hasn't always been easy, and the process hasn't always been smooth. Possessive jealousy (as well as envy, because one of us might score with a guy the other wanted) sometimes

seems as instinctually imperative as promiscuity, and can jump out of nowhere to scramble even the most doggedly rational mind. Jealousy is not
called a monster for nothing.

The monster's power to mess up our marriage has largely diminished
over the years, thanks to our growing trust in each other and our somewhat
stabilized sex drives, but it's surprising how it can still rear its ugly head.
The best long-term defense against it isn't old-fashioned fidelity, I think,
but complete honesty. From time to time you can bend or break any of the
other ground rules and probably be forgiven, but you'd better not lie about
it. Promiscuity can be negotiated. Deception can't.

keep having hot sex

Having outside sex never meant the end of our passion for each other. Long
gone are the days of doing it every day, in every possible position, on all
the furniture—but the sex is still hot.

Single friends of mine are dubious. Once, after Rick and I had particularly good sex, I happened to mention the fact in a letter to my friend
Andrew Holleran, who wrote back: "As for you and your lover having terrific
sex on Valentine's Day: *incroyable*. How do you do it? What IS sex like with
someone you've lived with for _____ years? It's an experience I can't even
grasp imaginatively. A body so familiar, etc., a person one has seen in so
many lights. WHERE'S THE FANTASY?!!"

In my head, mostly. While Rick claims never, ever to fantasize while
having sex, I do fantasize; I'm a porn writer, after all. However, when the
sex is good—and with Rick it is predictably, routinely, surprisingly yet not
at all surprisingly *good*—I reach that essential, wonderful, irreducible point
beyond fantasy, when I'm exactly *there*, in the moment. It's the very familiarity of the sex and the other body which gives me the security to sink
into that deliciously comfortable state beyond the protective pretenses or
uncertain expectations of sex with someone new. Yes, I know the thrill of
the hunt and the first contact, but some sex, with some men, gets better
over time. As for mystery, there is no lack of it: no matter how familiar
the Other becomes, the space behind his eyes will always hold a puzzle.
New bodies and new personalities are hardly necessary to tantalize me with
life's impenetrable mystery.

Advice? Continuing to have hot sex goes hand in hand with "Seek Guidance," above: The incommunicative periods are pretty much the low sex periods; the good times are the same as the good-sex times. Sex is sometimes therapy, sometimes the goal in itself; sometimes longed-for and absolutely necessary, as after a long separation, and sometimes utterly matter-of-fact, like watching a favorite sitcom on Thursday night; but it always has to be there, and I can't imagine any marriage succeeding or surviving without it.

Details? I shall give none, at least not here, and not as nonfiction. Like many porn writers, I am reticent to describe my own sex life. However, I will say that Rick and I have worked out a durable means of having very satisfying sex on a fairly regular basis—and this, despite the fact that ours is a mixed marriage: one positive, one negative.

be very brave

And now the hard part. To love is always to take a terrible risk. When I was young, the risk was mainly of rejection, that I might muster the courage to give my heart to someone only to have it handed back to me. What a small and superficial risk that seems to me now! As I've grown older, as I've witnessed the passing away of my grandparents, my mother, little Zoë, so many friends and colleagues and acquaintances, the risk of loving seems to grow greater and greater, for I've learned the hard, cold truth that even the people who love us back can be taken away from us.

And so the paradox: The more we love and cherish another person, the greater the rewards of the relationship and the deeper and truer the colors of the whole world become; yet at the same time, the more we love, the more vulnerable we become.

The shared memories are what I would miss most, I think. If Rick should leave this world, who else but me in all the world would remember that night we got thrown off the train at the French border? Or the way that Zoë relaxed from all the pain and became so beautiful when she died in our arms? Or the joyous afternoon I got the letter from my editor saying he wanted to buy my first novel? No one else will remember these things, because no one else was there. Rick and I have paid witness to one another's lives. Without him, half of me will be lost in time, and there will be no one, no one at all, to whom I can turn on a sunny afternoon in San Francisco and say:

"This weather, this light, something about it reminds me of that day in—"

"Rome."

"Yes! I'm flashing on this one particular place, a sort of grotto—"

"On the Palatine Hill."

"Was it?"

"Uh huh. Do you remember all those cats—"

"Just outside the Forum."

"And the old ladies putting out spaghetti for them!"

We laugh.

"Ummm, pizza rustica!"

"Like they had at Tivoli, with the potatoes and rosemary. Are you hungry?"

"Maybe. Look at that one."

"Where?"

"On the bicycle."

"Mmm, he used to work out at my old gym. I think he's a school-teacher. The fountains were shut down that day, remember?"

"Where?"

"At Tivoli."

"But it was still incredible. And then Hadrian's Villa."

"In the rain."

"It wasn't so bad."

"No, it made everything kind of soft and blurry—the ruins, the tall grass, the olive trees. But that pensione we stayed in, with the freezing linoleum floors!"

"And those churchbells at five in the morning."

"I wish we were there right now!"

"Maybe next spring, unless we go back to the desert."

"Yeah, maybe next spring . . ."

In my mind we talk back and forth, until, on the printed page, I lose track of which of us is speaking, but it hardly matters, so long as we're both here to speak a part; so long as there will be another spring when both of us will be here, alive, together.

———

The time between my writing these words and your reading them could be many years; at the shortest, it will be a matter of at least a few months. I think, as I write, of all that could change before these words see print. Mostly, I think of what could happen to Rick. How will I feel, to read these words in a book a year from now if my whole world has changed? Will I smile or weep, to read what's written here?

The virus looms over Rick and me. I shrug and say: Mortality hangs over us all. Just two weeks ago, driving across Utah, Rick and I had a terrible car accident—we went off the interstate and rolled over six times. Neither of us was badly hurt, but we could have been. It could have been me who died, and Rick who was left alone. The horrible risk imposed by the virus is nothing new; in a world where everyone dies, everyone is left alone sooner or later. All that life gives us is eventually taken away. There is no escape from the possibility of loneliness, no matter how lucky you are, or how clean you keep your karma, or how carefully you plan your life.

What I'm trying to say, I suppose, is go ahead and love, no matter how awful the risk. I gaze into the uncertain future, and I say to myself, and to you, with all the love I have: Be brave, be very brave.

larry
duplechan

sweet gregory
blue eyes

It's getting to the point where, when I am asked how long we've been together as a couple, I actually have to stop and think about it. It's like when I'm asked my age, and I have to pause; not only because lately I'm never quite sure if I want to divulge this information to strangers, but because as years go by and time blurs, smearing like a charcoal drawing under your elbow, I find I will actually forget.

As we spend our eighteenth year together, I often find myself thinking back over the circumstances which brought us together, and the people, events, and personal differences which have occasionally threatened (but so far—knock wood—failed) to break us apart.

I can picture (without the aid of the photographs of you I impulsively tore up and threw away after our first fight) the handsome blue-eyed UCLA senior in his high school letterman's jacket and entirely too much wavy light-brown hair parted (as some of my bitchier college friends used to say) "at the armpit." The boy with the muscular, slightly bowed legs and flat, Arizona vowels, but no discernible fey mannerisms, who I assumed was straight and consequently ignored for months, despite Tyrone Power-ish good looks and a pair of shoulders out to *there*. Happily, I was wrong—you weren't straight at all—not nearly—notwithstanding a penchant for wide-wale corduroy flare pants, Hush Puppies shoes, and unbecoming haircuts.

And the big surprise was your apparent interest in a slender, sloe-eyed, rather pretty, terribly effeminate black boy with a fluffy little Afro and wire-rimmed glasses, an androgynous young thing often mistaken for a woman. Years before I discovered Nautilus machines, years before I discovered that one really didn't *have* to call everybody "girl," you discovered me.

Obviously, a young man with an eye for potential.

I remember the time a certain blue-eyed boy brought a bunch of violets to my dorm room (a few of which I still have pressed between the pages of *A Pictorial History of the Talkies*). I might have fallen in love with that boy then and there, standing at my door wearing that letterman's jacket and a sweet smile that crinkled the corners of his eyes, flowers in his fist. Except I'd already fallen in love with him, the first time we kissed.

"How could you possibly know he was the one?" a co-worker of mine recently asked me. "You were just a kid," she said, quite accurately. "How did you know?"

"At the risk of sounding like a song by the Ronettes," I said, "the first time he kissed me—"

"Da-doo-ron-ron?" she said, with a little smile.

I nodded. "Da-doo-ron-ron."

We begin our own special calendar with that kiss, using its occasion as our anniversary date. It was March 30, 1976, and I've been yours ever since. And your kiss is still as sweet. It's a better sugar substitute than either the pink stuff or Equal with my morning cereal; and I look forward to it with an eagerness that surprises even me, when a certain handsome, blue-eyed, oh-so-gracefully maturing man comes home to me every evening, dressed much better than in college and with a considerably nicer haircut (albeit with a touch of distinguished gray).

Nearly eighteen years later, da-doo-ron-ron.

I remember the first time we said the "L" word. It couldn't have been more than a week—ten days, tops—after that first kiss. We'd spent as much time together as two full-time college students could manage without flunking out (though truth to tell, both our grades would suffer that semester), and while I hadn't yet broken the news to you, I'd already told several friends that I'd met the love of my life. ("Him?" they invariably said. "With that *hair*?")

It was in the front seat of your ugly green 70-something Ford Maverick with the hood that didn't match, following one of our typically protracted good-night kisses, when I decided I could wait no longer.

"I have something to say," I began. "And I know this is awfully soon. And I hope this doesn't scare you away. But . . ." And by now there were tears in my eyes. "I love you."

And you said, "Oh my God."

"What?" I knew it—I'd rushed things. I'd said the big "L" before you were ready. I braced myself for your hasty retreat.

"I'm so glad," you said. "I love you, too. I wanted to tell you a week ago, but I was too scared to say it."

And our good-night kiss grew ever longer.

I stand amazed that an entire generation of Americans has been born and received their driver's licenses since I first told you I loved you. I stand amazed that two people as vastly different as ourselves (and you and I both know the racial thing is the least of our differences, don't we?) have managed to hold it together through the years of Hamburger Helper poverty and paper-walled apartments with noisy neighbors living on our heads. Through the latter seventies and the eighties in their often bizarre entirety. Through your love/hate relationship with my abortive singing career and your love/ hate relationship with my semisuccessful writing career. Through sort-of monogamy, sneaking around behind each other's back, marriage counseling with that psychologist who informed us that nonmonogamous couples didn't really love each other anyway, out-in-the-open "swinging," the quickies, the three-ways, the boyfriends (yours, mine, and ours), and that infamous underwear party at Probe.

We've survived your parents' objections. We've survived my parents' objections. We made it through your turning-thirty crisis and mine. We made it through Carter, Ford, Reagan (twice), and Bush. Through it all, Baby, through it all. In the words of Rickie Lee Jones, It must be love.

I stand at least equally amazed that, contrary to the advice of well-meaning acquaintances who warned us back in the seventies that the passion we felt for one another at that time would mellow into a warm, platonic, sisterlike friendship long before this, we're hotter for one another now than I'd have thought possible after nearly two decades. After all these years, the sight of your naked ass or your nipples through a mesh T-shirt can still make my breath catch. You'll still call me at the office to let me know that between 8:00 A.M. and mid-afternoon, you miss me. And we can still make love that measures on the Richter scale; sweaty, slippery, slam-bang, tongue-sucking fucks that fill the room with our collective bodily funks and animal noises, and leave the bed too wet to sleep in.

I am yours. You are mine. We are what we are. And you (still) make it hard.

And so, relatively confident that the feeling is still mutual, and no less delighted by that knowledge than I was during the Carter administration, I'll say it once again:

I love you, Greg. With my heart, my soul. With my arms, my lips, my dick. With everything I've got and all that I am.

I love you.

the marriage of michael and bill

Two things happened to me when I was fourteen: I wrote my first poem and I tried to kill myself. These two events were related to another; I fell in love with a boy at school named David, and because I could not express my love to him, I turned to writing so that I could at least express it to the universe. But telling my secret feelings to a sheet of paper didn't make them any less secret, or resolve them or lessen their intensity. Like something deprived of air and light and nourishment, they spoiled, and the rot I carried inside of me became unbearable, hence the suicide attempt. The experience made me into an emotional eunuch, cut off from feelings, fearful of acknowledging, much less acting, on them. It was not until I was twenty-four and met the man with whom I shared the next decade of my life that I began to regain my capacity to feel. Bill and I separated after nine years, and the years between our meeting and our parting were not always easy or happy ones. But the life we made for ourselves was, in fact, a life, not the shadowy despairing existence I believed I was condemned to before I met him because I was queer.

I had known since I was twelve that I was a queer, that was the word I used to describe myself. After I inadvertently taught myself to masturbate, I was filled with physical desire for the bodies of other boys. I knew exactly what I wanted to do with them, having been taught sex by the adult relative who had taken me, unwillingly, into his bed when I was eleven. The knowledge was shameful to me but I was as powerless over my hormones as any other teenage boy, so I masturbated grimly, parading across my imagination the naked bodies of my male classmates who, by day, I barely spoke to. Unable to repress my sexual feelings, I succeeded in isolating them from everything else I knew and felt about myself. Sex became separated from emotion and who I was between the sheets, and what I felt there, had nothing to do with who I was by light of day.

Who was I? Back then I imagined myself to be vile and grotesque even as I made a point of being conventionally virtuous; the smartest boy in class, the best-behaved, the most respectful of his elders. My two selves were built on the shame I felt about my family. We were dirt poor. My stepfather was what Victorian novelists might call a "ne'er-do-well" who spent a great deal of my childhood in one jail or another leaving my hapless mother to raise six small children on handouts from her parents and Aid to Families with Dependent Children. I blamed myself for their misfortune and no one ever bothered to disabuse me of that guilt. I strove to be a model child, as if this would compensate for the dank house we lived in and the Thanksgiving baskets from the Salvation Army, but as nothing I could do relieved our poverty or made a more responsible parent of my stepfather, I was gloomy and sullen. To be queer on top of all this was the final, crushing blow.

Or so I thought until I fell in love with David, an ordinary fellow fourteen-year-old with pale skin, green eyes, and the wiry build of a runner. It was his quietness that first attracted me because, unlike my own silence, there seemed to be nothing behind it except contentment. Watching him in class, head bent, studious, or practicing sprints on the track, I suppose what I first felt was not so much wanting him but wanting to *be* him. As the year passed, my feelings toward him changed from envy to love. I can describe the physical symptoms of that love, the longing to be near him even when I was with him, the way he began to look to me like the handsomest boy I had ever known and how I tried to keep him talking just to hear his voice. What was going on inside is harder to put down because the tortured fourteen-year-old I was seems so far from who I am at thirty-eight. The love I felt for David softened the harshness with which I viewed myself and it opened up to me a possibility of happiness that I had never even considered. Love drew me out of myself and my misery with an almost physical force, as if I were being pulled out of the pit of shame and yearning I had dug for myself by strong, compassionate hands.

David didn't know any of this. He probably thought it was strange that I called him at home every night, but if I sometimes heard the puzzled annoyance in his voice, he was too well-behaved to cut me off. If he noticed how I mooned over him at school, he never said anything about it to me. Perhaps he was more innocent than I was and truly failed to understand what I felt for him, or, maybe, because he felt nothing like it in return, he was simply waiting for it to pass. But whether he knew or not, cared or not, he let me love him, and this was a kindness on his part for which I am still grateful. For my part, I knew that I couldn't go up and tell him that I loved him (how did I know? All my heterosexual conditioning, no doubt). So I wrote a poem and called it "For David." I don't remember what it said, but I had just discovered Shakespeare's sonnets (and was declaiming them in the backyard after everyone else was asleep) so I'm almost certain that it was in the style of "Nor gilt, nor marble monuments." But if love brought me hope of happiness, it also made me excruciatingly aware of the many obstacles to that happiness, not the least of which was my inability to say the words to him that might make the rest possible, whatever that was.

My classmates were beginning to enact the rituals of boy and girl, and if they were uncertain of how, exactly, to proceed, they need look no farther than the grown-up world of men and women. I had nothing to look to but the shameful memory of being fucked by a grown-up man who now ignored me. I didn't just want to fuck David, but there was nothing in my world or in my experience to teach me what else to want, much less how to go about getting it. The hope that I had felt when I fell in love with him curdled and one day I took a handful of phenobarbital and waited to die. The dosage was not sufficient. I lurched down the corridors of my school until a teacher, appalled by his best student's behavior, took me to the principal's office. My parents were called. I admitted what I had done and was taken to the hospital where the doctor looked me over and ordered my parents to take me home and put me to bed. A day or two later my stepfather told me, "Don't worry your mother," and that was the end of it.

After David, there were other boys I fell in love with, but it never again had the same rawness of hope and despair. The lesson I drew from those experiences was that love was a kind of sickness that distracted me from the hard work of being the smartest boy in the world, from my relentless reading of books I scarcely understood, and the grim business of surviving my family. My friend Robert Dawidoff has a phrase to describe gay men like me and him who sublimate their sexual longing and emotional need in intellectual accomplishment; he calls it "ambition disorder." That was certainly my pathology. I was driven to make up in outside achievement the inner deficiency I felt, and the harder I drove myself the more I accomplished until, at the age of twenty-three, this barrio boy from the slums of Sacramento, found himself at Stanford Law School, which numbered among its alumni two sitting justices of the United States Supreme Court.

At Stanford, I could be open about my homosexuality because it was a time and a place where this information scarcely raised an eyebrow among my heterosexual classmates. In a way this was less a matter of tolerance than indifference. My classmates were at law school to acquire a profession, a pursuit that left little time or energy to invest in prurient speculation. But, to be fair, it was also true that my classmates were smart, sophisticated people inclined toward laissez-faire in matters of personal morality. I was an erratic law student because I was bored by most of my classes and, for once, my hard-won discipline failed me. Instead of studying, I wrote poetry, drank, hung out at the Gay People's Union, and tried to get laid. My best friend was a stocky girl named Susan who wore men's clothes and had short hair but was, contrary to her appearance, straight. We'd sit in Contracts, conducted by a bored, supercilious teacher in a classroom shaped like an amphitheatre, and mock our fellow students. One day, we devised a contest called, "Find Mr. Stanford," the point of which was to identify the one male classmate who epitomized the bourgeois conventionality we pretended to disdain. The person we finally chose was a boy from Cleveland, someone so neat his jeans were creased. His name was Bill Weinberger.

There were only two hundred students in my class, and I knew everyone slightly, including Bill. But all I knew about him was that he was friendly and studious and he dated a girl Susan and I called "Barbie." I don't think Bill knew much more about me than my name. I was living with three male classmates who watched the comings and goings of my various "dates" with cynical amusement but treated me no differently than they treated each other. School was a struggle, and my dates never amounted to much more than sex but I was not unhappy. Biking around town on my green Schwinn, taking in old movies at the Varsity, pouring beer at my part-time job at a biker's bar in the hills above Palo Alto, I was what I had never been in my life before: young.

One afternoon in my second year, just before finals, I was sitting at my carrel in the library when Bill came up to me and said he wanted to talk to me about something.

"Sure," I said, leaning back in my chair.

He said, "Can we go someplace else?"

I had no idea what he wanted, but he seemed anxious, so I suggested we go for a walk. We ended up on the steps of the undergraduate library, and he said to me, "Janet Hall told me you were gay."

"I am," I told him, wondering what this was leading up to.

"I'm gay, too," Bill said. "I'm just coming out."

I would have been less surprised if my ancient Trusts and Estates professor had confided to me that he wore panty-hose beneath his suits. But Bill was looking at me expectantly, so I said, finally, "Congratulations."

I was the first man Bill ever slept with. That night, fortified by a couple of pitchers of beer, as we were rolling around on the floor of my bedroom, Bill said suddenly, "This is so easy." And he began to laugh. We laughed and kissed, and rolled around some more, and somehow got undressed. He laughed again when he came, from pure pleasure and happiness. I will always remember that moment because, before Bill, sex for me was no laughing matter. It was, instead, often drunken and always awkward with the inevitable negotiations about who would do what to whom and even when I got what I wanted and squeezed some pleasure from it I felt disconnected from the body beneath mine. The part of me that entered those bodies was the least important part of me, and I was conscious that the part of those bodies I entered led nowhere. I learned with Bill that sex could be more than contraction and release.

I have known Bill now for so many years, and from so many angles, that it's hard to remember how I saw him that first night. At six feet, he was four inches taller than me, with fair skin, a lean body, and a frizz of brown hair above a long, narrow face. His eyes were greenish-brown and his moustache was white at the corner of his mouth, the result of some deficiency in pigmentation. There was a gap between his two front teeth which he liked to say indicated honesty. As I learned over time, honesty was one of his great virtues, along with a total lack of malice, a corny sense of humor, and an even temperament that balanced my more mercurial one. As for me, looking at pictures taken at that time, I see that I was a rather pretty brown-skinned boy with big eyes and a wary mouth, thin from the five miles I ran each afternoon but a little soft around the middle. It was May 16, 1980, and we were both twenty-five years old; I was exactly six months older than Bill.

Two days later, Bill stopped at my house on his way home from running, carrying a yellow rose which he gave me, saying, "I think I'm falling in love with you."

I didn't hesitate. "I'm falling in love with you, too."

Finals were beginning and the school year about to end. I was going to Denver to work as a summer associate at a law firm there and Bill was working in Washington, D.C. Because the time was short and busy, and our feelings for one another were so intense, we didn't bother to explain to our friends what had happened; I just starting sleeping at his house, and he at mine. Our housemates accepted it without a murmur of protest or hint of surprise, though Bobby, one of my housemates joked, "Who else are you sleeping with, my second grade teacher?" I remember one afternoon we were making out in the backyard of my house. I looked up and saw a woman inside, peering out the window, the sister of one of my housemates. Later, thinking we startled her, I apologized to Eric who said, "It's your house, too." I moved through those warm days half-asleep, yawning through my finals.

We said to each other, "I love you," constantly. It was mostly erotic love at that point, but not entirely; another reason we couldn't keep our hands off each other's bodies was because touch alone reassured us that what was happening was real. Behind those busy fingers were years of lonely boyhoods, tormenting fantasies, dissatisfactions, confusion, yearning. We had each been adrift in the flood of our longings for love, normality, family. In this respect, we were no different from our heterosexual friends, but for us there was the anguish of wondering how these things could be achieved by two men. When we found each other it was as if, in an alien country, each of us had found someone who spoke his native language.

For me, those first weeks with Bill wiped away the pain I had carried from the time I was fourteen and had fallen in love for the first time, with

David. I saw that my actions, the poetry, the suicide attempt, were extreme responses to love precisely because I could not express it normally; that, indeed, I did not know what its normal expression might be. With Bill I learned I could love another man and tell him so, I could want another man and have him, I could dream of creating a life together and set about creating it. I wrote very few poems about Bill, and I never felt like killing myself. There was no need.

I moved to Los Angeles after law school because I'd been offered a job at which I wouldn't have to lie about myself in, of all places, the prosecutor's office. I was recruited by an openly gay lawyer, himself a Stanford graduate who assured me that my being gay would be no problem. During my law school summers, I had worked for private firms in Sacramento and Denver and hated the chilly, male atmosphere of those places. My class of city attorneys, by contrast, was half-female and included an African-American man and woman, a Japanese woman, three Jews, an Anglo man, and me. After three weeks of training I was put into a courtroom, handed my supervisor's phone number, for emergencies, and began a trial. Over the next four years I tried close to forty cases, not to mention bargaining innumerable pleas.

I was alone in Los Angeles that first year because Bill was clerking for a federal judge in Cleveland. It had been arranged before we met and there was no question of him backing out. The separation was devastating after our final law school year. We had lived in separate houses down the street from each other, going back and forth, eating together, studying together, sleeping together. Our third year at Stanford was a long valedictory, punctuated only by my anxiety about a job and the difficult mechanics of working out where we would settle. Bill wanted to go back to the Washington firm he had worked at but I insisted on staying in California. At times during that last year, I fell into the bleak depressions that were the downside of my manic drive.

Bill had been raised in an upper-class Jewish family in suburban Cleveland, his parents Austrian emigrés, his father a successful businessman. Bill and his twin brother were the youngest of four brothers who became, eventually, two lawyers, a doctor, and an investment banker. The pressure in his family to succeed was accompanied by encouragement and rewards for the effort. He had no understanding of the struggle education had been for me, or the terrible insecurity I felt about my ability. My depression sometimes rendered me speechless, something he found disconcerting and strange. On my side, I was so caught up in my private myth of lonely forbearance and travail I could not let go long enough to be rational about my misery. We had some rocky times in consequence. But for the most part our last year at Stanford was sunny and hopeful.

In Los Angeles, I shared an old, spacious apartment with a gay man who had graduated from Stanford a year before me. Luis was sleek, handsome, and popular. He came home from work every night, took a nap, and then went out to the bars and clubs in West Hollywood, seldom returning alone. Silently, I disapproved of his promiscuity and he found my monasticism annoying. I lived for my nightly calls to Bill and the long reassuring letters he wrote me. Once in a while in my loneliness, I went to a gay supper club called the Academy (the waiters dressed in military uniform) to hear a singing duo called Hal and David. David, the antic one, was famous for his rendition of the theme song from "The Patty Duke Show" which he sang with a psychotic intensity—but I went to hear the standards, "Bewitched, Bothered and Bewildered," "Lover Man," and "The Nearness of You," because they made me think of Bill.

He came to Los Angeles in the fall of 1982 to work at a big, stuffy downtown law firm. We kept the apartment I had shared with Luis. It was not the kind of place I had associated with Los Angeles, having imagined instead endless vistas of ranch-style tract houses and kidney-shaped swimming pools beneath smoggy skies. Sycamore Street, however, was lined with tall trees and two-story Spanish-style buildings built before World War II. Ours was divided into four apartments. Our second floor apartment was commodious and filled with light. The big square rooms had tall ceilings, banks of windows, and crown moulding. There were hardwood floors beneath the carpet, black-and-white checkerboard tile in the bathroom, a pantry, and a back entrance for deliveries complete with its own doorbell. Our landlords were an ancient Jewish couple from somewhere in Eastern Europe who took an immediate shine to Bill. We furnished the place with orange crate end tables, brick-and-board bookshelves, a white couch, and a dining-room set purchased on sale at the May Company, and we slept on a mattress on the floor of a room whose windows were shaded with paper blinds from Cost Plus.

We furnished the place with student trappings not just because we couldn't afford better furniture, but also because these objects from school

had happy associations for us, something we were in need of that first difficult year of living together. We found ourselves in a city that neither of us
knew well, at jobs that were a constant test of our competence, and without
the community of friends we had had at Stanford. We were alone with each
other, two men trying to figure out how to live together without any models
of how it was to be done. Not far from where we lived was the frenetic gay
enclave of West Hollywood—Boys Town, the locals called it—its main
thoroughfare lined with bars, its bathhouses still in operation. This was
what passed for the gay community in Los Angeles in 1982. We kept our
distance, knowing instinctively that we would not find our way there.

What were we to do? The thrill of erotic love had worn off. The petty
faults we had overlooked now became glaring; my messiness, my smoking,
Bill's impunctuality, his bossiness. The deeper problem was that we were
both men, neither of us accustomed to deferring to another man, each of us
used to making his own way through life, and both of us, in his own way,
unused to the intimacy that living together required: the confessions of
annoyance, anxiety, insecurity that people have to make to each other for
the thing to work. Above all, we both feared confrontation and anger and,
to avoid them, each of us swallowed his anger or vented it in silent resentment. There were family pressures, too. I seldom spoke to my family, but
the legacy of my growing up, the depressions, the panics, the feeling of
hopelessness persisted and attached themselves to my life with Bill. He was
close to his family, but he told me his parents disapproved of his homosexuality and blamed me for seducing him. In all the years we lived together,
his father never once mentioned me by name.

We got through that year for the simple reason that we needed each
other. Both of us had planned for grown-up life but neither of us was
prepared for it. Having spent most of our lives as students, we were used
to being coddled and rewarded for being smart. We were always certain of
the next thing expected of us, and we had few doubts we would accomplish
it. But now, it was assumed we were smart, and no one gave us points for
that. Nor did the grown-ups we worked for have the time or patience to
explain what we had to do to succeed in their eyes. We were expected to
figure it out for ourselves, and even when we did, good work was only part
of it. The harder part of our jobs was mastering office politics and navigating
the thickets of turf and personality, a task more daunting for Bill because
he feared his employers would fire him if he came out. It was easier for me,

working in a government agency where a certain amount of job security existed, but Bill had none.

In all this anxiety, the only thing we could count on was each other. Almost every night, because I got home first, I would have dinner ready, something simple, baked chicken and vegetables or pasta and salad. We would talk about our days over a bottle of Trader Joe's wine. Later, after TV or reading or some work from the office, we cuddled in our student mattress on the floor, holding hands beneath the sheets until we dropped off to sleep. I learned something from this about why people marry and stay married. There is a kind of animal comfort to be taken from the physical presence of another person, a feeling that satisfies an almost biological urge. It was the first time that either of us had experienced this, and it kept us going for a long time.

Within two years our life together had opened up considerably. Bill was at a different firm, one where he could be out. This gave him the confidence to explore the city's gay world. He was, unlike me, a joiner, someone whose natural gregariousness led him to seek out community. Through him, we became involved in a gay running club and a gay lawyer's group (he later became an officer in both), and the people we met there became our first friends. At this point, 1984, we had been together for four years. We were something of an anomoly among our gay friends of our age, most of whom were single. They called us "Michael-and-Bill," or "Bill-and-Michael" in the same breath, half-mocking, half-envious. I could never go anywhere alone without someone asking, "Where's Bill?" and it made me more conscious of the life we had together than when it was just the two of us. I was proud of that life, proud of him, proud of me and, as the first rumors of AIDS deaths surfaced in Los Angeles, grateful as well.

That year I turned thirty and it was one of the happiest years of my life. Everything enchanted me, even Los Angeles. The first couple of years I lived there I found its distances daunting and the ugliness of so much of it depressing. But 1984 was the year of the summer Olympics and the city was possessed by a celebratory mood. Everything seemed bigger and brighter and cleaner. We started looking for a house and discovered the city's hidden neighborhoods of hills and gardens and lovely old houses. We found our house in a tiny enclave called Carthy Circle whose houses had been built in the 1920s. At $184,000, the house on Moore Drive was much costlier than we had bargained for, but we loved the tall, half-beamed ceiling above the living room, the working fireplace, the domed dining room, the covered terrace, the sunny bedrooms. We bought it and moved in that October.

If someone had asked me then if I loved Bill, I would have said, "Yes, of course I do." But if I had been asked to define what I meant when I said I loved him, my answer would not have come as quickly. A marriage takes on an inexorable life of its own, spinning a web of obligations, expectations, relationships, history, so that the separate identities of the two who are married become submerged to some extent in the marriage. This is not, however, to be confused with intimacy, which may be, but isn't necessarily, a part of this marital web. Intimacy means "I show myself to you, the parts you'll like and the parts you won't," and you show yourself to me, and we trust one another not to run away from what we are shown. Bill and I had created an elaborate web at the center of which was our daily life together and when I said I loved him, that was what I meant, that we were together and had created a common life. But we were not truly intimate with each other. Each of us harbored pains and fears that we kept secret, not wanting to hurt the other or drive him away. Slowly, over the next five years, our secrets overwhelmed our marriage and made us strangers to each other.

Things began to break down over sex. After the first couple of years we had sex less frequently, but we attributed this to our busy lives rather than lack of interest. But after about five years, whether or not to have sex became a fierce, if largely unspoken, ground of disagreement. Bill never showed signs of lack of interest, but for me the physical act became difficult, and then distasteful. I responded to this the only way I knew how, by ignoring it, but eventually it could not be ignored. The question of sex became not whether we would have it, but why we didn't, and I felt the weight of it on me.

I now have some understanding of the forces that were at work within me back then. My adolescent separation between sex and emotion had not prepared for a long-term relationship in which I would be expected to merge the two. For me, the erotic and the familar were antithetical; exciting sex was sex without emotional obligation. There really was a point when I told someone that I had trouble having sex with Bill because I loved him. I said it, but didn't understand it, and I didn't say it to Bill, who, I thought, it would hurt. Something else was at work, too, about which I had even less understanding. My introduction to sex was being raped when I was eleven years old by a member of my family, someone I liked and trusted. I remembered the event but I ascribed no significance to it because in my family violations of one sort or another defined my relationship to my elders. In my family, children did not fully count as humans but occupied a status somewhere between toys and animals.

I rebelled against this devaluation by leaving my family, but this sense of devaluation stuck, and the only way I knew to fight it was to withdraw from whatever it was that rekindled that feeling. Sex had always been scary because sometimes it seemed a reenactment of that first terrifying, confusing experience. Terrifying because I knew that something was being done to me that I did not want to happen, confusing because I came, for the first time, and in that moment, the pleasure was as great as the terror. With Bill, as with others, sex both tempted and frightened me, and though I was conscious of that ambivalence, I was at a loss to understand why I felt it, much less what I could do about it.

This was the baggage I carried into our bed, and it was only my half. Bill had his own set of responses to sex, and though it is not my place to go into them here, suffice it to say they were as confused as mine. We never talked about any of it, though Bill sometimes tried. I remember, vividly, sitting on a hotel bed in New York near tears as he tried to get me to talk about why I didn't want to have sex with him. When I think about the two of us in that stark white room, trees swaying in the springtime breeze outside the window, the pain we both felt, I'm still filled with regret.

By the time we passed our seventh anniversary, May 16, 1987, our troubles were becoming terminal. Bill was now at a law firm he liked, one whose partners valued him, and he was on the partnership track. He worked six days a week, long hours. I had just published my first book a year earlier and was hard at work on the second, so that when he did come home, he was apt to find me writing. I worked long into the night, coming to bed only after he was asleep. Our sex life, nonexistent now, was not even spoken of. One afternoon, I came home to a message on our answering machine from our doctor's office, telling Bill that his test had come back negative. When I asked him about it, he said he had taken an HIV test and admitted that he had been having sex with other men. I had remained monogamous, less out of virtue than because the logistics of an affair seemed daunting. I was outraged, but also, because I felt tremendous guilt over my sexual abandonment of Bill, secretly relieved.

———

Around this time, I became painfully conscious of my drinking. I had been a sporadically heavy drinker since my teens when alcohol released me from the grimness of my adolescent life and later because it loosened my powerful inhibitions. In college, my two best friends and I, budding poets all, liked to pass around a bottle of scotch and declaim verses to each other. Of course I felt the effects the next morning, but I shrugged them off. After I turned thirty, however, the drinking got less convivial and the hangovers correspondingly worse. I quit for a month and became so irritable that I'm sure everyone around me was relieved when I finally gave up and had a drink. Disturbing elements crept into my drinking after that. When we went out to dinner or a party, I always had a couple of drinks at home because I worried there wouldn't be enough alcohol when we got to wherever we were going. I could no longer predict how many drinks would make me drunk, so I began counting them, or I would make myself drink a glass of water for every glass of alcohol. At night, after Bill had gone to bed and I was writing, I drank up our brandy, carefully replacing every bottle I consumed. I didn't think Bill noticed, but he did. He mentioned my drinking to a friend of his who was sober, and while this friend confirmed Bill's suspicion that I was an alcoholic, he also told Bill I would have to come to this realization myself. My drinking and Bill's silent disapproval of it became one more current of the bad feelings that flowed between us.

In December 1987, we went to New York for a long weekend. The first night we met some friends for dinner and then went down to the Village to a bar. I got so drunk that the next morning I was throwing up parts of my stomach lining, but not before I said things to Bill that were both pathetic and cruel. He sat with me all the next day, saying little, but the expression on his face, combining concern and disgust, made speech unnecessary. "I'm not an alcoholic," I told him, at one point, but when we got back to Los Angeles, I entered a recovery program.

When, a year later, I observed my first-year anniversary of sobriety, Bill and I were no longer living together, but we had not yet formally broken up. Once a week, we showed up at the office of a therapist who specialized in working with gay couples. He was a slyly witty man who let us each speak our piece in turn with a minimum of editorial comment. I remember his dim, cool office, quietly furnished with comfortable leather chairs and reproductions of Klee on the walls. His office window opened out to a busy alley and there was always a fair amount of ruckus going on out there. Inside, meanwhile, the cool, well-mannered exteriors Bill and I presented masked an equal amount of internal ruckus. As part of our therapy, I moved out, to a tiny studio apartment in West Hollywood, where I slept during the week, returning to our house on the weekends. The move had been painfully difficult but as I lay in bed, alone, I felt as much relief as I did sadness. I suppose I knew that this was not a temporary move, but a final one.

It ended in the therapist's cool office, with me accusing Bill of being selfish, self-centered, and incapable of changing. I said I had had enough. He didn't defend himself but said only that he had come to the session prepared to tell me that he wanted to end things, too. When our hour was up, we walked downstairs together, said good-bye, and went off in separate directions to our cars. It wasn't until two years later that I woke up one night seized by sorrow, thinking of our years together and how they had come to an end. What hurt the most was that I knew Bill was a decent, loving man, and so was I, and yet we hadn't been able to work things out. And I remembered how, when we had met, we told each other we would be together for life, and meant it. I remembered, too, how, on one of those early nights, I had looked into his eyes and seen such love that I had wanted to weep. And then I wept.

The end was not, of course, the end. After a few months of little communication, we began talking again. I sat in the audience when Bill had a wedding ceremony with his second lover, and then I sat shiva with him when Martial died. When I broke up with my second lover, Bill was one of the first people I called. I've gone through the period of calling him my "ex"; now he's just my friend Bill. The anger I felt at the end has been replaced with gratitude for what he gave me those nine years we were lovers. He gave me permission to have a normal life, something I could not have imagined when I was fourteen years old. I could not have pictured myself living in contented domesticity with a man I loved, and who loved me, in our own house and our own bed. Bill was not the first family I ever had, but he was the first family I chose. And for that, Billy, I am forever in your debt.

n i k o l a u s
m e r r e l l

---

nicholas

At the junction, where our trail meets with the intermediate, I slam Randy's errant ski into the snow, bend down to help untangle him.

Randy was raised in San Jose, in the diversity and anonymity of a city, so he could be a bit freer in the way he acted; he didn't have to be so concerned about what others might think.

It wasn't true for me. I was raised back in the mountains among loggers and Indians where everyone knew each other. It was important that no one know.

Not that Randy is effeminate; he's not. He's just a normal-acting guy who moves as though he is just as much at ease in the gym as he is behind his desk.

But not me. Like a child who made too many poses into the blowing wind, one time the posture stuck. Although I am not large, when I walk through public parks, people compliment me on how beautiful the gardens look; in lumber yards, they ask me where the 2 × 8s are stacked; and at the slightest injury, doctors ask to fill out my worker's comp claims, sure somehow that I operate heavy equipment.

A nasty little eight-year-old, this time a Honduran-American, slides to a near-perfect parallel stop, showers my boots with powder.

Randy likes adventure, but he's reckless. Perhaps it's his Mexican blood. With black eyes dancing and broadsword swinging, he would have no trouble jumping aboard an English ship. . . .

I like adventure, too, perhaps more than he does. But if I were to jump onto an English ship, I would want it to be into the arms of a handsome captain as, surrounded by a crew of admiring hands, we sail off to explore some faraway land filled with warm, dark, mysterious men who do warm, dark, mysterious things.

And I would want the hold of the ship to be filled with condoms. I like to be well prepared for every wonderful surprise.

The kid raises his sunglasses; his black eyes sparkle. Looking down at Randy, he laughs, "Rad, Dude."

It wasn't always this way.

The telephone rang at four in the morning. A man spoke in Spanish, introduced himself, "*Señor* Alfredo Palermo," and asked for Randy. "We have a son for you. He is three months old."

When we skied off the lift, Randy had shouted, "To the right." I'd followed, down the easy narrow trail, until it forked into two: both marked with double black diamonds, both expert slopes. In horror I searched for the map, found it. At the lift, we should have turned left.

Randy and I travel a lot and had seen the gangs of abandoned kids.

For me it wasn't so much about having a son, but to do a good thing for one of the kids—to help, to share, to give him a gift he would never have without us. Even though we were gay, we could offer him a home.

So we agreed: a boy for me—I already had two birth daughters from a previous marriage and had lost a son shortly after his birth. And a Latin American for Randy—with the death of his brother, Randy became the last of an old Hispanic branch who had come to California from Mexico with the first Spanish padres.

We had finished the necessary home study—while I pretended to be only a roommate—and as a "single" man, Randy was found eligible to adopt a child in the state of California.

We had it all mapped out. If only we had followed our plan. . . .

"We can do it." "No." "I'll just ski down around those trees and see what it's like." "No, once we start, we can't go back." "Just let me go down and take a look."

Although Randy and his parents wanted an infant, I was adamant: Divorced when my oldest child was five, I knew our limitations. Two men could never raise a baby.

He went down, disappeared around the trees, while I stayed up and contemplated our joint insanity.

With my tenative okay, he left for Honduras, and I reassessed the madness which had brought us to this place. There was the desire to share our material goods, our time, and our energy. There was the emptiness of the house that caused us to give too much affection to our dog. There was the chance of growing ourselves, and of showing the world that gay men are not just selfish, but can give and share the same as others. And as always, there was the adventure of doing something different.

"It's beautiful. We can make it; I know we can."

In Honduras Randy visited the home for abandoned infants where the baby was kept. There were eight babies in separate cribs in an apple-green room, all watched over by prepubescent girls who only touched them when it was feeding time or time to change their diapers. In three more months, if no one claimed him, the baby would be eligible for adoption in Honduras. Randy hired a lawyer on the spot.

Together again, I agreed. He was right: Ahead was a picture of beauty, of fun, of challenge. We both pushed off.

Optimism is contagious. I agreed to limit my classes to night school and to take care of the baby during the day. We painted a spare bedroom, set up a crib, bought blankets and baby clothes. And we named him Nicholas—anglicized after mine—and James—Randy's middle name.

Randy leaped ahead and down, and just as though he knew what he was doing, he skied down the bumpy chute and disappeared behind the trees.

Baby Nicholas James remained unclaimed, and in three months Randy returned to Honduras. Expecting two weeks of legalities and delay, he made arrangements to stay at the Episcopal Church's home for abandoned boys, *El Hogar de Esperanza y Amor*, in the capital city of Tegucigalpa and planned to visit the baby daily until he had final permission to bring him home.

Arriving for his first return visit, the director gave Nicholas to him, clad only in a cloth diaper and a blanket, and announced that he was to take the baby, that he was now his responsibility, but that the baby had been, and still was, very, very sick.

Then came his cries for help.

The United States requires a certificate of health before an adopted baby can be brought into the country. Randy immediately contacted the American Embassy. The officials recommended a doctor, and the doctor prescribed medicine to add to Nicholas's formula.

A drought had been gripping the city of Tegucigalpa, and back at the Episcopal *hogar*, water only ran from the faucets between seven and eight in the morning.

Each day he spent at Señor Palermo's house, but at night he returned to the Episcopal *hogar*, and having no crib, laid Nicholas in his suitcase and began the nightmare of scant four-hour feedings, and changing diapers for his first time—diapers of a baby struggling from diarrhea—unaided by moistened swipes or running water.

He called every day, often two or three times, telling of all the frustration and trouble, but how he had come to love Nicholas so much that he would never be able to leave Honduras without him.

There was the expected legal delay: The baby must be adopted in Honduras before he can leave the country. And he must be granted an entry visa from the American Embassy.

And there was the unforeseen delay. The First Lady of Honduras is also the head of *Bienestar Social de Honduras* and must sign all exit papers for adopted babies leaving Honduras. But Randy was the first single male to adopt, and she was rumored to have severe doubts.

After days of negotiation and postponement Randy was summoned to her office, and as he waited outside her door, his lawyer again presented his case. She signed the exit visa, but it was a hard bargain. The lawyer's brother was a legislator who was blocking one of her husband's pet programs. The baby was released, Randy paid the lawyer, and the president's legislative program moved ahead.

Randy called from the airport, almost in tears, barely coherent, announcing that he wouldn't give Nicholas up, announcing the victory, but also that, as they made their way to the airport, the lawyer had warned him the First Lady's signature sometimes would be "unrecognized" by the rifle-carrying guards, and not to be overly confident that the baby would be allowed to board the plane.

Around the trees, with him again, the beauty—the absolute beauty. Before us stretched the white and green of the mountains, the lace-edged blue lake . . .

At 2:00 on Sunday morning they landed in San Francisco. Looking down through the glass ceiling of Immigration, we watched—Susan, the baby's soon-to-be godmother; her boyfriend, Michael; and me. Tired, after a twenty-hour trip, Randy beamed up and waved, held up the baby carrier to show off our prize, but the baby had no eyes for us, only for his daddy. Two fingers in his mouth, a smug smile, and that animal-baby adoration as he stared, mesmerized, at his daddy's face.

A pack of snowboarding kids passed us, yelling, laughing, having fun.

In poverty-stricken Latin American countries, abandoned girls are valuable: They make acceptable servants, but abandoned boys soon become unruly and rebellious and are pushed into the streets. Out in the streets they form "rat packs" in which most live until they are killed or die.

In Honduras the death rate is highest for women in childbirth and for boys under ten.

The kids disappeared down behind another group of pines. We shoved off again, down the steep, open slope. I, then Randy, tumbled, formed two flying windmills of poles and skis.

Monday morning Randy left for the office, and I called the pediatrician's office for an appointment. "Who delivered the baby?" "I don't know. We just adopted him from Honduras. He's six months old." "The next available appointment is not until two weeks." "I'll take it."

The rest of Monday was a nightmare. Babies left alone in their cribs learn not to cry if they can see no one. They learn fast that crying is only wasted effort.

Nicholas would only cry if I entered the room, but the moment he saw me, he would start crying, and regardless of how I held him, regardless of anything I would do, he would continue to cry. The only exception was the four-hour feeding time when I would give him his Honduran doctor-prescribed three-quarter bottle of formula. And when he finished it, he would drop the bottle and begin to cry again. Only when I left the room would silence return.

When Randy returned from work, I met him at the door, almost in tears myself, and told him of the terrible crying. Randy entered the room and Nicholas broke into a great smile and cooed baby sounds while Randy held and walked him. He wanted only Randy, the only one who had held and played with him during his entire six months of life. And I was not an acceptable substitute.

The next day his crying continued, but the third morning, when I walked in, he had the hiccups. I imitated him, and he seemed to think my imitation was funny. When I entered later, he seemed to have the hiccups again, but I dismissed them and checked his diaper. He kept looking at me and, catching my eyes, would hiccup. I imitated him and he broke into a smile. Deliberately, he hiccuped again, and I saw that he had created a game. If I was no substitute for Randy, at least I had become an acceptable stand-in.

The weekend before the doctor's appointment, Randy's parents came over. They had been in Europe and were excited about seeing and helping to take care of the baby. But they only stayed a few minutes; they gingerly held the baby, then to our confusion and surprise, abruptly left.

Four skiers, blocked by our bodies, or maybe just interested, stopped to talk, to offer help, to warn us of the dangers, the obstacles ahead.

When the doctor saw Nicholas he was appalled and wanted to know why we hadn't brought him in immediately. I explained that I took the first available appointment, and in fury, he charged down to the front desk. When he returned he handed us a number and told us to call immediately, day or night, at the first sign of any trouble.

Then he began the examination. Nicholas had, according to the doctor, "with the exclusion of leprosy, every skin disease known to man, including scabies and lice." One of the medicines prescribed in Honduras was for epileptic seizures. Immediate tests showed them never to have occurred, but the medication had kept him and the other babies docile for their first six months. His body was ballooned on one side, shrunken on the other, caused from lying in the same position for months. He suffered from sensory deprivation, and in most ways his development was at the level of a newborn infant. And he was severely malnourished: just skin and bones with a big head. At six months and two weeks, he weighed only ten and a half pounds.

The doctor said to let him have as much to eat and drink as he wanted, to give him as much sensory stimulation as he could handle, and said at the close of his examination, "I don't want you guys to get your hopes up."

"What?"

"Babies in his physical and sensory shape usually don't make it."

Again and again we fell, cursing, laughing, retrieving our skis, helping each other back up.

Fighting words. I contacted Project Hope and they came to the house and worked with us on his sensory stimulation. Randy's parents, wiser than us and still reeling from their younger son's death, admitted they thought Nicholas would die and temporarily avoided becoming attached to him. But they rallied and joined the cause, delighting in his every improvement. In a year he could turn over by himself, and in less than two, he was walking. Project Hope announced that he had graduated from their program with honors, and although he would probably remain a year to eighteen months behind in his development, who on earth would really know or care, if at the age of thirty, he was really only twenty-eight and a half?

But not everyone was helpful. A group of skiers who had passed by us before, noticed us again, warned us, told us we shouldn't be here.

Some people have no trouble expressing their disapproval, even when not asked.

"When he starts school, how can he ever explain that his parents are queer?"

And the understanding, semi-educated thrust: "I wouldn't be opposed, except that I think every child should be able to decide for himself about his sexual orientation."

And two straight-haired men out in public with a dark, curly-haired baby can raise eyebrows, questions. "Whose is he?" "How did you get him?"

The suspicious looks, the exchange of glances, which say: "Maude, have you ever seen that baby on a milk carton?"

They told us the trail was too rough, the cliff too big, that we could never make it, that we—or someone—should call for the ski patrol.

Then began the age of the "terrible twos," the "terrorizing threes," the behavior problems and temper tantrums of every childhood. But to some, Nicholas's behavior had a very specific cause: He belonged to two gay men.

Randy has a way of flaring, of raising his middle finger, and dismissing unasked-for advice. I'm different: I wonder if what people say might be true.

"Two guys can't raise a baby." "You'll turn him queer." "You people can't have your own, so you recruit."

Psychologists call it internalized homophobia, and I suffered from a raging outbreak. What if he turns out to be gay? Will we prove them right, and he'll never have a chance to lead a straight life? Who am I to think two queers can raise a child? How can I take an innocent, foreign child and raise him in an abnormal, if not immoral, house? And how will he ever explain to his friends that he has two gay fathers?

When paralysis sets in, it's hard to do anything well.

We reached the cliff: Randy has a fear of heights. I coaxed him: "Come on. It's like the Olympics. Just push off and lean forward." But he wanted me to go first.

There is a strength that comes from years of acting, from years of wearing a mask. Once the curtain rises, the show goes on.

Nicholas, unlike me, probably could have landed and stayed on both of his skis. Nicholas, unlike Randy, probably could have landed and stayed on at least one of his skis.

As predicted, Nicholas remained a year to eighteen months behind academically, but that was not true physically. His body straightened to normal, and by the time he was five years old, he had gained enough weight to make it onto the doctor's childhood charts, and he had gained enough height to be tied with the average American five-year-old. And by seven years, he was excelling in anything athletic: soccer, cycling, football, basketball, skateboard, roller blades, ice skating, skiing.

I would have noticed earlier if it hadn't been for my preoccupation with the cliff. Below us lay nothing but a steep hill of moguls, those terrible mounds cut by expert skiers, stretching down, forming a maze of huge, white, teutonic tits.

Moguls don't bother Randy: He skis between and around them. He says they help him slow down and turn.

Not me: I run into them, run up them, sail off them, crash between them. . . .

But when Nicholas entered kindergarten, having two gay parents wasn't his problem: It was having no mother.

All the other kids seemed to have mothers: mothers who took them everywhere, who held them when they cried, who changed their diapers, fed them, picked them up when they fell. Randy was fun to play with, but it was I who was the daily caregiver, who ran to him whenever he was hurt or frightened, who rocked him, cuddled him, kissed his hurt away. And he heard other kids call their mothers "Mama," and he decided that was my name. He began to call me "Mama."

"No," I corrected. "My name is Papa."

But he dismissed my every correction and would chant, "Mama, Mama, Mama."

Finally I gave up, decided to be liberated. Why should I care if he calls me "Mama"?

We live on the east side of San Jose, which is populated by many handsome Hispanics. And in grocery stores I'm easily distracted—not that I would openly cruise when shopping with a child, but sometimes my eyes have a will of their own—and there was that moment, when standing next to the most handsome, most macho man in the store, when we both reached down for a loaf of bread, when his beautiful dark eyes met mine, flicked interest, and when he smiled . . .

And from far away, from the other end of the aisle came the shout, "Mama."

Instantly, all liberation disappeared and I grabbed my bread, quickly pushed my cart around the corner. But Nicholas found me: "Mama, can I have this?" And the handsome macho found me, too, but now he had a friend, both of them standing there, amused, as Nicholas continued his—from this time forward, forever and ever, absolutely forbidden—chant of "Please, Mama," "Please, Mama," "Please, Mama."

But my victory over the totally forbidden was not complete. On Mother's Day he came home with a paper cutout of a teapot. On the front was a little poem, which ended: "Don't get upset with me, just sit right down and have a taste of tea." Inside were stapled two tea bags. I kissed him, thanked him, and put it on top of my desk. Two weeks later it fell, and as I retrieved it, I noticed the greeting on the back: "Happy Mother's Day, Papa."

Now, where the trails finally meet, Nicholas helps dig his too cocky daddy out of the snow, and back once again at the cabin, we sit in front of the fireplace, Randy and I warming ourselves with hot buttered rums, Nicholas with cocoa.

"Papa, next year can I have a snowboard?"

"Sure, if it's okay with Daddy."

"Can I, Daddy?"

"Why not?"

"Yes!" he shouts.

He slides off his chair and sits on the rug at my feet. Then, wrapping his arms tightly around my shin, he rests his head against my leg, stares toward the fire, smiles, and lovingly mutters my forbidden name: "Mama, Mama, Mama."

There are times when he doesn't obey, and times when I pretend not to notice, not to hear.

jim marks

we three

"What do I call you? Who do I tell my friends you are?" Brian asked over three years ago. We were about a year and a half into our relationship, with another year and a half to go before he formally moved in with us. They were good questions, but I didn't have answers. I hate "ménage à trois," foreign and French with a lewd snicker behind it. "Trio" sounds like a Dolly Parton, Linda Rondstat, and Emmy Lou Harris album; "threesome" like a bunch of guys enjoying a one-night party. None of them sounds like the rather ordinary domestic life Nick and Brian and I share. Do we have to give it a name?

If it bothers me that I can't find a name for us, a gap in my memory is just plain embarrassing. I cannot remember how we moved from being Nick and Jim, long-time partners, and Jim and new boyfriend Brian, to Nick and Jim and Brian.

Oh, I remember the preliminaries, all right. The six months from the first time Brian caught my eye at D.C.'s only (semi) leather bar. The hiding in the shadows, watching him play pool, overcome with lust and longing and despair and a girlish shyness altogether inappropriate for my thirty-nine years. I remember our first conversation (I honed in on a chat with an even older geezer, and learned that Brian had a brother living in Florida who had become a Mormon—not your ordinary religious path for a black kid from an urban New Jersey family).

And I remember the night it became now or never. I bought him a beer and held his hand and knew in my excitement it would happen. How he was following me home and took a wrong turn. I laughed and thought, What sort of trick is this kid playing with me? I went back to where we started, and five minutes later he drove up, apologetic.

And again, I remember how I said to myself, This time I am not going to let my life be divided into two camps. Brian has got to meet and get to know and be nice to Nick and if that doesn't work, it doesn't work. You don't throw ten years out, especially when they've been a good ten years.

So I cooked a dinner, invited Brian to meet Nick. Brian and Nick talked music, then Brian and I went out to Baltimore. And then we had another dinner. And this is where I can't remember. Oh, I remember the sex, exciting and high-pitched and maybe too hurried, like this may be my only chance, let's try this and this and this. And, better, there we were, after, laughing and telling jokes and a great happiness welling up as I see a door opening and all of us walking through it. But from table to bed? Not a shred of memory.

jim

I think homophobia is not so powerful a hate as racism, because I came out as a gay man at twenty, yet it took me until age thirty-two to figure out that it was black men I was attracted to most.

Perhaps that is because I grew up in the back woods of North Georgia, where racism went hand in hand with a kind of familiarity—a living closeness—that made for far more intimate knowledge of black and white than happens in places like Washington, D.C., where I now live. In Washington, the white people, except for oddballs like me, live in a white world, and only venture in their little automotive bubbles from the sweet suburbs through the mostly black streets. Even living in a gentrifying, mostly African-American neighborhood like mine, I see people in the street, talk to the neighbor next door, but know less about him and his family, his wife and children, than I would have known in the unregenerated racist hometown of my youth.

I was raised by a black woman named Florence Johnson. From eight until six every day, she was the adult who ruled my life, who read to me and talked to me as she went about the house cleaning and ironing clothes. She was the one that would come and gather me up when my best friend, Greg, a bully, beat me up. When she got TB and was put into Batty State Hospital, we visited her, and she sent us wry little letters, with happy faces drawn on some of the O's.

Middle-class people in a little town like mine had a Florence in their homes, or, if they were a little poorer, lived near a black family, or worked in a business like my daddy's used-car dealership, where the white men did bodywork, and Luther the black general handyman, was a constant presence in the shop, listening to the stories and driving us kids when dad would send us on an errand—usually to repossess a car. "You haven't known the sweetness of life until you've been a black man on Saturday night," Luther told my brother on one such journey.

But if in that Faulknerian South black and white knew each other, that didn't mean racism wasn't instilled way down deep. The balcony of the town's lone movie theater was for "coloreds only." There were two sets of schools. My eighth grade Georgia history teacher—a redheaded Neanderthal whose real job was coaching basketball—lectured us on how ending segregation would lead to interracial marriages, and a lowering of the race.

My boyfriends—and I did have boyfriends when I was hitting puberty—were all white. Although I liked to think of myself as liberal, college—Georgia Tech, Emory University, Georgia State University—and then teaching, part-time at a local junior college and Georgia Tech, kept my world mostly white.

I was not a brave young man. Still, the summer I graduated college, I went to England and quickly overcame my fears and found my first "real" boyfriend. Within three years after that summer love, Patrick, my first lover, and I were winding up a prickly Atlanta courtship and preparing to move in with each other.

Looking back, I can glimpse who I wanted to be hiding behind who I was. One night of my first coming-out days, I spied a beautiful black man amid the three hundred white bodies crammed into Atlanta's then lone dance bar. I had terrible success picking up tricks in those days, but that night I didn't go home alone. My junior college job found me teaching English at the Federal Penitentiary for six months; I learned a lot about who goes to jail, and why, in our society, but I didn't learn enough about my heart to understand why some of those young men kept lingering in my mind more than the bright, athletic, and scholarly students of Georgia Tech. When I moved to Washington, I was astonished by the muscled black man I brought home my first night out.

But these were hints I wouldn't understand. Deep down, in a place I didn't think existed, I "knew" that white people were "superior" to black people. I knew it in the patronizing white liberal way—not inherently inferior, but disadvantaged by growing up in a racist society. Then, in Washington, I took a writing class, and a black woman in the class wrote rings around the rest of us. At a meeting of gay poets, all the white poets read poems that were dreck. And black poets Essex Hemphill and Michelle Parkerson simply blew up the room, so honest and real and heartbreakingly beautiful was everything they read. "I'll never write a poem like that," I thought. I was humbled.

I don't think it was an accident that within a year I'd embarked on my first relationship with a black man. I think I first had to stop listening to that song playing unconsciously in my mind, "White's better, white's better," before I could see a whole person in the black man whose bed I was sharing.

becoming a team

Brian, Nick, and I moved from "dating" to becoming an entity when we took our first trip together. In the summer of 1990, we flew out to San Francisco. It was a business trip for me, photographing the International AIDS Conference and writing about Black and White Men Together's tenth annual convention. For Nick and Brian, it was pleasure, a long weekend centered around the Gay Freedom Day parade.

On Brian's first airplane flight nothing went right; the plane delayed for hours in St. Louis at the gate and then on the runway. But sometimes it takes a bad start to make the rest of a trip seem good. The next day, Friday, we split up: I chased AIDS demonstrations and photographed speakers while Brian and Nick toured the city. I can trace their progress from Brian's photographs: my fat butt waddling down a steep hill as we walked to a bus stop to go into the city. Market Street. Chinatown. The Trans-

America pyramid, shot straight up. North Beach. When I caught up with Brian and Nick in the Castro, Brian was lit by a beatific glow that only a gay man on the eve of his twenty-seventh birthday in San Francisco on a high gay holy day could have. He and Nick had bought music, T-shirts, and clothes. Nick had taken Brian to the Gauntlet, where he'd had his ear pierced, and Nick had picked up a new ring for his nipple. Men spilled out of the bars onto the sidewalk in the long high summer twilight, the air brisk and fresh. Brian's eyes bulged as he watched sex icon Richard Locke casually chatting with friends. He wanted to sell everything he owned and move to San Francisco.

San Francisco was magic. Everywhere we went, we ran into old friends. On Saturday, our hosts, Dan and Abe, threw a solstice party, organized by a Faerie friend. As the sun was setting, the friend lit a bonfire. A dozen of us circled it in a line, chanting and tossing in herbs and incense and handfuls of powder that burned bright blue or green or red. We drank wine punch, ate barbecued chicken, and dug out bread from the bonfire's ashes and ate it warm. Conversation in the garden grew more and more animated as darkness settled and Dan called us in for desserts arrayed upon the marble-topped table. Later, Dan confided his secret for a perfect party: "Add just a touch of acid to the punch bowl: It gives everything such a nice sparkle."

Sunday morning, we went into the city: Brian and Nick to the Gay Freedom Day parade, I to photograph the conference, disrupted on its last day by a major demonstration. I caught up with them at a corner of Market Street off the Tenderloin. They'd made friends with a grizzled, gray-haired veteran of the leather scene, a regular contributor to *Drummer* magazine, who was supplying them with running commentary, parade history, and advice and previews of the afternoon's street fair. He gave Brian a tiny metal clothespin to put on his jacket lapel.

Wandering the fair spread out in front of City Hall, we came across a tent where a local photo shop was offering free photographs. What the hell, we said, and took our first group portrait. Later in the week, when I went to pick up the print, I was startled (and a little pleased) to see that ours was one of the pictures the store had put in its Market Street window. To myself, I look gray and washed out, wearing an old Polo shirt and a wan attempt at a smile. Nick is bright-eyed and red-cheeked, a tie-dyed T-shirt exploding across his chest, pumped up from years at the gym. And in the middle of us is Brian. He's wearing an EAT SHIT AND DIE T-shirt, his black leather jacket, and Drummer baseball cap, a look of transport on his broadly smiling face.

nick

Nick grew up across the street from Mount Moriah A.M.E., the oldest free black congregation in the state. At the end of the block in its circle stood St. Anne's Episcopal, a brick-steepled English chapel, home to the city's finest. The historic preservation people were just getting around to preserving the homes built by the signers of the Declaration of Independence. The State House hummed a few months of the year; the Naval Academy had its ebb and flow of dress whites. Down at the raffish waterfront, where crabmen caroused at night in what was then called Hell's Point, his moma and papa ran a family restaurant in an old mercantile building. In those days the space smelled of fish and rotting produce from the old city market. When hurricanes and nor'easters would come past, the streets around the crumbling harbor would flood, and all the merchants would put sandbags at their doors.

I learned what it meant to grow up between Mt. Moriah and St. Anne's one holiday meal with Nick's family. Nick's sister and her husband and family were there. She's a slim, immaculately groomed woman, unfailingly kind to her brother's friend. When her other brother ran for mayor (and won) she became a Republican to vote for him, and having money and businesses, stayed that way. We somehow were talking about the old-line men's club next door. "I remember when we were just greasy Greeks," she said.

Nick's dad has saved a framed picture of Nick playing his violin in the school orchestra. He's a sweet, sad-eyed Greek boy. You can tell the cleft palate has made him shy and self-conscious. He's the baby, his father in his mid-forties when Nick was born. There wasn't much money growing up, but after his parents retired and Hell's Point became The Harbor; when the annual yacht show got bigger and bigger, and they built a Hilton on the other side of the water; as the crabbers stayed away and suburbanites moved in and buildings old enough to have housed George Washington acquired a certain cachet, money quit being tight. Mom and Pop retired, and the family leased the building (at a very good rate) to a restaurateur who renamed it "The Reynolds Tavern" and added a raw bar whose bright copper and brass and polished wood shone in the skylit afternoons.

Nick became an accountant who, as the years rolled by, became a computer person. He's worked for law firms ever since I've known him. He owned his own apartment when I met him in 1979, which impressed a man who had been living in rented spaces for all the fifteen years since he'd left home.

If a gay man is someone who can turn a few chairs into something stylish and neat, Nick isn't a gay man. When I met him, the living room couch was a messy mattress on a box spring. He had a Formica-topped dining room table and four tubular chairs with marbelized vinyl seats and back. There was a cage with a friend's gerbil in one corner. The main focus of his bachelor pad was his college stereo system and his already large collection of albums. Never any shortage of marijuana.

I have a picture of Nick, scrawny and long-bearded, in a pair of shorts flecked with paint, perched on top of that apartment's refrigerator the day we painted it brown and blue. Somehow, it's hard to connect that boy with the gym-pumped man I live with today. When he's sporting a moustache, he looks a little bit like the stereotypical strong man of a turn-of-the-century carnival.

If my first marriage was a meeting of interests, a long, extended, always elaborated conversation, this second partnership has been more a shared emotion. Patrick, my first husband, and I would go to a movie, and then talk about it for hours afterward: story, structure, dialogue, campy lighting, whatever we'd see in it we'd share. Go to a movie with Nick, say, "What'd you think," and you get back, "I liked it" or "I thought it was good." Nothing more.

I know Nick as much through the music he collects as through his words: Depeche Mode and Blondie about the time we first met, Talking Heads and Martha and the Muffins and Everything but the Girl and R.E.M. We traveled to Florida and back listening to tapes of Dolly Parton, Linda Ronstadt, and Emmy Lou Harris, and of Paul Simon's *Graceland*. We've gone together to concerts of Ladysmith Black Mambazo and Sweet Honey in the Rock and Duretti Column.

When we were first going out, we liked to drink manhattans. On weekends we'd drop acid and wander through the Washington Cathedral or drop into the Phillips Gallery to sit and watch the Rothkos undulate.

Then we'd go home and make love and follow it up with a bubble bath. "The room's humming, Jimmie," Nick would say to me.

Nick says it's because he's a Cancer that he's a nurturer. He sold the apartment, and we bought a house. In the late eighties, when credit was high but easy to get, the market going crazy, we bought a second house and rented out the old one. We made an agreement on how we'd split expenses: Nick's the breadwinner with the job that brings in a decent income and family property that drops a big chunk of cash into his account every January, so he pays the bigger portion. But we both pay a fair share of what we earn.

He's seen me through unemployment and temp work and two years of work-obsessed gay journalism and another seven years as a freelancer and now two and a half years as an editor of a gay magazine, almost a respectable "real" job.

When I fell in love with Bernard, a black man, Nick drank too much and would fly off into rages. I remember the winter nights I lay beside Nick and wondered what I would do, how I could go through another day, and if I could survive if I shattered my life again and tried to start all over. When that love ended, I put Nick through my grief and despair, and when I fell in love yet another time, this time more crazily and dangerously, breaking up and making up every three or four days, Nick had grown into the role of the person I could count on to stay sane when I wasn't.

Now that Brian's in our life, we've become like, well, a mother and father. Brian's the link that was missing in our relationship. We worry about his finances and health, and talk about the advice we should give him. We meet his boyfriends and occasionally feed them dinner. Nick calls him "our baby."

meeting the in-laws

In the spring of '91 we took another trip. It was a part of a rough time for Brian. Brian had had his own keys to the house for at least six months by now, and although he didn't live with us, he came and went freely, and rarely went more than a few days without spending the night.

Nick had helped him find a job in the mail room of a giant downtown

law firm, its offices maybe a dozen blocks away from our house. Then the
law firm, which specialized in mergers and acquisitions, took a good long
look at their bottom line and freaked. They fired some 5,000 employees
nationally; Brian was one.

Brian simply vanished for a week after he was let go, and we went
berserk. When he finally surfaced, anger over his absence alternated with
the search for ways to give him support.

Nick and I hoped a trip south would cheer Brian up. First stop was
Charleston. I think the hosts at the gay guest house where we stayed were
much amused by our little threesome, although they made a point of not
making a point of not batting an eye at three gentlemen traveling together.
They put us in the Key West Room—all wicker and chintz and Hemingway
novels. The first night, we went down to meet the other guests having a
drink while watching a Charles Pierce video. There was a "bunkhouse" with
a porn room adjoining the showers and "the California suite" on the ground
floor, a hot tub out back.

The one Charleston gay bar we tried out that evening held interest
solely as a matter of anthropological curiosity. Long and narrow, it was, in
theory, a private club. Booths lined one wall opposite the bar. The clientele
was mixed men and women. The preppy young men wore shirts so stiff
with starch they looked like they would crack under a quick blow; the
women wore dresses or pantsuits with necklaces and earrings and makeup
and teased hair. Even the young men had that spoiled southern genteel
alcoholic air, cheeks ruddy with drink, blond hair longish and lank, bellies
soft if not yet round. The room roiled with tight little whirlpools of gossiping groups of three or four pointedly ignoring everyone else. Brian, the
only black man in the bar, didn't take long to pick up some bad vibes. We
admired the CD jukebox, then split.

As we left Charleston Monday morning, one of the guest-house owners
snapped our picture in the bright Carolina morning sun. They sent us a
print along with a refrigerator magnet the following Christmas, and Brian
put it on the fridge, pasting on the picture a word balloon that read, "Bosom
Buddies."

After a stopover in Atlanta, the three of us visited my parents in
Northwest Georgia for a night. Brian had looked forward to the visit with
no little anxiety. He is, after all, an urban Yankee kid, venturing into the

deep rural South. There was, in his mind, a Klansman behind every tree. My parents live on twenty acres of hill a mile outside town in a big, sprawling house at the crest, with a big porch looking off to the east.

Call me a coward, but we don't "name" what we are and thrust it into our families. Although my parents have known Nick since we first became a couple, we didn't and don't talk with them about our relationship. Ambiguous identity, free-floating, unnamed, a question that's maybe not even asked, has its advantages. Without an in-your-face name Nick and I can go home as a "son" with his "friend."

During Brian's visit, my dad suspended his Southern racial bigotry, didn't talk about *those* people in Atlanta stealing government money. Brian even went with Dad on the ritual walk in the pasture so the city kid could see cows up close. (Within minutes, Brian could imitate the cows' mooing so well they followed him whenever he called.)

The next day, we all ate barbecue together at the restaurant across the highway from Dad's business, a rural town village center. Was there any tension under the surface of these family rituals? To be honest, I don't think it bothered my parents to break bread with a black man in public—pillars of the community, sure of their place, don't worry about losing status, and the South where a black person could make news eating in a restaurant is dead and gone. But long afterward, I asked Brian if he'd been nervous, and he said yes.

We finished our trip having Greek Easter with Nick's family at his sister's home in northwest Virginia. Around the table as we passed the lamb and the potatoes and the beans and the *pastisto* and the *dolmades*, there wasn't any talk of *mavros* (darkies). If the family had no intention of giving up their Republican party affiliation, they didn't waste any breath on talk of "family values" with us—three bachelor traveling companions and a divorced woman cousin sharing the ritual spring meal.

brian

Brian grew up in urban New Jersey in the projects. His mother had a lot of children; his father was absent after they divorced when he was seven. At school, he was overshadowed by his elder brothers, one a football star, the other, in his words, "a musical genius." He tells stories about how he helped his mother run the house, cook and care for the babies. He found out about gay bars (and older men) at a very young age. Once he was in a gay bar when his mother entered to buy some beer to take home, and he hid until she was gone. He read *The Village Voice* to learn about where to go in New York City. He nursed his first lover though alcohol detox, and moved with him to Washington.

It took three and a half years of dating and building a relationship until Brian finally moved in with us. While Nick and I don't have any reservations about the three of us being a group, it's hard for Brian to reconcile his living arrangement with what he thinks is "right." One night, Brian and I started talking, and he said he loved me and Nick but he'd always thought that, one day, he would "have someone of my own." He wants our relationship to be monogamous (or, I guess more accurately, bigamous), but Nick and I, our ideas shaped by seventies sexual politics, resist.

I think the closest we've come to losing Brian to "someone of his own" was right after the March on Washington. I knew that Brian had met a hot man by the way he came home on that Thursday night before the march, packed a bag in a state of high excitement, and vanished. About a month later, "Ted" came to visit. Rather than not see Brian for a whole weekend and then some, I told Brian to invite him to dinner, and we'd all go to a party together.

One meeting, and I knew Ted was the stuff of Brian's dreams. West Point graduate. Hispanic. He wore his balding hair a little shaggy in the back, was Brian's ideal bear shape. Obviously bright, articulate, capable, macho. He'd scoop Brian up with one hand, and I could tell Brian had a brand new skin and it was tingling.

I can't recall feeling anything but a sense of inevitability so strong it made every other feeling irrelevant. Nick and I both knew this guy was "right" for Brian. The week Ted visited Washington, Brian would call me up and I'd try to josh him about all the sex he was having, and he'd get very quiet and serious. "Ted's nice, Jim," he said. I know, I said. "No, he's really *nice*," Brian said. All that remained to see was whether Brian was "right" for him.

Fortunately for us, Ted lives a long way away. Ted had a boyfriend, a bodybuilder. The boyfriend made surreptitious calls, threw scenes. The romance cooled, although I bet Ted and Brian would jump each other's bones in a minute if they were alone in the same room together.

I don't think we consider ourselves as pioneers or as innovators. Still, we fall into patterns as we figure out how to live together. I was leaving work one day when I got into a conversation with some of my co-workers. Somehow, I ended up telling them that I usually do the cooking at home. Who does the washing up, they asked? Oh, Nick does that. He does the laundry, that's his therapy. And what does Brian do, they wanted to know. Oh, he keeps us entertained.

I was trying to make a joke, not be hopelessly patronizing. What I mean is that what Brian contributes to the household is, well, its life. As Nick and I settle into the cocoon of middle age, he brings new people into our lives. A music enthusiast with a mania for disco, he comes up with incredible albums. He goes out to the clubs and tells us what's hot and what's not. He tells jokes and keeps us from getting stale. Like me, he can't match Nick in terms of income, and like me he contributes his fair share to the household. He gives us someone to worry about and to help out.

Our happiest nights will find us flopped about on our big bed like a litter of hound dogs, watching, inevitably, the 10:00 P.M. "Star Trek" reruns. Nick and Brian will nip at each other, wrestle with me, fart and make a fuss about it. Then Nick and Brian start playing Warf and Captain Picard. Brian is Warf. "Request permission, sir," Brian says, his Warf voice deep and gruff, "to bite your nipples, sir!" We all break up in laughter.

further family adventures

As I write, we've been seeing Brian for almost five years, living together a year and a half. We're beginning to come out of the closet about who we are. One night at the Eagle, Brian introduced us to a friend as his "nontraditional family unit," Nick's pet phrase for us. Nick has a bit of swagger about the whole thing; when a gym buddy asked Nick if he had any pets, Nick hollered back, "Pets! I have two lovers, I don't need pets!"

This fall, we sealed our relationship with a trip back to San Francisco. It was a great vacation: Folsom Street Fair, wine-tasting up the Napa Valley, a mud bath in Calistoga, sunset in Sausalito, dinners with friends, another trip to the Gauntlet.

Midweek in our stay, the night of the full harvest moon, we went to Everlasting, an out-of-the-way tattoo parlor recommended by a friend. We told the artist what we wanted, in general terms—it had to have an element repeated three times—and he began sketching. No, we didn't like that: Could he do something more abstract? The designs he came up with didn't look right, until I said, Could you put three sort of yin and yang shapes in a circle? Yes, he could do that. A few quick strokes of his pencil, and we were all agreed, that's the design. All told, it took about two hours for him to tattoo the three of us: Nick had the sperm shapes black, the negative space he left untattooed. I have the same part of the tattoo black, but the negative space red. And Brian has the negative space red, but the figures are turquoise, to show up better against his black skin.

All the remainder of the week we happily sported our tattoos while we worked out at the Market Street gym, and showed our friends while visiting over lunch and dinner. People ask all the time what it means. Brian's come up with the best response: He says it's based on a Japanese wave design, and it symbolizes unity.

Walking down Market Street from the Castro on the last night of our trip, we passed a frame shop. In the window hung a child's kimono picturing three cranes, one brown, and, above it, three Japanese medallions in a design quite similar to our tattoos. I knew I was going to be broke the next day.

Packed and freighted and shipped out to my work address, the kimono arrived about two weeks after we returned. Nick and I borrowed a friend's truck and brought it home. We unscrewed what seemed like a thousand screws, dusted off the gold frame, hung it right where I knew it would fit on the wall next to the fireplace.

Just as we finished, Brian sauntered downstairs, admired our handiwork, and exclaimed, "Oh wow, our marriage certificate is here."

Some time ago, Nick bought a new tea kettle and retired the old one for watering plants. The new one was shiny silver, with a matte black handle, and, unlike the old kettle, was a whistler. Actually, it has three holes in the lid, and when it's worked up a full head of steam it makes a chord. It reminds Brian of Philip Glass, and, a sucker for all kinds of interesting sounds anyway, he just adores it. The first time Nick heard it, it startled him—he hadn't realized that he'd bought such a weird noisemaker.

Ever since the doctor has taken me off caffeine, the kettle's seen a lot of action as I use it to boil up water for my mandarin orange or lemon zinger teas. One day about a year ago, when we were all in the kitchen as I was cooking and Nick was setting the table and Brian was horsing around, the kettle started its chordal whistling. Nick sounded a note just a pitch above the basic chord. Brian chimed in above that and, after little wavering, I managed to find the note above that. Now, whenever the kettle boils and we're all in the kitchen, we find that chord, and hold it. Ah-h-h-h-h . . . until I pour out the water for my tea and the sound trails away. That's the way I like to think of us, three notes in an odd harmony.

rock climbing

New Paltz, New York, lies about ninety miles north of New York City, just beyond the southeastern edge of what my father's family simply called "the mountains," as if Jews of his generation could conceive of no other high altitude retreat than the one selected and duly civilized by Grosingers. On maps, New Paltz sometimes falls into the green-shaded area of the greater Catskills, though properly speaking it is the Shawangunks, not the Catskills, against which New Paltz rests. You can see the Catskills from New Paltz, but you have to climb the Shawangunks to do so. Here, just outside of town, great sloping slabs of quartzite conglomerate shove themselves out of the earth at intervals steady enough to form a range. These mountains are small enough to be of human scale, but their eruption out of the earth was sufficiently violent to create a series of sheer and spectacular cliffs. For this reason New Paltz is home to some of the world's best rock climbing.

   Thom Scheuer is a rock climber. He is also the head ranger at the Mohonk Preserve, the wildlife refuge and climbers' Arcadia that surrounds a Victorian-era resort hotel, the Mohonk Mountain House. The hotel sits on the back rim of the Shawangunks on the edge of a high lake. If you go for a hike with Thom, he will explain to you how, a century ago, a vast area around the Mountain House had been completely stripped of trees to provide firewood for the mammoth hotel, and how much of the rest of the Preserve's woodlands had once been farmland. He might take you off the trail to where the remains of a tiny stone farmhouse lie crumpled in the brush, trees shooting around and through its walls. If he really likes you, he will invite you to go with him and help haul deer carcasses out of the woods during hunting season or retrieve a lost, spooked hiker on a dark autumn evening.

As far as the carcass hauling is concerned, you won't have to touch the stiff and bloody deer. Thom just wants the company. He tolerates loneliness, but he needs fellowship to become fully himself. On these trips into the woods, Thom might tell you lurid rock climbing tales from the 1960s, when he and his friends formed a daredevil counterculture climbers' group called the Vulgarians, the purpose of which was to cheat death and drink excessively, all the while sticking it to the stodgy, rule-abiding climbers who ran the sport in those days. He was an adman then. Thom's specialty was the set of rules and regulations governing the representation of United States currency in advertising materials, and he's proud to tell you how he chucked it all for the woods. He connects with you through these stories and, through the telling, makes you part of his past.

I was introduced to Thom by his son Ethan. If Ethan and I had gotten married, I would be Thom's son-in-law.

"Just don't act like you own the place," Ethan told me before our first trip to his father's house, an eighteenth-century farmhouse, the oldest on that side of the Wallkill River. Thom's resident guests were famously rampant—the house was scheduled to sleep nine assorted persons that weekend, though in fact the actual total was fourteen, if you count the two who ended up in the barn—and I was being warned not to be problematic. "If you want something, ask for it. You'll get it, but ask first. Don't just start grabbing beer out of the refrigerator. At the end of the weekend, he might ask you back. That's how you'll know if he likes you."

I was keyed up. We had been together all of two weeks. Ethan was twenty-four, I was thirty-four. He had just graduated from college. I was losing my hair. We had met on a phone sex line. Now I was meeting his family.

"So let me get this whole thing straight," I said. "Exactly *who* is going to be at this house?"

"Okay, my father; his girlfriend, Linda; my brother Kif—his real name is Chris but we call him Kif (I started it when he was born because I couldn't say Christopher—Kif, Kiffer!); my little brother Thommy; he has Attention Deficit Disorder; that means he's wired all the time; maybe Linda's daughter, Amanda . . ."

"Wait—who's Thommy's mother?"

"Patt, my father's second wife. Where was I? Oh . . ."

"Wait! And your mother lives *where*?"

"In New Paltz. In town. We'll go over there some time, probably for dinner on Saturday. Oh—and Jenny, Kif's friend from high school. She rents a room now. This guy Bob also rents a room. He's middle-aged. And Jenny's friend Liz. I think that's it. Oh, and a dog, and a cat, and a goose."

"A *goose?*"

"Yeah, it's really disgusting and mean. My father loves it."

When we got out of the car, the goose, effective guard animal that it was, strutted directly to Ethan's leg and bit it firmly and with self-evident expertise. After knocking the goose squarely in the ribs with his suitcase, sending it stumbling away screaming, Ethan muttered, "Go ahead, get AIDS, I don't care."

There is something grotesque about a goose's bill, the sawtooth edges erupting out of rubbery-looking animal material that is neither bone nor flesh. The skin on Ethan's leg had in fact been broken by the goose's bite, and although his shin was not bleeding, blood had risen to the site of the wound and shined brightly through his pale skin. Better him than me, I thought.

Ethan greeted his father in the kitchen. "Your damn goose bit me."

"He was just kissing you," Thom said. "Welcome to New Paltz." He put out his hand and smiled broadly through a gray beard. The house was pandemonium. Ethan's brother, Kif, who had just finished his junior year at college, was coming out of the bathroom wrapped in a ripped Sesame Street towel, and his younger brother, Thommy, who was then nine, tore around in a wet bathing suit, yelling, singing, and being told to bother someone else. There were at least three other people in the kitchen, and I heard noises coming from upstairs. Thom said, "Let's go ahead and destroy this chicken on the grill. Kif, will you go up and throw the goose in the barn so we can eat outside?"

My own family is small. I am an only child, and we had no pets. We did not barbecue food. As my father explained, we had a modern house with two ovens, one electric and one gas, and therefore didn't need to build a fire just to eat. When guests came for dinner we served them cocktails in the living room. We did not do outdoorsy things. We read *The Progressive*, *The New Republic*, *Gourmet*, the Sunday *Times*, and, in the late sixties, *Ramparts* and *The Village Voice*. We sat inside, on chairs, when we ate. When my mother and I shucked corn, we did it at the kitchen sink.

At Thom's house, people shucked corn while sprawled on the lawn, taking care to avoid the many blotches of slimy green goose shit that darkened the grass and spotted the flagstone walk. I was delighted and horrified at the spectacle that was Ethan's father's house.

"Dad, you know I don't eat meat." Ethan was starting in.

"Oh. Well, there's some leftover fish. Would you like that? There's some spaghetti too—no that has meat in it—how about tuna? We can make tuna salad!" Thom began wildly pulling open cabinet doors.

"No, it's fine," said Ethan, having achieved his aim. "I'll just eat a lot of salad."

"And corn!" Thom shouted. "We have lots of corn!" To me, he said, "Would you like a beer? Some wine? It's cheap box wine but it's not that bad."

"That wine is terrible," Ethan said. "Take the beer."

At the end of the meal, after the sun had fallen behind the trees and the lightning bugs were blinking, everyone systematically hurled their corncobs into the woods. Having been accused once too often of throwing like a girl, I was careful to backhand mine as if the cobs were frisbees. I had tried to make sure Ethan's dad knew the score before we arrived. "He knows we're fucking, right? No surprises?" Ethan responded by telling me that he hadn't planned to bring the subject up for discussion. "I just want to know how to play this," I persisted.

"I don't know what he thinks and I don't care," Ethan said. "Don't worry about it."

Ethan and I slept on a single mattress on the floor of his old bedroom, a small, narrow room made even less accommodating by a slanted roofline which cut the space of the room nearly in half. Late that night, since it was only the second weekend we spent together, we went at each other with an energy derived from mutual appeal and prior frustration. Ethan was fair-skinned, I am dark; Ethan was slender and boyish, with thin shoulders and a small waist. I need to shave every day, and I make it a point to buy belts that are a few sizes larger than they should be so the excess leather makes

my hips look smaller. I wanted him the moment I saw him, and his desire
for me made me breathless. With the house so full of people, strangers
whose good graces I had several reasons to seek, I made it a point to clamp
my jaws together to keep from alerting Ethan's father to the particular
elation I felt under his son's hands.

We were sleeping with easy contentment the next morning when the
door burst open and Thommy entered the room in mid-sentence.

". . . do last night? Why are you still sleeping?"

"Thommy, go away," said Ethan.

"Why are you sleeping together?" He was staring down at me.

From my position on the floor, I looked up at the child's face and wondered what he saw when he saw his brother naked in the hairy arms of a thirty-
four year old man. "Because it's fun?" I said. Apparently satisfied, Thommy
exited, leaving the door wide open. Staying low to the ground, I crawled forward off the mattress, stretched toward the door, and pushed it until it
clicked shut. "This isn't New Paltz," I grumbled. "It's Woodstock Nation."

The week before, when Ethan told me that he was HIV-positive, I
asked him if his family knew. His parents did, he said, as did the older of
his two brothers. I wanted to know how they dealt with it. I needed a
blueprint to follow. "I guess they worry," Ethan told me, "but they act as
if it doesn't exist."

How could they act as if it doesn't exist, I thought to myself righ-
teously, little grasping that I was doing precisely the same thing and that
none of us had much choice. We spent almost every night together. I got accustomed to the homeopathic remedies he took and bit my tongue about his
doctor's insistence on high colonics and juice fasts. Whenever he had a fever
or a night sweat or a rash, I panicked, quietly and to myself, while he took it
as a matter of course and went on with his life. I told one friend that
Ethan had no T-cells, and the rest of the time I acted as if it didn't exist.

At the end of the weekend, just before we headed for the bus station, I
was walking across the yard when I came upon Thom peeing into the bushes.
He said over his shoulder, "Come back sometime—any time you want."

Through the summer and into the fall, we spent a number of weekends
in New Paltz. It was a healthy escape from the city, even if Ethan's chief
sport in the country was needling his father. Glad to get to know people
who were familiar with Ethan's emotional tics, I took a bad misstep on one

occasion and joined in what seemed to be just a momentary, good-natured roasting of the eldest son. Later, by ourselves, Ethan spun at me. "Don't you *ever* side with them against me."

As the weather grew colder, we stayed in the city more. We would go for walks and to the movies, to Indian restaurants and health-food stores. As it happened, we had both been exchange students in high school—Ethan to Sri Lanka, I to Finland. We both liked seeing the world outside of our spheres, but Ethan was especially open to the ideas and sensations of a radically different culture. He took India and Sri Lanka into himself; he loved reading books by Indian authors, and when he cooked Indian food he got it right. He was charmed by the Thai chili peppers I grow on my windowsill. He used them in curries. "This is so romantic," he said the first time he picked them, and he threw his arms around me and gave me a kiss.

A year after my first trip to New Paltz, in late July, Ethan suffered what appeared to be a nervous breakdown. It began with a touch of insomnia and escalated over a weekend to something much more extreme. Manic and confused, he rambled on and on about a collection of images and ideas that had few ties outside of his head but that had clumped, deep in his brain, into a pure, personal religion: butterflies, moths, ambidexterity, learning, teaching, masculinity, and the Hindu god Siva. We had been fighting for weeks. He insisted on quitting his job and said he didn't care about losing his health insurance. He had already lost his apartment—a bad sublet deal—and was living with me. In a matter of days, Ethan descended into feverish despair, though he did not see it that way. He was getting to be more than I could handle. Angry and terrified, I plotted ways to ship him back to Thom and say . . . You deal with him.

Ethan's mother, Sandra, is quieter and more self-enclosed than Thom. Until very recently, she was difficult for me to read. That first weekend in New Paltz, she served us steamed sweet potatoes, brown rice, carrot juice, sesame seeds, and broccoli, looking me straight in the eye throughout the meal but saying next to nothing. The portions were small. I was so hungry I couldn't concentrate. Maybe I was just too shy to ask for more. At that meal, which was held in her dining room and served on beautiful floral plates, and for a long time thereafter, Sandra was pointedly opaque in dealing with her son's boyfriend, direct in her inscrutability. Thom, on the other hand, could be easily caught stealing glances in my direction with an expression that nevertheless stated the matter with slapping bluntness: *What do you want from my son?* When Ethan fell apart, I called Thom.

The central images of insanity that punctuated the week of Ethan's breakdown are as sharp in my memory as they were when they appeared as a sequential series of cruel facts:

Ethan told me in the middle of the night that I was an incarnation of Siva and he refused to take no for an answer. We wrestled for control of a bottle of tranquilizers in his room at Thom's house. In the emergency room of an upstate hospital, an immense psychiatrist declared that he was having Ethan committed but provided us with no indication of a course of treatment. I had to beg Ethan, who was particularly obstinate, to lower his voice in the emergency room right up to the moment when Thom and I hustled him out the door and into Thom's car. The psychiatrist called the police on all of us because we departed the hospital grounds. Thom and I explained to Ethan that if the police showed up at Thom's house we would hide Ethan in the woods. A neuropharmacologist friend of Thom's intervened, long distance, and the police were called off, but the following day I noticed, abruptly and with idiotic surprise, that Ethan had turned thin and gray and appeared to be dying. I assured him that he was not dying. After finding a neurologist who knew about AIDS, we rushed Ethan back to the city on a steaming Friday night and secured him a hospital room. Together, Thom and I heard the term "AIDS-related encephalopathy" for the first time and understood fully that Ethan was not yet dying but would likely die. I cried in Thom's arms, grasping his shoulders and the knowledge that he was propping me up the way a father supports a son.

To Ethan, my own parents seemed enigmatic and remote. Fifty-five years older than Ethan, my quiet father took on a grandfatherly quality in his eyes. My mother, a few years younger and more talkative, still remained doubly bound in Ethan's view by the conventions of an earlier time and the physical limitations of its standard-bearers. Their slow walking frustrated him. His gentle voice never rose to the occasion of my father's hearing aids. When they arrived in New York for a long weekend, Ethan would soon grow restless, irritated by my prickly regression back into a tiny, well-worn family life that not only predated him but promised to outlive him as well. One thing he could never get over was how obsessed we are with food. After two nights of rigorous New York restaurant eating with my folks, Ethan would make other plans.

Still, my parents faced Ethan's illness with honesty and tenderness, and he valued that. He enjoyed their generosity, was impressed by their seamless desire to include him in our familial set. I think he was amazed that he could stroll out of the bedroom in the morning and join his boyfriend's parents for coffee and toast. Of course, they were spared the insanity. The medication had worked almost immediately; the Siva period lasted only a week or so, though it gave way to a moving-target phase in which no one was safe, his parents, brothers, and I each popping up randomly and without warning into his line of fire. But, as the neurologist predicted, he settled after about eight weeks into a state of subdued normality that lasted through the winter and beyond. In the spring, before the lymphoma got him, we traveled back home to western Pennsylvania for Passover. He fell for the good china, the platters, the whole get-up. He took pictures of the cold poached salmon I made, and he couldn't get enough of my mother's matzo ball soup. Back in New York, when I made it for him, he polished it off, saying, "It's not as good as hers," and I thought, Of course not, the wife's matzo ball soup can never compete with Mother's, even if it happens to be *my* mother's, not his.

Sandra warmed up under the crisis of Ethan's illness, but she will never be a soup maker. She is a reader. Mary Gordon, Anita Desai, Michael Cunningham, Dorothy Allison, Ann Tyler. For Sandra, life is an internal and consequently unfathomable act. Hers is lived in consciousness, not in social events. After Ethan died, she told me that she originally had difficulty with his sexuality, her son with men, but that she came to understand that her own immutable ethos applied to Ethan as well. "Nothing should stand in the way of the individual making his or her way through the world," she said. *"Nothing."* As she repeated the word, her hand sliced through the air and came to rest on her dining room table. He had said to me once, "You like my father better." I said, "I understand your father better." It was not until Ethan was dying that I understood Sandra, who connected with Ethan's consciousness with an ease that did not come naturally to Thom. Now, when I want to feel Ethan's spirit outside of myself, when I want to hear his voice, I call Sandra.

In late March, seven months after Ethan got out of the hospital following his breakdown, the two of us went to France. We spent four days in Nice, drove around Provence, and then went to Paris. On our last night there, my parents treated us, by prearranged plan, to a magnificent and thunderingly expensive dinner in an ancient restaurant. Ethan started with a pâté of fresh goose liver. I had ravioli filled with langoustines. For the main course, Ethan had scallops wrapped individually in phyllo dough, and I had sweetbreads that were nearly caramelized in a dark, essential sauce. We finished with cheeses, a chocolate ganache and a white chocolate mousse, *mignardises*, and two chocolate truffles. Drunk on the best wine we had ever tasted, we clung to each other ferociously in our hotel room, coming prodigiously and with uncommon exhilaration. I have never been more contented.

When we got home I told Thom that I knew something was wrong. The neurologist, describing Ethan's streamlined argumentativeness the summer before, had used the word "disinhibition," and although as Sandra noted, "He was always disinhibited," I saw it subtly creeping back in France. In May, he started getting pains in his legs, and by the end of June, he sat for hours, alone and confused, unable to remember his medication or decide what to wear. One week later, in the hospital, just before the lymphoma was diagnosed as the latest element in the onslaught of diseases, Ethan climbed into bed and stayed there, unable to climb out. We took him back to New Paltz by ambulance at the end of September, and he died on November 6. Thom was on one side, holding his left hand, Sandra was on the other side holding his right, and I held him around the middle.

A few weeks earlier, Thom and I had taken a hike together. We had to get out of the house, it was too much. There was someplace Thom wanted to show me, he said, but first he'd make me an assistant ranger for the afternoon and have me drive one of the small blue Mohonk pickup trucks while he retrieved a larger vehicle from out on the trail. On the way back, he'd lead in the big truck and I'd follow. Predictably, Thom is a speed demon on the road, even while navigating rutted dirt trails in the middle of a nature preserve. The pint-sized truck I was attempting to steer flew off each bump and into the cloud of dust kicked up by Thom. We parked at a spot I recognized from a hike with Ethan. "It's up here," Thom said, marching off the trail and up a hill. The day happened to be sunny and cloudless, and the leaves had turned. He led me through some brush, across some rock, and up. At the top of the hill, through a stand of yellow trees, was a ledge, and over the ledge was a monumental precipice. We were not facing the Catskills but rather the flat plain of the Hudson Valley, a vast crisp emptiness in the clear light of day. Thom had a look of euphoria, and I knew how he felt.

I thought I would never climb rocks. Fear of heights is not the problem. A dread of falling is the problem. And a mule-like resistance to trust, an understandably vital element of this particular sport. But I have a young cousin, a fourteen-year-old, who likes being outside and whose terrors are not mine. His parents are divorcing, and I worry about him. In an impulsive moment at Thanksgiving I told him that we would go rock climbing this summer and that Thom would teach us. Ben took to the idea, so I told Thom, who was thrilled. A few months from now, on some warm weekend, Ben and I will go up to New Paltz and Thom will not only show us the ropes but attach them to us all and, with them, bring us up and down the side of a cliff. I trust that we will survive.

michael lowenthal

everything possible

The image of the family tree has never worked for me. It's a beautiful idea: a growing network of branches, all connected by common fibers, ever spreading, ever reaching up and out to cover more sky, to create more safe shade. A family tree brings to mind summertime picnics, a brood of children gathered underneath the bright green leaves. But this is not me, not my family. Whenever I try to fit my family into this vision all I can see is a Charlie Brown Christmas tree, withered and bare.

My family has always seemed like a limited resource, nonrenewable. There was only so much of the original blood to start with, and every time some is lost, that's it. Gone forever. Our history is one of diminishment, closed options, constant weedings out. Of the numerous family members living in our German homeland, which would be spared the concentration camps and make it to safe ground? My grandparents were lucky; because my grandfather was a rabbi they were able to escape to New York in 1939 on one of the last nonquota visas. There were still losses, though, more choices and narrowings. My grandfather had two sons: The first, Peter, died at Bergen Belsen in 1945; the second is my father. Ours has been a family of few children and frequent divorce. There has not been a new baby born in more than twenty years.

I am the only male child of my generation with the name Lowenthal. And I am gay. Will the name end here?

When I came out, my gayness seemed like the last nail in my family's coffin, rendering my grandparents' miraculous escape from Hitler futile. I didn't let this interfere with my self-esteem. I was fiercely proud of being gay, one of the most visible gay activists at my college. Still, I couldn't help thinking: They endured that hardship just to see it all end two generations later?

Then, for the first time in my life, I acquired a new family member. After so much taking away, there was an addition, a flowering bud. John wouldn't show up on a conventional family tree. He is my lover Chris's brother. Or, as we affectionately call each other, my brother-out-law.

John is also gay and he lives in San Francisco. Before I met him, I had never ventured into the world of gay culture. A "gay man from San Francisco" was a creature of mythical proportions to me, something I had only read about or seen on TV. I had no sense that I might in some way be connected to him or his world.

That I had no experience with gay culture before I met John may sound surprising or even impossible, given that I already had a steady boyfriend and was a gay rights activist in school. Let me explain.

I attended Dartmouth College in Hanover, New Hampshire, a relatively isolated community in the midst of rural New England. I came out during my sophomore year, and by the time I was a senior I was spending almost as many hours on gay activism as on my schoolwork. I helped develop antihomophobia "road shows" and presented them to first-year students. I orchestrated sit-ins to protest CIA recruitment on campus and lobbied to get ROTC barred from Dartmouth. I wrote a political column for the school newspaper, and when they started censoring me I helped some friends found Dartmouth's first queer newspaper, *In Your Face*.

If it sounds like I was at the center of a whirlwind of gay politics and culture, it's just the big fish in a small pond syndrome. My gay life consisted entirely of the other dozen or so openly queer students in this conservative rural enclave. For all my bravado as the Big Queer on Campus, I had never (with the exception of a single pride parade in the small town of Northampton, Massachusetts) had direct contact with gay culture in the larger world. By the spring of my senior year I had still never been to a gay bar or bookstore. I had never been inside a gay person's home. In fact, aside from the single openly gay professor at Dartmouth (who served as advisor to the gay students' group), I had never met an openly gay adult.

In this atmosphere, gayness was more an activity for me than an identity. When I was at a homophobia road show or sitting in at the administration building, I was "gay." But when I was, say, performing in the jazz band, I was a trumpet player. When I was in class, I was a student. The extremely small size and isolation of the gay population at Dartmouth precluded any sense of my gayness that transcended other categories.

Looking back, this was a terrifying void. Here I was committing myself to a life of open homosexuality, spending a great amount of energy lobbying for my right to exist as such, and all the while I had no personal experience to show me that such a life was truly viable. I was queer by faith alone.

I met John in March 1990, three months before my graduation, when I flew to San Francisco for a conference. Chris couldn't accompany me on the trip but he called his big brother—with whom I'd never even spoken on the phone—and arranged for me to stay in John's apartment.

On the plane to San Francisco I paged absentmindedly through the in-flight magazine, trying to convince myself that the imbalance in my stomach was attributable entirely to air turbulence. For the first time I would see what it was like to be gay outside the confines of a college environment. I would enter the mysterious, dark world that to this point had existed for me only in magazines, books, and rumors.

Compounding my trepidation about my first foray into the world of gay culture, I was terrified of meeting John. Chris had prepared me with numerous stories about his brother: mild-mannered preschool teacher by day, famous gay actor by night. But I was unpracticed in the "meet the family" routine, and I knew the Hogans took family seriously. Their family tree is a towering oak: Chris and John are two of six siblings; they have twenty-three first cousins on one side alone.

At the airport I boarded a SuperShuttle and gave the driver John's address. It was late, and dark, but the driver was able to point out the important sights as we drove up the peninsula and into the city: Candlestick park, the ticky-tacky row houses immortalized in the song "Little Boxes," the string of lights that he assured me was the Bay Bridge.

I had been to San Francisco once before, five years earlier, when I had just turned sixteen and was only "out" to two ex-girlfriends. I had been so terrified by the city's queer reputation and by the possibility of my secret being discovered that I walked through the streets with blinders on, missing all the sights. Now, driving up Highway 101 to make my first pilgrimage to the queer mecca as an openly gay man, I stared searchingly at the passing darkness. This time, I wanted to see it all.

The shuttle corkscrewed its way off the highway and into some sort of warehouse district. Interspersed with the drab industrial-looking buildings were occasional flashes of neon announcing late-night bars and clubs. This was a far cry from the scenic "Frisco" I knew from movies and TV. Where were the friendly cable car conductors hocking Rice-a-Roni?

Just as the buildings started to get taller and slightly more upscale, the driver pulled over and let me off. We were on the edge of what I would learn is the Tenderloin. I found the door with the correct number, but it was being blocked by two huge-seeming black prostitutes in identical lipstick-red dresses. I couldn't tell if they were women or men dressed as women. (I didn't know yet to check their feet and hands.) Feeling stupidly young and touristy with my backpack and duffle bag, trying to be courteous without returning the hookers' seductive grins in the wrong way, I stepped past them to the building's directory and pushed the tiny black button next to John's name. I climbed the flight of stairs slowly. Butterflies were slam-dancing in my stomach. I almost fainted when it was Chris who answered the door. Except it wasn't Chris. Not exactly. The hair was slightly shorter, and he was wearing a Jell-O-green bowling shirt I knew Chris didn't own.

"John?" I asked, feeling like the dupe in a bad sitcom identical-twin switcharoo episode.

He shook my hand warmly. "Hi, Mike. Come on in."

I'd been briefed that the brothers were very similar, but the resemblance was truly uncanny. John looked just like Chris except slightly more suave, more stylish, more Big City. He had the same "dark Irish" features: penetrating brown eyes under thick eyebrows, crow-black hair creeping away from the temples, beard shadow all the way above his cheekbones.

"How was your flight?" John asked, and the familiar Iowan Hogan twang put me enough at ease to manage a one-word response.

"Long."

John carried in my bags and took my coat. He pointed me directly to the daybed where I collapsed, trying not to stare at the first gay man's apartment I had ever visited. For a few moments I reverted to my pregay self and experienced the thrill of the dangerous and forbidden: I was *inside* the home of the freak. I was astonished how small the place was, hardly bigger than my college dorm room. I was overwhelmed by the kind and number of decorations, like some museum of strange taste.

John must have caught me looking. "Oh, they're just a few knick-knacks I've picked up," he said. "Here, I'll show you around."

The living room/bedroom was about as wide as the ceiling was tall. Displayed on a low cabinet was the dead Kennedy collection, including the commemorative JFK bust mug with drinking hole doubling as gaping skull wound. "I never actually drink out of it," John confessed. "There are limits to my disrespect." An Elvis shrine occupied another corner of the room. John glossed over the bottle of ELVIS cologne and went right to his pièce de résistance, the full-body bourbon decanter/music box (young Elvis). To get a drink, you had to decapitate the King and pour the liquor through his neck. John wound the key and I waited expectantly for "Love Me Tender" or "Heartbreak Hotel," but instead I was accosted by a shrill rendition of something resembling the Salvation Army theme song.

Next was the claustrophobic kitchen, a neon splash of color, every inch of available space crammed with John's collection of ceramic fruit-and-vegetable dishware. There were ear-of-corn butter melters, a cabbage-shaped borscht tureen, and an entire window display of tomato cups, bowls, and saucers on shelves constructed of Hunts and Contadina cans. "What's this?" I asked, holding up a piece that resembled a petrified pale green cigar. John looked wounded. "Celery stalk, dear. You don't think I stir my Bloodies with the real thing, do you?"

We returned to the main room. I thought I'd seen everything, but John opened one last door revealing a room the size of a large closet—just big enough for a single bed—the walls painted a dismal seasick green. John gushed an explanation: "I was flipping through color chips, wondering what to choose, and when I read the name of this one I just knew I *must* live in a room painted"—and here he concluded with a grand Carol Merrill flourish—"'Invitation to Paris.'"

I was trying to take everything in, trying simply to observe, not to pass judgment. But as I stood there, staring at the puke-green walls and the garish clusters of tchotchkes, I found myself thinking with amazement, *he lives this way* all *the time.* Then a question: *Do you* have *to decorate like this to be gay?*

It was past midnight, so we decided to go right to bed. "We can sleep late," John announced cheerfully. "I'm taking tomorrow off to show you around the city. Think of any places you especially want to see."

John stretched some sheets onto the daybed and showed me where the extra blankets were. We took turns in the bathroom and settled down to bed. As tired as I was, I stayed awake for a few minutes, watching the patterns of city light filter through the blinds and dance on the ceiling. I smiled at the prospect of sleeping late and wondered if I would have taken the day off if the situation were reversed.

I also thought about the only other times I could remember sleeping so close to a stranger: my first night at college and my first night at summer camp. Both times I had been as terribly nervous as I was now, but for a completely different reason. Then, I had been terrified that at such close range the other guys would be sure to discover my secret. Who could tell what they'd do to a fag in their midst? Now, I no longer had my secret to hide behind. I was a self-proclaimed fag, and so was "the other guy." I had the simultaneously thrilling and terrifying sensation that this was my life, for the rest of my life. I had chosen this and there was no turning back now.

Eventually I closed my eyes and allowed my breathing to slow down. The unfamiliar sounds of a city rocked me into a fitful slumber filled with dreams of airplanes and butterflies and fairies flying over the Golden Gate Bridge.

"Don't be afraid to stare," John said as we emerged from the MUNI subway station. "That's what the Castro is all about." "Okay," I said, but as we embarked on our tour of gay San Francisco, part of me had the desperate urge to cover my eyes and turn right back underground. We walked past a street musician dressed as a monk, singing Gregorian chants for pocket change, and a man dressed in black leather from cap to boots. A couple of drag queens—one in a Cher wig and the other done up as Dolly Parton—leaned against a wall, lighting cigarettes. My first thought was that these people must be hired to stand here and look the part, like the costumed attendants at Colonial Williamsburg.

Turning the corner, I was confronted by a bustling street scene that was at the same time shockingly new and utterly familiar. The men in leather jackets holding hands on the crowded sidewalks; the big neon CAS-TRO of the movie theater; the street sloping gently down for a block, then ascending the dramatic hillside dotted with pastel-colored houses—I'd seen this exact view so many times before. This was where the mourners march in *The Times of Harvey Milk*. This was the picture that flashes in the box behind Tom Brokaw's head whenever there's a news story about gay men or AIDS. This was the quintessential image of gay America. And I was inside the picture.

Observations about the diversity of the gay community are by now cliches: *We are everywhere, From all walks of life.* But as someone whose entire gay existence had occurred in a homogeneous group of a few Ivy League students, the Castro made me experience these truisms as shimmering revelations. It was dizzying to see so many gay people of so many different types.

I was especially stunned to see people who were clearly gay simply going about their regular business, that is, not "being gay." There were gay bikers, gay police officers, gay cappuccino drinkers. My activist persona had espoused this phenomenon as a theoretical possibility without ever being sure it was true. Now I saw that it was, and just how fabulous it could be.

Walking with John was like having my own personal tour guide. He pointed out the bar on the corner, noting it had been the first gay bar with clear glass windows facing onto the street. He made sure I stopped to admire the ultratasteful window display of the gay-owned hardware store. We browsed in a leather shop, then in A Different Light bookstore—food for body and soul.

John knew everybody on Castro Street. Every few steps he pulled me close to whisper, "That's X, he's a well-known gay playwright," or "Y directed the show I was in last year." There was a lot of nodding and waving going on. Eventually we came face-to-face with one of the men John had pointed out. John greeted him with a kiss and then turned to introduce us. "This is my brother's lover, Mike," he said.

My brother's lover, Mike. When John spoke those words, everything else stopped. Suddenly, I was transported back to the time in junior high when I stayed with my cousin's family for a few days and accompanied him to school. The other kids greeted me with glares and scrunched-up faces, keeping their distance until Andy announced, "This is my cousin," and I was instantly one of the gang.

Outside of my own small family, I'd never been introduced as anybody's anything before. John's choice of phrase was probably not even conscious, a simple description of our relationship, but for me it made all the difference in the world. I felt he was claiming me as my cousin had, lending me his badge of his admission.

I was also startled by John's calling me and Chris "lovers." We'd been together for a full year, but in the parlance of our predominantly straight college culture we were always just "boyfriends." I already got the sense from my brief time there that in San Francisco, calling a couple "lovers" didn't necessarily say anything about their relationship; it was simply standard language, the way people in the gay community talked. And that's exactly what was so amazing to me. When John said "my brother's lover, Mike," I heard myself being included in that community. I had credentials. For the first time I felt gay not in theory, but in practice.

The next few days were a wonderful voyage of discovery. I imagined I had been one of those babies stolen away from their parents and raised in the forest by wolves. Now, returning to civilization, I had to be introduced to my own family, my own culture—people, places, ways of being that were frighteningly strange and new, but that also, somewhere in the recesses of my mind, struck a comforting chord of recognition.

Over meals of Thai food, Vietnamese, Mexican—all the cuisines I couldn't find in Hanover—John and I had long and animated conversations. We traded coming-out stories, tales of first romance. John talked about what it was like to live in San Francisco after growing up in the Midwest; I wondered aloud if I could ever live in a big city. He told me about his own introduction to gay life, feeling like Alice stepping through the looking glass, and it put me at ease that this thoroughly self-assured, elegant gay man had once been a gawking first-time fag like me. I found myself already addicted to John's bizarre sense of humor and his sweet, infectious laugh.

After dinner, John was my guide into worlds I had only read about. The first night we went to the Rawhide, a gay country bar. I was petrified and spent most of the time hunkered against a wall, wondering how an Oxford shirt and khakis, so ordinary as to be invisible at Dartmouth, could be so glaringly out of place here. (I've since come to understand that a man without Levi's in a gay bar is strange enough, but a man without Levi's in a *country* bar is downright sacreligious; having never been in a gay bar *or* a country bar, at the Rawhide I was in double jeopardy.) After a few cheap American beers I relaxed enough to sing along with John when our mutual dreamboat Randy Travis came over the speakers. But when John asked if I wanted to go out onto the floor I said, "No, thanks, I never dance." It was enough for me simply to observe the regulars. I found myself picking out a two-stepping couple and staring at them for minutes on end, enraptured by the sheer sight of two men with their arms around each other, smiling, gliding around the room.

The next night John took me to a biker bar, where I tried not to stare at the man in full leather (including executioner's hood) seductively finger- ing his nipples in a dark corner, or at the guys biting each other's necks so hard I could think of nothing but praying mantises and their sexual prac- tices. In the dim light of the bar I watched these men and wondered who they were in the daytime. Did I know them? Could this be who I was? Later, we cruised the strip on Polk Street, where John explained that the young guys in too-tight jeans normally charged thirty dollars, but for fifty they would have sex without a condom. I studied their faces as we walked past, realizing that most of them had not yet reached my age, and that some never would.

Under normal circumstances I would have felt extremely awkward about drifting in and out of these places, worried I was invading other peoples' worlds. With John by my side I felt less like a thrill-seeking tourist than a novice preparing to take his vows. I loved the feeling of being taken places by John, being shown the ropes by a more experienced hand. I dis- covered as we moved from restaurant to bar to club that I couldn't help but extend this, couldn't help thinking how natural it would be for John to carry my initiation one step further—into bed. In fact, I soon realized that everybody else just assumed John and I were "together." When we entered a restaurant, the maitre d' would lead us to a private table near the back. In the bars, men would start to cruise one of us, then notice the other and write us both off as taken. I found that I enjoyed letting people think we were on a date. I liked the assessing stares, the special treatment.

More important, there was a large part of me that wished John and I *were* on a date. There were times during our conversations when I had the urge to reach across the table and hold John's hand or run my fingers through his soft, black hair. I imagined what it would feel like for him to hold me.

Then I would catch myself. This was *not* a date. John was not my boyfriend, he was my boyfriend's brother. This was a completely unexpected form of self-denial. For years my options had been limited by being in the closet and by living in a rural town with almost no openly gay men. Now, here I was in San Francisco with an attractive, available, openly gay man— and I *still* couldn't act freely on my desires. I had gone from the limitations of complete inexperience to the double constraints of monogamy and "incest" in one fell swoop, without passing Go.

As confusing as it was on one level, I also derived a great amount of satisfaction from this clear boundary. When John and I returned to his apartment each night and climbed into separate beds, I had the wonderful security that his offer of initiation carried no expected payment—sexual or otherwise. His gift was free and unconditional.

As I drifted toward sleep on the last night of my stay, I listened to the still unfamiliar rhythm of John's breathing and imagined—as I have so many times in my life—what it would have been like to grow up with an older brother: someone to sleep in the bunk above me in our shared room, to teach me how to shave, to help me get ready for my first date, someone who would guide me through all the important passages.

Now, with John next to me, I felt I knew something about what that would have been like.

Three months later I was briefly in San Francisco again, this time touring with a brass quintet, once again leaving Chris in New Hampshire. John met me at the end of our concert on Fisherman's Wharf and I flaunted the fact that I was the only one of our group to have family in the city. I beamed as I introduced him to each of the other musicians: "my lover's brother, John."

John had an evening rehearsal for his latest play, so we'd planned just to meet for dinner. We went to a Chinese restaurant in the Castro where John was a regular. The hostess, a bird-thin forty-something woman with a smile that threatened to bust her jawbones, kept interrupting us to catch John up on the latest news of her family, the restaurant, her hairdresser. When she finally left, John imitated her bouncy way of talking and told me he'd nicknamed her the Chinese Mary Tyler Moore. When he sang the theme song—"Who can take a nothing day and suddenly make it all seem worthwhile"—I laughed so hard I spit tea through my nose.

Our talk was not entirely light-hearted. I had graduated from Dartmouth only a week earlier and I was full of doubts. Would I find a job? Would Chris and I be able to stay together after school? Was it possible to be openly gay without moving to a city? John was as good at giving serious advice as he was at making me laugh. Without false optimism or pat answers, he convinced me that everything would work out for the best. He made it clear that whenever I had questions I could call on him and he'd do his best to guide me through the rocky shoals of adult gay life.

Dinner ended earlier than expected and I decided I had time to sit in on the first half hour of John's rehearsal. The play was no *Hamlet*, more like a gay "Bewitched." John's character is dating a man whose lover has died, and the gag is that the jealous ghost returns, visible only to his former lover (Watch out for the floating ashtrays!). Despite the sitcom level of the play, as I sat alone in the darkened theater I was filled with an intense pride. For the first time I understood why my mother used to embarrass me to no end by announcing to near-strangers, "Did you see my Michael at the band concert? Wasn't he fantastic?" Now I wanted to run up to the light-board operator, the props manager, anybody at all and shout, "Hey, that's my brother up on stage. He's really good, isn't he?" In my imagined dialogue, and in my mind, I had already conflated "lover's brother" to simply "brother."

In December 1991 I had business in San Francisco and this time I brought Chris along for an extended vacation. It would be the first time he, John, and I would all be together at once. The first day we headed straight for the Castro. As we rode the subway this time I felt not anxiety but pure childish excitement, the way I always had as a kid when we returned to our summer home on Cape Cod after a long winter away. On Castro Street I felt like an old hand. I walked confidently from shop to shop, chatting with the store clerks as if this were my neighborhood. "See that place?" I said to Chris, pointing to the building on the corner. "That was the first gay bar with clear windows facing the street."

That night we went back to the Rawhide and I insisted we arrive early enough for the two-step lessons. I wasn't going to be satisfied just watching the regulars strut their stuff any more. Now I wanted to twirl.

At the early hour we showed up the crowd was split between beginners and a few die-hard urban cowboys. I was about the only person not wearing boots and a bolo tie, but I was determined not to let my self-consciousness defeat me this time. The dance instructor was a cross between a drill sergeant and a stand-up comedian, and he managed to put me at ease as we fumbled through the first few steps. Soon I was concentrating so hard on the slow . . . slow . . . quickquick rhythm that I had forgotten all about my inappropriate dress. In one of the dances, you stepped through an entire cycle with one partner, the last motion of which was to be handed to the next man in the circle. I started with Chris, moved on to John, and then got passed through a series of complete strangers who managed, with the simple touch of their hands on my shoulder and waist, to make me feel as if we'd all been friends for years.

My favorite were the line dances: a sea of blue jean–clad men packed into tight block formation, clicking our heels and slapping our thighs in perfect synchronization, as if we were marionettes moved by the same pair of hands. I'll never forget the exhilaration of realizing that if I fell in any direction I would literally be supported by men.

In the next few days John led us through an exciting battery of queer activities. We watched a strip show by "Joey the Brooklyn Dream" at N'touch, a gay Asian bar. We hogged the karaoke machine at The Mint, competing for best rendition of "Stop in the Name of Love." On Christmas Eve we went to a concert of the San Francisco Gay Men's Chorus in the old Castro Theater. But in the midst of this whirlwind of urban fun and adventure, the high point of the trip for me was our quiet Christmas morning in John's apartment. I have always had mixed feelings about holidays. The part of me that has always longed for a large extended family warms at the idea of the kinship gathered for a special occasion. Because my real family is so different from the idealized image in my head, though, the few times we have celebrated holidays together I have often been disappointed. Our Chanukah, for example, supposed to be an eight-day festive celebration, has deteriorated to a fifteen-minute struggle to remember the Hebrew blessing for lighting the candles.

From what the brothers had described, the Hogan family Christmas is a meticulously rehearsed ritual, with assigned roles for everything from who walks downstairs first to who brings the creamed onions. I was worried that

I would feel excluded from the festivities, the only person who doesn't get the joke; plus, it wasn't even the right holiday. But because we were not the "real" Hogan Christmas anyway—we were just three fags in San Francisco—we were able to pick and choose what seemed most appropriate from all of our various traditions.

The first item in the Hogan ritual is a parade of the children, lined up from youngest to oldest, marching downstairs from their bedrooms into the living room. Somewhat limited in John's small apartment, we improvised, piling into his walk-in closet and marching proudly into the main room. "Christmas is such a great time to come out of the closet," John joked.

Our Christmas meal was a brunch, with imported cheese, oranges drenched in kirsch, and—in deference to my Jewish heritage—smoked salmon. There was no Handel's *Messiah* or English boys' choir in the background; Patsy Cline and Randy Travis held the day.

After brunch we opened the presents, normally an unpleasant experience for me. I hate the awkwardness of waiting while somebody unwraps a gift, the impossibility of anything but a disingenuous-sounding response: "It's just what I've always wanted!" But the tone of this gift exchange was different. First I opened an intriguing cylindrical package that made no sound when I shook it—and was delighted to find a gleaming can of G.I. Joe Foam Soap. (Later, Chris unwrapped his companion gift, a bottle of Barbie Bubble Bath.) Subsequent rounds brought me two dreidels (another tribute to my heritage), a much dog-eared copy of *Hot Dean, Hung Hunk*, a roll of SILENCE=DEATH stickers, and a Felix the Cat T-shirt.

Chris and I gave John a joint present that we had been excited to find at our local flea market. It was a set of four ceramic jelly bowls in the shape of an apple, an orange, a grape, and a plum—a lovely addition to John's kitchen collection.

The final present—the only "serious" gift—was one from John to Chris: a painted ceramic tile of two Keith Haring figures dancing together under a giant red heart. I assumed at first that the tile was meant as a depiction of Chris and John, sharing their love as two gay brothers. But as I looked more closely, I thought it could just as easily be a symbolic marriage portrait to honor Chris's and my love for each other. Or maybe the joyous figures were John and me, dancing together at the Rawhide.

I realized at that moment that a crucial transformation had taken place. There were only three of us present for this holiday celebration, not the sprawling assembly of siblings and cousins and uncles I had always envisioned in my idealized image. There was no elderly patriarch or matriarch, no brood of children. There was no steaming turkey, none of the requisite components of my romantic family holiday fantasy. Yet I felt the way I always imagined I would feel if I were part of such a picture. I didn't need the fantasy anymore because I had my own reality to replace it.

It has been a year and a half since that last trip to San Francisco. In that time I've continued my initiation into the gay kinship, now able to find my own way without John's assistance. I've attended pride parades in New York, have been to gay bars in that city as well as in Boston, Washington, Seattle, Quebec, and most recently Norfolk, Virginia. There was never any question that I would attend the massive March on Washington for Lesbian, Gay, and Bi Equal Rights in April 1993.

I grew up less than a mile outside of Washington, and one of the greatest benefits is being able to return for events like the March and stay at my mother's house. Because my mom is such a good sport, I always know I can invite as many friends as can fit on the various pull-out couches or find sleeping bag space on the floor. For this march, seven of us descended on the place. The one who came the farthest, and whose presence meant the most to me, was John.

We joked a bit about the unusual arrangements. John said he'd tried to explain to his friends where he was staying but he'd gotten bogged down on apostrophes: his brother's lover's mother's house. He slept in my sister's bedroom, just across the hall from my own, adding a strange tinge of reality to my earlier fantasies of having grown up with him as my sibling. But our relationship had progressed from my first trips to San Francisco. This time I was the guide, showing John the sights in Washington, teaching him the ins and outs of the subway system, introducing him to my friends. I was no longer John's idolizing younger brother; now I was a peer, a friend on my own terms. I was especially glad I could "share" John with my mother and vice versa. They got along famously, so well that by the end of his stay John felt comfortable calling her from downtown and asking her to rummage through the kitchen garbage to locate a scrap of paper with a trick's phone number.

The day of the March was unforgettable. Even in the suburbs where we boarded early in the morning, the Metro was like a moving gay bar. Strangers joked as if they'd been friends for years, asking one another to rub suntan lotion on their backs. It was simply assumed that everyone was on our team. When we emerged from the station downtown and walked past the White House amidst a stream of thousands of other marchers, I wondered for a moment if we would storm the place. There were so many of us, it seemed we could do anything.

The actual demonstration was secondary to the sheer excitement of being there. We watched from the sidelines for a while, and then our group scattered to do our own things. My mother marched with the Parents and Friends of Lesbians and Gays, while Chris and I went to the Mall to listen to the speeches. John roamed in the crowd and then opted for the quiet dark of the National Aquarium.

We regrouped as the sun was setting at a junior high school near the Capitol where the Flirtations, the gay a capella quintet, were giving a benefit concert. Everybody in the auditorium was flushed with sunburn and the thrill of having made history, the atmosphere somewhere between a high school reunion and a religious revival. The show was delayed, and so we waited, sweating in the stuffy hall, telling anecdotes from the march. We babysat for two little boys while their lesbian mother ran to the McDonald's across the street.

When the Flirtations finally walked on stage we all leapt to our feet, and for a moment it seemed as if the crowd would surge forward in a crushing wave. We wanted to touch the excitement, to hold it in our hands. The Flirts, usually impeccable professionals, were visibly nervous. How could they possibly sing well enough on this day? But with the first bracing chord of five-part harmony the jitters disappeared.

The concert was a furious blur of singing and applause. I remember my hands stinging terribly, and not caring. I remember standing up after almost every song. Most of the audience knew the Flirtations' repertoire, and we mouthed the words as they sang. At one point I was convinced that we were all creating the music, not just the performers. They were merely conduits for our collaborative crystal sound.

Near the end of the show the group sang Fred Small's "Everything Possible," a lullaby for the next generation of children: "You can be anybody you want to be, you can love whomever you will. You can follow any country where your heart leads, and know I will love you still."*

As they sang the words, I thought about the path on which my own heart had led me, a path away from my family, away from everything I knew, all the way to another coast and back again.

At the last note we rose as one and stood, arms around each other, tears streaming down our cheeks. It was a perfect moment, one I wished I could preserve forever, frozen like a beautiful amber crystal. With my mother pressed close on one side of me, and Chris and John on the other, I had a new vision of my family. No longer did I see a decaying tree. Now, I envisioned a sprawling chain of us, linked by apostrophes: son, son's lover, son's lover's brother, son's lover's brother's lover . . .

This new vision of family still doesn't "solve" my dilemma, doesn't completely eradicate my feeling of obligation to my grandparents. I still wonder if the genetic lineage, the Lowenthal name, will be carried on, and what will be lost if it is not. But the kinship that surrounded me that night has shown me I was wrong to give up entirely on the idea of family. I'm not sure how long the chain is, or where it leads, but for now it's enough to know that I'm part of it, and a chain always has more than one link.

* "Everything Possible." Words and music by Fred Small, © 1983 Pine Barrens Music (BMI). Used by permission.

looking for
brothers

barney, chris,

and me

I have made brothers out of my two oldest friends. I'm not sure where the line between friendship and brotherhood is drawn and crossed, but it has to do with trust and time.

Barney and Chris and I have surface things in common: We were raised in comfortable upper-middle-class circumstances. We all attended prep school, Chris in Ottawa and Barney and I in Western Canada. Chris went on to the University of Toronto, the Sorbonne, and law school. Barney went to the University of British Columbia. Although I would eventually wind up at Toronto with Chris, I have always preferred travel to classrooms, and I became a journalist.

Of the three of us, Barney is the most handsome and patrician, scion of a boaty Vancouver family, perpetually rugged and tanned, ex-college rower, classic prep. Chris is thirtysomething, a blond-haired blue-eyed fast-track attorney who still looks like the rugby player he was. He is the best educated and the most athletic.

Barney and I are gay. Chris is ebulliently heterosexual. He and his partner, Claire, have a small perfect miracle of a little blond boy named Alex. He is the very image of Chris in miniature. Sometimes when I look into the baby's face, when I hold him and look in his eyes, I see Chris there,

and me sometimes too. Alex takes me back to a point almost before memory.
But I knew and loved Chris and Barney before I held the trusting, sleeping
weight of the baby in my arms. Alex is the next generation of my family,
but before him there was the three of us.

I met Chris in 1969 when I was nearly eight. He was seven. My family
and I had just returned home from five years abroad, diplomatic postings
in Beirut and Havana. I saw Canadian snow for the first time that winter.
I met Chris when our mothers signed us up for swimming lessons at the
old YMCA in Ottawa, a fetid chlorine swamp that made our skin itch and
our eyes burn whenever we swam there. On our first day there, Chris and
I discovered that we preferred to swim *under* the water. We looked slyly at
each other across the water, past the bovine, obedient eyes of the other
children that were riveted on the beefy young woman charged with teaching
us to swim. We already knew how to swim. The trick was moving this
slow hour forward so we wouldn't die of boredom.

Suddenly, we dove. Closing our eyes to the chlorine and our ears to
the swimming instructress who shrieked at us to *pay attention!* we pushed
down through the gray water. We touched the pool's slippery tiled bottom
with our toes and sealed the bond of our friendship, open palm to open
palm, in that silent watery cave. There were no words underwater. We
didn't need any. That was the beginning. We were expelled from the swimming class in disgrace until we could learn to behave properly. We always
knew how. We were just judicious about showing it.

Our friendship over the next four years was very nearly exclusive. We
attended the Child Study Center. We slept over at each other's house regularly. His mother became my first standard of glamour. She was blond and
effervescent, and the first time I saw her, I thought she must be his older
sister. She either cooked the sort of elegant meals that children are almost
never served (which made me feel terribly grown-up), or she ordered pizza
or Kentucky Fried Chicken. She wore make-up and perfume, sometimes
even jeans. She laughed a great deal, and she always treated Chris and me
as though we were the two most important little boys in the world, little
adults capable of any greatness or ambition, no matter how far-fetched. She
allowed me to bake at her house, and encouraged me to write my stories
about vampires and ghosts on her portable typewriter with the blue keys,
at her elegant antique writing desk, always praising the result.

With Chris, not talking was as expressive as talking. We would just be together, and that was enough.

When my father received news of a posting to the United Nations in Geneva, my first wrenching thought was that I was going to have to leave Chris. The night before we left for Switzerland, while my parents oversaw the final packing up of our belongings, I stayed at Chris's house. We swore that we would stay best friends.

"Always?" he said solemnly. His eyes were very blue and serious, lashes dark blond, darker than his hair.

"Always," I said. "Write to me. Write to me every day. I'll never have another friend like you, not ever."

Chris was at the airport to see us off with his mother and father. He and I crammed into a photo-booth and took a string of photographs. Children are trained to smile for cameras, no matter what, even if it's an unnatural, stiff rictus. The photograph of us showed two smiling boys, one blond, one brown-haired, grinning bravely into the machine that snapped our picture.

We moved into a rambling white villa outside Geneva, at the top of a hill which sloped gently down from our lawns toward the railroad tracks and the shimmering blue of Lake Leman. On summer days, when the sun was hard and brightly crystalline, I would lie on warm fragrant grass, writing letters to Chris and reading the ones he wrote back to me. His life, our old life, seemed far away. I loved my new school and the international set of friends I made there. I skied the French alps in the winter. I roamed Europe with my parents in the summer.

And I discovered an attraction to men, which frightened and confused me. I dated girls, of course, but one night after a dance, my date kissed me full on the lips and slipped her tongue inside my mouth. My eyes were closed, and as her tongue met mine, a horrible vivid image of some blind mole or rat peeking it's head out of its den and blinking in the sunlight suddenly rose up, and I recoiled. I never saw her again.

When I returned home to Ottawa at the end of the four years, Chris was the first person I called. I felt changed and grown in more ways than one, and desperately wanted something familiar.

Chris had changed physically: The chunky little boy the kids at school had teased and called Christophat was now a sleekly muscled youth. I spent as much time with Chris as I could that summer. In the mornings, I stayed home and helped my parents unpack and open our house. As the golden August afternoons drifted past, Chris and I caught up. We went to movies downtown, and cycled through Ottawa along the Rideau Canal. In the evenings, grown cooler now, we sat on the porch swing, sometimes talking, sometimes not, while the blue twilight air filled with the scent of flowers from my mother's cutting garden and the smoky memory of barbecue. In September, I left for boarding school.

St. John's Cathedral Boy's School in Selkirk, Manitoba, was run by a lay branch of the Anglican Church. It was dedicated to an exceptionally traditional education for boys: sports, school, muscular Christianity, and manual labor. The end result was supposed to net, according to the literature, a "complete man": devoutly Christian, free of outward manifestations of class distinction, with a work-ethic filched from John Calvin, and a disdain for the fripperies and gloss of "worldly things." Homophobia, as a matter of course, ran as thick as grease throughout everything the school taught.

I was moody, undisciplined, "overly sensitive." St. John's would fix that, read the school's jolly prospectus. It would make a man out of me. Besides, I was a legacy: My macho cousin Brian had attended St. John's. It was as tough as they said, he told me grimly. When I feebly asked about an arts or drama program, he muttered something about being careful not to get "labeled" on my first day.

Once there, though, the thought of quitting or running away never occurred to me. By that first winter, I had fallen in love with the wild, flat beauty of the prairies. I thrived on the long snowshoe hikes over frozen fields and lakes. And the second year I met Barney, and my life changed.

My first glimpse of him was from a distance. He and three other boys were carrying a heavy war canoe up the riverbank to the school after their 300-mile, three-week Newboy Canoe Trip. Something caught in my chest, fluttered there and held. I saw broad shoulders, an open, handsome face caked with sweat and dirt, and dark-brown hair, almost black. He was fifteen, I was sixteen. His clothes were filthy and damp. I found myself watching his back, his shoulders and the loping, long-limbed way his body moved beneath his grubby clothing. At fifteen, he had the look of a medieval warrior-prince, with a face from a nobleman's carved-marble sarcophagus in some ancient French cathedral. I learned his first name. *Barnaby* rolled off my tongue like inky music. I learned his double-barreled last name. He was from Vancouver. He missed his family. Even then, Barney had a man's beautiful speaking voice: mellifluous, dark-brown, with no scratchy adolescent breakage. As autumn swept inexorably toward winter, he lost his tan and his dark hair and eyes lay in shattering contrast against his pale skin. As the prairies turned yellow-gold and brown, and, finally ice-white, our friendship deepened.

I would watch his large, muscular hands as he wrote or ate. He played sports with a facility I did not have, which assured him a speedy entry into the collective body of the school. He had a spectacular blasting laugh which was impossible to ignore, impossible to at least smile at, if not join in.

We became lovers that first winter. When he seduced me (and I so wanted to be seduced by him) it was in an atmosphere of warmth and safety, as well as burning need and urgency. He was my friend before he was my lover, and his lips and hands on my body were the first, and, even now, among those I remember best.

We were also seduced by the school, however, and the terrifying guilt we felt was fueled by the intense, almost fundamentalist, Christian ethic that prevailed at St. John's. If anything, though, Barney was more caught up in the school's soul-searing Christianity than I was, and our sexual relationship ended.

"It's over," he said when I cornered him outside the darkroom one night after lights-out. "It's wrong. This is not what I want for my life. I can't see how you'd want it either."

"Barney," I said, not willing to plead, but not believing either, not wanting to believe, that it was over. "Just . . . well, tell me why. Why not? I mean, you started this. You can't just . . ."

"Well," he said with chilling finality, "I am. No more. It's over. It's wrong."

"But what about me?"

"I still want us to be friends," he continued implacably. "I love you *as a friend*. But I don't want this life."

Smoking with rage, I wished him dead. "Bastard," I said.

"I feel sorry for you," he replied calmly. "Really, I do. I hope you find what you're looking for."

He began to pick up girls at the roller rink in Winnipeg on Sundays, and would brag about it back at the school on Sunday nights the way the other boys did. I would grin and guffaw and backslap. I would join the others in goading him on to details of his conquests, feeling cold and numb and jealous.

On the day I graduated, Barney sat with our friends and cheered for me. He had brought a chirpy young woman to my graduation whom he introduced as his girlfriend from Vancouver.

"I love her," he confided jubilantly.

"That's great, Barney," I lied. "I'm so happy you've found what you were looking for."

"There's no one like you, no one," he said earnestly. "I love you, you know? You're my best friend."

"Yes," I said. "I know."

"Don't forget me?"

"No," I said. "Never."

I was scheduled to leave in three days. I changed my ticket that day, and left that evening on a night flight to Ottawa. The prairies vanished beneath a veil of purple sunset clouds as the DC-9 streaked toward Ontario. Below me, I saw the sparkle of lights: farms, gas stations, truck stops. Then, nothing. Darkness.

I was cold. I gathered the airplane blanket around me and closed the plastic window-shade. The flight was long, and I didn't sleep.

I returned home to Ottawa and Chris and vowed that my real life was about to begin.

I was definitely not ready for college. The idea of another four years lived in close proximity to people not of my choosing depressed me. I had been modeling in Ottawa and Montreal for the past two summers, with some success, and I had vague plans to go to Paris for a little while and work there. My friend Lesley Durnin (who would eventually become a star on the European circuit as the eighties unfolded) was already there. She urged me to join her, and I planned to do just that, come September. I spent the summer working on a new portfolio for Paris, and spending time with Chris.

As the first fragrant coolness of late August nights came to Ottawa, we walked the dark streets of Rockliffe Park, past tall hedges and the large, tasteful houses of the district, talking. As we have since we were children, we lapsed into our silences and just walked. I preferred the companionable quiet to the possibility that he might not have understood the depths of my despair over the turn my life had taken. To reveal Barney would have been to reveal my sexual secrets, and, to my way of thinking, risking the love and friendship from Chris that I had come to trust for thirteen years. I could not risk it.

I went to Paris for three months. I lived in an apartment with a view of Montparnasse. It was here that I was first made love to by a man, with a man's authoritative touch. He was older than I was, probably thirty, a languid Southerner with a sculpted, well-muscled body and smooth alabaster skin. We met at the American Church of Paris, after services, and I took him home with me.

Barney and I had been inexperienced and greedy in our passion, made savage by adolescent lust and the impossible suppression of our desires. Here in Paris, on my narrow bed by the open window, with the garnet-toned late afternoon sunlight flooding my bedroom, there was no brutal rush and friction. I appreciated the man's unhurried touch as he held me, and his mellow southern voice which sounded to me like cream pouring.

I was home in Ottawa in time for Christmas, and I called Chris within hours of landing. My time in Paris had made me stronger. We sat in his dark living room late one night in front of the fireplace, with the lights of the Christmas tree sparkling like brilliant jewels in the corner. He had lifted a bottle of Chianti from his parents' collection. Dizzy with wine and the fire's heat, the story of my double-life came tumbling out. I spoke of the loneliness and pain of keeping my desires to myself, of hearing words like "queer" and "faggot" hurled by my peers who called each other words like that as a matter of course, and me always wondering if my secret was out.

Chris reached out and hugged me close. I felt myself enveloped in a spreading warmth that drew the pain from me like yarrow. As so often before, we didn't speak. Then Chris asked me why I had taken so long to tell him something he already knew. At that moment he became the only human being alive who knew all of my secrets, and loved me more because of them. But I did not go into specifics. I did not mention Barney by name.

I moved to Toronto in the New Year. There, surrounded by the omnisexual rush of an international city, I found a home.

I danced shirtless until the early dawn hours at The Manatee and Katrina's. I sought out leather bars like 18-East and The Barn, luxuriating in the contrast between the WASP propriety of my upbringing and the smell of poppers, sweat, beer, and leather which etched the parameters of my night hours.

Chris moved to Toronto later that year, and we both enrolled at the University of Toronto.

I wrote lugubrious poetry. He played varsity football and intramural rugby. I lived at Knox College, a gothic ivy-encrusted pile which, by some bizarre, cheerful recipe of fate, housed several pumped-up varsity swimmers, a pallid clutch of sexually repressed Presbyterian seminarians, and a loud, pro-active gay clique of which I became a founding member.

One night in the fall, late, long after the bars were closed, I was strolling home to Knox through the gay district south of Wellesley with my friend Bruce. We were both in our cups and feeling rosy. The moon was high, but the street was dark and deserted. Toronto was then, as it is now, a fairly safe city, but a flurry of bashings were not unheard of around Halloween. Bruce and I walked quickly along the dark street lined with trash dumpsters and concrete apartments. Suddenly the predawn silence was shattered by raucous bellowing, followed by a series of crashes.

"Shit," said Bruce.

More crashes. Rugby songs, drunken male voices. I turned around. Up the street and closing in, I saw the twisting shadows of five brawny campus jocks with fire in their eyes, jacked full of alcohol and testosterone. They were roaring and knocking down mailboxes and newspaper stands, singing lewd ditties and bellowing about beating the other team and getting pussy.

"Fuck," I said.

Bruce was as camp as a pink plastic lawn flamingo, both in appearance and manner, and my profile on campus was no secret by that time either.

"We are going to die," Bruce sniveled.

"Shut up and walk faster."

The roaring came closer, then suddenly stopped. I could hear grunts, and panting. I didn't turn around, didn't dare. I kept walking. Our shoes sounded like hail against the sidewalk.

"Hey!" bellowed one of the voices. "Stop!"

I paused. It was a familiar voice, a warm voice made coarse by liquor and triumph. I turned around, and started to laugh.

"Hi, Chris," I said. "Nice evening?"

"We won, 'fcourse," Chris growled in drunken-jock indignation.

"What're *you* doing out here so late?" He looked at me reproachfully, as though I had violated some curfew and exposed myself to danger from God-knows-who by walking down this street unprotected.

"Hey, buddy, you know these guys, buddy, man?" rumbled the barbarian horde behind us.

" 'S'Mike!" Chris slurred indignantly. " 'S'my brother." This was all they needed to hear. I was hoisted in brawny arms, and dragged cheerfully forward. The bellowing resumed. Apparently my new best friends and I were going to get drunker still, and hunt for pussy together. *Crash!* Another newspaper-box met concrete.

"You know these people?" whispered Bruce in awe. These were real rugby jocks, not bar poseurs in workout drag.

"My oldest friend," I said. And that is how I was escorted under guard back to Knox College under a high October moon, through the dark streets of Toronto at the height of bashing season.

I had, by then, resumed tentative communication with Barney who, not surprisingly, had hit the wall in his quest for full-time heterosexuality. We still danced defensively around each other over the telephone, but when we saw each other the summer of my sophomore year, there was no denying that we were still deeply entwined in each other's lives and fortunes. As two gay men, we spoke the beginnings of a common language which filled the space previously occupied by his pious sympathy and my feelings of abandonment and impotent, jealous rage.

I dropped out of school that year to try to become a writer. I had published several articles in commercial magazines while at school, and I was finding academia stuffy and repressive.

I went out to Vancouver the following summer to visit my parents, who had retired there. I had gained some weight, and Barney could not resist remarking on it. The erratic writing, eating, and sleeping habits of a freelance journalist had cut into my workout time, and it showed. Barney, the competitive rower, looked fabulous. He had bought an old cabin cruiser and refinished it. He lived aboard full time, which struck me as glamorous and romantic. To boot, he had become one of those born-again homosexuals who, once released from the confines of internalized homophobia and denial, blossoms. It was as though he had invented homosexuality. Bronzed and glorious, he snapped and danced his way through the summer, setting me off in a way that was most unflattering.

A pattern was established that summer that would last us well into the decade: a need to be together, supportive of each other's lives and work on a superficial level, wanting it to be deeper, but unable to let it be so. We were sometimes viciously competitive, often privately smug in the face of each other's failures. My weight problems and the lessened self-image that sprang from them were the perfect counterbalance to his inability to maintain a successful relationship or commit to a career path. But there we were, bound by joint histories and a terrible, bruised love for each other.

Once, at my house in Toronto, his lover blackened both of his eyes for an infidelity. I was downstairs when it happened and I claimed that as my excuse for not interfering. Some darkly jealous, uncivilized part of me had always nurtured a cancerous desire to strike Barney, to hurt him, cause him pain, see blood flow. Aloud, I coldly wondered how long he thought he could get away with abusing the parameters of his relationship with his lover.

"So like you," I added cruelly. "You've always treated people who love you badly."

My sympathies were squarely with the lover, who represented himself to me as the victim of Barney's shallowness and insensitivity, language I could relate to. I fell for the line, fell for the lover, and I silently invited him to become my hammer.

The phone rang one night at my house. It was Barney. He was hysterical.

"Calm down," I told him. "Calm down and tell me what happened. Barney, calm *down*."

"We were fighting," he said harshly, his breath coming in shallow hitches. "A bad one this time, really bad. A bad fight. Nothing I do is ever right. It wasn't his fault. It was my fault."

Their fights became more violent and intense. When Barney entered therapy and did in fact begin to become strong and whole, the lover, threatened by the rebel strength, escalated the abuse. Their last fight (and Barney related the story with a chilling detachment which horrified me) ended with Barney escaping to spend the night locked in his own car.

He called me from Vancouver the night he ended the relationship. His voice on the telephone was strong and clear, and only the slightest bit hesitant as he told me that he was single again.

"I thought you'd be disappointed in me," he said. "It looks like I've failed another relationship."

"Why on earth would I be disappointed in you?" I said, shocked. "You got yourself out of a horrifying situation, and you did it all by yourself. That's great, Barnyard. Why would I be disappointed? You're strong now. You've made yourself very strong, and it suits you."

"I feel different," he admitted.

As Barney healed, I healed, and our friendship healed. He had learned to open himself up to me, dispensing with the glossy, superior patina that had protected him from the world, and from me. I had learned to admit my jealousy and resentment of him, and my initial resistance to support him through the holocaust that his relationship had become.

"The luckiest families," he said sagely one night over the telephone from Vancouver, "the rare ones, grow together with everybody learning at the same time. That's always been a rough point for you and me. We've never been at the same point in our development. One of us has always been ahead of the other."

"And now?" I was curious.

"Now we're starting." He paused. Softly, he said, "It's great."

I agreed. "How's the bachelor life?" I asked. Barney had been single for some time. In the past, he had defined a large part of his life by the men in his relationships, but this new Barney was fiercely independent, which heightened his attractiveness a hundredfold.

"Hmmm," he said. "I'd rather be single than be involved with someone who can't carry their weight without being cruel. Your relationships always seem to work," he mused. "I've always admired that about you."

"Well, Barney," I sighed, "you seem to be able to manage everything else. You cook gourmet meals, you dance like liquid sex, you live on a *boat* for Christ's sake. And you're so handsome it sets everyone's teeth on edge. . . ."

"You'll turn my head," he interrupted slyly. "Well, then, I guess that between the two of us, we make the perfect person. Your talent and wit, my style. We should inhabit the same body."

"Fine," I said tartly. "As long as we use yours."

On his last visit to Toronto he stayed with me. We slept in my bed, and we stayed up and talked until late. Before we fell asleep, we held each other close. When we touched, we felt the weight of years: I slept with him in the same bed, feeling his body's heat, and was warmed by it. It drove me to nothing but peace. When I reached for his hands, or held him and smelled his hair, there was almost a blood memory of being one, bound by trust and time. Last year he met his partner, Doug, a man of both strength and kindness. There is talk of a commitment ceremony next year. I have come to care for Doug, and I think of him as a brother-in-law. As much as anyone deserves the things that matter to them, Barney deserves this happiness. For me to believe that, to want his happines as sincerely as I want my own, is the final atonement for our years of disharmony. Our family grows. It is the natural way of things.

As for Chris, I see a great deal of him these days, now that he is a father. An entirely new dimension has been added to our relationship because of the baby. I now have a nephew. I have become Uncle Michael.

I am more likely to be at Chris and Claire's these days than out clubbing. Alex's birthdays, Halloweens, and Christmases are the new rituals of my life. I can remember when Alex first stood up and walked, and when he first spoke. He can now say something that sounds like *Micha*, and I confess that I am utterly spellbound. He touches my face with his chubby fingers and laughs, sounding so much like Chris that my heart feels as though it will leave my body.

I can't help feeling that watching Alex grow, and being part of that growth, will keep me from growing old myself.

My nephew, Alex. My brothers, Chris and Barney.

At night sometimes, before sleep, I move my mind across the years and gather about me the tapestry of our lives together as though it were a quilt. It warms me with every breath, every heartbeat. Chris and Barney. Light and dark. Both essential.

eric latzky

summer at
the beach

a memoir of friendship
and fire island

I'm not sure why we left it to the last minute, but there's the rationale that
you get the best deal if you rent late. Then, again, some people say you get
the best deal if you rent early. All I know is this: It was one week before
Memorial Day and though Matthew, his boyfriend, and I had talked about
renting a house for the month of August, we hadn't done anything about
it yet.

It was definitely a Saturday when Matthew and I boarded the ferry in
the town of Sayville and rode across the Great South Bay to Cherry Grove,
Fire Island. If the holiday the following weekend marked the official opening
of the summer season, the chilling rain made it feel more like winter was
just around the corner. Meryl, our broker from At the Bay Realty, ran us
around from house to house, anything that was left—two bedrooms, one
bedrooms. We even looked at studios, though I can't imagine why we
considered that possibility.

Matthew worked a deal, his calling in life. "What about the broken
window?" he asked. "Throw in the first tank of propane free. . . . How
about an extended season?" I concentrated on aesthetic matters, my own
area of expertise. I looked at kitchens, bathrooms, and decks. I opened
closets, checked out space. I was mentally fulfilling an agenda of require-

ments: sunlight in my bedroom, an outdoor place to write and paint, the perfect set-up for nightly barbecues and healthy tomato vines. All the trappings of some kind of home? If so, an idealized one, the family members chosen rather than assigned.

That same day, just a few hours after our arrival on the island, a little shocked at the unexpected outcome and too impatient to wait for the next ferry, we hired a water taxi to speed us back across the bay to the mainland. How had it happened? We'd gone to Cherry Grove with the clearest of intentions—a month on Fire Island. As we pushed off from the dock, for three times as much money as was planned, we'd just signed a lease on Hot Seat, our tenement at the beach, home for the next four months.

A foreword to a summer at the beach. (Read to the tune of the Rolling Stones' "Some Girls.")

In high school, a mutual friend called us midgets. This, because we drank coffee and smoked cigarettes. We were a little short, it's true, but we were only fifteen. And I'm sure the clothes we wore were outside of the standard for boys in the Bronx, ca. 1977—rose-colored Annie Hall sunglasses, Fiorucci jeans two sizes too small, and fine cotton collarless shirts from Mr. Europa, the Bronx's own answer to Bloomingdale's. Anyhow, we were much more interested in the time we were spending in Manhattan since, by then, we were officially gay, boyfriends, and so far out into the day and night, the closet was a dim memory if ever it existed at all.

The slow, quiet things in life I can understand—nature, an aimless walk, the long-awaited completion of a painting or a novel. I never really did like speed, in drugs or in business. Fast things strike me as devoid of substance.

A business trip—a convention in Anaheim, California—separated that Fire Island rental expedition and the actual beginning of the season, our summer at the beach. By then I didn't want to go, I just wanted to be out at the house, but the trip was planned, and since both Matthew and I had our individual commitments to be there, at least one wouldn't be jealous of the other. And also, we agreed to return with enough hotel signature towels to fill the linen closet of Hot Seat. On this point alone the trip was successful.

At the convention, I tried to work, but my mind was filled with images of waves and strolls on the beach. And my friend Amelia, a fellow conventioneer, seemed to be as distracted as I was. So, after conspiring briefly during lunch on the third day of the convention, we jumped into my rental car, abandoned Anaheim, and obtained the keys to her parents' terraced, oceanfront apartment in Malibu, code name: Barbie's Malibu Beach House. The location was perfect—within nose-shot of Granita, Wolfgang Puck's newest restaurant, where, lucky us, we were able to secure a reservation for a late dinner. I flew back to New York the next morning after arranging, over dinner, that Amelia would join us on Fire Island some time in July. The shape of the summer was becoming clear—house guests and all.

The first full weekend of June, a few days after returning to New York, Matthew, his boyfriend, and I hired a car to take us on the first big trip from the city to Sayville. The three of us, their very young and extremely energetic cairn terrier, Charles, as in *Prince* (my new nephew), two pounds of French roast coffee, a few bottles of extra virgin olive oil along with an entire kitchen including my proper Charlotte Russe mold, suitcases full of clothing, linens, my computer, a library full of books, a sketch pad, and a set of pencils. It's amazing what you can fit into a Lincoln Town Car when you really try. Charles did not enjoy the ride, and he let us know it the whole way out, but he did discover, almost immediately, that he liked the beach, as well as just about everyone on it.

Whatever the house might have lacked in grandeur was more than made up for by our enthusiasm. We spent that Saturday and Sunday scrubbing, cleaning, planting, arranging. We went back across to the mainland for a shopping spree at the local K Mart—a barbecue, strings of deck lights, citronella torches, beach chairs, sunblock. We bought soft drinks by the case: Diet Coke for them, mineral water for me. Monday morning when I opened my eyes, the sunlight filtering through the curtains on the windows above my bed, I was moved to tears by the beautiful quiet and the quiet beauty of the house, my home, and the thought of a whole long summer at the beach with my friends.

An important historical note for a summer at the beach. (Read to the tune of Lou Reed's "Vicious" at certain moments, and to the tune of "Conversation," by Joanie Mitchell, at other more tender moments.)

Right from the start, a kind of competition informed our friendship

—Matthew took the lead, I rebelled and surpassed him, he came up from behind, I moved away in a new direction. He followed, I followed, he followed, etc. It was always like this.

We met in the spring of our freshman year of high school. The first and only girlfriend of my life, Suzanne, whose aggressively dominant kisses in dark rooms of sixth grade parties had made an indelible impression on me, had become Matthew's girlfriend that early high school spring. Suzanne, in fact, introduced Matthew and me, but we were standoffish for the next several months. It must have been Matthew who designated me the enemy. Perhaps he imagined I was invading his territory. Knowing myself, I can't imagine that I had anything but a twinkle in my eye for him.

It was a busy summer—Matthew and Suzanne had broken up and I went to California to blossom. My father had moved there a couple of years earlier and since then, twice annually, I retreated to Malibu, the land of sunshine, movie stars, and buff blond surfer dudes in rubber suits. This lovely combination of local tourist attractions was not wasted on me, even at that young age.

That fall, the beginning of sophomore year, things started to thaw. Somewhere around November, Matthew and I began to spend time together, in school and also on the weekends. He wanted to talk and we would look for secret, secluded spots in the school building. I wondered if he had scouted them out in advance. He never seemed to have a lot of trouble finding them.

On an early winter day, the first revelation, Matthew to me: "I have to tell you something. I'm . . . I'm . . . I'm bisexual." Two days later, me to Matthew: "I have to tell *you* something. I'm . . . I . . . I think I'm the same." One week later, Matthew to me: "I wasn't being completely honest. [Blurts this out] I'm gay." Maybe another week goes by, me to Matthew: "I wasn't being completely honest either. [Blurts this out] I'm gay too."

Our time together turned from conversation to making out. I began to spend every weekend at his house. Often he would tell his mother that we were staying at my apartment and we would disappear into Manhattan —to the prime of Studio 54, to the Central Park South apartment of Christopher, a hair dresser who had adopted us, to . . . anyplace that we thought was glamorous. I'm sure what our mutual friend said was true, we must have really looked like midgets.

————

Matthew and his boyfriend were mostly out at the house for long weekends, leaving the middle days of the week quiet, time I spent working on a second novel, making drawings, swimming, and taking long walks on the beach. In the late afternoons I would often hang out at the restaurant in the middle of town, sort of writing, but mostly watching the slow parade, wandering people, the arrivals of the boats carrying vacationers and true islanders.

The first time Tony and I had an actual conversation I almost started to laugh. He waited tables at the restaurant a few days a week and we'd sort of been saying hello to each other whenever I'd go by. I hadn't quite figured out what his work schedule there was yet, but I thought he was very cute—small, Italian, long dark hair—so I was in the process of scouting out the situation. That one afternoon as I sat there with pad and paper, not writing, he came over to talk to me. It was a pretty standard opening line: "So, what do you do?" I told him that I'm a writer. Then, without a trace of self-consciousness, he gave the smile I could never resist and said, "Oh you're a writer. Write a play, you should write a play. We need more plays." It didn't take long to learn he worked in the theater, a production stage-manager for Broadway. And it didn't take long for that endearingly frank openness to win me over completely.

Cherry Grove is like Strawberry Fields—nothing is real. So with only a few lines in the sand to cross we found ourselves spending time together. We cooked meals, went swimming, took Olga, Tony's shar-pei, to chase the deer at the bay at sunset. She never caught them and always got upset by it. Olga was on the clumsy side. We watched television—the summer Olympics and the political conventions—we walked into town at night for pie and ice cream, and slept late almost every day. In the mornings he bought the papers and made blueberry pancakes while I went through my hour-long ritual of awakening. We walked in the garden at Ship's Deck, his curved luxury-liner of a house, waiting for the tomatoes to ripen. We plotted to steal the lilac from a house we disliked on the next walk, but each time I really threatened to do it, he backed down and wouldn't let me.

On weekends, I picked blueberries from the mammoth bushes on the property at Hot Seat. At night I baked cobblers and we prepared barbecues—all of us plus an assortment of houseguests. It seemed like we never got to dinner before nine, nor dessert before eleven. And only then did we begin our card games around the kitchen table which were inevitably disrupted by the dogs getting into trouble—foot-tall baby Charles making unwelcome sexual advances toward poor, big, awkward Olga. Oh, how she wanted so much to be treated like a lady.

This was the way the summer went. What was I looking for? A place? A home? All the time I wondered if it was fantasy or an earnest dream.

Two pivotal moments many years before the summer at the beach.

1. Greenwich Village, a cold late autumn day. *(Read to the tune of Thelma Houston's "Don't Leave Me This Way.")* I think I started wanting out when he started talking about the rest of our lives. At sixteen it wasn't an idea I could get my mind around. I mean, in some way, the thought that Matthew would want that with me was beautiful, but there was so much both of us had never had and done—anonymous sex, other boyfriends, and everything else. When I told him, he cried and pleaded, and he might have won out because certainly I loved him; but somehow, without fully understanding the implications, I realized that for the first time ever I was making a decision about my own future.

2. New Year's Eve, one year later, the Paradise Garage. *(Read to the tune of "You Make Me Feel (Mighty Real)" by the one, the only, Sylvester.)* Warhol was there when we found each other again. I was walking through the tunnel hallway with vertical pinpoint spotlights that separated the room with the big dance floor from the room with the juice bar and fruit bowls. I can't remember what I was on, but my head was down and when I looked up, there was Andy, ghostlike, a vision, his straight, white, chopped-off hair luminous, lit from above. Our eyes met, froze for a moment, fifteen seconds. I leapt out of the hallway and there was Matthew. We danced together, then we left together. We went over to the east side for dinner and champagne at 4:00 A.M. Then I brought him back to my apartment, well, my mother's apartment near Gracie Mansion. We slept together that night but we didn't have sex, and we woke up in the new year, friends.

Matthew had this thing about *S*s. We played a lot of Scrabble that summer and Matthew saw *S*s as powerful. With them, he explained, you could add on to the end of a word, in particular, a good word that someone else had already made, making their word plural and gaining all those points in addition to making your own whole new word that ended in *S*, getting those points too. Matthew had a thing about points and he loved to win.

One afternoon, I laid down an *S* at the end of his last word and proceeded to build my own a-z-u-r-e-s onto the end of it, working my way clear across to the edge of the board, right over a triple-word score box. I leaned back in my armchair on the deck where we were playing, exhilarated and a bit drained by my literary triumph, and looked up. How spectacular, how infinite nature is, I thought, that there exists a spectrum of even a single obscure color.

I counted my points in a somewhat studied way, admittedly adding some uncharacteristic gesture. I counted out loud, slowly, gleefully. "Ten," I said, "seventeen, twenty-three, plus the triple-word score." And that didn't even include the original word. A *Z* is, after all, a ten-point letter in and of itself. But I could sense something was wrong—all was not well across the table. I looked up. There was Matthew, erect in his chair, peering over at me, his eyes tight, barely slits. "I'm going to challenge that word," he said finally. "There's no plural of *azure.*"

I couldn't believe it. We checked the *Scribner-Bantam English Dictionary*, "the biggest bargain in desk dictionaries" by it's own dubious admission, and there was no separate listing for a plural *azures*. Of course it is a noun and a noun can be pluralized. He wouldn't relent, though, so not only did I lose all those points, not only was I penalized a turn under the rules for losing a challenge, but I felt strongly that the beauty of my word had been seriously tarnished by this erroneous attack. And despite all this injustice, he seemed genuinely pleased with himself.

A few days later he called me from the city to say, a little sheepishly, with a hint of apology in his voice, that he had purchased a proper *Scrabble Dictionary* and that he was wrong after all.

An abbreviated chronology of an old friendship, pertinent to a summer at the beach. (Read against the epic backdrop of DJ's special extended dance mix including but not limited to "Ceremony," by Joy Division; "Boys Don't Cry," by The Cure; "Just Can't Get Enough," by Depeche Mode; "Our House," by Madness; "Ocean Rain" by Echo and the Bunnymen; "Enjoy Yourself," by The Specials; "Tainted Love/Where Did Our Love Go" {12-inch single}, by Soft Cell; and "True," by Spandau Ballet.)

They called us "the boys"—me, Donald, and Matthew—seen nightly at Hurrah, the first and premier post-disco, rock-'n'-roll video nightclub. We capped off many an evening with our own *parties* at 4:00 A.M. on the deserted dance floor, invitation required. Quaaludes, as I recall, are a very social drug. After a taxi ride downtown, the party often continued at the

Mudd Club. Or maybe Berlin had already opened. Everyone's parents must have stopped asking questions by then. To us nothing really mattered since we had no plans past the age of thirty, maximum, anyway.

College was a bummer right from the start. For one thing, I lived on speed just to maintain the grueling schedule. I spent most of my time disappearing back into the city to meet Matthew, go out all night and catch the 6:20 A.M. train back up to school. Three months into it, for my eighteenth birthday present to myself, I dropped out. That January, Matthew and I signed the lease to the apartment on Avenue A. Four rooms for $500. It seemed like a huge amount of money at the time. I was mugged at gun point in the vestibule of the building two weeks later. Hurrah closed suddenly but the divine little Jefferson, the perfect nightclub in the loft above the old Jefferson theater, opened. There, we would walk out onto the marquis to watch the sunrise. In March, Donald returned to New York from abroad and moved in with us. "The boys" were back together again.

We got our hair cut at Jungle Red Studios in TriBeCa but it wasn't being called TriBeCa yet. Huge G.I. Joe flattops held up with butcher's wax. They stayed that way for a week. My small, selective nineteenth birthday party was a turning point—my first shot of heroin at the Lower East Side salon of a friend. It was like a miracle, the first time the needle went in. I can still feel it. Before too long, I had my first habit. Matthew fell in love and moved to the heartland. Dorothy in the wheat fields. We gave up the apartment, Donald moved one block uptown and I moved seven blocks downtown, into the palatial Ageloff Towers. The day after Thanksgiving that year, I went to see the world, in search of the truth. I found it in Paris in the form of opium.

Matthew broke his leg and moved back to New York. When I returned to the city, Donald and I became business partners doing the thing we knew how to do best—party. We coordinated special events at the Limelight, the church cum nightclub, enormous extravaganzas—William Burroughs's seventieth, Shirley Maclaine's fiftieth, etc. It became increasingly difficult, however, to keep a full calendar and maintain a heroin habit at the same time. Clearly something had to go.

Donald was the first to fall. We sent him off, abroad again, and I continued a pared-down schedule for at least another year. Matthew came to see me on the eve of my departure for Los Angeles. He'd been for his first visit to *the farm* and he looked absolutely fabulous. I was sure he'd taken up eating again. Nodding out only occasionally, I listened to him extol the virtues of the sober life. He insisted that everyone should pay a visit to *the farm* at least once in a lifetime, if only for the experience. Days later, when I came to in my hospital room, smack in the middle of detoxing from a nasty heroin habit, it was warm and sunny and I saw palm trees outside the window and mountains in the distance. It was late February and where I'd come from it was terribly cold. This confused me. But whatever happened in L.A., it must have worked, though I still don't know why it took me five years to move back to New York.

Matthew had made a few more trips to *the farm* and eventually it worked, too. He'd been with his boyfriend for a while by the time I made my triumphant return to the big city. They generously invited me to hang my hat on their sofa for three months while slinging words at *Interview* magazine and looking for a place of my own.

It's not that I didn't know money meant a lot to Matthew but I didn't understand to what extent. Sometimes, it seemed to me that Matthew's strategy in life was to play both or many ends against a middle. As if he believed in discord. Divide and conquer. And he had a fantastic capacity to remain cool under infinite pressure. This was both deceptive and disheartening to me—he often came off as if little in life was really all that important to him.

The events of that rental expedition day a couple of months earlier happened so quickly, and it was only now I was coming to understand that the high life at Hot Seat was somewhat beyond my means. Matthew had laid out a good part of the money for the house at the lease-signing, and I'd agreed to pay back the remainder of my share at a certain rate on a certain schedule. I was beginning to fall behind and this was causing tensions between us which, one morning, erupted into a fight, each of us biting the other's head off in our own uniquely snitty ways. Mercifully, at that point, the weekend was just about over.

Before Matthew left the island, I suggested that we meet in the city that week to talk—about money, but also about our friendship—and he agreed it would be a good idea. Our meeting at a café one midweek late afternoon started out on a very cold note, despite the searing heat and humidity of New York in July. We were in our corners, across a tiny marble table. Eventually we came around, called a truce, and found some common language. He asked me what I could realistically afford and I told him I'd call him the next day with an answer.

I asked him how he felt about our approaching thirtieth birthdays. About having survived so much together, being up and down simultaneously and separately. At one point I started to cry, involuntarily, something I hadn't done in years. I told him that somewhere in the course of fifteen years I'd come to see him as a kind of family. It seemed to make him very uncomfortable.

Tony and I made our way through the summer. We took trips to the mainland to see wonderfully awful movies at huge Long Island shopping malls. We went to plant nurseries and pet shops, farm stands and supermarkets. One rainy afternoon we took a wrong turn in a town I'd never heard of and discovered the Entenmann's Bakery factory-and-outlet store. This is it, I thought, the thing I'd been searching for—after years of dragging around the ball and chain of my devoutly cosmopolitan existence, I felt finally, and without shame, suburban.

So there we shopped. We bought cookies and cakes and sweet rolls and garbage we never intended to eat—Tony couldn't refuse a bargain, unlike me who took some sick pride in forever paying the highest possible retail price for anything and everything. We headed back to the ferry, stopping along the way at a farm stand to buy the glorious fruits of summer, the foods of August that never really found their way to the single little grocery store of Cherry Grove—Jersey corn, white peaches, sweet ripe tomatoes. I always wanted to stock up, get it all in. And I'd been promising to invite Matthew and Michael over to Ship's Deck for a proper summer dinner, a homemade pie and a late-night card game.

My timing was a little off with the invitation. Tony and I had been having a rough time that week. In our way, we fought without ever raising our voices. I guess we were looking for a way to communicate with each other, something we were never very successful at. The day of the dinner was particularly strained—maybe we were discovering that what each of us wanted in the long run was not necessarily compatible with the other. It must've been early evening before I asked Matthew if we could postpone dinner until another night.

The following morning I woke up to Tony and Olga outside my bedroom window at Hot Seat and a spectacularly perfect Fire Island day—the *azures* of the sky, the heat of the sun with a cool breeze, the just-audible sound of the waves crashing in the distance beyond the house. In his sexy, pseudo-tough-boy way, Tony suggested that maybe we should have the dinner that night, quickly squelching the smile on his face by adding, however, that he wasn't doing any of the cooking. Then Olga bestowed upon me one of her rare, frugal yet sloppy kisses.

Later, after a solo walk on a pristine beach at low tide, I reextended the invitation for dinner. Matthew's answer was not immediately forthcoming. He sat back in his chair on the deck, taking an extra moment before looking up from the paper he'd been reading. Then he asked, half teasing and half seriously, if I was going to cancel at the last minute again. Before I could be sure why I felt a tiny bit stung by the question, I replied, saying that I wasn't intending to, and he accepted the invitation. In my usual, excessively slow way, several minutes passed before it occurred to me that he'd never asked if things were all right between Tony and me.

Contemporary observations on an old friend, pertinent to a summer at the beach. Also, contemporary observations on the evolution of a friendship. (Read to the tune of "Why," by Bronski Beat.)

Over the years he changed. And, of course, I changed. We both changed in our own separate ways and this caused changes in the way we related to and dealt with each other. But changes, especially with those closest to you, often take a long time to perceive.

I couldn't say at what point our identities as adults emerged, though it must have been sometime after the wild days were over. That it took years for the wild days to end probably caused some complications. We'd been through so many periods and phases together, but the real shocker was seeing each other for the first time back in New York, our youth behind us, fully formed people looking ahead in our own individual directions.

I never stopped to think about the possibility that the differences between us might become problems. Looking back on all the years, having always found a way of allowing for, tolerating, dealing with, and respecting, I suppose I just assumed we would always be able to do that for each other.

After our meeting back in the city, we made our peace or called a truce and moved languorously into August. The ocean grew warmer, gigantic jelly fish washed up on the beach, and the bluefish began to run, at times making the sea look as if it were boiling. The corn became plentiful—silver queen, butter and sugar. We ate it by the bushel. We attended a symphony of timeless evenings, the rich sun on our skin, peach pies cooling in the kitchen.

Donald had come to visit during his call to the port of New York on yet another world tour, having long abandoned the city as home. We were able to pry our friend Lea away from her desk at the magazine in the city for a weekend or two. Amelia had come to spend a week and do some work with Matthew. What indignities she suffered at our barbed wits for her tofu sandwiches and lack of interest in a big, rare steak on the grill. She retaliated with her own cleverness—I have some memory of nights spent on the couch rather than in my own very expensive bed.

Probably September is the most beautiful month on Fire Island. Even more than August, the naturally exquisite landscape is mellowed just that much further by a summer of wind and sun and the relentless salt air. There's a sense of exposure at that point on the beach, a kind of native, emotional fearlessness. A barefoot summer, without clothes, without rules, without times—it transforms you in magically unspeakable ways.

Without our realizing it, Labor Day weekend had arrived. We were all out there, along with swarming numbers of other worshippers at the altar of the end of summer. We'd begun to think about lugging the contents of Hot Seat home. Even though we had almost a full month left on our lease, we figured if we hired a car a couple of times, did it in a couple of trips, it would make the whole thing easier. At that point, Matthew was still insisting on somehow bringing the six-foot ficus tree he'd bought for the deck back to the city. For this, even his boyfriend told him he was crazy. We agreed that late Monday afternoon, Labor Day proper, we would have a car meet us at the boat on the mainland.

Tony had guests out that weekend and he decided to have a barbecue on Monday which we all attended, a real barbecue with hamburgers, potato salad, Coca-Cola, and ketchup. In it's own silly way, it was one of the best afternoons of the summer. It was just what it was—easy, simple, without a care. We got along, we laughed and chatted, we drank and ate. And somewhere around 5:00 P.M., the residents of Hot Seat stood up and said thank you, that we had to run to catch the boat. I don't remember sensing it before that moment, that slight, almost imperceptible chill in the air, the first bell warning of the beginning of the end of the summer.

It was at that moment, too, that Tony and I looked at each other and excused ourselves to the garden for a few moments alone. I'm sure we didn't say anything profound to each other, no big declarations or promises. We both knew I'd be back out in a few days and that really there was still plenty of time left to our summer. I asked him to check on my tomatoes in my yard, hugged him, stood silent for a few more minutes, and returned to the others on the deck. But the presence of that chill in the air was intensifying. There was something about its persistence that stayed with me. I felt it the whole way back to the city.

A postscript to a summer at the beach. (Read to the tune of "We'll Let You Know" by Morrissey.)

I spent a good part of the month of September at the beach, but I don't recall seeing Matthew out there. We spoke on the telephone, to say cordial hellos and to make plans to close down the house. As the month went on, though, he made it more and more difficult to get in touch with him. Days went by before he returned a call. And then he only had a moment to speak. He was abrupt. At times, it seemed, even rude. Of course, everyone was gearing up, getting back to work, and Matthew, more than anyone, embodied the ideal of true New York manic pace. Still, I felt dismissed, shut out by my oldest friend, and I began to wonder why I was continuing to make an effort to communicate at all.

Eventually, toward the end of the month, the deepening chill in the air signaling a full-fledged autumn, I packed up the Charlotte mold, dismantled my computer, took the drawings off the walls, cleaned the house, and caught a ride back to the city with Tony.

I'd been talking about turning thirty all summer. Perhaps, in part, because it was never supposed to happen. And all of a sudden, there it was, my birthday, two weeks away. I spent an evening looking at myself in the mirror, at the lines around my eyes, the shape of my face and the weight of my body, thinking back on all the years, all the times, the darkness and the life. Thinking, finally, I wasn't dead after all. I realized in a breath that I looked better and felt stronger than in all of the thirty years of my past.

I planned a small dinner for close friends at a favorite restaurant on the outer edge of SoHo. Lea, sweetly, offered to take charge of the invitations and arrangements. The guest list was obvious. Until it occurred to me that, since Matthew and I were practically not speaking to each other at that point, I had to decide whether or not I wanted to invite him and his

boyfriend. At first it was shocking to me that I would even consider ex-
cluding them, but when I thought about how the summer had ended up,
and in particular how cold Matthew had been during the last month, it
made a little more sense. After thinking about it carefully for a couple of
days, I decided to invite them. I just couldn't imagine allowing a difficult
period of months to invalidate a friendship of such historic proportion. It
seemed wrong not to ask them to be part of such a milestone in my life.

Tony picked me up at my apartment in a suit and escorted me to the
restaurant where many of the people I love waited—some who knew each
other and some who were meeting for the first time. The evening was casual,
comfortable. People moved around, talked to each other warmly, and celebrated my birthday. All except for Matthew, who was coy, cynical, as if he
were there to entertain, to make a cameo appearance. He never came over
to where I was sitting to spend a few moments with me as everyone else
had done throughout the evening, but waited for me to come to him.
Though this bothered me, I wonder if I really expected much more.

October grew cooler. In the country and the city, the leaves began to
turn, to change from green to ruby to ochre and float gently from the trees
to the ground. Downtown, T-shirts and cut-offs were replaced by wool
blazers and leather jackets. Plays premiered on Broadway and off, new restaurants booked weeks in advance, people rushed from office to event, and
gallery openings spilled out onto cobblestone streets. Telephone lines
swelled with the sharp talk of business and gossip. In those weeks leading
into November, communication between Matthew and me deteriorated further until, eventually, it was reduced to a series of curt faxes greeting me
at my office in the mornings.

We both knew we had to talk. I thought it would be best if our
meeting took place in neutral territory. Matthew asked if it would be all
right to take Charles to the dog run in Washington Square Park. He said
we could sit on a bench while Charles played, which we did that damp
evening at the edge of winter. There we were, the two of us, in black jeans
and motorcycle jackets, one barely looking at the other, the breath of our
words visible in the clear, heavy, cold night. Matthew told me that he saw
the next few years of his career as vital, and that if he was going to enjoy
his life later on it all depended on him making it happen now. He said
plainly that he couldn't afford to let anything stand in his way. I listened
to this, quietly. My feet were wet and I was getting a chill, unwilling to

dress properly for the season. It occurred to me that somewhere, maybe over the course of the summer, I had lost my trust for him. He said that maybe old friendships just run their course, that friends grow apart. But a voice inside me said that wasn't exactly it. All I knew for sure was this: I was the only person left in the world who knew him and his history as a peer. What was it, I wondered then, that he felt he couldn't afford with me?

We arrived at a distanced, negotiated peace, knowing we had business together and people between us. December came around and for his thirtieth birthday he decided on a huge party at a small nightclub with a North African theme, literary in its own invented way. The room was packed when I arrived—smoke-filled and full of absolutely everyone in the downtown universe as well as several special guest stars. After the hour it took me to work my way across the room, stopping for endless chats with friends and acquaintances, I discovered that even Matthew's family was there. It was wonderful to see them again. Later, when things had mostly quieted down, I walked over to give Matthew a kiss, wish him a happy birthday, and say good-night. On my way out, Lydia, another lingering guest, stopped me. "Oh," she said with a look of surprise, "I thought we were all going to dinner." This time it took me no time. I was so quick I almost had to laugh at myself. I'm sure it was completely innocent on her part. I'm sure she just didn't realize I hadn't been invited.

christopher c. cornog

letting it in

My friend Stan just left. Nothing special happened. We ate dinner. We talked with friends around the table for a while. When the others went home, Stan stayed and helped me assemble a small oak table. It was a birthday present to myself, from some overpriced mail-order catalog. I'd been coveting it for months, and when my father sent me a check on my birthday, I couldn't resist ordering it. I could have put it together myself, but it was more fun to do it with Stan. We watched TV, then went for a walk. We ate sherbet. Nothing special happened, and yet I felt something tonight I'm not sure I've ever felt before, or at least haven't felt for a long, long time.

Stan and I have been friends for over five years. My thirty-nine years to his thirty-five make us contemporaries, although sometimes when we talk I feel the subtle impact of my minor maturity: TV shows from childhood I remember more clearly; political assassinations (and a war) I felt more personally. This has never been significant to me, and I think much of what I sense speaks more to the realization that Stan and I simply pay attention to different things in life. Probably we always have, always will.

We both live within a few miles of Concord, New Hampshire, a city that maintains many qualities of a small town. Stan is a native of the area; I am not. I moved here after finishing graduate school almost fourteen years ago. Our paths seemed to cross regularly through the years. Stan and I knew several people in common. When we officially met, I didn't need to identify myself as a gay man, nor describe the general circumstances of my life, as this information seemed to have already circulated quite sufficiently by word of mouth. He never needed to tell me he was straight, and married. Such is life in a small town.

I think Stan and I were aware of each other for quite a while before we met and said our first hello. At least *I* was aware of *him*, and I didn't like him very much. That's not exactly accurate. He was one of those men who shifts my knee-jerk hypercriticism into high gear. He looked too good, too smooth, too comfortable in his body, too confident.

On an emotional level, I related to Stan as the competition, and at least one of the things I thought we were competing for was the attention of women. Some version of this archetypal sparring match had been in place since high school for me, particularly with the prettiest and most popular girls. Back in high school, girls were always telling me how unusual I was (for a boy). I was so different from other boys. I loved feeling special. I became addicted to it. I wasn't aware at the time of how much I'd learned from my thwarted, buried desires.

I'd make the girls laugh. I'd offer them sage advice about how to handle the brutes they'd been socialized to date. That's the kind of guy I imagined Stan to have been when he was in high school—dating and screwing around with all the pretty, popular girls that I *talked* to. They came to me when guys like Stan were done with them.

I figured out much later that at least one of the reasons I formed such close friendships with girls in high school was the simple fact that pretty and popular girls usually had the best-looking boyfriends. It was really them that I wanted to be closer to. I was aware of my attractions to men back then, but I hadn't really eroticized (or labeled) these glimmerings yet. And there were no models.

I noticed Stan initially because of his looks and his attitude. Stan is nice to look at. He knows it, too. Medium height, generally fit, great curly brown hair, soft-blue eyes, and an incredible smile. And he'd flirt with anyone—even me. I could tell right away he was one of those guys who probably went several times around the block on a wink and a smile. This

is what I thought from a distance. Usually, that kind of swaggering turns
me off. All too often there's a fairly uninteresting and rather puny personality behind such body-based self-assurance. I sensed early in our friendship
that Stan was different, and I hesitated to throw him into one of my
straight-boy categories. He didn't quite fit the empty-headed picture that
I often painted of men in the world. I also thought I felt some interesting
energy between us even before we were introduced. It was more than just
significant eye-contact, the kind of silent exchange gay men are so hyper-
aware of. Maybe it was just me; it doesn't really matter anymore.

In the beginning, I thought Stan was difficult to talk with, and probably not worth the trouble. Our interactions felt like maneuvering through
a minefield; make a misstep, and *pow!* Stan would set me up for ridicule.
It usually went something like this: Stan would say something that wasn't
true (or made no sense), and then laugh when I took him seriously, or tried
to understand what he meant. It was a game I didn't particularly like, even
though I knew he meant no harm. With Stan, this was a game that existed
on his terms only. A few times I set him up for what felt like a similar
believe-this-and-you're-a-dumb-shit form of ridicule. Maybe I played too
hard, but Stan didn't seem to enjoy it as much as laughing at me.

None of this playful posturing really mattered, because Stan was
straight. If I had learned any lessons in life, one was not to get emotionally
involved with straight guys. Straight guys just couldn't handle friendship
with gay guys. Maybe, to be fair, it was the other way around. Even when
I respected the sexual boundaries (whatever they are) it seemed I always
wanted something more than straight men were willing to provide. I wanted
time, talk, and something to look forward to. Something more than evenings when the woman allowed them out. Straight men love to use their
wives and girlfriends as mothers. It's not that I'm against checking things
out with significant-others. It's the way it's communicated that bugs me:
"I'll have to ask [the woman]," so many straight men say, "or I'll get in
trouble."

Yes, there were times in my friendships with straight men when I
thought about at least one little sexual experiment, just for the hell of it.
My unspoken rule with straight men in this area was not to be the person
to initiate sexual activity. In retrospect, few friendships survived the experiment, so I learned to be extra cautious, and a bit more emotionally guarded
when I sensed sexual interest. It wasn't that I didn't encourage sexual energy

and fully participate once the dance was under way. It was just that I learned over time to expect subsequent abandonment. Postcoital flight.

So it was axiomatic that my relationships with straight men could only go so far, or so I thought. In the beginning, as far as I could tell, Stan showed little interest in me. While I enjoyed his company, I didn't go out of my way to see or talk to him. Throughout my adult life, my friendships with straight men usually developed because they pursued me. I want them to do most of the work . . . initially. Emotional investment isn't worth the energy when the eventual payoff is some form of abandonment.

I certainly bring my own fears and cautions into relationships with straight men (indeed, the whole straight world). Since junior high school I knew that I never wanted to put myself in the position of being directly rejected. I've never, ever said to a straight friend that I wanted to have sex with him, even when I thought I did. No, that initiative had to come from him.

I remember one guy—someone I'd met at the local Y several years ago. He insisted he was straight, but also insisted on a little sexual play. This guy thanked me after our (only partially satisfying, but quite lascivious) rumpus on his living room floor (he had an orgasm; I did not). "Now I know I'm not gay," he said afterward. What a piece of work he was! Six months later he married some girl he knew from college. It probably serves me right, this toying with the sexually confused. Such activity certainly keeps me from exploring my own sexual confusion. Looking back at my history with straight men, I'm amazed at how often it happened—that deliciously awkward conversation and the torrid coupling flowing out of it.

I'm also amazed at the times when I said no. Sometimes I think I got off on just knowing the desire was there, without the act which would ultimately confuse the desire, let alone ruin the friendship. It was also emotionally satisfying to challenge what I believe to be the general assumption among straight men that gay men will have sex with anyone or anything (at any time).

With Stan, I didn't sense sexual confusion as much as I sensed pure, diffuse sexual energy. Throughout our friendship, I am astounded at the quantity of our sexual talk. Often humorous, sometimes flirtatious, always a bit titillating (at least for me), we talked about sex and sexuality with each other in even our earliest conversations. In retrospect, these conversations feel just a wee bit like the exchanges I never had in my high school locker-room—as if this sexual banter with Stan gave me vicarious participation in a fraternity where I never had full membership, and reflected a time and place where I never spoke.

When I was building my house, Stan was my electrician. I talked with him during this period more than our previous haphazard contact had allowed. I guess I could say that this was when Stan and I became friends. I remember being struck by how bright and creative he seemed to be as an electrician, and how impressed the designer of the house was with his work (he called it "elegant"). Stan was always clear and direct, at least when it came to wiring a house and dealing with a neophyte home-builder. He had a good memory, and would work through the process of positioning all the wall outlets and light switches in a methodical and logical way. He'd patiently remind me about what I'd already decided when I questioned something he was doing. He was also one of the few contractors who agreed to a price up front, and never asked for more than what he had said the job would cost.

What finally made me sit up and really take notice was when a friend told me that Stan and I were going to the same therapist. I guess you could say I suddenly fell in love with the possibilities. It was amazing how powerful this little bit of information was at the time. It was the possibility of really making contact with another man—gay or straight—that fueled my new fascination. I didn't think that anything sexual would evolve. After all, Stan was married, with a child on the way, all the traditional heterosexual trappings that speak of a settled life and psyche. Our therapy connection added an entirely new dimension to our conversation. Making a commitment to long-term therapy is hard enough. Discovering another man involved in a long-term process felt very special to me. Finding another man involved with the same process felt extraordinary.

After this revelation I began to pay more attention to our conversations. I took a few more carefully calculated risks. Around this time I was asked to help form a men's discussion group at the Unitarian Universalist Church, and I immediately put Stan on my short list. My motives were not entirely honorable, in that initially I saw the men's group as a safe forum through which to get to know Stan better. Other issues, like "self-exploration" and "exploring men's issues in a group setting," were secondary. A men's discussion group was the ideal umbrella, I thought, to make contact without being engulfing, without freaking Stan out.

Initially at least, Stan was harder to freak out than I expected. We started to get together for dinner before our group meetings. Our conversations seemed to come easily, both of us talking about our jobs, our families, and life choices. Stan and I are different in many ways. We have often remarked to each other what an unlikely pair we make.

I am a writer, working in advertising and marketing. Head work. My hands are soft and groomed. Stan's hands are rough, and lined with the grit of his labor. Primarily an electrician, he also can function quite competently as a carpenter, plumber, auto mechanic. A true jack-of-all-trades. He knows how to use the tools that cut and shape material. I know how to describe the experience with words.

After several months, I realized that I'd begun to treat Stan much like my gay friends, talking to him about relationships and sex in direct and clear terms. Sometimes I would share my feelings about men, and speak of the sexual tensions I was aware of in my daily life—business associates that seemed repressed, mutual acquaintances who seemed to be struggling with their sexuality, that kind of stuff. Sometimes it was more directly flirtatious on my part, like when I'd describe someone to Stan as "almost as cute as you." Stan didn't seem to mind. He seemed to like it. He would share similar observations and information. Our quasisexual repartee evolved naturally and spontaneously.

When I changed jobs, my new office was within a short walk of the local YMCA. I started to encourage Stan to join me for aerobics, or do sets together in the weight room. He didn't respond with much enthusiasm. I was puzzled by his reluctance, but didn't push it. I had thought that the Y was another context where we could meet and spend time together. Maybe he saw the Y as his territory, and I was encroaching on it. It was these conversations about the YMCA—the twentieth-century archetype of homoeroticism—that eventually brought out Stan's discomfort with my sexuality, and blew my mind.

Some of this was certainly quickened by the way I talked about the Y. I found out later how nervous some of my comments made him. I told Stan I wanted to start wearing my contacts again, because it was frustrating not to be able to see when taking a shower. I mentioned the parallel for him as taking a shower in the women's locker room, and not being able to see. I told him that I found the steam room incredibly sensual and relaxing. I told him how exciting and bizarre I found the weight-room atmosphere of grunting and groaning (and preening and posing) men. Yes, I got a bit carried away.

After a few weeks of this, Stan initiated a conversation. Since Stan didn't often take the initiative in emotional conversation, this was significant. This is another characteristic of straight men. They will talk about inanities forever if you let them. Stan can go on and on about the technical details of daily life, but rarely about something that is emotionally challenging. When he does talk about something emotional, it is more often than not stated as a fact: "I'm depressed about [my job or my wife]." There's seldom any elaboration or exploration. Maybe all men are programmed this way. I know that Stan presented himself as a listener in his relationship with me. He loved to respond (and offer advice about) my emotional gyrations. On topics more substantive than his work schedule for the week, and what he had done that day, he usually relied on me to draw him out.

As I recall, the conversation took place before one of our group meetings. We had arrived early, and were walking around the church grounds. It was about a week before the six of us were traveling to Maine for an overnight camping trip. Stan and I were strolling through the church parking lot on our way to a path through the woods when he spoke.

He said that he was aware of pulling back from his relationship with me. I was startled by this, because I wasn't aware of any kind of withdrawal on his part. My first thought was that this was yet another time when I was too wrapped up in myself to notice that a close friend was moving away from me, but it wasn't unusual for me to be the one to call, to initiate conversation, to plan an evening together. There wasn't a sign of discomfort on his part that I could recall over the recent past. I said all this to him, but he pressed on. Stan said that ever since I'd changed jobs and joined the Y, he'd started to feel differently about me. He said he was nervous about being at the Y with me. He was nervous about the possibility of being naked with me in the locker room. He said he wanted it to be absolutely clear that there was no possibility of a sexual relationship with me. "It's not in the cards," he said matter-of-factly, as if our friendship was a poker game. Up to this point our friendship *had* been like a poker game, with all the bluffing and bravado that is part of a game of chance. Stan was calling the hand. It was time to show our cards.

I was in shock throughout this discussion. My responses felt disembodied, defensive. I did what I often do when surprised by hard information—I asked lots of questions. It's hard to separate now my feelings in the moment from the rage that consumed me later. I know I didn't want to believe Stan was saying and feeling this stuff. I also felt that Stan was accusing me of doing something, and I felt innocent. I was innocent and felt very guilty at the same time. Guilty of what? Did I love him? (Maybe I did, I wasn't sure. What did it mean if I did?) Did I ever let him inform my fantasy life? (I had, once or twice.) Did I want to believe in the possibility of a sexual relationship, even when I knew all along that one wasn't possible, or particularly desirable? (Anything is possible, isn't it?) Was something ending here?

Stan was killing an illusion, that's one thing I could palpably feel ending. This was also something I knew I could deal with, even if I didn't like it. What felt so hard at first was that this was an illusion I wasn't aware I was carrying. I could accept the finality of his no, but this was a no to a question I wasn't aware of having asked, a no to a desire I'd never fully explored myself, let alone put out clearly to him. I also knew that Stan was responding to something else, something inside him that had little to do with me. I was just a vehicle, a catalyst that brought it all tumbling out. I didn't like this part of the dynamic. I didn't like what I was hearing; I didn't like it at all.

As we talked I could feel myself struggling to understand the specifics. "What did I do?" "Why didn't you say something?" "What did you think I was going to do, jump you in the locker room?" In response, Stan said that he thought this was "his stuff," that there was nothing that I had done or said.

I was reluctant to let go of my role in all this, and no matter what Stan said I insisted on holding onto powerful feelings of rejection. There had to be a reason for what he was saying, and the reason involved me, who I was on a very basic level. "It probably would be a good idea for me to see you naked in the locker room," I said. "You're not really my type. I would get completely turned off, and that would be the end of it." My feeble attempt at a joke was a desperate effort to save face. Stan was always telling me to "lighten up." This seemed to be my cue to show him how "light" I could be.

I focused all my energy on keeping my lid on tight. (*Don't show him anything: Keep your head; Flee! Flee! Flee!*) I persisted in feeling guilty, a reaction that lasted hours after the exchange had ended. I'd had several variations of this conversation before, and for a while my entire life felt only like a long daisy-chain of unrequited involvement with straight men. I did sense that this conversation was just a gentle prelude to something else . . . like telling me to get lost for good. If Stan's words were leading up to a more permanent kind of good-bye, then I wanted to get a few licks in while I still had the chance.

My resolve to keep it light started to crack as soon as I realized how completely upended I was feeling. I was also increasingly pissed that Stan had brought this whole thing up fifteen minutes before our group meeting. We had to end it when we were just getting started. I was pissed at his cowardice. Another illusion blown. I preferred to see him as unafraid of this stuff, unafraid of me.

Later that night it hit me: I didn't know who Stan was, and this thought frightened me to the core, because right behind it was the realization that I didn't really know who I was either. I didn't really know what I wanted from Stan, and I also didn't know what to do. I hated myself more thoroughly in that moment than I had since the most painful days of my adolescence, when I was just beginning to admit to myself that I'd never get married; that I was fundamentally different from all of my friends. "What had I done?" I asked myself. I'd set myself up once again. I let myself care about someone who could only see my queer sexual energies.

Stan thought I was after his dick. The thought went round and round in my head like a mantra. Though unlike a mantra—a supposedly soothing incantation to higher awareness—this was pure self-torture. I was furious that he'd think such a thing. Except for our mutual flirtations, I thought I had been so careful. I had never, ever said anything that would lead to this impossible conclusion. Of course, with all this energetic defensive posturing with myself, I had to admit, eventually, that a part of me was after his dick. Then new questions came tumbling out: Why was this so hard to admit to myself? Why was this such a shameful realization? This was just a part of me, an idea I'd tried on. I suppose a part of me did want to touch him all over. This wasn't something I ever intended to act upon. This was a fantasy, a harmless run-of-the-mill fantasy. Stan had just told me a definitive no to something I wasn't really asking for, and he was also encroaching on my fantasy life. What was most galling of all, this was a fantasy I'd never (fully) let myself explore. I'd never really let myself have fun with it. Out of respect (and fear), I'd kept masturbation and Stan in separate categories, categories that had overlapped only a couple of times. Now the thought of a romp with Stan felt more like a nightmare than a wet dream.

I could feel myself numbing up. I didn't want to examine any of this with Stan—or with myself. Becoming numb is a coping mechanism I'd developed into an art form, an automatic response to pain. If I can make myself numb, the whole mess will slowly recede into the background. Numb is also a very effective sleeping aid, the ultimate refuge from feelings.

That night I dreamed about a house that was built very precariously on a hill overlooking a beautiful stream. I knew the house needed repairs, and even thought that I knew how to repair it, if I could only get inside and find the tools, and find the others who would help me. I was climbing an outside stairway that was also very rickety, and I fell several times during my assent. I knew that inside the house were some very nice gay people. I wasn't sure that I knew them, but I knew—in that wonderful dream way —that they were friendly and would take care of me, help me, if I could only find my way in.

I could see them inside, having fun (without me). They didn't seem to see me or hear me. I didn't call out or knock on the window. It didn't even occur to me to draw any attention to myself. I didn't want to let them know that I was outside, trying to get in. I wanted them to see me. I wanted them to see me first. When I got to the top of the stairs there was a landing with empty boxes on it, as if the people inside had just moved in. There was a door, but no bell. There was no bell to ring. I'd come to the back door (I'd made a mistake!). I looked down the long flight of unstable stairs I'd just climbed, not wanting to go back down and look for the front door, where there might be a bell to ring. I looked again at the door in front of me. The knob was brass, almost black from disuse. I thought that it would look spectacular if I polished it. I knew that to get inside I needed to walk in unannounced, without warning. I would be barging into something already underway. I was late. What if they didn't like that? What if they didn't like me?

We finally talked, Stan and me. Our weekly routines together were difficult to alter, and I wasn't prepared to cut off contact completely. I briefly entertained the notion of dumping him—walking away. I could "pretend" I was fine, when I was absolutely devastated inside. I'd practiced that scenario since elementary school. We had dinner the following week, as usual, before our men's group meeting. I admitted that I had been behaving badly. I apologized for being a jerk. I shared some of my slowly dawning awareness about where my behavior was rooted—in previous rejections, my sense that his words created an insurmountable barrier between us.

Stan and I recovered from this episode slowly, and if resolution means that the issue of our sexuality has gone away, then we're far from resolution. Between gay men and straight men—perhaps for all men looking for intimacy—sexuality is one of those things that needs to be revisited repeatedly. At least that's how it seems with Stan and me. The challenge is getting past the gonads. I told Stan recently that I just want to talk about who we are, about what our lives *feel* like. That's where the distinctions (and connections) feel truly rich to me. Gonads are fun, but they aren't where the real mystery is.

I felt something new in my life tonight, and in my relationship with Stan. It seems like such a simple feeling, but it is remarkable. My feeling is new and crisp and all mine. Tonight, when Stan and I were eating dinner and talking with the others gathered round the table, I caught Stan looking at me. There was nothing remarkable about his look. His eyes just met mine, and held for a moment. I felt a flood of emotional warmth wash through, and thought *this person cares for me.* I could feel my eyes fill with tears . . . not because I felt sad, or glad, or anything other than that I knew I was feeling something. It felt new, and accurate. It didn't feel like I was making it up. It didn't feel like I was using it as a platform to launch myself into a fantasy. This feeling had nothing to do with sex or sexuality, but had a simple purity to it that didn't immediately veer off to my crotch. "Caring." What's the big deal? I just felt it. My friend cared about me. I cared about him. I just let it in.

paul bonin-rodriguez

a cloak and dildo story

My friend Mack has a stock of dildoes in his closet. A lifetime supply in a rainbow of colors, a myriad of sizes and shapes. Enough to divert an army, should the army need diversion and not be able to supply its own.

D rations. That's what they could be called. Coming on the end of C rations, which are food. Food, then sex. Who then would say it's not a logic-derived organization?

Yet Mack is straight, or so I've been led to believe in our four-plus years as friends, and the dildoes have never been an issue before, because until now I never knew about them firsthand. Now that I do, all has changed: I wonder why he's depending on D rations and dating women when the real thing is only a stroke, a kiss, a condom away. Even more so, I wonder if I want Mack now because I had the chance to get to know him as just-a-friend long before his 8- and 9-inch distractions ever put him in the realm of sexual possibility. Or do I want him because there's no glory greater than the conquering of a straight man?

It's not that I'm proud of how I found out or that I think that closeted dildoes alone are enough to indict him for closeted queerhood. There's more to it, and that can only be revealed in the telling of the whole story.

We met in ballet class. I was his teacher. He came with his then girlfriend. He was fleshier then, not fat but not toned. He was thirty-eight, slim, brown-eyed, black hair graying at the temples. I thought him attractive. There were only four students, none of them very good. Mack was the worst of the bunch: arms and legs shot mutinously from the center of his body, not yet contained by centrifugal force. He stayed after class and asked, shuffling his feet as he did, would I teach him privately?

I did it because he offered $25 an hour, more than I made from the entire class, more than my dancer's salary. Actually, I dropped the class and kept him. Was it sexual instinct or just a business decision? The first time we worked together, I had an erection beneath my baggy sweats. Maybe it was the tension of the situation, the aloneness, my hands on his body, freely adjusting, the absence of his girlfriend, Tracy, who seemed suspicious of me from the beginning. Maybe it was the fact that he had a girlfriend, and yet he wanted to submit to me.

For the next couple of years, we met two to three times a week in different studios. I got to know his body well. And to a certain extent, at least from the waist down and especially from behind, I helped form it. He was grateful for all I had taught him about his body. I had changed his posture, he said. I had built his abdominals and made him more erect. I had made him feel more attractive.

In our second year together, he gave me a datebook for Christmas. He said it would help me keep appointments (a funny comment, since I had yet to miss one with him). A nice enough one, I thought, black calf leather. Until Alice, another dancer who worked part-time in the shop where he bought it, confided, "He spent over two hundred dollars on it."

Then he bought me some time with his massage therapist, an old lover of his, I later learned.

"He speaks so highly of you," she said the first time I met her. After I had seen her several times, that "he speaks so highly" became, "Mack says he could fall in love with you if he were actually going to fall for a man—it's because he thinks so highly of you."

And still I didn't see it happening—perhaps because no gay friend had put it into a comprehensible construct like, "He's doing this because he wants to do you." But I was beginning to be curious about his interest in me. For his own part, Mack talked only about women in my presence. He seemed to favor those who were almost twenty years younger than him, girls closer in age to his own daughter and son. These ingenues he replaced regularly, never going out with one for more than a week.

Once or twice he mentioned giving me tickets to a dance performance because his girlfriend for the week had canceled out. He wouldn't come with me though, he was just passing the tickets on.

"I won't use them otherwise," he would say.

Then I became friends with George. George owns a restaurant. For two years he employed Mack's ex-girlfriend, Tracy, whom I had not seen since that first day in ballet class and who had not been his girlfriend much longer after that. George blurted it out for her, plain and simple. "Tracy says you're fucking Mack," he said.

"I'm not," I said. "I've never even thought of it."

I meant, of course, that I had never thought it possible. Though in some late-night situations, I had thought of nice variations to his grande pliés or stretches on the barre.

"Why would she say a thing like that?" I asked.

"I shouldn't say anything," he said, which meant he would.

"You must promise never to tell," he added, which meant I wouldn't—promise.

"When she was dating him," he went on, "she looked in his closet one day and found a box stuffed with dildoes—"

"That's nothing," I interrupted, trying to sound very knowing, "there are straight men who like stimulating the prostate."

"—and male porn mags and Jeff Stryker's *Power Tool*!"

"So maybe the women like the porn," I said definitively, but already I was thinking about the fact that *I* don't even own a Jeff Stryker video.

The information was then filed away in my bank of denial for months and months. Mack took up weight lifting to work his upper half. His trainer's name was Steve. Whenever I saw him he would tell me how Steve was exhausting him with multiple straight sets. "Steve really knows about bodies," he'd say, or "Steve's really working me hard."

I began to wonder if Steve now sported a wallet or had visited the massage therapist. What messages had she passed to him? Mack started going to other ballet classes, too—he was good enough for that by then—but all of those teachers were women, over thirty and married. I wasn't worried.

Then he bought an exercise machine, one strictly for abdominals, and he asked me to help him learn it. "Steve doesn't do anything with my abdominals," he said. A friend thing, I thought, something I didn't have time for, but it would be nice to see him again on a regular basis. And he was looking good.

Learning it required going to his house, sitting on his bed and watching a video. The first time went off without a hitch. He reclined against the pillows of his king-size bed. I sat on the front end. He actually fell asleep, but I woke him to do the workout. He apologized and explained Steve had really worked him hard early that morning.

The second time I came over, he said he had to leave because he had forgotten an appointment. "Go ahead and watch the video, do the workout," he said.

I was in his room again, alone this time. There were books all around. All of them, in some way, had to do with pleasuring a woman, *The Joy of Sex, The Joy of Sex Revisited, Beyond the Joy of Sex, Getting Past the Joy of Sex, Returning to the Joy of Sex*. I mused that his need to research indicated a need for inspiration and instruction.

The closet was to my left. A few paces away. I had only to open the door and look inside. The answers were waiting for me there: Jeff, my subliminal substitute, might be there. And if he was, Mack was undoubtedly in there too, a sentinel perched over his box of secrets, perhaps looking for Steve after having grown tired of me. Four years could be easily explained. It would be as easy as opening the door and peering in.

When I was in junior high we watched a film version of Frank Richard Stockton's short story, "The Lady or the Tiger." It goes like this. Some guy gets wrongly accused of something, and during the trial, he is afforded the possibility of a second chance. Placed into a coliseum, where everyone can watch, he must open one of two doors. Behind one, a ravenous tiger; behind the other, a compliant lady. The story ends as he's about to open the door.

Sex or death. The perfect tease. An unarticulated ending for a group for which sex remained largely unarticulated, anticipated, and mysterious. How ironic that it should be shown to junior high–level boys, as our hormones were raging out of control. Erections came as sudden and inexplicable phenomena, obvious to anyone looking down. Formica could be titillating then. Some of us died of embarrassment every time it happened; others proudly displayed their wares. Imagine what havoc Jeff Stryker could have caused.

That was the first time our sexuality became an extremely important part of our external identity. Some felt a need to strut some sort of sexual promise against threats of "faggot." Some of us hid unnoticed. Mack told me that when he was young he was skinny, gawky, unattractive, and he had a hard time convincing girls to go with him. I was fat, androgynous, unattractive, and didn't feel a need to convince girls of anything. We'd both redefined ourselves physically since then. I did it earlier. He was just coming around, but was he coming out too?

Now I do not think that being gay is the result of not having been a macho dude in junior high. My questions were based on Mack's own enthusiasms for me, then his trainer, on George's story, the massage therapist's words, and especially those tickets that were passed off to me when Mack's acceptable dates had backed out. He was trying too hard to be the antithetical queer, and in doing so, he gave it far too much reverence. Guilt by extreme and self-conscious disassociation. In making such an effort to block his closet doorway, Mack was illuminated by its light—backlit, sinister, seductive. Steve and I were both courted by a phantom. I didn't know what Steve felt, but I found it stimulating.

What I do claim about sexual identity is that, in its initial stages of definition, it is an outward reflection of an assumed stereotype—one is either a lady or a tiger. Only later, with the persistence of real sexual feelings, does that identity take on variations—so that the lady ends up with a tiger's head, the tiger a woman's breasts. Some never stop acting the strict part of lady or tiger, despite what urges toward variation they feel. And it is those acted veneers that can undermine friendships much more than fully dealt-with feelings.

As friends, Mack and I guarded our doors from each other. He did it because that was part of his identity. I did it because Mack hadn't budged an inch, and I wasn't going to be the first to jump, or so I thought.

Two days later, I asked the massage therapist, "Is Mack gay or what?"

She told me that when Mack was divorcing his wife of twenty years AIDS was just becoming an issue, and it scared him from pursuing his interests in men. She believed the feelings were there, but she didn't think he would explore them.

If that was the case, then Mack was equating sex with death, thinking that in choosing one door he would automatically spring open the other.

Another day came. He asked me over to exercise, but when I arrived, he told me he'd forgotten he had another appointment. He would have to shower and leave. Familiar enough with the exercises, I skipped the video and went to the room where the exercise machine was placed, leaving Mack to undress in his room down the hall. There was some tension, yes, but his shower was far enough away. We were two continents, and even speculation of what could happen if the two collided seemed a waste of effort.

Until he came to the room where I was working. Wearing only a towel, he walked into its adjacent bathroom, leaving the bathroom door open, and turned on the shower.

Now I am learned enough to know that this was a classic porn scenario. Jeff's played it out, I'm sure. If he hasn't, Matt has, Ryan has, Dallas has. The real question was, Would I? Should I? Could I join the legions of porn starlets in a moment of hasty talk and even quicker action?

Would I have the gumption to strip, stroke, prepare, then pull the shower curtain aside and say in my most stilted porn prose, "Hey, dude, you look like you could use a little help in there"? Then step in and go down on his tumescent dick?

Art must imitate life, and vice versa, right?

My heart was pounding fast. I hadn't had this feeling since way back, maybe college, when on the eve of my first experience with sex, I questioned the plausibility, much less the possibility, of it happening to me.

I had gotten hard lying against the Naugahyde surface of the exercise machine. Act or talk. It had been so long since sex was unpredictable. And this line, between friend and lover, or even just fuck buddy, felt such a thick one to cross. What would be behind that curtain, the lady or the tiger? Did I want compliance, the possibility of matrimony, or perhaps just a good tumble with a meat-eater?

Rolling off the machine, I walked to the bathroom door and spoke.

"Mack, is this some sort of trial? I mean, you in here, this door, me. Am I supposed to seduce you or something?"

His head popped out from the curtain. He had it gathered and draped around his shoulders. I imagined his half-erect dick behind it.

"Excuse me?"

Water dripped from his chin and saturated a mauve towel mat on the floor.

"You, me, here," I said, "Am I supposed to climb in with you?"

"I never considered that . . . you've shocked me. You know all the women I date think you're gorgeous."

Slam.

"That's fine," I said, "but what do you think?"

"Honestly," he said, "I've never thought of it happening."

Slam.

"I'm going to go, then," I said. "This is too much; my heart is pounding very fast."

"I'm very flattered," he said.

Time to think. I had been victim to the awkward prose without the porn payoff. I felt a need to run, to swim, to do something so that my body would catch up with my galloping heart. The tension of near sex, when it happens over a longtime attraction, easily defies the cynicism of past experience. More often than not, that cynicism alone usually provides a formidable, if not impenetrable, obstacle that prevents the near sex from being considered—the obstacles built from years of experience in moments of feeling a fool.

Which I felt again.

But what I was racing toward was an understanding of how Mack could get so close to me that consummation had become important. And it occurred to me that, because he was supposed to be just a friend, I had let him sneak into my life unobserved, without a lot of the cumbersome negotiating that I would impose on a lover. So when I turned to face him, he was closer than others could have gotten.

Usually, it went the other way around: I met someone, had sex, then decided it was far too uncomfortable to date. Luckily, they were often preparing to move out of town.

Walking home from a rehearsal later that same day, I stopped to see an ex-lover who's a communications consultant. He said that I overlooked the obvious. Mack, he said, had to have thought of it. We all just do. The shower, the open bathroom door, all of that was deliberate. And all of it, he stated, had demanded action, which I had failed to take.

Slam. Slam.

I gave it time so I could sulk.

Mack called two days later. I was at home, though only for a few moments before leaving for an out-of-town performance.

"I wanted to call you," he began, "to make sure everything's okay."

"It's fine," I said. "I just wanted to be honest about the situation, deal with it immediately. What I said I felt at the moment."

"You know I care about you," he hesitated. "I mean, I love you, man."

"Hey, no skin off my back," I said. "Gotta go, Mack. I'll talk to you when I get back."

"We can have a class then."

"Sure, no problem."

In Mack's closet, I found a bucket of cleansers—scouring powders, disinfectants, sponges, and rubber gloves. Underneath it, a lidded box filled with dildoes and male porn mags and a video or two. I found it all when I went in there searching for some betrayal of the truth. In doing so, I betrayed his trust, because it's really not my business that he presented a scoured, straight version of himself to the public and kept something altogether different underneath. And certainly the more dynamic lie came from me, the one who purported "to deal with it honestly," but who had the glimpse of Mack's closet backing him up. In forestalling the sex and speaking instead, I had kept my closet door fairly bolted.

I have a friend who says that the difference between lovers and friends is that one draws the line at sex with friends. I found myself wishing that Mack and I had sex and then dug our way out to friendship again.

Two days later we went out. He told me stories of his youth, about his father who was a womanizer, about his mother who made him her ally against his father. He was painting a picture of someone who was devoted to correcting his father's past, when in truth, he was only repeating it.

Then he added, almost as a non sequitur, "You caught me by surprise, I don't know what I would have done if you had acted. I don't think I would have resisted."

I sat silently, not sure where to pick up, not willing to make myself a fool another time. His door had opened just enough to let a little light in.

r a n d y   b o y d

a whole new world

They don't have a name for this one.

We're not father/son. Oh, I offer the kind of advice a dad might, but I would've had to have been one horny and physically mature animal at the age of twelve to have sired him. We're not big brother/little brother either. True, when I spot him a couple of bucks for a haircut or wrestle around with him on the floor of my apartment, I have flashes of a healthy sibling relationship; but it would take a miracle worthy of Oprah or Phil to make us related by blood: an Indiana-born black man with two black parents and a young Latino from El Salvador conceived by two Salvadorans. Yet, the term "best friends" somehow seems lacking, especially considering how we do things like dedicate love songs to one another to express how we feel about each other. And we're definitely not lovers. I'm gay. He's straight.

No, the world has yet to come up with a name for a relationship between a thirty-one-year-old black gay man with HIV and a nineteen-year-old straight Latino boy who spent a good part of his teenage years in the mean streets of Los Angeles. Nor has the world invented specific roles we're supposed to play with each other. That's something we've had to do since the day we met.

Our friendship began at the place where many of my post-college friendships have blossomed, the gym, and for the first time in my life, the old cliché about finding something when you least expect it came true for me. I was coming out of the gym's showers after a morning swim, stark naked and minding my own business since I was in the midst of a year-long depression and wanted no particular involvement with anyone, romantic or otherwise. But the instant I landed in the drying-off area, this dripping wet, chiseled torso (accompanied by equally wet dark gray shorts) and two of the brightest, most intrigue-filled eyes smiling right at me shook me out of my world, and like the chosen in *Close Encounters*, I followed the light in my unabashed nakedness.

Before I even reached him he said hello, his voice ripe with a combination of confidence and nervousness. We exchanged the standard "how was your workout" lines, then he promptly shifted to a more personal gear. "I play football for my high school," he boasted, giving his motivation for working out, and as he filled me in on his upcoming senior season and two-a-day practices in the sweltering August heat, I stood there, half listening to his vague, L.A.-Latino accent, half trying to recover from the shock of being caught up in conversation with this handsome young man who was a good deal shorter than my six-foot-four-inch frame with smooth boyish skin and jet-black hair and big brown eyes.

But his most prominent feature was not of the flesh. It was his lone earring. In his right ear. Now, any straight guy will tell you, *right* is wrong, as a girl who assumed I was straight once put it at the start of the hetero earring craze; and in all my years, I have yet to see a straight man wearing jewelry in the right ear unless it was accompanied by a qualifier in the left. But was this young man gay? And so open about it while on the high school football team? The earring intrigued me as much as his genuine persona. I wanted to ask him about the shiny loop right then and there, ask if he was over eighteen and willing to get to know a thirty-year-old man; but those questions never filtered into the conversation, which went from the locker room to the parking lot where he nervously said good-bye (nervously, he later told me, because he'd already realized I was gay by the wide-eyed way I looked at him).

Emerson, he said was his name, a bold, curious name that only added to the mystery. Over the next few weeks I began to look for Emerson at the gym, believing the earring symbolized one of two things: He was gay and might be interested in dating, or he wasn't gay, but the fact he wore an earring in his right ear meant he was one helluva person whose story I wanted to know. Because of my tenacity, we began running into each other and doing a few sets together, our rapport always congenial and relaxed. After finding out he was indeed eighteen, I decided to broach the subject of sexuality. I told him I was a writer and subsequently made it known I wrote about gay subject matter. "You see, I'm gay," I explained. As if I told him I preferred hamburgers to pizza, he took it in stride (later he would tell me it was my honesty that made him feel comfortable about what he had already figured out on his own). In that same conversation he also came out as a straight person (I asked) and later, in the parking lot, I inquired about the earring. "I'm doing it as a protest," he said, "to say to people it shouldn't matter if I'm straight or gay. I'm still me." An eighteen-year-old young man, senior in high school, straight-identified, on the high school football team, in urban Los Angeles. Right then and there I knew I was dealing with someone very special. I confessed my attraction to him, stressing the fact that I would also respect his preferences. "That makes me feel pretty good," he said.

Our friendship began a steady climb upward after that night. Because he couldn't afford them, I bought him a new pair of workout gloves to show my appreciation for who he was. For that I got a spontaneous hug in the moonlit parking lot of the gym. It may as well have been Christmas morning.

Shortly thereafter, our friendship catapulted to an even higher plateau, once again while in the parking lot after a workout. I was down after hearing of another writer's death by AIDS. "Tell me everything you're feeling about it," Emerson offered. And so I told him that I'm a fellow soldier in the war and any death by AIDS, especially someone I know, is like a loud reminder that even though I'm relatively healthy, I could be next. Emerson reacted like a veteran caregiver. He listened and sympathized. He wasn't scared, wasn't shocked, didn't run away or give the slightest hint of judgment. He was more knowledgeable about the virus than some gay men I know, an education he'd received voluntarily through programs at school. "Why didn't you tell me sooner?" he asked, an odd question considering our friendship was still in its infancy. But that's Emerson, void of pretenses many people take for granted, still full of innocence despite a rough background I was as yet unaware of.

That night, as if a new purpose had entered his life, he promised to stick with me through anything I had to go through, that he would make me laugh, that he would be a good friend. He told me I had already been a good friend to him, that I was a good role model, that he saw my strength and I was good to have in his life.

The moment served as a watershed for each of us letting the other into his life. Our workouts together became standard, as did phone calls where we talked for hours like teenagers do. On weekends he'd come over and we'd watch movies late into the night, and it became routine for him to rummage through my closets, staking claim to my old clothes as if it were his birthright.

Emerson also began to open up to me about his own life. A bit of a loner like me, he was still deeply wounded from the recent breakup with his girlfriend of three years, the love of his still young life. We spent many a late night talking about his newfound loneliness, the guilt he felt for the mistakes he'd made in the relationship, and the relentless pain of seeing her in the hallways at school with her new boyfriend. He also talked of his family. He hadn't seen his biological father since he was old enough to remember and had only recently reestablished contact with him by phone from Florida. He also told me of the stormy relationship with his mother who more than once threatened to kick him out and didn't seem to understand that, as Emerson put it, "it's hard being a teenager in today's world."

During one of our marathon phone chats, he also informed me that in his middle teens he was no stranger to gangs and painted for me a picture of his wonder years that was straight out of the "Eleven O'Clock News" on any given night in Los Angeles. It was enough to make a college-educated, suburban-grown gay man think of running away; but the anger-filled life he described was incongruent with the intelligent, tolerant, maturing young man I was getting to know, and this college-educated, suburban-grown gay man wasn't about to go into hiding.

Besides, the more he talked about it, the more I understood his involvement in gangs. From the age of twelve, he was basically left to sort out the world for himself: no father, a mother who when she wasn't busy working seven days a week as a housekeeper only knew how to dole out negative attention, and an invisible stepfather who never cared enough to step into the role of Dad. No one paid attention to this growing boy. No one answered all the questions he had about life and the world. No one gave him a hobby, an interest, anything to live for. So he turned to another readily available family that taught him how to survive the harsh environment in which he lived.

And still Emerson is one of the fortunate ones. He realized he didn't want to live a life of violence forever and possessed enough inner strength to do something about it. When his family moved from L.A. proper to a less-dangerous barrio in the quasi-burbs of the city, Emerson, on his own, seized the chance to clean up his act and severed his ties to gang life (a bold and dangerous move in and of itself because leaving a gang can lead to death if the wrong people ever see you again).

When we met he was at the tail end of his transformation, still looking for purpose and guidance. I like to think I helped him in his search and on many occasions he has credited me with just that. When he'd tell me about the pain of his past, I'd offer a supportive, nonjudgmental ear. When he'd ruminate about his dreams for the future, I'd become his biggest cheerleader. "Now I want to go to college," he'd say to me as a demonstration of his changing values. "I want to own my own business. I want to study medicine, law, psychology, everything. I want to be important." Spoken like a boy who just discovered he too could play on the best playgrounds of life. "You can do it," I'd tell him, then offer my father's most important words to me. "You can do anything you set your mind to." To which Emerson would say: "I believe you."

It was this belief—in me and my words—that instantly became one of his greatest gifts to me. He saw the good in me just when I wasn't sure I saw it in myself anymore. My life was in a tailspin when I met Emerson. The optimism of surviving HIV had eroded along with my T-cell count, which was still livable but nowhere near invincible. Also fading was my stock in the network of friends I had tried to create for myself in the gay community. I'd done support groups, service organizations, bars, sports teams, picking up people/friends on the street. But years of effort hadn't come close to yielding a true "be-there" friend or a lover and, in short, I was bitter. I thought the only thing left in my life was getting ready to die. Until I met this youth, so innocent and in need of guidance, believing in my words, coming to me for advice, wanting to spend hours at a time with me, needing me. In my "old age" youth has always owned a special place in my heart. Some of it could be labeled aesthetic, but much of it also has to do with bittersweet feelings for my own lost youth, plus a longing for the adventure called parenthood (after all, were it not for the virus, I would be actively considering the idea of adoption).

Clearly, Emerson and I needed each other and what started out as a gym friendship quickly became so much more. I began picking him up from school and we did his homework together. I became the first person ever to ask to see his report card. I talked with his college advisor so we could get straight exactly what he needed to graduate. He became more and more involved in school, each day enthusiastically telling me about an essay he wrote, a field trip to a local college, a girl who was "fine."

In these instances I felt like a father figure and at first we both relished the idea. The early highlight of this came when together we bought him an organizer to help him organize his changing life. With my help, he picked it out with the kind of caution one might take buying a first car. Then, with me by his side, he filled in the dates and details with the enthusiasm of someone finally putting down roots in the world. A truer father/son moment was never had, prompting the first verbal acknowledgment of this aspect of our friendship, followed by an unspoken attempt on both our parts to play the traditional roles to the hilt: authoritative parent and obedient child. This lasted about forty-eight hours. After two days of strain and tension, we both realized I couldn't have authority over him. He wasn't used to it; he'd lived for eighteen years without someone always telling him what to do. We settled for being friends.

I still feel like the mentor/father figure on many occasions, like when I took him to open his first bank account or when I'm driving him around while he's looking for a job; but there are plenty of times where we're like two brothers playfully poking each other in the gut, or two horny pals, driving down the street, lusting after men for me and women for him. Then there are times, like when we call each other practically every evening to say good-night, that we feel so close and passionate about the friendship it seems as though we're having a romantic relationship without the sex.

The many roles we step into are both a source of fulfillment and challenge. Early on we realized we had to define our own relationship. We had no role models or modern-day mythology for a friendship like ours. But that hasn't stopped us from living life, from doing things like going ice skating (both of us for the first time), or me taking him to his first college football game, or us renting a Cadillac with me as the chauffeur for him and his date on prom night. We create our own brand of fun, like driving around late at night, either down the crowded neon-lighted streets of Hollywood and West Hollywood or the quiet, mostly deserted streets of our own neighborhoods, talking about life as we know it. It was here, on one of our late-night drives, where he initiated something that's become commonplace in our friendship: dedicating love songs to one another to express our appreciation for the friendship.

It was only natural that the more I ventured into Emerson's life, the more I became involved with his entire family. Hilda, his mother, and Henry, his stepfather, don't speak much English (I don't speak Spanish) and at first were very guarded around the older black man seen giving their son rides and doing homework with him in their apartment. To my surprise, Emerson told the stepdad I was gay weeks into our friendship, partly to gauge his stepdad's reaction, partly because Emerson is just that open and honest about things. "They're okay with me as long as they don't try anything," the stepdad said.

Emerson's mom, the true head of the house, is another story. We're unsure as to the extent of her knowledge, if any, of my sexual orientation, but from day one I've had an uphill climb with Hilda. At first she'd hang up on me on the phone and talk about me in Spanish in front of my face, forcing Emerson to defend his friendship with me. Then, one day, Hilda's truck broke down and I gave her a ride to work. Just the two of us. Between the awkward moments of silence we talked in broken English and I told her I was college educated (i.e., not a street thug trying to corrupt her son) and tried to get her to see that said son was changing for the better. In addition, I helped Emerson get her truck repaired that day and we both picked her up from work. Hilda and I have gotten along ever since. If tension does come about, it's the kind any two family members might have, with both of us as insiders.

From day one I have been accepted by the kids in Emerson's family. Brother Ricky, five years younger than Emerson, looks up to me the way a young boy into sports might look up to a tall, black athlete. He also envies my friendship with his older brother. He wants to tag along wherever we go, is elated when he can and dejected when he can't. A slow bloomer in the adolescent game, we're waiting till he blooms a little more to tell him I'm gay, although we're confident it won't be a problem. Sister Marlyn, two years younger than Emerson, has blossomed enough to know. I told her while giving her a ride to her boyfriend's house. A prankster who's always fearful of becoming the victim of a prank herself, it took her a few hours to actually believe I was gay. When she realized it was no joke, shock took over; but despite her ignorance about gays, she quickly learned not to judge or treat me any differently.

I've also become quite friendly with two cousins, Jonathan and Eric, who are five and seven years old and spend much of their time at Emerson's family's home. In their eyes, I've become part of the family landscape. I teach them French, they translate the adults' Spanish for me; we sing songs from Disney movies, they rattle my nerves as only kids can do. After watching a news story about gays in the military, Emerson told them what a gay person is, but we have yet to tell them I am a living, breathing example. No need to right now.

I've become so familiar with Emerson's family I merely walk into their apartment without knocking and it's not entirely uncommon for me to be there without him. With my own clan two thousand miles away in the Midwest, they fulfill some of my need for family. With my camera I videotape the kids, knowing the value of capturing their tender years. I give rides to school. I go to family parties where even though I'm the only non-Latino in sight, I'm always welcomed. I become involved in family conflicts, sometimes solicited, sometimes not.

Perhaps the apex of my involvement with Emerson's family came when for two scorching weeks, *we all* went to their homeland of El Salvador, which was only a year or so removed from the civil war that ruptured the country. Why did I go? It was a family outing, naturally.

Home in El Salvador was Agua Caliente, a very, *very* rural town that seemed to be merely one never-ending dirt road. Power came in the form of generators; running water was nonexistent. The family house was an adobe-style cluster of rooms that let in an army of tropical monsters parading as bugs. Seeing as though he left Central America when he was a small child and my most exotic trip was to Paris, this was both Emerson's and my first real foray into third-world living. A day into the trip we weren't sure we would survive the elements. A week into the trip, however, we were pouring buckets of water over our heads for showers and using the bathroom down by the river as if it were old hat.

We also made lasting connections with the people of Agua Caliente. For Emerson, it was a spiritual return to the land of his birth. Seemingly the whole town remembered him and told him stories of his childhood. For me, I was very much a stranger in a strange land. Not one person spoke English and I got the feeling many of them had never seen a black person. Still, I encountered nothing but friendliness and warm smiles. And Emerson, Ricky, Marlyn, Jonathan, and Eric all did a lot of translating.

The children of El Salvador were storybook memorable. Some sort of natural order dictated that most of the town's kids gather at Emerson's family's home early in the afternoon after school and loiter there until late in the evening. Emerson and I turned this idle time into a virtual summer camp with him and me as camp counselors. We played musical chairs and hot potato and organized races. Somehow I got to telling them stories in English, stories they didn't understand but loved anyway because I peppered them with exaggerated sound effects which they had to repeat. I also sang songs to them and before long I couldn't take a step in Agua Caliente without a child pleading to me: "Randy, *historia* [story]." or "Randy, *Que cantes* [sing]."

Because of the legacy of political violence, which never touched us but nonetheless shadowed the trip, my being gay was never brought up. But it didn't seem to matter. In fact, most of the time, unlike back in the States, my sexual orientation was relegated to the back of my mind. I was just me, no labels. There were tears all around when we left Agua Caliente. Someday Emerson and I plan to go back.

The trip to El Salvador only solidified my presence in his family's life and their presence in mine. Now, like true families, we can't seem to escape being involved in each other's lives. Emerson is the oldest child and true crisis-solver in the family, but if he's unavailable, Marlyn and Ricky sometimes turn to me or both of us at the same time. And Emerson and I continue to find adventure. Shortly after he took me to his world of El Salvador, I took him to the gay pride festival in Los Angeles where we had a ball, and his sentiments afterward fell along the lines of: "I forgot I was straight. I was just me, no labels."

Without a doubt we've had our share of quality moments, like his high school graduation where I felt like the proud father videotaping every moment of my son's big day, even when it bothered him to the point of distraction; but we've also had our share of conflict. With all our differences—age, race, background, sexuality—battles are inevitable and can usually be traced to one of those differences, with age being the number-one culprit. He's more flexible; I'm set in my ways. His life is constantly changing; my life is ready for the comfortable groove of my thirties. When he makes decisions about things young people have to make decisions about—college, drinking, dating, jobs—I try to give him just the right mix of the benefit of my experience and the freedom to choose his own course and make his own mistakes, but, of course, I don't always conjure up the perfect mix and like a true teenager, he'll let me know about it.

But most amazing perhaps is how we resolve disagreements. After the initial blow-up, we refrain from attacking one another, try our best to express our feelings in a calm, frank manner, then understand that our conflicts come from our differences which come from being two different people with different needs and different ways of operating. With that in mind, we try to come to a common ground by forgiving and understanding the other person, then being more considerate of that person's needs. Like any relationship, our fights can be filled with intense, passionate anger, but it's clear to us the only way a friendship like ours can survive is through communication and work. And it works. I'm not sure we've ever had an argument that didn't end in a hug or an "I love you" over the phone.

That's why we keep growing and going, and with Emerson's ever-evolving life, new territory meets us head-on seemingly every week. Now we're about to face the adventure of college and his increasing independence from me as a natural result of his growing up. Also, he's ready to love romantically again, and, for the first time, one of us is actively searching for lasting intimacy outside our friendship. Just like everything else, we deal with this honestly: I admit I'm scared of losing all or part of him; he admits he's scared of losing all or part of me; we both agree to try our best to work it all out.

From the very beginning I've made a valiant effort to realize that I cannot completely base my life around a growing young man who's busy trying to find his own niche in the world, and this knowledge can be a source of pain when I envision the emptiness of having even one less ounce of him in my life. But accompanying the pain is the stone-cold fact that if I want this boy to be his own person and grow up as healthy as possible in mind and spirit, I have to give him as much freedom as my imperfect, needy soul can give him. That's a hard pill to swallow sometimes, especially knowing how wonderful a life we could make for ourselves were we to dedicate eternity to each other. But I do want him to be his own person and grow up with a healthy mind and spirit; more than anything I wish for *us*, and that's the weapon I use against my own fears of abandonment —that and the idea that just maybe I can fulfill the needs of mine that he can't/won't meet by putting myself back out there in the world and becoming involved again, as terrifying as the prospect is.

And his independence doesn't have to mean our relationship will become ancient history. A boy always needs his father figure. Brothers still need brothers. Friendship survives with common bonds. We dream of the day when we both have spouses and I'm a grandfather-figure to his children. We talk of living in adjacent houses and being one big happy family. One way or another, we plan to find a way to stay in each other's lives.

Fate willing.

AIDS is as much an underlying theme of our friendship as Emerson's growing up. The virus is always with us, when I get too tired at the gym, when we envision the glorious day he graduates college years from now, when I come to him crying and panicked at a sudden bruise that we hope is just a bruise. Any conversation about health or the future is tinted with the prospect of a full-scale war between the virus and my body; but just the mere mention of our friendship ending this way can render both of us teary-eyed in a millisecond so we try to stay away from speculation and instead concentrate on what we do know: I'm here and I'm not guaranteed to die of AIDS. If the war does escalate, however, there's no doubt in my mind he'll be there for me as promised, between doing homework or raising babies or whatever he's doing at that time. He'll be there.

But that day may never happen. Instead we plan to keep building on this whole new world we've created. And one day I want to look back and tease him about how much of a teenager he once was, how he used to change his mind from minute to minute, how he used to drop everything just for the briefest sighting of the female anatomy, how he was so strong-minded that sometimes, it felt as though if I said the sky was blue, he would say it wasn't just to contradict me.

In the meantime, though, we'll continue to enjoy and be challenged by a friendship neither one of us would have thought possible the day before we met. And we'll continue to define it for ourselves and those around us. We almost always avoid referring to the labels society might hang on us. Father/son, big brother/little brother, best friend—they all come up short in describing what Emerson and I are. And so we fall back on a word we made up, a word that evolved when he was bringing to an end one of our nightly good-night phone calls. Half his brain wanted to call me buddy, the other half brother. And out of his mouth came "bruddy." Since then we've been bruddies. We don't say it too often because it sounds rather corny. But until the world comes up with a better name, it'll have to do.

adam levine

roots

It's late on a clear blue summer afternoon, and I pause in my weeding, look around the garden at some of the flowers I've worked so hard to grow—a sedum named Vera Jameson and a phlox called Franz Schubert, a coral bell named William Bartram and a rose called The Fairy—plants that, if they're not actual members of my family, I feel a special kinship with.

This garden, in the Spruce Hill section of West Philadelphia, was my first love, the first thing outside myself to which I dared to make a commitment, in which I dared to put down roots. While toiling on this tenth of an acre over the past ten years I've found my place in the world, become part of an extended family of friends and neighbors who care about this community—and I also found the lover and the cat with whom I now share my home.

The Spruce Hill Garden ornaments a corner lot at 44th and Locust streets where two brick rowhouses once stood, houses that were undermined by an underground stream and torn down around 1930. The empty lot remained a rubble-strewn, weed-choked eyesore until 1961, when the newly formed Spruce Hill Garden Club got permission from the owner to clean and fence the property, level it with a thin layer of topsoil, and plant it with trees and shrubs and flowers.

I was almost twenty-five, about to break up with a long-term girlfriend and take my first steps out of the closet as an openly gay man, when I got involved with the garden in 1983. I had been living in the area for seven years, the first four as a student at the nearby University of Pennsylvania. I know I had seen the garden before, but it never interested me until that spring. Struggling to make it as a freelance writer, I was always on the lookout for saleable story ideas, and on a sunny April day I walked by the garden and added up the scene like this:

Ancient man tending beautiful flowers in the midst of a gritty city = good story.

I interviewed the ancient man—Stanley Woodward, an eighty-seven-year-old widower who had been the garden's volunteer caretaker since 1965—and in May my brief article appeared in the "Our Town" section of the *Philadelphia Inquirer* Sunday magazine. Shortly after, because I needed the money and Stanley needed a strong back, I began working as his assistant for five dollars an hour.

In June, as Stanley's guest, I attended the annual picnic of the Spruce Hill Garden Club, a group of mostly-old women with a handful of mostly-gay older men, one of whom was Gene Smith. That picnic was my first introduction to a side of Spruce Hill I'd barely noticed before—the permanent residents who form the neighborhood's backbone amidst the constant comings and goings of hordes of student renters. I was already three years out of college, but I still counted myself among that transient student group. Even as I began to set down the first tentative tendrils of my roots here, through the garden and the garden club, I didn't see them as such. I considered myself mired, not rooted, stuck in a place where I had no desire to stay. I longed for greener grass that I imagined existed in cities I had visited only briefly, falling in love with their pretty surfaces, romanced by the new—the same way I longed for perfection in the men I met during the first few years after I came out. I never moved away from Philadelphia, but I did move from man to man back then. I would latch onto a fresh body as the novelty of the previous one wore thin, after I had known him long enough to see some of the messiness that lay beneath his pretty face, which was often an illusion itself, conjured up by drink and the dimness of the bar, dissipating like starlight in the bright of the morning-after.

———

When I try to trace my path from that unsettled state to where I am now
—living with one man for the past five years, eager to buy a house in this
city if only I could make a down payment—the lines of this convoluted
genealogy all lead back to Gene Smith. If the garden is the roots of my new
family tree, then Gene is the trunk, from whom all the branches and leaves
and acorns emanate.

Soon after we met at the garden club picnic, Gene got me a job doing
yard work for his neighbor, Christine Palmer. Whenever I was out in Mrs.
Palmer's yard, Gene would stand on his side of the fence and talk to me
while I worked. We became friends that way, and the next summer, after
he convinced Mrs. Palmer to rent me one of her apartments and I moved
in next door, I quickly got into the habit of visiting Gene in the late
afternoon a few times a week, when I needed a break from writing, or was
bored, or lonely. We would sit in his kitchen, sipping cheap sherry from
coffee mugs, talking about ourselves, gossiping about the garden club members and other people I was just getting to know. If he had enough food
Gene would often invite me to stay for dinner, and to return his generosity
I'd bring him cake or applesauce I'd made, or loaves of a particular raisin
bread that he loved. He collected Ritz cracker proof-of-purchase seals so he
could buy me a telephone, advertised on the box, that looked exactly like
a bottle of Heinz ketchup, which he knew was one of my favorite foods.
Among other things, I gave him a "stamp licker"—a white canister on
which were painted luscious red lips, through which, at the turn of a knob,
a long damp red tongue would emerge. I never saw him use it for stamps,
but he loved the licker for its lewdness.

Gene became the nurturing, supportive parent I'd never had, a combination father and mother in whose eyes I could do no wrong—a too-
positive view, for sure, but one I far preferred what I perceived as to my
real mother's uncaring aloofness or my real father's unreachable expectations.
Gene had given up his dream of making a living as an artist years ago, a
disappointment that may explain why he was so enthusiastic about my own
creative aspirations. He had had only a few secretive affairs in his sixty-plus
years, so it must have been heady for him to live next door to an openly
gay young man and watch me trot a series of boyfriends right through the
front door, not caring who in the neighborhood might see—and I spent
entire nights with them, too, a pleasure that Gene had never shared with

any man. In daylight hours I would bring these men next door, seeking, and always getting, Gene's parental approval.

Though we never spoke of our friendship in such terms, looking back I can see that I loved Gene, and that he must have loved me, too—as the son he'd never had, perhaps, or maybe he had a crush on me that I failed to notice because he never made it obvious. Unlike other older gay men I've met, Gene never engaged me in any discomfiting sexual innuendo, he never made a pass at me—though one afternoon I thought he did.

"I want to show you something," he said, leaving me alone in his kitchen for a minute, and when he returned I gasped, or jumped out of my chair—I don't remember exactly what I did but my shocked response was what Gene had hoped for, and he laughed hysterically while removing the plastic yellow daffodil he had dangled from his fly.

In the spring of 1985, it was Gene who encouraged me to take over the care of the Spruce Hill Garden. The previous summer Stanley Woodward had gone blind and was moved into a nursing home, and when no one from the garden club stepped forward to take his place it looked as if the garden might go the way of several other vacant lots the club had cleaned up and planted and then abandoned over the years.

That August I worked in the garden on my own, clearing the beds of the worst of the weeds, but without Stanley's direction I didn't know what else to do. The following spring I began removing the winter's accumulation of leaves and trash, but I quickly realized how many hours Stanley must have put into this job and figured that, even at my meager wage, the club would go bankrupt if I was paid for all my time.

I told this to Gene, and he urged me to do the work as a volunteer. I pled ignorance, I said I didn't have the time or knowledge to take on such a job, but he overcame my resistance by promising his help. He also hinted that if I didn't do it, nobody would, and I think that's what hooked me— the idea that I was needed by this tiny fragile plot of land. I saw myself as the Chosen One, the Saviour of Our Most Precious Plants, the trowel-wielding exorcist who would search out and destroy the demon weeds and keep the garden from backsliding into horticultural hell.

I remember Gene's patience as he led me down the brick path of his own beautiful garden and recited the names of his many unusual plants, a trip we made over and over since only one or two names would stick each time. I remember his pleasure as he watched my first tentative efforts in the Spruce Hill Garden, nodding and smiling each time I looked over my shoulder for his approval while planting the cuttings and seeds he had given me. With his help that year I dug and planted the first two of many new beds I would eventually create in the garden, and gained the confidence to continue working the following spring—on my own, as it turned out, because Gene died suddenly, of lung cancer, on Easter Sunday 1986.

From Gene I learned something my nuclear family had never taught me: how to share. Sharing the bounty is one of the responsibilities of a gardener, and I've done it well, giving away hundreds of plants—and many hours of free advice, too, since in the past ten years I've gone from knowing and caring nothing about flowers to making most of my livelihood from horticultural work.

And my tangible offers of flowers and information are just the most obvious part of this bounty. The garden itself is a gift, my way of making the world a better place—one tiny corner of the world, anyway.

Gene also taught me how to receive: plants or silly gifts or knowledge or love, all of which he offered me. The Spruce Hill Garden, now three or four times as full of flowers as when Stanley Woodward took care of it, has certainly benefited from this lesson. I bought some of these new plants at nurseries, but many have been given to me by gardening friends. I look around the beds and, besides the plants that Stanley and others put in before my tenure, I see a dianthus from Blanche, geraniums from Margharita, ferns from Pam and Sue, hostas from Bella and Ruth, a butterfly bush from Liz, and hellebores from Sylvia, all of whom I met through my work in the garden. I see the many plants I received from Gene, two of which I especially love because they reseed themselves year after year, needing no assistance from me: Johnny-jump-ups, a type of pansy; and a pale blue flower called the forget-me-not.

The garden is also home to dozens of plants that I got from my mother, who has always had a beautiful garden, one I refused to work in when I was growing up, not wanting my shaky sense of masculinity to be tainted by association with flowers. My newfound interest in horticulture became our first tentative connection after years of estrangement. It provided us with common ground for discussion, a safe way for her to begin giving to me again after I had been rejecting her offers of anything for years. Her gifts of flowers opened the way for us to share more intimate things, enabling us, if not to become mother and son again, then at least to become friends.

Without my commitment to the Spruce Hill Garden I probably would have left Philadelphia long ago. That's why I say the garden holds the roots of the extended family I've found here—not because all my friends are connected directly to the garden, but because without it I would have ended up somewhere else, found a different lover, hooked into a different family. I sometimes wonder where I might have gone, and if my life would have been better or worse—but I didn't go, I'm here, and after eighteen years it doesn't matter why, my roots are planted deeply now.

I sometimes use the garden as a refuge from the pressures of the world, a place in which I can escape the complicated desires of humans and deal with the simpler needs of plants. Unlike most people, most of the flowers respond to my care by happily blooming, and those that suffer from my neglect don't scream at me or call me names, even if I snip off their branches, lop off their heads.

But other times I love the exposure the garden gives me. It sits on a well-traveled block, adjacent to a supermarket and across from a laundromat, sandwich shop, pizzeria, and Thai grocery. Only one hundred feet long and thirty-five feet wide, its cyclone fence only three feet high, the entire plot is visible from the surrounding sidewalk. I'm there several times a week through the gardening season, out in the mud of March before the first robin appears and sometimes still doing fall clean-up on brisk December days, and often I feel as if I'm on stage or in a cage, a spectacle on display, with passersby looking in and watching me work as if they've never seen anyone mow a lawn or dig a hole or pull a weed. In my public role as "The Gardener," I've received near-unanimous praise, far different from the other roles I play in my life. And while most of the kind words are directed at my flowers, I know (even if the praiser doesn't) that they are also meant for me, because a garden can't long survive without a gardener.

I've met hundreds of people during my decade-long tenure in the garden—old people and young people, gay and straight, black and white and yellow and brown and even some with purple hair. Some of them I've gotten to know intimately, others I just know by their smiling faces when they pass me on the street, but all of them give this neighborhood, for me, a comfortable small-town feeling. Maybe that's as much a fantasy as my longing for the perfect man, as much a delusion as when I thought I could be straight. I know this isn't a small town, that it's only a small part of the big bad city where people sell drugs and rape and mug and murder, and where I might be the next one caught in the crossfire. But that's how it feels to me sometimes: homey. I go into a local market on a Saturday morning and have conversations with four different people I met through the garden. I'm not only privy to the neighborhood gossip but also the subject of some, I'm sure. I've been here long enough to have seen mewling toddlers turn into surly skateboard-toting teens, teens grow up and trot off to college, students graduate and buy houses and have children and become middle-aged like me, and older people (and some who aren't so old) go gray, go bald, and die. Sometimes I feel as if the garden's constituency— people who may know me and like me or only know and like my garden —are watching over me, protecting me, as a proper family should.

In the spring of 1988 I ended the last of a long series of relationships with insecure artists like myself that dated back to my coming out. I remember telling people that what I really wanted was a "normal" lover—good-looking, of course, but one with a regular job and clear goals who would trust what I said and love me for what I was able to be.

On a cool March morning, when I was working in my garden, I met such a man, though I didn't know it at first. He was tall and thin and beaky-nosed, fashionably dressed. His name was Tom, and he told me that he was a landscape designer, that he lived a few blocks away in an apartment I might have noticed because the porch had been blanketed by moonflower and morning glory vines the previous summer. He offered to help me in the garden, adding that he had admired it ever since an old girlfriend who lived nearby had first shown it to him years ago.

Tom gave me his phone number, I said I'd call him, and I admired him as he walked away, wondering what his story was. I had a couple of old girl-friends, too, but I never mentioned them to guys I was interested in, so this threw me off the scent, made me think that Tom was straight. I was afraid it might scare him off if I told him I was gay, so I didn't—and while slipping back into the closet may not have been the proudest thing for me to do, I don't regret a minute of the time I spent there with him.

Instead of jumping straight into bed, we got to know more about each other than the particular curves and thrusts of our bodies. We worked side by side in my garden, went to orchestra concerts, spent hours talking and laughing—time that we've collectively come to call our "first date." We didn't have sex until two months after we met, not until Tom casually mentioned that his best friend was gay, which made me feel comfortable telling him that I was gay, at which point he said that he was gay, too. By that time we had become close friends, which has proven to be a far more solid foundation for our relationship than any sexual attraction.

The first thing Tom and I did, the morning after we first had sex, was receive the delivery of a truckload of limestone at my garden, for a wall that he had designed and helped me build. Two years after we met at the garden, Tom and I moved into the apartment we now share as a family with Sheba, a stray cat we rescued from near-starvation in the garden. We found the apartment through a friend who lived on Woodland Terrace, where I had moved because of Gene Smith, whom I had met because of the garden.

I used to think that I was at the center of my universe, but for now, I know that the center is my garden.

And I say "for now" consciously, because the garden won't always be at the center of my life. Things change, and if Tom and I move out of the city, to a house with land for the trees he dreams of growing someday, I'll lose the garden, that's true. But I won't lose the friends I made while tending it, or all that I learned about plants and myself. The time I spent will not have been wasted, even if no one takes my place and the garden is eventually abandoned and goes back to weeds.

The garden lured me out of hiding, out of the closet in many ways, and now I don't need it so much anymore. I still love tending the flowers, hearing the unsolicited praise of passersby. But the garden is no longer the only good thing I do or the only place I feel safe, as it was ten years ago. Little by little over that time I've been chipping away at the stone wall I once hid behind, until now that wall is more like a fence, a three-foot cyclone fence with a gate around the side. Most people don't see that opening but I point it out to certain friendly types, inviting them to come in and join me, in my beautiful garden.

I'm in my garden on a sunny afternoon, taking a break from weeding, stretching my arms to the sky. A familiar old woman slowly makes her way past on the sidewalk outside. One arthritic hand grips the garden fence, the other tugs on a creaky metal cart laden with groceries. She knows me only as the young man who takes care of the garden, and though I don't even know her name I consider her one of my neighborhood grandmothers (not all of whom are women). Some of these old people sing praises to me and my work, taking a grandparent's pride in my gardening accomplishments. A few stop and bend my ear, complaining about the bad state of the world or the neighborhood or their health, while others try to make sure I won't end up in their orthopedic shoes. Every spring an old woman named Marie catches me kneeling on the cold damp soil and chides me, "That chill's gonna get into your bones, you'll get arthritis for sure if you keep doing that! Get a pad under those knees!" I smile, thank her for the advice, and as she walks stiffly toward home she looks back and says, "Mark my word! I oughta know!"

On this day my nameless grandmother pauses and tells me in a voice as quavering as her gait that my flowers are beautiful, that the garden is like an oasis, like the Garden of Eden. As always her praise sounds effusive to me, especially when I look at the garden she so admires and see nothing but work to be done—weeds to pull and grass to cut and flowers to dead-head and roses to prune and on and on and on.

When she finishes paying her compliments, I'm tempted to fall back into my old self-deprecation, to give credit to God or the weather or the Garden Club, to some way, any way, take the focus off me—but I stop myself this time, manage to choke back this fit of false humility. Instead, I look around the garden again and can almost see it as she does. I can almost admit that maybe, just for today, it's really as pretty as she says.

I tell her, "Thanks, I'm glad you like it."

"No," she insists, "thank *you*." And then she smiles and totters on her way, my flowers waving in the soft summer breeze—taking their bows, perhaps, or maybe nodding their heads, telling me:

Yes, Yes, Yes.

christopher
b r a m

george and al
and john and others

The first image is a bedroom. Double mattress and box springs sit on the floor, under the window whose white security bars suggest a room in a mental hospital. It's the same bed Draper and I still share. Odd how much has and hasn't changed in eight years.

Credits, white on black: *George and Al.*

The bedroom again, another angle. A portable movie screen hangs on the wall over the bed, like an empty thought balloon in a comic strip.

Credits. *A Film by*

Almost since the night we met, Draper and I talked about making movies. He was an art director and I worked in a bookstore but we both loved films with a passion that could be requited only by making one. In our first years together, it was a bedtime story we told each other, concocting plots and scenes and characters while we lay under the blankets.

George and Al was our first film. It's thirty minutes long, shot in Super 8 and transferred to video. I wrote it, Draper directed it, and most of our friends became involved in one way or another. People often say that film-making is like being in a family, an intense yet temporary family that dissolves as soon as the project is completed. Because we worked with friends, this particular family preceded and survived its making.

It's a movie about making movies. Draper plays George, a gay man with a camera who thinks he can control his life if he gets it on film. We had a Super 8 sound camera. Draper loved the grainy texture and painterly colors and I suggested we make the homemade roughness part of the story. A fictional documentary, the film consists entirely of footage shot with George's camera.

It begins with our empty bedroom, then morning-after glimpses of different men in our bed, guys that George brought home the night before.

First there's Yarrott asleep on his stomach. A hand reaches into the frame to draw the sheet off Yarrott's ass. Everyone who's seen the movie comments favorably on Yarrott's ass. He and Draper have known each other since kindergarten in Nashville. "I'm not into that," Yarrott grumbles and rolls away from the camera, wrapping the sheet around him.

Then there's me, in close-up without my glasses, croaking sleepily that I want to be left alone. I was a last-minute replacement when a friend chickened out.

Next comes Nancy's husband, sitting up and glaring as the camera bobs toward him. Nancy is a poet who worked with me at the bookstore. Long before we began *George and Al*, she had a dream where Draper and I were shooting a movie in our apartment. "And I thought, How practical of them." She didn't mind loaning us her husband, and he didn't mind playing a gay man so long as he could keep his T-shirt on. He snarls, "If you don't turn that damn thing off, I'm going to shove it up your nose."

And then comes Al. Waking to the cold, obtrusive eye of a lens, his first response is to ask, "What kind of camera is that?" Immediately, he and George seem to be made for each other.

Al is played by our good friend, John.

Where do I begin to describe John? He is such an important, complex part of our life. We met him twelve years ago, when he and Draper took an acting class at Herbert Berghof Studios. He adopted us, or maybe we adopted him—I can't remember exactly how the friendship gained momentum. He's a few years older than we are, with more lives than his two cats, Cyrano and Rimbaud, combined. He has been a teacher, a bartender, a salesclerk, and a chef. His family tree is Italian—Sicilian to be precise. He's also an ex-monk, in and out of the Jesuits once, the Benedictines twice. As the names of his cats suggest, he's very well-read. In addition, he is the only opera lover I know who can talk to agnostics without sounding like a

baseball fan citing batting averages. He makes opera exciting even for me
and Draper, who're hardly opera queens but, as Draper says, mere ladies-
in-waiting.

Another day, another room in our apartment: the living room this
time and our ruptured camelback sofa. George has invited Al over to film
him secretly, shyly keeping himself out of the frame. Al spots the hidden
camera, laughs, and drags George into the shot: What's good for the gander
is good for the other gander. For the first time, we finally see George, or
rather, Draper. It was only eight years ago, but he looks even younger, with
a short curly haircut like a fox terrier. George is painfully, convincingly
self-conscious. Draper dislikes performing unless he has a character to hide
in, but he included bits of himself in George, gestures and simple phrases
—"I'm starved"—that now seem like quotes from the movie whenever
Draper uses them.

George and Al become lovers. Draper is small and John is large—he
was forty pounds larger than he is now—a friendly bear with a full beard.
They are not anyone's idea of a hot couple. They do make a good comedy
team, however, which is probably a truer model for a long relationship.

George and Al have a dinner on the roof of our five-floor walk-up,
with two friends played by Jennifer and Larry. Behind them is an airborne
Greenwich Village landscape of low roofs and chimney pots. A few larger
buildings stand above the tar-paper plain like great chests of drawers.
George leaves the camera on and joins the others. (In reality, I stood at the
tripod and watched everyone through the viewfinder.)

Larry is the lover of a former Episcopal minister who's one of John's
best friends—gay ex-priests seem to be ecumenical. Larry supported himself
as a housepainter, but he was and is a real actor, at his best when he's
pretending to be someone else. He has a barking laugh and looks like a
handsome farm boy.

Jennifer goes back much further. She studied design at Pratt Institute
with Draper and is another art director devoted to other arts. She loves to
sing and worships Patsy Cline. She has a striking face—cheekbones, lipstick,
and dark hair—and natural spontaneity. Her character keeps letting slip
things George has told her that he hasn't told Al, including the fact that
he's in love with Al. "This part is perfect for me," Jennifer said when she
read the script. I didn't have the courage to confess that I based the character
on her.

Everybody slow dances against the sunset to "Someone's Rocking My Dreamboat" by the Ink Spots. George and Al dance together. That was the contribution of my friend, Mary. We showed her some unedited footage when she was visiting from Boston, explained how it would be put together, and she said, "But we never see them being affectionate."

The affection continues into the next scene, where the lovers wordlessly dance around each other while fixing dinner in our narrow kitchen. George had wanted to film the two of them in bed, but the intimacy of cooking is the most Al will agree to expose. George's invasive mechanical eye is finally becoming a problem for Al.

Then comes the skunk party.

Ever since we saw a child in skunk pajamas at the Halloween parade one year, Draper had wanted to have a party where everyone would be dressed as skunks. Never getting to it in real life, we incorporated the scene in the movie.

You would not believe how hard it is to find a dozen people willing to dress as rodents. Draper and his friend Julia assembled the outfits: cardboard stiffened tails, black hoods, and, for the stripe, lengths of white boa. Worn with black clothes, they were quite effective. But only a handful of friends had so little vanity they would agree to wear them.

It was one of the hottest days of July when we gathered on the roof, dressed as skunks but sweating like pigs. Nancy from the bookstore was there—this was not what she had in mind when she dreamed we'd make a movie. My cousin Maureen, who works on Wall Street, willingly offered herself—she had just come out and we'd set her up on her first date (it wasn't our fault the woman turned out to be a lunatic). Our downstairs neighbor Cook was enlisted. "This isn't a disco body," he told us, referring to his multiple sclerosis, but he was happy to stand off to the side, a sultry skunk with sideburns and a cigarette. Neighbors in surrounding buildings leaned out their windows or loitered on the fire escapes, wondering what the hell was going on. Draper shouted, "Action," and the skunks began to dance.

Jennifer and I dance on top of the hut over the door leading downstairs. I was slimmer then. Jennifer looks good even with a white stripe down her back. She was a wild, exuberant dancer, not noticing until we were done that we gyrated inches from a five-story drop down an air shaft.

"It's so Fellini!" Larry exclaims.

"Yeah. Fellini's *Bambi*," Al grumbles miserably. He agreed to the party because he thought he could have fun with George. Instead, George treats the party as a photo op, and Al as just another extra.

Al suddenly snaps, exploding at the camera. He and George get into a fight, still dressed as skunks, their argument shakily filmed from a distance by Larry. Al is sick and tired of the way George uses their life as camera fodder, and is fed up with how George always calls the shots.

Is any of this autobiographical? Yes and no. None of the truths here are literal. Like George, Draper makes movies, but he's never wanted to use us as raw material. In fact, I'm more like George than Draper is, including snippets of reality in my novels.

More important is the question of power addressed by the story: Who calls the shots in any relationship? Draper and I seem to take turns. It's how we handled *George and Al*. Writing the screenplay, I was open to suggestions, but the final decisions were mine. Directing the movie, Draper was receptive too, not just to me but to John and others. All final decisions were his, however, and he's an exacting perfectionist. John took to calling him "Erich"—in homage to Erich von Stroheim—but Draper was never cruel or manipulative. He simply had a very clear idea of how a scene should play and insisted we get it right.

After I wrote the script, my role was reduced. I operated the camera for shots where Draper appeared, but he gave detailed instructions on what to film. I occasionally played devil's advocate.

"You sure you want a medium shot here?"

"Yes! Trust me."

"I trust you. Just wondering if a long shot wouldn't—"

He gave me a look that could only be translated into the Ring Lardner phrase: " 'Shut up,' he explained."

Collaborating with a loved one has its dangers, creating whole new areas for quarrels. But arguing over which lens to use or how to pace a scene is much more interesting than arguing over more personal matters, such as why I never clean the bathroom.

In the next scene, George is in bed. With Larry. George wants to film himself having sex, and if Al won't oblige, Larry will do. Once the camera is turned on, however, George has second thoughts.

I shot this perched with the tripod on a very wobbly table. Despite what one might think, filming sex is not sexy. I was too worried about

focus and exposure and sound to enjoy seeing a cute guy pluck at the
waistband of his underpants. Or to be jealous that my boyfriend was beside
him. Not until the film came back from the lab and Draper ran it through
the projector did I catch traces of those feelings.

Our chief difficulty during the scene was a fear of giggles. It was the
situation, of course, but also the dialogue. When George says he's not in
the mood, Larry offers to go ahead without him. George considers it, then
decides no. Larry promptly says, "All right. You want to go eat?" I burst
out laughing when I wrote that line. Larry burst out laughing when he
rehearsed it. Nevertheless, whenever we screen the movie, nobody has even
chuckled. I assume they're too busy hoping Larry *will* masturbate.

At this point, filming on weekends and holidays, the project had gone
on for six months. A new reality began to creep in. As Al grew more
irritated with George, John became more annoyed with us. It wasn't
method acting. He'd been very excited when we first told him about the
movie and asked him to be in it, but you're asking a lot when you commit a friend to a project that goes on and on with no money involved, only
friendship. The situation wasn't helped by the fact that we were a couple
and John was single. John has had boyfriends in the past, but generally he's
single. We were two-against-one, and a couple is a confusing animal for
somebody who lives by himself, not one person, but not quite two either.
We had our own little wars, resolutions, and intimacies that did not include
John. And at the end of each session, no matter how well we worked together, John went home alone. He was too loyal to quit, and he continued
to give his best on film, coming up with new ideas and fresh bits of business
that brought a clumsy scene to life. But he became more despondent off-
camera.

We renewed friendship between shootings by sharing things that had
nothing to do with the work in progress. John is a wonderful cook and
frequently had us over for dinner. Draper and I couldn't compare with him
there, but we duped a porn film as a Christmas present, customizing it for
John by replacing the cheesy disco soundtrack with selections from Verdi.
None of us can hear "Libiamo" from *La Traviata* now without thinking of
bleached-blond surfers humping on the hood of a car.

We also tried matchmaking, but Draper and I are not very good at
that. My friend Cedric came up for a visit from Virginia. A musician and
writer, he was to provide music for the movie. I went to college with Cedric

but never suspected he was gay until after we graduated and mutual friends reported the news. A gentle, longhaired chain-smoker who loved Mozart, Kafka, and Frank Zappa, Cedric seemed too original for anything so obvious as repressed sexuality. He cut his hair and shaved his beard when he came out, revealing a gentle, square-jawed face. He remained as unique as ever though, as original as John. We thought they might hit it off. Alas, they were too original for each other, and too similar, both of them smart and tall and locked in private dreams of what they wanted in a boyfriend. While he stayed with us, Cedric kept apologizing for the repeated trips he made to Gay Treasures, a nearby store that sells old pornography, to stock up on magazines that didn't exist back home.

After George sleeps with Larry, he and Al continue to see each other, although Al refuses to let George film him anymore. George films him on the sly one day, following Al to his job and around town. There's a sad, wrongheaded desperation in George's stolen glimpses of Al. The shots of Manhattan from the summer of 1986 look oddly historical now.

Then comes the scene that's the heart of the movie. Using George's camera as an answering machine, Al leaves a message. His soulful, rumpled face filling the frame, Al explains what he feels about George, and about his camera. "When you film me I feel like an object. When I film you I feel like a servant. We have to find a way to work this out."

And they do. Their solution is to invent a fantasy together, their own fictional movie, a short Charlie Chaplin parody.

When Draper and I first met, one of the things that tightened our bond was a love of silent movies. German expressionism, Soviet epic, American melodrama, we enjoyed them all. But we had a special affection for Charlie Chaplin. We knew his work thoroughly, from the early shorts through *The Kid* to *City Lights*. And Draper could do an uncanny Chaplin impersonation. He not only looked like Chaplin in makeup and costume, he could catch the inventive spirit of him, the coyness, pathos, grace, and malice. One of our bedtime stories had been to imagine a gay Chaplin film—the Little Tramp is so polymorphous that it's not much of a stretch. John made a perfect Chaplin partner, the larger foils played by Mack Swain, Eric Campbell, and others. Just as we found a use for our skunk party, we found a place here for Charlie Chaplin. The movie is a scrapbook of shared fantasies.

Iris-out on our roof again, this time in black-and-white. Mack Swain and Chaplin are roofers. Chaplin is in love with Swain, who cares only about his work. Chaplin bats his eyes and dreams of bliss—and is hit on the head by the roll of tar paper swung around by Swain. During lunch, Swain in baggy clothes and droopy mustache sits down to devour a loaf of bread stuffed with sausages. Unable to take his eyes off his beloved, Chaplin mistakes a pot of glue for mustard and daintily spreads some on his own little sandwich. He tastes it, shudders, sniffs the sandwich, then sniffs the pot. He tosses the sandwich aside to happily inhale the glue. He jumps up for a wild dance of leaps and poses and pirouettes—Draper's mother taught ballet—and hops up on the parapet, thinking he can fly. Terrified for his pal, Swain climbs up to coax him back to safety. Glancing down at the five-story drop, Swain gasps and slips. He clings to the bricks for a moment, then falls. Chaplin screams for help, pinches his nose and, as if his beloved has fallen overboard, jumps in to save him. The bodies drop together. Blackout. And Chaplin comes to, in Swain's arms. They're still on the roof, their fall a glue-sniffer's hallucination. Iris-in on Chaplin and Swain's embrace. The end, of the movie-within-the-movie, and the movie itself.

It's a terrific sequence. I knew it was good when I wrote it. I'd originally intended for George and Al to break up, split apart by the camera. But when this slapstick love-death unexpectedly came to me, I felt that two guys who made anything so weird and wonderful had to stay together.

What was a joy to write, however, was a dog to shoot. I thought I made our work easier by setting the sequence on our roof. Draper wanted it to have the even, shadowless light of silent film, which was achieved by shooting under gauzy tents of muslin. We found we could get the same effect by filming on overcast days. But cloudy skies sometimes clear up and sometimes rain. Day after day, Draper and John put on their costumes, clown-white makeup and black eyeshadow, then sat grumpily in our living room waiting for the weather to change. Months later, on rainless overcast mornings, Draper or I still said to each other, "Looks like a good day for Chaplin and Swain."

Weekend after weekend, we climbed up to the roof and shot the damn scene. Take after take. It's surprisingly difficult to achieve such standard shtick as the head repeatedly ducking in time to miss being hit by a swinging object. But bit by bit, we put it together.

The project had gone on so long now that I became John's ally in impatience. I'd finally sold my first novel and was busy with rewrites, but

Draper expected me to put my work aside whenever he needed a cameraman. I was not in a generous state of mind the afternoon we threw George and Al off the roof.

Using Styrofoam heads and clothes stuffed with newspaper and weighted with old shoes, Draper and Julia built lifelike dummies of Chaplin and Swain. Jennifer told us we could use her roof for the drop—there was too much traffic on our street and we didn't want to give an innocent passerby a stroke—but she had to work that Saturday. John too said he was busy. So it was just Draper, me, and the dummies. We lugged the figures out to the street and hailed a cab. It was the morning after another Halloween parade and the driver gave us only the briefest of jaded looks.

We hauled the dummies up to Jennifer's roof and Draper went down to the street to set up the camera. I waited for his signal, wanting only to get this over with. I had to keep myself hidden behind the wall so "Erich" would have no reason to complain. I rolled the Swain dummy over the edge. I couldn't watch its fall. Only when I heard it hit the ground did I begin to sense anything strange here. I tossed the Chaplin dummy and, as the figure left my hands, it suddenly wasn't just Chaplin but Draper in effigy. My heart jumped into my throat. I heard a heavy thud and thump, and my heart broke.

"Cut!" Draper shouted from the street.

I timidly looked over the edge, a guilty emotional wreck when I saw the twisted Chaplin on the pavement.

I was kinder to Draper over the next few days.

The filming was over but the movie wasn't finished. It still had to be edited, the soundtrack mixed, and music added. Draper spent the next weeks bent over the editor as if at a sewing machine, contentedly lost in his work. He involved yet another friend for the sound, Chad, a sweet-tempered audio wonk who lived in our building's basement with his girlfriend, the super, before they broke up. Chad had been helping all along, sharing advice and microphones. Cedric returned to town to record the music.

I was present the afternoon they taped the score in a cluttered little studio off Times Square. Cedric played the piano while watching Chaplin and Swain on a video monitor. Usually so laid-back and dreamy, Cedric grimaced over the keyboard, twisting his body and juggling his hands, frantically improvising phrases that brought out details, stitched them together and made a brilliant piece of music in itself. Even the technicians were impressed. When he finished, he took a deep breath, sat back, and resumed his sheepish, self-deprecating calm.

It's hard to say when *George and Al* was finally done. If it had been commercially released or shown at a major film festival, that might make a good end to the story. But nothing ever came of our movie. Too short to be a feature, too long to be used as filler, too experimental for television, and too narrative to qualify for the New Queer Cinema that came into being a few years later, our creation never found a home. Which is sad considering how much work we put into it. Draper had been protectively realistic from the start, quipping that it might lead to a career for him as a Chaplin impersonator, available for shopping mall openings and children's parties.

There was no gala screening for the cast and crew. The closest we came was the night we showed it to John. He hadn't wanted to watch himself until the thing was completed. We met at Chad's studio. Jennifer was there, although she'd already watched her scenes. We didn't bother to dim the lights, only pulled a few chairs around the monitor.

Seeing a worked and reworked movie with someone who's seeing it for the first time forces you to watch with fresh eyes. I discovered that night that it was a real movie. I couldn't tell if it was good or bad, but it was funny, dramatic, and unpredictable, with a life independent of the people who made it.

When it was over, I was pleased, Jennifer ecstatic, Chad and Draper satisfied. John, however, sat very quiet, very still. He remained quiet while everyone praised his performance. He complimented Draper on a job well done and went home.

Over the following week, meeting first with me and then with both of us, John discussed what he felt, a mix of admiration and deep disappointment. He liked the movie, was impressed Draper had pulled it off, but—and he said it first as a joke—he couldn't help feeling that what had been his show was stolen at the end by Charlie Chaplin.

He hated saying that. We had always talked about it as *our* movie. John apologized for what he felt; Draper and I tried to assure him it was his movie too. But there was a grain of truth in what he said—people who see *George and Al* usually begin by praising Draper's Chaplin—although Draper never intended to steal the show, and it's not like anyone gained anything in the end except experience.

A few months later, we were all reduced to supporting players when

John left a videocassette with an agent at William Morris and the man's only response was, "I know somebody who'd love to meet the blond with the nice ass."

Looking back on it now, I see there was more than injured pride in John's dissatisfaction. It had none of the egotism of an upstaged actor. He never mentioned—didn't even seem to notice—how good he is in the movie. Acting is an odd business, a slightly masochistic art where people offer up their faces, bodies, voices, their very selves, as raw ingredients. Even the most experienced actors dislike watching their performances, and John was new to acting. His personality was too rich and deep for him to step out and blithely regard himself from afar, or to split an expendable performing self from his real self, which is what more typical, light-footed actors seem to do. Maybe that was another cause for his growing unhappiness while we shot: He was defenseless. John had offered us a piece of real self and then, when he found the experience more disturbing than he expected, was too generous to take it back until the movie was finished.

Part of the appeal of filmmaking is the attraction of working with others, a sociable creativity instead of our usual artistic solitude. The Italian director, Ermanno Olmi, called it, "This idea of making films around a table together, not just to live, to eat, but to look into each others eyes." That, of course, is a director talking. Other people at the table will have a different opinion. But the idea retains its appeal, even now when I know the dangers of mixing the personal with this mechanical art. We looked into each other's eyes for several months—Draper, John, and I and the rest—saw things we hadn't seen before, and continued, changed in great ways and small.

When I watch *George and Al* now, it's a photo album of a past that remains connected to the present.

Since then, Draper has made three more short films, each better than the last. He is gearing up to direct a feature next. He no longer needs his boyfriend behind the camera, but works with professionals, which is fine by me. I remain involved from outside, offering ideas, screenplays, and a sympathetic ear.

Meanwhile, Jennifer bought a video camera and is interviewing women for her own documentary. Chad handles the sound for trade shows, continues to work with Draper, and has a girlfriend who's a first-rate theater director. Nancy and her husband moved to Seattle. Cedric finally moved to New

York, where he writes short stories and plays piano for dance classes. Larry appeared briefly on Broadway in an evening of Thornton Wilder one-acts.

And John, despite *George and Al*, continued to act. He performed with Karen Allen in an off-Broadway production of *The Miracle Worker* and began to work as a movie extra. He put acting aside three years ago, saying only that he did not have time for it since he opened his catering business. But that's him in *Prizzi's Honor*, holding the bag of silver-plated golf clubs at the Mafia banquet. John Huston, in his rolling, mouthful-of-plums voice, told the cameraman, "And be sure you get this man's face. He has such a marvelous face."

a l a n   b e l l

alex, hassan,
and michael

When we first came back from the 1993 March on Washington for Lesbian, Gay, and Bi Equal Rights many of the straights at the office said, "We looked for you on television." A co-worker unfolded a copy of the *Los Angeles Times* and aimed a finger at a photo of the crowd scene around the Capitol Mall. "Point yourselves out," she said.

Alex and Hassan talked excitedly and displayed handfuls of pictures. Michael stood around and smiled. I talked as well, but not too much, my telling squeezed through a narrow shaft, the partially open closet door's tentative band of light. I snipped details, shaved edges, avoided the personal, conveyed the political. Worse, I found myself pandering. Of all the particulars I could have relayed to a married colleague, about friends I'd bumped into or the transcontinental romance I'd initiated, I selected something safe: "Several of the marchers wore T-shirts that had the words STRAIGHT BUT NOT NARROW printed on them." Brian nodded, repeated the slogan, and said, "I could wear something like that!"

By any measure, I believe I am fortunate. Usually—not always—but usually the straights at the office are supportive. If I still shutter a small part of myself in the closet, that's my doing. By contrast I would bet that most gays and lesbians are completely closeted at their places of work, and with good reason. In our homes, bars, and organizations we're in control, but unless we're self-employed or independently wealthy, most of us must work for someone else for a living. Usually that employer is straight, a person who may or may not be sympathetic, and without the protection provided by laws that prohibit discrimination on the basis of sexual orientation, "We're at their mercy," is not an overstatement.

At most of my jobs I've been a minority of one (as far as I've known). At about half these positions I've felt comfortable enough to disclose myself to the few co-workers I believed I could trust. But only in my current assignment, with the Los Angeles Department of City Planning, have I felt almost literally free—certainly not the same kind of freedom enjoyed by straights who live in a world designed for them—but a freedom nevertheless, the most amount of freedom I could imagine possible in an environment where heterosexuals are the majority. I feel this way because of my gay friends—Alex, Hassan, and Michael—and the fellowship we've created.

Thumbtacked to a cork bulletin board at the office are two snapshots of me, two among many photos of friends and colleagues. The top picture captures a bright, smiling, and friendly Alan, framed by downtown Los Angeles's turquoise and silver skyline, while the bottom picture displays a grim and professional Alan, glasses filled with glare, standing posed in front of a gray partition. Posted beneath both images is a caption that declaims, *Yes, he DOES smile.*

Look closely at the bottom snapshot, past the foreground and into the background, and you will notice something odd. An anonymous hand on the other side of the partition holds up a life-size photocopy of my beaming face. If you were to inspect a blown-up version of this snapshot you'd notice that the photocopy has been doctored, that my lips have been colored red and my hair streaked with fast and furious lines of blue. A twisted metal clip and pull-off aluminum tab fashioned into an earring dangles from my paper earlobe.

The anonymous hand belongs to my friend Hassan, a colleague who emigrated from Iran to attend UCLA, where we both graduated with degrees in city planning. Hassan tells me that this icon of me, this symbol of his affection for me that is the closest that I've ever gotten to drag, is part of his permanent collection, an essential element in the collage of pictures, posters, and other artifacts he transports to each work site.

Hassan has transferred to the Department of Public Works. What we miss most is the opportunity to drop by his desk, like next-door neighbors, and exchange chit-chats about nothing at all and then—with just the start of a hand gesture or the beginning of a sentence—detour into an intimate discussion about our personal lives.

Let's continue the office tour. Alex, a management assistant, and Michael, a graphic artist, also splash color on their drab government-issue equipment.

A work-in-progress grows on the side of Alex's bookcase: a photograph of a shirtless and smirking Marky Mark modeling Calvin Klein underwear; postcards and cutouts of pop singer Madonna posed in lingerie; and a safe-sex poster that reads, in a huge font, WHAT THE SMART DRESSED MAN IS WEARING: CONDOMS. Taped to the middle of the poster is a blue Trojan brand prophylactic.

Alex is the youngest and favorite child of immigrant parents from Yugoslavia and the youngest and most doted on member of our group. During the week Alex alternately complains about the tedium of his job and entertains us with tales of his Saturday-night adventures at local dance clubs.

Around Michael's work space and on his drafting table objects of his own design appear and disappear. Two examples:

A T-shirt for "Clean Needles Now," an AIDS prevention organization, displaying a cartoonish but faceless blond wig. A blazing headline reads, "Bleach It!"

A flyer for an upcoming concert starring Billy Wisdom, the pseudonym for one of Michael's best friends, depicting a fantasia of sleek air-ships and needle spires, all aflame.

Originally from Idaho, Michael has a disposition so refined of rough edges that no one, to my knowledge, has ever made a derogatory remark about him, short of gentle kidding. Yet there are some apparent, seeming contradictions. Michael never deviates from his precisely plotted daily schedule or compromises his strict vegetarian diet. For twenty years he's worked for city bureaucracies, since he was a teenager, but as a former guitarist for The Romans, a post-punk L.A. surfer rock band popular in the late 1970s, he has a glamorous past.

My own desk area is beige and barren of signature. My friends tease, pull me away from assignments, and persuade me to take breaks. In the lunch room, while talking about last night's "Star Trek" episode, we match personalities with show characters. "Spock," they decide. Who else but Alan Bell could be a Vulcan? No question about it, and later Michael makes a Spock nametag for me.

Four years previously, when I first started working for the Planning Department, I never would have imagined myself in such a scene, joking around at the office with some of my best friends. Back then I was temporarily placed at a desk in the cartographic section, away from the other city planners, the only space available in overcrowded City Hall. My job was to help develop a plan for managing Los Angeles's then exploding growth. The cartographers, for the most part, were older, taller, heavier, and hairier. All men, they spent most of the day talking about sports or women or the situation comedies they had watched on television the night before. They made maps with sharp instruments, corrected errors with motorized erasers.

I have to confess, these men conformed to my stereotype of the typical antigay bigot. "What did you do over the weekend? Do you have a girlfriend?" I feared they would ask. While I was certain I wouldn't lie if they did, I wasn't sure if I wouldn't opt for the easy solution, the gender-free nonresponse, the safe innocuous mumblings that can be interpreted by anyone any which way.

Circumstances interceded, obliged me to open my voice. A colleague visited, another city planner, *a known homosexual*, and when he left, prompted the cartographers to conduct an entire floor show of pantomime and impersonation, limp wrists and mincing steps, swishing hips and curlicued voices. I turned around in my chair and watched their mockery. Familiar territory, huh? In fact the performance seemed so rehearsed that I wondered if these men had borrowed their antics from an Eddie Murphy skit.

That evening I fussed over what I would do, finally deciding that I would speak to the culprits in the morning. I called them out one at a time and talked to them in the hallway, told them I was gay and that I found their behavior offensive, and not to do it again. Waves of apologies and wide-eyed expressions. "Hey, we didn't know!"

I doubted the sincerity of these regrets, the overeager attempts to establish nonhomophobic credentials. "We were just joking!" One offender confided that his aunt was "you know, that way" and that he loved her dearly. Fortunately, there were no more incidents. Still, I looked forward to the day when I would be moved to a different location in City Hall.

By the time I first met Alex I had finally been transferred to new and permanent quarters away from the cartographers. I was hunched over the computer writing a report when Alex's supervisor tapped me on the shoulder. I turned around, distracted, and saw before me the personification of earnestness, a good-looking young man dressed in a two-color leather jacket, button-down shirt, and tartan tie. We were introduced. He's so uncertain, I thought. Struggling . . . hasn't come out . . . has to be gay.

But of course I couldn't be absolutely sure. On my previous job I had invited a new employee out to lunch, not with lascivious intent, but simply because, so far as I knew, I was the only gay on the workforce. I wanted the company of somebody like myself and was confident that this young man would fit the bill. I asked him if he was gay. "No," he said with finality.

"Not even a little bit?"

"No," he repeated.

I realize now that if I'd asked Alex early on about his sexual orientation he would have said "no" as well, considering the question to be a form of accusation.

As with Alex, I first met Hassan at the computer. Only a few grains of conversation were required to confirm what we both knew by instinct, that the other was gay. Casually we dipped into talk about what-we-did-over-the-weekend, and while our mutual insertion of the word "boyfriend" into the discussion was too obvious to be natural, at least it spared us the ritual of having to ask, callow-faced and naively, "Gee, are you a homosexual too?"

A few months would pass before we became friends. In fact, I wasn't even sure if I liked Hassan at first. He was too obvious for my taste. Instead I preferred Michael, whose quiet personality was more like my own. But now that I look back I realize that my initial ambivalence toward Hassan could be explained by a single lingering concern, that if I associated with him everyone would assume that I was a homosexual too.

Nevertheless, Hassan intrigued me. Somehow his bravado seemed more like part of a design rather than just another personality trait. Unfortunately the anxiety of "I wonder what people will think," even though I had successfully confronted the cartographers, had not completely abraded.

One day Hassan and I went to lunch at the downtown Security Pacific

Bank Building cafeteria and the conversation about work shifted into a discussion about our respective boyfriends. While we talked I scanned the somber, feeding, middle-class faces of bankers, tellers, and secretaries. We poured out confidences to each other, and as I gratefully divulged, I also felt, like a stomachache, the fearful turning of questions. Could we be overheard? Why was he talking so loud? I misinterpreted the stray head movement, the pair of eyes that accidentally burrowed our way.

If it took time for my friendships with Alex and Hassan to develop, that was not the case with Michael. When we were first introduced in City Hall's ornate elevator lobby, I immediately liked him. Congenial and unpretentious, he wore thrift-shop castaways: baggy brown slacks and a lime green patterned shirt—nerdy guy wear made fashionable by virtue of its age. With a couple of other gay men in the Planning Department we started going to lunch every day.

Coincidentally we both had large circles of friends and acquaintances that intersected at many points. It became a standing joke that if Michael knew someone I was bound to know him as well. Example: Michael's cousin from Idaho was the lover of my lover's best friend.

Michael was not only the trendiest dresser in our group, he was also the most talented. A while back The Romans reunited for a marathon weekend AIDS benefit at Al's Bar, a gritty space located in downtown L.A.'s warehouse district. For three hours I milled around the dark bar, catching bits of each performance, when finally, to claps and cheers, The Romans entered stage left. While his adoring crowd of friends screamed their approval I watched Michael slam a guitar across his hips and croon out lyrics, eyes closed.

For the first year of his employment with the city Alex was the subject of intense and gossipy speculation, though he managed to maintain a discreet if not coy distance. But I could tell he was struggling with the issue of his sexuality. Sometimes he relayed to me the vivid details of his dreams, which often had violent overtones. Once I told him, "Well, that's your dark side manifesting itself." Pleased with the idea, Alex arched his eyebrows and twisted a smile onto his face.

Other than that I seemed to intimidate him. We often had occasion to work together and sometimes, while standing in front of my desk, the goofiest of grins would appear, his eyes would shine brightly, and he'd bow oddly, folding his torso as if it were a piece of paper, while laughing in a kind of honking style.

Once I asked him about this behavior. "Alex, why are you always bending over in front of me?" I tried not to put any spin or unintended meaning into this query. "I don't know, I don't know," he said, red in the face, embarrassed and giggling.

Hassan was more direct. "Are you gay?" he asked Alex one day when the two of them went to lunch. "No," Alex said, flustered. "I don't know. I do know but I don't want to talk about it."

Around this time an older closeted man in the Planning Department befriended Alex. They started dating and soon became lovers. Three years later Alex told me that at the beginning of their relationship he and Doug (a pseudonym) had both subscribed to the idea that the closet, while confining, was a cozy and comfortable place to live. Doug actively disliked Hassan, Michael, and me, the openly gay men in the building.

Doug and Alex started to argue, Alex questioning Doug's wish and apparent need to remain closeted. At the same time Alex visited us more often, especially Michael, who would eventually take him to his first gay nightclubs in West Hollywood.

Soon thereafter Alex confided to Michael that he was gay and that he was seeing Doug. Michael said, "I thought so." After coming out to Michael, Alex went back to Hassan, who'd laid low during this whole time, and also told him about Doug. I didn't find out about the affair until after it was over, when I was forced to guess who Alex had been dating. I sorted through several names before I identified Doug but when I did so I made a sour expression. "Oooo," I said. "How could you sleep with him?"

We made sure Alex was included in all the "boys' lunches" and invited him to all of our parties. But he was still remarkably shy, standing around with his hands in his pockets, barely saying a word.

We decided that what he needed was a really good lay to erase the sour aftereffects of the introductory affair with the ultra-closeted Doug. Once we pulled him into our circle and told him what we'd just been discussing. At first he smirked, then seconds later a smile emerged.

I suggested to the group that we throw Alex a coming-out party. Everyone immediately endorsed the proposal. I offered to have it at my apartment. Michael volunteered to design the invitations, which we all agreed should feature a caricature of Alex stepping out of a closet. Hassan said he'd coordinate everything.

As it turned out we never did host a coming-out party for Alex. Inertia had set in, and when the notion resurfaced we realized there was no longer any need. Alex was now thoroughly out. Long sideburns framed his face and a single ring pierced his left ear. He'd thrown away all his old clothes and replaced them with black boots and wide belts, blue jeans and work-shirts. Alex had not only disclosed his sexual orientation to his mother and father but he'd also persuaded them to attend meetings of Parents and Friends of Lesbians and Gays.

Michael, Hassan, and I were the first openly gay men Alex had ever met. Later he said that each of us, in our own way, had been a role model for him. Michael had taught him how to dress and introduced him to the coolest clubs. I had counseled him about his career. Hassan had shown him how to be outrageously out. A role model himself these days, Alex volunteers for a community education program, visiting area high schools and junior colleges to speak to students about what it's like to be gay.

The supportive office environment we enjoyed at the Planning Department didn't develop by accident. Certainly we possessed many advantages, mainly the city's ordinance prohibiting discrimination on the basis of sexual orientation, civil service protection, and liberal straights, but none of these factors, by themselves or in combination, could explain how or why this situation evolved. The necessary ingredient was leadership, which Hassan supplied in abundance.

"If I act like a big flaming faggot maybe other people won't feel as uncomfortable about being openly gay," he told me once. "Maybe they can take incremental steps in coming out."

I remember a story Hassan recounted to me one day that illustrates his leadership style. At one of his unit's staff meetings the topic of discussion had changed from routine business to the personal. Turn by turn each person had talked about his or her private life, but rather than murmur something about his mother or siblings or some similarly safe subject Hassan had instead talked about his lover of several years, in much the same way that everyone else had talked about their husbands or wives.

A co-worker folded his arms and turned to Hassan and said, "What I don't understand is why gay people feel they have to talk about their sexuality all the time." Hassan replied that he hadn't been talking about his sexuality but rather about his spouse, there's a distinction, and that what he'd just said was no different in kind or degree from what anybody else had just said. "You have a point there," the colleague conceded.

This story both amazed and frustrated me. The man's admission was reluctant, at most a tentative agreement to consider the proposition that gays and lesbians should enjoy the same social freedoms as straights. Why wasn't he embarrassed? Why wasn't he apologetic? Replay the words, *You have a point there*, and you'll hear a different melody, the implicit assumption that homosexuality is shameful and queers should keep their perversion concealed. Ordinary music, part of the background of oppression so low-toned it's barely audible.

I measure the degree of my outness by how comfortable I am around straights, and thanks mostly to my gay friends at the office I've made steady progress in that domain. Just over a year ago I instinctively still pulled back, hid in small bottles from heterosexuals, as if they were appalling secrets, the specifics about the men I dated. Meanwhile, Brian, the married colleague who could wear the STRAIGHT BUT NOT NARROW T-shirt, listened to Alex's weekend dance club stories, not with voyeuristic intent, but with genuine care and interest. While they conversed, Brian asking for all the details and Alex supplying them, I remained silent, still living, for that moment, in a closet.

Lately though I've started to loosen up, in very un-Spocklike ways. After Hassan transferred he gave me a poster of Pope John Paul II which I taped to the front of my desk. Inspired, I decided I would organize my desk as an ironic religious counterstatement to the ever-growing sex display on the side of Alex's bookcase.

Since Hassan gave me that poster of the pope I've also taped to the front of my desk a brochure printed by Billy Graham, *Will It Be Soon?*, a religious tract concerning the end of the world; a full-page newspaper advertisement published by *Focus on the Family, In Defense of a Little Virginity*; and a souvenir from Michael, something he'd bought for me while he vacationed in Mexico, a laminated holy card bearing an image of The Blond Jesus.

Nongay colleagues visit and stand before my desk, their eyes flickering like candle flames in a drafty church, and sometimes they get it and sometimes they don't. "I didn't know you were religious," an engineer, someone I've worked with for years and who knows that I'm gay, says casually.

"Of course I'm not," I reply. "This is meant as high camp. Irony." The engineer looks at my desk and then at Alex's bookcase, pauses, and then laughs. "I get it," he says.

More evidence of progress: I've started to drop hints into the social conversation stream that I'm not a completely asexual creature. While Alex and Brian talk, I mention that I'm "divorced" and now date. Gender is not hidden. When Alex tells Brian stories about my behavior at gay dance clubs ("Brian, you should have seen him, I've never seen him so friendly. How many beers did you have, Alan? Three?") I don't automatically flinch. I tell Brian about a date that didn't work out. Brian looks up, shrugs, and says, "Better luck next time." Such perfect banality. He's used to it. He doesn't care.

I think these perfunctory reactions reflect a remarkable achievement. Brian is a married and basically conservative young father of a one-year-old son, but he's interested in our lives. When I talk about Brian to my gay friends outside of work their faces usually register suspicion. Why is he so concerned? I tell them, Well, he just likes us. It's not at all what you think.

At the office we have a circle of men who take morning coffee breaks together, half gay and half straight. Lesbian and gay Los Angeles city employees recently organized an association to press for domestic partner benefits and better enforcement of the nondiscrimination ordinance. I served on the by-laws committee of this new group and told the straight members of the coffee circle about my role. One day Brian and another member of the coffee circle walked up to me and said they wanted to join this new organization. "Are you kidding?" I asked. No, they weren't. I said sure, we don't discriminate, all you have to do is sign a statement saying that you agree with the objectives of the association. "We agree," my straight friends said, and smiled. "We want to be dues-paying members."

His last day on the job we took Hassan out to a Mexican restaurant, our final "boys' lunch." As usual I was late, finishing up a report. That morning Alex had given Hassan his farewell present, a life-size stand-up cutout of cartoon character Betty Boop, which Hassan promptly installed just outside his new cubicle at the Department of Public Works.

"Come on, Alan, we're waiting," Michael said, his voice inflected with mock impatience, with forgiveness for the way I can sometimes act. I left my desk and walked to the front part of the office. "Bell?" Hassan said, and squinted at me. "Come on, Bell. We're going."

Alex could hardly contain himself. When he got excited he practically levitated, one hundred and fifty pounds of floating boy. Suddenly he started hugging us. We all laughed and piled into the elevator with the enthusiasm of youthful and mischievous stowaways. Michael had made an oversized going-away card for Hassan—which each of us had earlier inscribed with messages of tenderness, love, and friendship, and regrets that the office would never be the same without him—and decorated the cover with a vintage stock photo of a pretty Soap Girl. Beneath her eye he had colored a single golden tear.

jesse g. monteagudo

notes of an adopted son

The search for family and community takes us in different directions. In my case the search took me to an alien faith and to a people I had no direct connection with, neither ethnic nor cultural. At the age of twenty-three, after growing up in a Latino Catholic culture, I became a Jew. My conversion to Judaism was part of an ongoing process of redefining and rediscovering myself, both as a gay man and as a human being.

In 1492 Spain's Catholic monarchs, Ferdinand and Isabella, expelled the Jews from their country. The Edict of Expulsion left Sephardic (Spanish) Jews with no choice but to leave their country or convert to Christianity. Many who converted, called *conversos* (converts) by the authorities and *marranos* (pigs) by the masses, were closet Jews who practiced their ancestral faith in secret. Others married into the general population, including the nobility, and merged into the Spanish bloodline. Because of this mixture it is estimated that most of us who are of Spanish descent have Jewish (and Moorish) ancestry. Though I have no proof of Jewish ancestry, I like to think that I do, and that my conversion is a return to my Jewish roots. But this is speculation. My ethnic background, as much as I can tell, is Spanish, French, German, and North African (from the Canary Islands), but not directly Jewish.

My introduction to Judaism and to the Jewish people was a gradual process. As a boy in pre-Castro Cuba, I did not know any Jews, though the island had a small but vital population of both Sephardic and Ashkenazic (Eastern European) Jews. Cuban Jews flourished in spite of an atmosphere of anti-Semitism that the Cuban people, an explosive mix of Spanish and African (with everything else thrown in for good measure), inherited from our Spanish ancestors. Jews were not legally allowed in Cuba until its independence in 1902, and those who came afterward were hated as alien immigrants or as agents of U.S. imperialism. The Spanish term *Judio* (Jew) had such negative connotations that Cubans who did not want to seem prejudiced often used the term *Hebreo* (Hebrew) to describe a Jewish friend or Jews in general.

The Cuban Catholic Church, till 1959 predominantly Spanish, was anti-Semitic. It was also, before the Revolution, in charge of much of Cuba's educational system. My second grade class was run by a notorious (though not atypical) clerical bigot who taught his students that the Jews were Christ-killers who were expelled from their homeland as punishment for their crime. Having learned about the State of Israel in another class, I quickly noted that the Jews *have* a homeland. The monk, not used to feedback from impertinent seven-year-olds, tartly noted that Jews were still scattered about and went on with his lecture.

Not till I came to the United States in 1962 did I meet any Jews. My father, like many immigrants to South Florida, got a job at a Miami Beach hotel that was largely frequented by Jews. During the sixties the Jews in my life were tourists whom I encountered in the hotel where my father worked, and where later I held a series of summer jobs. To the adolescent me, the Jews were strange but interesting people, often immigrants like myself; mostly elderly people who spoke a different second language (Yiddish), had different tastes in food, liked books and movies and the theater (as did I), and practiced a religion that circumcised their sons but managed to survive without Jesus, Mary, the saints, the Pope, priests and nuns, and with only half a Bible. I also learned about the State of Israel, as dear to them as fighting Communism was to us Cubans, and about the Nazis who murdered six million Jews during World War II. Like Jews, middle-class Cubans (known throughout the hemisphere as the "Jews of Latin America") prized education, hard work, family, and community, values that I inherited from my parents and my surroundings. Like the Jews of Miami Beach, the men and women of the Cuban *diaspora* were then creating a dynamic community in exile—across Biscayne Bay in Little Havana—which, like Jewish-American communities everywhere, combined our ancestral traditions with American values and ideals.

Little Havana too had its Jews, men and women and children who like the rest of us fled Cuba to escape the rigors of Communism. Many flourished in *El Exilio*, a term which, like the Hebrew *diaspora*, is full of meaning for those who speak the language. To those of us who grew up in Little Havana during the sixties, Cuban Jews were not Jews but Cubans, so much like us that they did not impress me the way their distant cousins on the Beach impressed me. In fact, Jews and Judaism were not priorities with me during my crucial decade. These were the years when I discovered my essential difference; the fact that I, like a Jew in an anti-Semitic society, was something that everyone around me despised.

The story of my coming out as a gay man in a homophobic society has been told before. Though homophobia is not unique to Roman Catholicism—it is a trait that is shared by other faiths, including traditional Judaism—it seemed to be especially hypocritical in an institution where so many of its spiritual leaders were gay. One of my uncles, now deceased, was a closeted gay man who joined a religious order in order to avoid dealing with his homosexuality. It was obvious to me, as a student in a Catholic school in Miami, that many of the priests, nuns, and monks were gay. In fact the Catholic tradition of clerical celibacy encouraged men and women who were homosexually oriented to enter the religious life, where marriage and children were not expected of them.

The sixties were uncertain times, when my emerging sexuality and my developing intellect clashed with established beliefs. I began to question a Church that condemned all its masses to impoverishing overpopulation, its women to second-class citizenship, and its sexual and intellectual dissidents to excommunication and hell. Though I continued to believe in a God, I gradually lost faith in the Trinity, the Virgin Mary, the saints, a supposedly infallible Pope, and a priesthood that claimed supernatural powers. Though I continued to think well of Jesus, he seemed to be no more than a man— a devout Jew who wanted to reform his people but not start a universal faith, and certainly not the Messiah. By the time I graduated from Catholic high school in 1972, I had ceased to be a Catholic, though I continued to be a nominal Christian, albeit a nonbelieving one, for some time.

All this turmoil might have made me, like so many other "lip-service Catholics," an unbeliever who continues to pay lip service to his Church, if only as a place to be married and buried in. But I was not satisfied with a "solution" that to me was no solution at all. My college years, the years in which I came to terms with my sexual orientation, were also years of spiritual searching, when I explored several spiritual options, from atheism to Holy Roller. I even dabbled in Scientology, perhaps the worst mistake of my life, for the Church of Scientology was not only homophobic but also centralized and regimented to a degree unheard of even in the Catholic Church.

Now I realize that my spiritual road, through many detours, was taking me toward Judaism. My admiration for the State of Israel translated into deep affection for the people who made the Zionist dream a reality. The Jewish ability to survive for centuries among hostile Christian or Muslim populations struck a chord in a man whose sexual affinities made him something of an outcast. I found in the Jewish traditions of justice, as expounded by generations of prophets and rabbis, an ethic by which I could live. Like King Bulan of the Khazars, a Russian prince who converted to Judaism in the middle ages, I compared Judaism with Christianity and Islam and found Judaism to be first, not only in age, but in its beliefs, traditions, and rituals. Judaism gave humanity the Torah, the Sabbath, a strong moral code, and a one-to-one relationship with a unitary God whose uniqueness was diluted by trinitarian Christianity. While other religions stress the afterlife, Judaism is oriented toward the here and now; study and good works are honored for their own sakes and not as conduits to heaven.

And Judaism was more than a religion. It was a way of life, practiced through the ages by a "chosen people"—more precisely a *choosing* people— who, though not quite a "race," were an extended (if quarrelsome) family that went back in time to Abraham and Sarah and forward into the untold future. Life-cycle events, daily rituals, and annual holidays alike served to bring the Jewish family, whether in Israel or in the Diaspora, together with one another and with our ancestors. All this struck a chord in me.

My affinity for Judaism and for all things Jewish might have never carried me over the threshold to conversion had I been heterosexual. As a straight man, I would have almost certainly married a Cuban woman, or at least a Latina, and raised our children in our parents' faith. As a gay man, and thus a rebel against society's sexual and gender mores, I had less of a reason to remain rooted to my religious and cultural heritage. I am not alone in this regard. In my twenty years in the lesbian and gay community I have known many women and men who have changed their faith, not only to Judaism (or Christianity) but also to Unitarianism, Islam, Buddhism, Santeria, Wicca, and other cults.

There was another reason why being gay influenced my decision to choose Judaism. That was my need to find a family and community that would take the place of a Cuban-Catholic culture that I was no longer quite comfortable with and which would not accept me on my own terms. The gay bar scene, as I experienced it, left me empty, and the Metropolitan Community Church would have me believe in a theology that I could not accept. Judaism, on the other hand, represented a community that I could accept, admire, and emulate. Though traditional Judaism was too sexist and homophobic for my taste, I was attracted to Reform Judaism, a forward-thinking and progressive branch of Judaism that, at its best, combined Jewish traditions and ideals with modern realities. Reform Judaism's stance on lesbian and gay rights is more progressive than that of any branch of Judaism except Reconstructionism and any Christian sect except the Unitarians and the MCC.

During this formative period (1973–76) I developed friendships with many Jews, both gay and straight. Steve was an attorney and singer whom I met in a Miami bar and who became my lover for several years. It was early 1976, a memorable year for several reasons, not the least of which being the start of my involvement in lesbian/gay politics. Steve, as it turned out, was active in Congregation Etz Chaim, Miami's lesbian and gay synagogue, where he served as a cantorial soloist. Though I'd heard about Etz Chaim, I had never been there, so I accepted Steve's invitation to go with him to shul. The rest is history.

Congregation Etz Chaim, then the Metropolitan Community Synagogue, was founded in 1974 by gay and lesbian Jews who were not comfortable with the Metropolitan Community Church. In the spring of 1976, services were held at the YWCA building in downtown Miami. The synagogue was run by the lay leadership, then for the most part consisting of the synagogue's founders. Since congregants came from all branches of Judaism, service leaders tried for a mix of Conservative and Reform. Etz Chaim did not have a rabbi at that time, or a permanent home or any of the accoutrements one expects to find in a temple.

Though organized as a synagogue, Congregation Etz Chaim drew lesbian and gay Jews who were not religious but who had strong ethnic and cultural links to the people Israel. Some came to Etz Chaim for the services; others came for the social events—Etz Chaim's annual drag shows, featuring the "Fabulous Yentettes," were already notorious; and virtually everyone looked to Etz Chaim as a place where those who are "twice blessed" could be out of their double closets, free to be gay and Jewish in a world that was often anti-Semitic and mostly homophobic.

Though I had been to synagogues before, this was the first time I attended a "gay" synagogue. I remember being greeted at the door by David, a lovable old bear who took me by the hand and introduced me to everyone there. A stranger in a strange land, I was fortunate already to know some of the people there, including Steve and Jay, one of the synagogue's founders and then its president. Someone put a prayer book in my hand and a yarmulke on my head and I sat down, looking at the incomprehensible Hebrew script in front of me (fortunately for me, the prayers were also transliterated into English script). I sat (and stood) through the services, led by Jay, Steve, and Howie (another founder), following the time-honored prayers of the Sabbath liturgy. Services were followed by the *Oneg Shabbat*, literally "joy of the Sabbath," and actually an after-service social with plenty of food, coffee, and shmoozing (conversation). For many congregants, an Etz Chaim *oneg* was the social highlight of the week.

All the roads that I traveled in my life, whether they be sexual, social, religious, or communal, came together that night. Though I could not explain it to myself, I knew that this was where I belonged. Etz Chaim was different from other synagogues, not only because it was gay but because its friendly and informal nature encouraged participation from the congregation. It was clear that the members of Etz Chaim, joined by shared ethnic, religious, and sexual identities, cared for each other and looked to each other for support, assistance, and camaraderie. Here was the family I was looking for and the community I never had!

I was not the first gentile to be active in Congregation Etz Chaim, nor was I to be the last. But I wanted to do more than sit on the sidelines, as a clever *shaygetz* (gentile partner) in a nominally interfaith partnership. Howie, a devout man who was a member of both Etz Chaim and Miami's largest Conservative synagogue, noted my interest almost before I did. He came up to me one night and asked me if I was interested in pursuing a conversion. Without a thought, I said yes.

Judaism does not proselytize. Christian and Muslim leaders forbade their coreligionists from converting to Judaism under pain of death. Traditional Judaism discouraged conversion, though it might have accepted the conversion of a non-Jewish partner as an alternative to an interfaith marriage. Because it is a faith so intimately tied to ethnicity, conversion to Judaism is problematic to many people, both Jew and gentile. I could never become a Jew, they would say, no more than I could become a Black or an Eskimo. Not being the son of a Jewish mother, I had no automatic membership in the covenant of Abraham. Nor could I claim to be a part of the Jewish "race." How could I, who did not have the bloodline, the parentage, and the education of a born Jew, claim to be part of the people Israel?

I did not let those qualms stop me, any more than I let my Cuban birth keep me from becoming an American. Though I was not a native son, I begged to be adopted by the family of Israel. I knew that Judaism brought with it commitments and obligations as well as pleasures and blessings, that the Jews are disliked by many, that the time would come where I would have to prove myself, that my Jewish identity would always be in doubt. But I proceeded.

It was not easy. Some Reform rabbis perform "quicky" conversions that are convenient for the convert but are not recognized by the vast majority of Jews. An Orthodox conversion would have been ideal, for it would be one recognized by all branches of Judaism. However, the issue of my sexuality impeded such a move. Instead, Howie referred me to the rabbi of his Conservative congregation, a learned and affable man who was not fazed by my gayness (though we would later part company over his opposition to Dade County's gay rights law). The rabbi had done his share of conversions, so he was able to tell a sincere commitment from a convenient sham. Once he was satisfied as to the sincerity of my quest, the rabbi put me through a rigorous course of study in Jewish doctrine, history, rituals, and law.

Today the Reform movement conducts regular "Introduction to Judaism" classes for would-be converts. This was a service that the Conservative movement did not provide in 1976. Though Steve and my Etz Chaim friends helped, I was basically on my own. The conversion process took six months of hard work, from May to November 1976, a time in which I was also occupied with my secular studies at Florida International University. By the end of that period, the rabbi decided that I was ready to convert.

Of course I had to be circumcised. As the living symbol of God's covenant with His Chosen People, it was a ritual that no male convert could do without. (In the case of an already circumcised male, a symbolic pinprick to the penis is performed.) In Judaism, ritual circumcision, the *brit millah*, occurs when the boy is eight days old. But I was a twenty-three-year-old man, with an adult male's normal-sized penis. How would a *mohel*, used to clipping eight-day-old babies, deal with me? The solution, as it was, was worthy of King Solomon. I was checked into a Jewish hospital, where the *mohel* made the first cut and said the blessings while a Jewish surgeon finished the job. Needless to say, I was knocked out through the entire ordeal, though I (ouch!) felt the effects of the *brit* for several weeks after. I was even able to get my health insurance to cover most of my "surgical" circumcision, for reasons of health, of course.

Having been circumcised, I was instructed to pick a Hebrew name. I chose Yeshuah ben Abraham, the Hebrew translation of my birth name plus "son of Abraham," the surname that is traditionally given to converts who don't have a Jewish father. Since then I have added "ben Sarah" to my name, in honor of our first matriarch. I also appeared before a *bet din*, a rabbinical court that examined me, asked questions, and formally granted my conversion. Last, but not least on my agenda, was a dip in the *mikveh*, a ritual bath that is taken by Orthodox Jewish women after menstruation or childbirth and by everyone upon conversion. The temple's *mikveh* was closed for repairs, so I had to take my ritual bath al fresco at what turned out to be the local gay beach. Though it was not the first or last time I skinny-dipped in Virginia Key, it was the only time I did so in full view of two of our most revered rabbis and cantors. Fortunately for the course of my conversion, there were no police officers or former tricks around to witness my ritual bath.

Now formally a Jew, I (Yeshuah ben Abraham) proceeded to arrange my life accordingly. I became more active in Etz Chaim's congregational life. Having achieved at Etz Chaim first with my conversion, I went on to become this synagogue's first *bar mitzvah* (1979). I also served on the synagogue's board, on and off, for the past fifteen years, most notably as president from 1989 to 1991. Though my political, social, and literary interests have taken me elsewhere, Congregation Etz Chaim continues to be my second home, and the Jewish family that I never had. It was there that I met my lover, Michael, a teacher, musician and lovable bear of a man who combines all the qualities that have attracted me to Jewish men for so many years.

All in all, and in spite of lingering doubts (in myself and others), my search for family and community has been a successful one. But it is not the end of the story. To choose Judaism is to devote a lifetime to becoming a Jew, a process that is never complete. Each day I learn something new about my adopted people and the Jewish community, gay and nongay, which is now part of my life. Nor have I ignored other aspects of my life. I even reconciled myself to my ethnic and cultural background, even as I realized that I will never be the nice Cuban boy my parents wanted me to be. And though I shall never have Jewish children in a physical sense, I trust that through my work and my example I shall be able to touch a new generation of lesbian and gay youth, Jewish or otherwise. Nothing would please me more than the knowledge that I will leave this world a little better than it was when I got here. That is what family and community are all about.

arnie kantrowitz

family album

The best photograph of the three of us—Jim and Vito and me—was taken on a weekend cruise ship in 1986. All of us are wearing glasses. Vito is on the left, in a white jacket with a pink-striped knit black tie, hands nonchalantly parked in his pockets, flashing his toothy grin below a full moustache. I'm in the middle, my beard surrounding a quietly contented lips-together smile. I'm several inches shorter than the other two, wearing a beige tie that's invisible against the beige shirt I cleverly chose to wear under a beige jacket, as if I were trying to disappear. Jim is on the right, his pale clean-shaven face with its hard-to-read expression set off by the dark shirt and jacket he's wearing with a startlingly white tie. His left hand, like mine, is hanging straight down. His right hand is around my shoulder.

The three of us, along with my lover, Larry, had joined a gigantic boatload of homosexuals sailing south of the equator to see the long-awaited return of Halley's Comet, which turned out to be a faint, pinky tip–sized smudge between two dim stars just over the first mate's shoulder, and binoculars didn't help. All three of us kept a framed copy of the photograph in our apartments. It wasn't that we loved the trip, although we did have some fun changing clothes every twenty minutes and getting seasick. It was just that it was the best picture the three of us had ever taken. It was our favorite family photo.

Vito Russo, Jim Owles, and I met early in 1970 in GAA (the Gay Activists Alliance), which was the largest militant gay liberation organization in the United States. It was a kind of extended family. Over two decades later, its members still feel bonded to one another. Jim was the president and served as a young father figure to the hundreds of energetic activists who attended our weekly meetings. I soon became vice president, showering the membership with my maternal affection; and Vito, the eternal youth, chaired the Entertainment Committee, which he invented so he could show us movies. It was impossible to say no to Vito, so there wasn't any point in discussing it, but as it turned out, his movie festivals were an important part of our liberation. He taught us to be angry at the false ways in which we were depicted, and that rage helped to energize our attacks on our oppressors and cement our community together.

There is an eight-by-ten photograph shot in the grainy black and white in which history used to be recorded. It shows one of the crowded meetings in GAA's Firehouse. The three of us are strategically sprinkled among our many friends and cohorts, reveling in the labyrinthine gay politics of the day. But I prefer individual snapshots of that era: Jim, young and slim, hurling himself against a line of dark-coated policemen in front of New York's City Hall in one of GAA's first demonstrations; Vito, his eyes ablaze with rage, arm extended with pointed finger, screaming his guts out at the City Council members who voted against our civil rights bill; I, head down with my long hair flying, pursued by a mounted policeman, his massive horse hot on my heels, just before I got arrested at another demonstration in front of City Hall.

A few years after our daily involvement with GAA had subsided, the three of us found ourselves embroiled in the movement again when we volunteered to work on the Christopher Street Liberation Day Committee that was responsible for arranging the annual Gay Pride March. It was to keep it a political march rather than allow it to degenerate into a celebratory parade that we decided to work on it ourselves, but our work, which was emotionally exhausting, ended up as a series of heated discussions with a committee full of colorful eccentrics about what was the best design for the 1976 official lapel button and whether we should capitalize the word "gay" in our official correspondence. We gladly relinquished our positions at the end of the season, and eventually the annual march did turn into a parade, with floats and bands and glitter, but who has the heart to be angry at such fun?

We had been soldiers together in the great war, and that would bind us together for life, yet aside from that we had grown to love one another unconditionally. The main thing, aside from how much we enjoyed each other's company, is that we knew how to look out for each other. When Jim got beaten up at a demonstration, Vito rushed down to help me put salve in his grotesquely swollen black eye (which made a powerful photo in the *Daily News*). When I had my gall bladder out, Jim came to the hospital every day. (Vito had a little trouble with hospitals back then.) When Jim's glasses were broken, I knew his type so well that I cruised for him as we walked down Christopher Street. If Vito had no money, I brought him bags of food. If he had an extra ticket to a critics' film screening, he took me along, and when one of us had a vacation place, he invited the other two.

Like many people who love each other, we developed our own pet names. At some point Vito started calling me *"Cher Arnaud,"* perhaps an affectation picked up on one of his many trips as a lecturer on film. For short, he called me *"Cher,"* and some of his letters began, *"Cher Cher."* How could I ever match "Dear Dear?" I wondered, but remembering that Cher's early partner was Sonny Bono, I simply changed the spelling to reflect V's bright personality and began my letters, "Dear Sunny." Vito and I were the only two people that the more formal Jim allowed to call him "Jimmy," and although he always called Vito by his full name, never "V," he and I had a special pet name for each other. It began when we started imitating a generic suburban couple named Harry and Midge, but in spite of our decidedly unfeminine manners, each of us always seemed to be Midge, whining at her husband: "Harry, I told you to bring the umbrella, but you knew better than the weatherman, didn't you?" Eventually, the game ended, but we kept on calling each other "Harry" in normal conversations, and laughed when everyone except Vito was confused.

While we were all single, we went out dancing every Saturday night and afterward we went out to play separately, but we met for brunch religiously on Sunday afternoons, after which we would watch movies—or tapes of Judy Garland, if Vito could talk Jim into it—and we would play our favorite board game, Risk, the object of which was to take over the world. We played without mercy, shouting and accusing and plotting against each other, and actually driving other people to tears if they had the temerity to join us. No one dared leave the table even to go to the bathroom because the other two would immediately begin plotting against him, not necessarily to win, just for the pleasure of making him worry. Then we would laugh because we knew each other's moves so well that we could anticipate each one yet still get excited and enjoy ourselves, the way that long-term couples can still get aroused by the same old sex.

We played other games like Uno, a seemingly simple game of matching colors and numbers to see who could get rid of the most cards first. But we arranged a "Killer Uno" double deck, and our main aim was to torture each other by arranging the penalties so that one of us would get stuck with a huge number of cards while the others laughed in triumph. In the game *Milles Bornes*, where the cards represented mileage in an automobile race, our pleasure came from putting obstacles like "out of gas" and "punctured tire" cards in each other's paths. We played poker, too, but even though the stakes were real nickels and dimes, we were in it for the conversation and the fun, not for the money. Our favorite trick was when two of us spotted the third one considering whether to raise the bet. We would urge him onward, hoping he would risk too much and lose, so we could laugh at his greed. To shouts of "Bet the ranch!" we would hold one arm out and make forward circles with the other hand, to indicate that we were reeling in the sucker. I'm sure these playful little customs don't make us sound very nice. The only thing I can say in our defense is that we were equal-opportunity demons. We were well matched, so none of us got stuck all of the time, and all of us got stuck some of the time.

We knew each other's weaknesses well, and although we never judged one another, we knew exactly how far we could go with our constructive sarcasm, and we always went exactly as far as we could without making our victim really angry. The conversation around the game table was pierced by well-aimed darts composed of indelicate reminders about our unfulfilled dreams, our lost loves, and our vices, whose details we all shared. "Kantrowitz will have to live three hundred years to read all the books he buys," Vito might observe; or Jim might casually let slip, "After Vito leaves them, they take the veil," referring to one of Vito's lovers who joined an Indian cult after Vito found someone to replace him; or I might remind Jim about the time he had been accused of stretching the truth when he was president of GAA and he had retorted, "Don't bother me with your Sunday school morality!" It was exhilarating. At least it kept all six of our eyebrows raised a good deal of the time. All of us could take it, and all of us could dish it out. If one of us was especially effective, all of us would purse our lips with an exaggerated smacking sound, and with both hands outstretched, palms down, we would strike our fingers against our thumbs to imitate a 1950s matron in rhinestoned harlequin sunglasses at a New Jersey swim club, snapping her pocketbook closed to emphasize the fact that she had had the last word.

When all of us needed to escape at the same time, we went together to three movies in a row, including a double feature if we could find one. All of us had a soft spot for old movies, so we used to haunt the rerun houses. Vito loved Judy Garland, Jim loved Greta Garbo, and I loved Bette Davis, so we all had to indulge each other; but all of us loved *Gone With the Wind*, and we saw it again and again, at first on the big screen and later on videotape. (I'm talking about sixty-four times for me alone by actual count!) Eventually we developed an entire language from lines in the movie by taking them out of context and applying them to incidents in our own lives. I'm not talking about the obvious ones like, "Frankly, my dear, I don't give a damn," or "As God is my witness I'll never go hungry again." Ours were the more esoteric lines. If Vito was calculating how to encounter someone he'd taken an interest in, Jim and I would quote Mammy warning Scarlett about visiting Atlanta: "Mr. Ashley'll be comin' home to Miss Melanie, and you'll be settin' there waitin' for him just like a spider!" Or if I started complaining about my aching bones, Vito and Jim would smack me right between the eyes with Prissy's advice during Melanie's childbirth: "Mama says if you put a knife under the bed, it cuts the pain in half." Jim was an inveterate nostalgia buff and invariably thought the past superior to the present. Whenever he started admiring turn-of-the-century Vienna or automobiles of the 1930s, Vito and I would chorus Scarlett's admonition to a forlorn Ashley amidst the squalor of post–Civil War Reconstruction: "Oh, Ashley, don't look back. It only tears at your heart till you can't do anything but look back."

There is a snapshot of the three of us on the way back from the movies. We are standing on Christopher Street, half a block from Sheridan Square, the heart of west Greenwich Village. Vito's smile is not obscured because he had no moustache that year. Hanging from his shoulder is the worn fringed suede shoulderbag he carried wherever he went. Jim's long bangs are swept to the side across his forehead just above his eyebrows. And I have my head shaved and am wearing round red glasses

with a moustache that droops an inch below my chin and points toward the em-
broidered, rhinestone-studded dungarees that express my liberated spirit. I am in the
middle in that picture, too.

I always wondered whether we so often arranged ourselves that way for aesthetic balance, or because somehow I was the force that held the other two together. But that's a touch of arrogance on my part. Just as I had a relationship with each of them, they had a relationship with each other. In fact, they had sex with each other a couple of times when they first met. That's the way things were back in the seventies. We said hello with our dicks. First we went to bed with whoever turned us on, and later we exchanged names. Casual tricks often turned into lifelong friends. In my case, I never had sex with either one of them. We discussed it, but we agreed it would have seemed incestuous. We had met each other and become "sisters" first. Or maybe it was simpler than that. Maybe we just weren't each other's type, except for our souls.

The thing I loved most about our family was that we could always tell each other the truth. We were always supportive of each other's efforts, but we never let one another get away with fooling ourselves for long, at least not in matters of the heart. Sometimes we had lovers, sometimes not. When we did, they never came between us—except for one noteworthy incident when I didn't talk to Jim for three months because I was jealous—oh, and another minor scuffle when I asked Vito not to hold hands with his lover in front of me because it made me feel lonely. They were a little more relaxed about the subject than I was. Vito had serious relationships with at least five men while we were friends, and Jim slept with three of them. I didn't even consider sharing my lovers. I did participate in ending some of V's affairs, however. He had trouble saying good-bye to people, so I had to be the one to tell a couple of his boyfriends that their relationships were over. Jim thought the whole practice was shocking, and I was more than a little relieved to resign from the job of hatchetman. I had four relationships of my own during that time, and Jim had one or two also, but he preferred to save his semen for everybody else in town—not that Vito and I were saints of monogamy. We all had so many notches in our bedposts that they looked like totem poles.

Our various love affairs never complicated our relationship with each other, however. We simply included our lovers in our family, sort of like brothers-in-law. Most of them came and went, but we stayed. We used to imagine what we'd be like decades later when we were sitting in our three rockers on the front porch of the gay old-age home, boring each other to tears with our stories of the good old days back in GAA. We had already started yelling at each other for telling the same stories too many times when we realized we were only in our thirties.

We belonged to one another in a way that we had never belonged at home. I was sure, when I was a child, that I had been born into the wrong family, as if my mother were a cuckoo who had put her egg into some other bird's nest. It was true that some of my relatives looked like me, and I did have one sensitive uncle, but no one in my immediate family thought like me. None of them read books, none of them believed the movies were more real than life, and no one but me really seemed to care what color the slipcovers were. I was always in search of a family to belong to. As a boy, I adopted my friend Gerry Beatty's parents because even if they didn't care too much about their slipcovers either, they had books in their house, and they held conversations with actual content. I learned a lot of my view of the world at Gerry's father's knee, including a sense of social responsibility that in later years turned me into a gay activist.

When I finally started coming out (which took nearly thirty years since nobody I knew had the blueprints for growing up gay), I got a lot of different reactions, most of them positive. I had met both Gerry and Don Kalfus in the first grade, and we had stayed friends through high school and college. Many nights, after dropping off the girls we were dating, we would sit for an hour or two in a double-parked car and talk about our hopes and fears—their dreams of the girls they wanted, and my fear that I would never get married. I was the best man at Gerry's wedding and an usher at Don's. As far as I could see, they didn't even get flustered when I came out to them. Maybe it was because they are basically such decent people, or simply because they loved me unconditionally—or maybe it was because they had already figured out my story, but we just went on being friends, and they let me know I would always be welcome in their homes.

Gerry's parents said they weren't thrilled about my sexual orientation, but they certainly didn't love me any the less because of it. If anything, I imagine they were disappointed that I wasn't going to marry Gerry's sister and become their son-in-law. Years later, Gerry opened the eulogy at his father's funeral by saying, "Few of you know that my father had *two* sons, myself and my friend Arnie . . ." After the funeral, I called my own father and said, "Dad, I'm only a few blocks from your house," and he said, "Have a good trip back to the city." My mother's enlightened reaction to my announcement was to sprinkle salt on my head to protect me from the "evil eye."

The only ones who gave me a really hard time about coming out were the people I had least expected it from: my aunts and uncles. I had thought my place in their ranks was secure because it was my birthright, but some of my relatives saw me on national television saying I was glad to be a homosexual and developed a consternation that lasted for twenty years. It began with nothing too serious. They simply declared me dead. They soon relented, but I was still exiled from the family's one annual gathering, the Passover seder, and I had to find other places to go. That was when I realized that water was thicker than blood.

I was living in a gay commune at the time of the Passover debacle. A group of us who had met in GAA had sublet a very old house in Manhattan's SoHo district. It had a garden and half a dozen fireplaces and six or so tenants at any given moment. We left the cleaning of each bedroom up to its resident, and since there was no actual living room, the kitchen was our common space. We took turns shopping and cooking for the group and cleaning up after ourselves once a week. It was there that I made a Passover seder of my own for the only time. I experimented with the traditional dishes I loved, like the carrot and prune mixture called *tsimmis*, served alongside chicken fat slathered onto tasteless matzoh crackers with half a raw onion, and everyone, whatever his ethnic background, was very encouraging to the only Jew at the seder.

The commune had some of the elements of a family. The older, wiser members counseled the younger members. We gave lovely parties that went on for days and attracted fun-loving strangers whom we had to kick out of our beds if we wanted to sleep. Eventually, during a sabbatical year away from my job at the college, I realized that I had become so immersed in our gay household that I hadn't spoken to a straight person for months, so I made a concentrated effort to reach out to my other families.

Some contact happened naturally when my mother died suddenly, and Vito drove three of my housemates and me to southern New Jersey for the funeral. My brother and I fell into each other's arms to weep, at last beginning the process of getting closer. I lived in a different world from my relatives, and many of them didn't recognize me because they hadn't seen me in so many years. Having my gay friends at the funeral helped me to get through it, but they left when it was over, and I found myself alone with the strangers I was related to. After three days, when I was ready to leave, Jim came down on a bus to bring me back to reality.

Jim was part of the commune for a while. He moved to the top floor, which he shared with me, and because I was so close to him, I grew less involved with the rest of the household. Vito was our real family, not the commune. There was never any question of that. When Jim and I felt we'd had our fill of gay liberation meetings and New York hassles, we decided to set out across the country to look for a place to open a little book store with a coffee shop in it. Vito bravely threw us a farewell party and spent the whole evening crying in the bathroom. Then he promised to meet us at the train station to say good-bye, but of course he never showed up. We stayed with Jim's relatives in Chicago, and we stayed with gay activists in Minneapolis and Madison and Vancouver and Seattle and San Francisco. We stayed in hotels in Billings, Montana, and Portland, Oregon. We walked the streets and cruised the bars and ate in the restaurants, and when we were finished, we decided to go home. Jim stopped to revisit someone he had met in Minneapolis, but I headed straight for New York. (I had secretly kept a subway token in a locket I wore around my neck during the whole trip. I guess I wasn't ready to give up on the big city yet.) Jim showed up a couple of months later, explaining that winter in Minneapolis was very cold.

Vito kept a little distance from us at first. It was hard for him to trust us after we had abandoned him. But it wasn't long before we were as close as ever. We developed our own annual traditions: the June gay pride march, summer trips to Fire Island, the August concert with fireworks in Central Park, an October ride to see the autumn foliage. The three of us preferred to be together on holidays, so it didn't matter what our various families thought. We had to have our veal shank at the Cafe Vienna for Christmas and an extravagant Thanksgiving at Vito's place.

A photograph of Thanksgiving at Vito's includes the three of us, all beaming. We are surrounded by Vito's lover of the time, Bruce Parker; Baby Jane Dexter, a larger-than-life cabaret singer, wearing the outsized earrings that are her signature; Arthur Bell, the sharp-tongued Village Voice *gossip columnist, who died a decade back; Adam Reilly, one of Vito's friends from the world of film studies, who died several years ago; and an assortment of several gay waifs who had nowhere else to go for the holiday. All of us are gathered around the table set up in Vito's crowded living room. One of Vito's gourmet feasts is spread before us: water chestnuts wrapped in bacon strips, cream of broccoli soup, the traditional turkey brimming over with succulent stuffing, sweet potatoes with tiny marshmallows and tangerine wedges (and white potatoes whipped with cheese, especially for Jim), beans with blanched almond slivers, fresh apple cider, homemade pumpkin pie and mince pie and a chocolate soufflé. Everyone obviously feels at home.*

Norman Rockwell wouldn't have known how to paint our Thanksgiving dinners. We didn't look like the ideal American family of red-cheeked grandparents and happy tots with similar features. Vito was Italian and came from a large, close family that loved to squabble. I was a Jew: My parents had divorced when I was fifteen, and I had had little reason to see my relatives since my mother's funeral on one side of the family and the Passover battle on the other side had severed our connections. Jim was German-English: His father had abandoned the family when Jim was a baby, and he never truly got over it. We weren't too good at total accord, ourselves. Our annual dinner always included a discussion that went something like this:

"Isn't this turkey delicious? It's so moist and tender," I'd begin.

"Not like that goose you ruined three years ago," Vito would respond. "It tasted like a football."

"*I* ruined the goose?" I'd say. "I'm not the one who roasted it for twelve hours. You're supposed to be the cook here."

"I'm the one who had to eat the miserable thing," Jim would add.

"Then *you* cook," Vito would say.

"Not my job," Jim would protest.

"Oh, Mr. Macho can't get his hands greasy," I'd observe.

"The apple-chestnut dressing is delicious this year," Jim would reply in an effort to change the subject.

"Oh, *I* did that," Vito and I would chorus at once.

It never really mattered who was right. Good-natured bickering was our tradition, and we loved it. Vito's parties were worth the trouble. Jim and I never stopped grumbling about the time he got us to decorate a large green Styrofoam cone with olives and mushrooms and radishes and cheese squares and rolled-up pieces of ham and salami and roast beef all painstakingly speared on toothpicks until the whole thing became a Christmas tree of hors d'oeuvres. I told Vito it was one step away from the chopped-liver swan I'd seen at a bar mitzvah, and Jim refused to eat from it, but Vito thought it was very nice. Then he made us decorate the real tree, ignoring my protestations that I should be exempt because I was Jewish.

It was at a party at Vito's house in January 1982 that I met a handsome doctor named Larry Mass for the second time. He reminded me that we had met at the baths the summer before, but someone distracted me with an effusive greeting, and when I turned back to find Larry, he was lost in the crowd. It wasn't until the following summer that I met him again at the baths, and that time I didn't let him get away. We began a daily relationship that has so far lasted eleven years. The first time Vito and Jim came over to our place for dinner, I was nervous, but I didn't need to be because Larry is a good cook. Soon we were all spending as much time at our place as we were at Vito's (Jim's place was too small for entertaining), and we followed our dinners with card games and the inevitable game of Risk. Larry became my home, but Jim and Vito were still my family.

It wasn't only our love affair that made Larry and me stop going to the baths. The whispers of an epidemic were growing into a dull roar, and Larry told me that our lives would be changed forever. The first physician to write about AIDS outside of the medical press, he was one of the original founders of Gay Men's Health Crisis (GMHC), whose volunteers filled out insurance forms and scrubbed floors and established support groups for the sick; so I was sure he knew what he was talking about, and we settled down.

Jim's great love affair had taken place in the early seventies with a lawyer named Lenny Bloom. He'd had a lot of offers since then, but never one he wanted to settle for, so he continued to play the field, and I was concerned for his health.

"Don't worry," he assured me. "I don't do anything that's unsafe. Besides, I think this epidemic has been blown out of proportion by the media. It's not like *everybody*'s going to die."

"Jim," I said soberly. "Our whole world is going to crash around our ears. There's no way to blow that out of proportion."

He looked pretty glum at my announcement, but it was clear he didn't want to discuss the subject any further.

For a while, Vito continued his late-night excursions to The Glory Hole, an anonymous promiscuity palace, and I was concerned for his safety. However, not long afterward, he began an affair with Jeff Sevcik, a willowy blond poet he'd met in San Francisco, and I heaved a sigh of relief. Jeff moved into Vito's New York apartment, but they had difficulty sharing the cramped space, and he eventually moved back to California while Vito, Jim, and I returned to our political activism.

There are photographs of us at a demonstration in front of the offices of The New York Post. *In one I am with Jim, holding up a sign that says "Support the Gay Rights Bill." When it was used to advertise a film called* Rights and Reactions, *I felt like a poster boy. In another, I'm standing next to Vito with my sign held so high that all you can see is the top of my leather newsboy cap. We decided that the* Post *was a rag because of the way its editorials fulminated against us, so we got everyone to bring rags, and we deposited a huge pile of them on the newspaper's doorstep.*

The public panic about AIDS was growing. Parents were keeping their children home from school for fear of an unnamed pupil with AIDS; bars and bathhouses were being closed by the city; and the press was full of horror stories and ugly political cartoons that demonized gay men as unclean disease bearers. Vito asked me and Jim to come to a meeting to discuss what we could do to respond to the climate of fear that was being created, and although all of us had had our fill of meetings and organizations, we joined five other people at what became the founding meeting of GLAAD (the Gay and Lesbian Alliance Against Defamation) and spent the next year in a whirlwind of crisis phone calls, street leafleting, subcommittee organizing, mass gatherings, angry demonstrations, and an endless succession of executive committee meetings. I'm proud to say that GLAAD has grown into a nationwide organization that is still monitoring the press for homophobia and educating the public about who gay and lesbian people really are. But after a year of such exhausting work, all of us needed to return to our personal lives.

One spring day Vito called me and said, crying, "Jeff's got Pneumocystis." I dropped everything and rushed to his house, where he was already packing. He closed his apartment and moved to San Francisco to nurse Jeffrey through his AIDS. Jim and I flew to California to visit and offer what help we could, but then our whole world came crashing down. Vito was diagnosed with AIDS himself.

Knowing how emotional his family was, despite the fact that he was becoming a nationally known AIDS activist, Vito didn't tell his parents he had AIDS for two years. Even when they came to the memorial for Jeff at Vito's apartment, the subject of Vito's health was not to be mentioned. I had discussed it with my own family, however, and that turned out to be an unwise decision. At the end of that year, my father died after a long illness. As soon as I heard, I rushed down to my brother's house and once again was plunged into an alien world.

When the rabbi came to ask about our family so he'd have something to say, he asked if we were married. "I am," my brother responded, and he spelled out his wife's name.

"And you?" the rabbi inquired of me.

"I consider myself married, but I'm not sure you'll approve," I said. "My lover's name is Larry."

"That doesn't bother me," he assured me.

"Fine, then when you mention my brother and his wife, you can mention Arnold and his partner Lawrence." Rabbis, I knew, love formality. He agreed.

I called Larry and told him we would be welcome as the couple that we were in front of the whole family.

Before I returned home, my brother cautioned me, "Please don't ask your friend Vito to come. I don't want him in my house."

"But why?" I asked, truly mystified.

"Because he has AIDS."

"But you can't catch AIDS from casual contact," I protested.

"They're not sure. I don't want to take any chances."

I decided not to ask Jim to come either because there was no point in making him travel a long way just to feel uncomfortable, so I expected Larry to be my only support since all the other guests were my brother's friends and our relatives, who somehow belonged more to him than to me. I was pleased when Larry's mother came to the service, and surprised when my childhood friends Gerry Beatty and Don Kalfus showed up as well. I had been to their fathers' funerals years before, but I didn't even realize they knew my father had died.

"Why don't you ask them to come back to the house?" my brother offered.

"You mean my straight friends are welcome, but my gay friends aren't?"

"It's just the AIDS," he said.

"What if *I* had AIDS?" I countered. "Would I be unwelcome in your house?"

As the funeral proceeded, the rabbi mentioned only my father's brothers and sons. There was nothing about wives or lovers. I was invisible. As soon as the first evening's prayers were over, I went home to where my real family could comfort me. I didn't tell Vito about why he wasn't welcome until several years had passed.

There is a photo of the three of us at a restaurant in Washington, D.C. We are laughing, but you can see the seriousness in our eyes. We are there for the second national gay pride march as we had been for the first. And in a similar photo taken the following year, we are there to view the AIDS quilt, which is a painful reminder of the deaths we have already experienced and the deaths that are yet to come.

The summer after my father died, Larry and I rented a house on Fire Island for three months. It was a bigger house than we needed, but we wanted to invite Vito as our guest for the summer. Jim had suddenly lost his roommate to AIDS, so of course he came out to visit, and so did Craig Rowland, a member of Vito's support group at GMHC; but in spite of the company, Vito spent most of the time sitting quietly on the couch, depressed. Our one activity was playing cards in a nearby house that had been rented by three of our friends, all of whom had been diagnosed with AIDS, and all of whom are now dead.

To celebrate my birthday that year, Larry and Jim and Vito took me out to dinner. They arranged to have the waiters bring out a cake with a candle and sing "Happy Birthday," but evidently no one had told them what my name was. To make matters worse, my little family was leaving all the singing up to the waiters, so the song went: "Happy birthday to you, happy birthday to you. Happy birthday, dear . . . Ee-Ee, happy birthday to you!" For the next three years whenever they wanted to get a rise out of me, they would call me "Ee-Ee." I can't say I was especially gracious about it, but at least I continued to take them out to dinner on their birthdays —minus the singing.

There is a photo of Vito's forty-third birthday party at his parents' house in New Jersey. I am giving him a lot of presents, and he is marveling at my taste in gift wrap. He's looking happy but haggard. Jim is looking concerned.

It was a nice party. Half a dozen of Vito's friends drove in from New York, his brother Charles joined us with his wife and their three grown children, and there was much food and merriment until Baby Jane sang Vito's favorite song for him, and the tears in her eyes reminded us that it could well be his final birthday. At times like that we trotted out the black humor game that we used to survive such situations. We called it "The

Man with No Feet" after the proverb about the man who complained he had no shoes until he met a man without feet.

"I'm getting a headache," I'd begin.

"What should I say?" he'd respond. "I have Kaposi's sarcoma in my bone marrow."

"But I feel some nausea, too."

"I have AIDS, and I'm going to die," he'd say triumphantly.

"But I'm going to lose my best friend," I'd say, and I'd hold up my hands and imitate the closing of a purse to indicate I'd had the last word, while everyone else present looked on, appalled at our bad taste until we laughed out loud at our own irreverence.

He did have one more birthday, but the celebration was subdued. During his last summer, Vito was quite ill and was hospitalized twice. I was able to stay with him in NYU Medical Center's Co-op Care unit the first time. He had pneumonia, and I had to pack him in ice and rub him down with alcohol when his fevers spiked to 105 degrees in the middle of the night. Jim came to visit only once. It was hard for him to contain his tears, and he didn't want to cry in front of Vito.

Between trips to the hospital, V was able to squeeze in a short visit to Fire Island. His brother Charles spent the first two days there, and then I came out to take over. The three of us had one evening together, and during it, Vito was exhibiting some of his meaner side. Like many AIDS patients, he had to express his rage because the life that was so precious to him was being stolen from him so early. He would become irritable and sarcastic and demanding, and I would do my best to put up with it because who else could he take it all out on besides me? "I suppose you'd rather be out at the movies than cooped up in here with me," he'd say, but I wouldn't answer.

"Try to eat something," I'd say.

"Don't you wish you could lose weight like me?" he'd gloat darkly.

And if all else failed, he'd attack me for wearing socks the same color as my shirt. "Nobody's done that since 1963," he'd say. "It's disgusting."

Charles and I took a walk to the beach, and he asked, as we sat down to talk, "How can you put up with him when he's like that?"

"I have to," I replied, "because I love him."

Vito did say endearing things as well. Once, when Larry and I were having a tiff, Vito murmured: "Be kind to Captain Butler. He loves you so."

Tears sprang to my eyes immediately as I recognized Melanie's death-bed advice to Scarlett in *Gone With the Wind*. "Stop dying," I said. That was when he officially changed my nickname from "Cher" to "The Good One." He even wrote it on the score pad when we played gin rummy.

Late that summer, Larry and Jim and I took Vito on a tour of New England. We stayed in Vermont and Maine, and on the way back we stopped in Boston to visit Craig Rowland, the only other surviving member of Vito's AIDS support group. They joked blackly about the time when they "used to be alive," and the company of a peer seemed to cheer Vito up. As close as we in our little family were, Vito's new identity as a person with AIDS had created a distance between us that couldn't be bridged by love alone. He needed not only our support, but the support of people who were facing the same thing he was. Once that support was gone, it was difficult to go on alone. Craig committed suicide a couple of months after Vito's death.

We made our last trip to see the autumn leaves together that year. Larry took a photo of Vito and Jim and me standing near the Hudson River in an upstate town called Cold Spring. None of us looks happy. We all know why the picture is being taken. Larry says we look like the autumn leaves of gay liberation.

As Vito grew sicker, I enlisted the help of his many friends and arranged a schedule so that he never had to be alone. Some of the people who loved him the most, however, had difficulty seeing him. His mother came several times, but mostly she confined herself to phone calls to tell him of her love and to tell me of her pain. We still talk regularly. Jim came so rarely that Vito remarked on his absence. I took him to lunch to ask what was wrong, and he made up a flimsy excuse about being angry over something V had said years before. I didn't press him, knowing that his strength was only a brittle shell. He did visit occasionally, and several times he did some errands; once or twice I even got him to stay with Vito for a few hours. When Vito was close to the end, however, Jim became a second line of support, taking me out to dinner and watching compassionately as my tears dripped into my food.

During Vito's final days, I was reading his last movie review in The Advocate. *I looked at the accompanying photo of a smiling, healthy Vito, and I looked at his emaciated form in the bed, and I rushed from the room.*

Vito's will expressed his family priorities. Aside from a few specific bequests to friends and the disposal of any remaining cash to charity after his expenses were settled, it read:

> I direct that all my home furnishings including all the contents of my apartment . . . are to be distributed and or disposed of at the discretion of and pursuant to the wishes of Arnold Kantrowitz, Lawrence Mass, and James Owles. . . . Said Arnie, Larry, and Jim may keep for themselves any and all of my home furnishings. To the extent there remain items they do not wish to keep they should distribute such remainder as they see fit being mindful that my parents Angelo and Angelina Russo and my brother Charles Russo should be extended the courtesy of reasonable requests which may have purely sentimental value.

He included his instructions for a memorial, which said:

> It is my expressed wish that such a party not be permitted to provide a forum for my relatives to grieve. My friends are instructed to terrorize my relatives at this occasion by refusing to discuss anything but motion pictures and gay rights.

Later, Vito's brother expressed the pain that Vito's priorities caused him: "You don't know what it's like to lose a brother after forty years."

"He named me next of kin," I said quietly.

Half of Vito's ashes were mixed with what remained of Jeffrey's ashes and strewn in a park in San Francisco. The following September, on a quiet weekday afternoon in late summer, according to his instructions, a few of us traveled to Fire Island to strew the rest of his ashes. Larry made a triangle of lavender "sterling silver" roses to cast into the water. I read a short remembrance. There were still tears. Jim was there. Vito's brother and two cousins came. The rest of the mourners were friends.

It took me a little more than a year to get past the initial loss. My respite turned out to be brief, however. Five months later, Larry sat me down on the couch, and with tears in his eyes for the pain he knew I would suffer, he told me that Jim had suddenly become clinically paranoid. Jim's rage was deep and powerful. He imagined he was being watched and listened to and followed. He told Larry that he'd known he was HIV-positive for years, but he'd kept it hidden because he couldn't tell Vito while he was dying and he couldn't tell me while I was looking after Vito. In the psychiatric unit where he was placed for observation, he imagined that his roommate was actually his long-lost father, released from years of imprisonment. The doctors determined that he had been drinking alcohol and smoking grass heavily enough to have blackouts and that his reclusive behavior was the "isolating" typical of substance abusers, so I understood at last why he'd seen so little of Vito during his illness. Although he regained his sanity within a week, he began to cough and have spiking fevers, and then began the horrible déjà vu, as I escorted him through test after test that Vito had been through, only to arrive at the same conclusion: Pneumocystis, which meant that Jim, too, had full-blown AIDS.

I went to see him every day for seven weeks until he was better. Old friends from GAA appeared, too, loyal to the extended family we had once been. Jim had some good months, but then the whole thing happened all over again: the dementia, the rage, the pneumonia, and finally the release. He didn't lose his sense of humor, however. Discussing a story in the newspaper about organ transplants, I mused, "I wonder how I'd feel with someone else's organ inside me."

"You ought to know," Jim replied. "You've had enough of them."

"You wouldn't talk to me that way if Vito were here," I said.

"No, I wouldn't," he answered. "It would be worse!"

Larry was able to take us to the Berkshire Mountains for a vacation, where he treated Jim to a hot-air balloon ride, something Jim had long dreamed of doing. He looked depressed throughout the experience, yet when he returned, he started telling everyone it was one of the highlights of his life. But his AIDS kept progressing. On Gay Pride Day, 1993, Larry and I found him in his apartment, feverish, his face enveloped in an angry red rash and scaly white patches, too weak to get to the bathroom. For the third time, I put him in the hospital, where he was diagnosed with toxoplasmosis.

I tried to encourage him to savor every remaining moment of his life by repeating a story that Vito had told me about a man who was hanging onto a cliff with jagged rocks below and a tiger in pursuit above when he saw some wild strawberries growing out of the cliffside. "So he grabbed them, and he ate them," Vito used to say, ". . . and you know what? They were delicious."

After five short weeks, Jim slipped into a coma and died. I was his primary beneficiary as I had been Vito's, and I presided at a memorial service for him as I had for Vito. Afterward, four of his closest friends and I scattered his ashes into a waterfall in Pennsylvania. Each of us tossed a lavender "sterling silver" rose into the rushing water, and we watched them catapult over the edge.

While cleaning Jim's apartment, I came across a picture of him. He's young and slim, and his hair is long. He's standing on the steps of New York's State House in Albany, addressing a crowd of enthusiastic gay activists. The sun is in his eyes. In the intervening years he gained a good deal of weight and became a portly man. Before he died, he became slim once again, and it broke my heart. What is left of my family? Nothing but old photographs?

My relatives and I have finally reconciled after all these years, and now Larry and I go to Passover seder at my uncle's house as a couple. The first time we appeared we ran into a slight snag when my aunt introduced the family to her friends: "This is my daughter Cathy and her husband Ken; this is my son Jeff and his wife; this is my other son Andy and his girlfriend; this is my niece Adrienne and her husband, Roger; this is my nephew Arnold; and this is Larry." I decided not to get angry but to educate, so I explained to her that it made us feel unreal to be introduced separately after more than ten years of working at our relationship. The next time, I think she'll refer to us as "life partners" or at least as "friends," if "lovers" isn't a comfortable term for her. I'm willing to go the extra mile to keep my family ties.

You may have heard that old saying, "You can't choose your family, but you can choose your friends." Maybe it's possible to do both. Now that my family of gay friends is disappearing, I find myself reaching into other areas of ymy life for love and support. First, of course, is Larry. We are a family of two. I'm still making new friends, but I notice they tend to be women, both heterosexual and lesbian, rather than gay men, who are in shorter supply. A few months ago my boyhood friend, Gerry Beatty, his sister, and our old friend Don Kalfus invited Larry and me to brunch at a lovely suburban restaurant. Over coffee, I spoke to them all about the landscape of AIDS. "It's like being a survivor of the Holocaust who's lost his entire family," I explained. Gerry's voice answered quietly, "We're your family."

In Jim's AIDS dementia, he spoke of opening a rerun movie theater to honor Vito's memory. It may not have been a practical idea, but it

certainly had heart. So did Vito's mother when she wrote to me upon hearing of Jim's illness:

> You feel so alone without them—you are not alone; they are
> with you always. They are beside you with that special love you
> all had for each other.

It's true, in a sense, that I'll never be alone. Although gay families come to
an end after one generation, that doesn't mean that they disappear. There's
an old movie called *Three Comrades*, the story of three friends and the woman
who marries one of them. By the end of the film two friends and the wife
are dead, and the surviving friend is seen walking with the ghostly figures
of his comrades on either side of him. I tried that image on as I was walking
down the street the other day, and it seemed to fit. I can't waste time asking
unanswerable questions like why I should be the one to survive. All I know
is that Vito and Jim will always be a part of me.

*I am standing on a small hill, staring bleakly into the future, but the sparkle
in my eyes is restored when Jim whispers into one ear and Vito into the other the
saccharine observation that ends* Gone With the Wind: *"After all, tomorrow is
another day." Then, delighted with their own impishness, both of them strike their
thumbs against their fingers and smack their lips to make the sound of a pocketbook
closing with absolute finality.*

contributors

a l a n   b e l l was born in Sacramento, California, in 1956. He is a graduate of UCLA, where he edited the gay and lesbian student newspaper *Ten Percent*. He had an essay included in *Sister and Brother: Lesbians and Gay Men Write About Their Lives Together*. He is currently working on a collection of short stories and a novel. He lives in Los Angeles.

p a u l   b o n i n - r o d r i g u e z, a former dancer, is the writer and performer of *Talk of the Town, The Bible Belt and Other Accessories*, and *Love in the Time of College*. Since 1992, these monologues have toured to major venues and earned him a national reputation as one of today's most insightful and innovative artists. Portions of *Talk of the Town* appear in *Men on Men 5*. Now living in San Antonio, Texas, he has worked as a writer/producer for the nationally syndicated Latino documentary series "Heritage," and as an instructor of English at Palo Alto College.

r a n d y   b o y d is a native of Indianapolis, Indiana. A 1985 graduate of UCLA, his fiction has appeared in *BLACKfire* magazine and the anthologies *Certain Voices, Flesh and the Word 2*, and *Sojourner: Black Gay Voices in* *the Age of AIDS*. His essays and nonfiction work have been featured in *Au Courant, The Washington Blade*, and *Frontiers*.

c h r i s t o p h e r   b r a m , a novelist from Virginia, has lived in New York City since 1978. He is the author of *Surprising Myself, Hold Tight, In Memory of Angel Clare*, and *Almost History*. He also writes screenplays, book and movie reviews, and was a contributor to *Hometowns*. His newest novel, *Father of Frankenstein*, published in April 1995 by Dutton, is based on the life of James Whale, the 1930s movie director.

m i c h a e l   b r o n s k i is the author of *Culture Clash: The Making of Gay Sensibility*. His articles on sexuality, culture, AIDS, and politics have appeared in *Gay Community News, Z Magazine, Fag Rag, The Boston Globe, The Advocate, The Village Voice*, and *Radical America*. His essays have appeared in more than a dozen anthologies including *Gay Spirit: Myth and Meaning, Taking Liberties: AIDS and Cultural Politics, Hometowns: Gay Men Write About Where They Belong*, and *Personal Dispatches: Writers Confront AIDS*. He has been involved in gay liberation for more than twenty-five years. "I'll Cry Tomorrow: Susan Hayward, Summer Nights, and the Scent of Memory" is dedicated to the memory of the poet Walta Borawski, his lover of nineteen years, who died in February 1994.

c h r i s t o p h e r   c.   c o r n o g is a partner and copywriter at an advertising and marketing firm in Concord, New Hampshire. He has contributed and edited articles for the New York City, San Francisco, and New England *Pride Guide*, and has worked with many regional nonprofits in the development of articles, promotional materials, and fund-raising programs. He lives in a cooperative household in Canterbury, New Hampshire.

l a r r y   d u p l e c h a n is the author of four critically acclaimed novels: *Eight Days a Week* (Alyson, 1985), *Blackbird* (St. Martin's Press, 1986), *Tangled Up in Blue* (St. Martin's Press, 1989), and *Captain Swing* (Alyson, 1993). Duplechan's work has appeared in *The Advocate, The New York Native*, and *Black American Literature Forum*, and in the anthologies *Black Men/White Men* (Gay Sunshine Press, 1983), *Revelations: A Collection of Gay Male Coming Out Stories* (Alyson, 1988), *Certain Voices: Short Stories About Gay Men* (Alyson, 1991), *Hometowns* (Dutton, 1991), *A Member of the Family* (Dutton, 1992), and *Calling the Wind: Twentieth-Century African-American Short Stories* (HarperCollins, 1993).

j o h n   g i l g u n is the author of *Everything That Has Been Shall Be Again, Music I Never Dreamed Of* (nominated for a Lambda Literary Award in 1990), *The Dooley Poems*, and *From the Inside Out*.

w i l l i a m   h a y w o o d   h e n d e r s o n was raised in Colorado. He has been a visiting fellow at Yaddo and is a former Wallace Stegner Fellow in Creative Writing at Stanford. He has taught creative writing at Brown, Harvard, and the University of Colorado at Denver. His fiction and essays have appeared in a variety of periodicals and anthologies, including *Men on Men 3* and *The Faber Book of Gay Short Fiction*. He is the author of the novel *Native*.

a n d r e w   h o l l e r a n is the author of the novels *Dancer from the Dance* and *Nights in Aruba*, and *Ground Zero*, a book of essays.

a r n i e   k a n t r o w i t z is associate professor of English at the College of Staten Island, City University of New York. He was vice-president of Gay Activists Alliance (GAA/NY) and a founding member of the Gay and Lesbian Alliance Against Defamation (GLAAD). He is the author of *Under the Rainbow: Growing Up Gay*, an autobiography; his essays, poems, and stories have appeared in *The New York Times, The Village Voice, Gaysweek, OutWeek, QW, Poets for Life, Personal Dispatches, Hometowns, A Member of the Family, Leather Folk*, and other publications. He lives in New York City with his lover, Lawrence Mass.

m i c h a e l   l. is a writer well known in the gay and lesbian community. He writes here anonymously in observance of the twelfth tradition of Alcoholics Anonymous, which states: "Anonymity is the spiritual foundation of all our Traditions, ever reminding us to place principles before personalities" (from *Alcoholics Anonymous*, Third Edition, 1976, p. 564).

e r i c   l a t z k y is the author of *Three Views from Vertical Cliffs*, a novel. His articles and essays on contemporary art, literature, and culture have appeared in the *Los Angeles Times, L.A. Weekly, Interview, Bomb*, and other publications. He has lived in Paris and Los Angeles and currently lives in New York City, where he was born.

a d a m   l e v i n e, of Philadelphia, is completing a collection of short stories and working on a novel. Previously he worked as a reporter for the *Gloucester County Times* in Woodbury, New Jersey, and as a freelance journalist. His articles have appeared in *The New York Times, Ford Times, The Philadelphia Inquirer, Sew News, Organic Gardening*, and elsewhere. He also runs a small garden maintenance business and is treasurer of the Spruce Hill Garden Club.

m i c h a e l   l o w e n t h a l is a writer and editor living in Boston. His stories and essays appear in many anthologies including *Men on Men 5, Sister and Brother, Flesh and the Word 2, Best American Erotica 1994*, and *Wrestling with the Angel*. His work has also been published in more than twenty periodicals including *The Advocate, Lambda Book Report, The James White Review, Yellow Silk, Art & Understanding, The Evergreen Chronicles*, and the *Boston Phoenix*. He edited John Preston's final book, *Winter's Light: Reflections of a Yankee Queer* (University Press of New England, 1995) and is currently working on a short story collection and a novel.

j i m   m a r k s is senior editor of *Lambda Book Report*, a Washington, D.C.–based review of contemporary gay and lesbian literature. He attended Emory University, where he graduated with honors in English, and Georgia State University, where he received a Ph.D. He taught English at Georgia Tech, and worked as a staff reporter for *The Washington Blade* and as a freelance news photographer and feature writer for *The Advocate, OutWeek*, and other publications.

n i k o l a u s   m e r r e l l was born in Spokane, Washington, and raised in Idaho. An Episcopal priest, he received a B.A. from the University of Idaho, attended graduate school in Mexico City, and received an M.A. from Santa Clara University in counseling psychology. His essays have appeared in *Hometowns, A Member of the Family*, and *Wilde Oaks*. He now lives with his lover and their adopted Honduran-born son in San Jose, California.

j e s s e   g.   m o n t e a g u d o began his writing career as a contributor to *The Weekly News* (Miami). His reviews and essays have appeared in *Lambda Book Report, Alive!* (Miami), *The Front Page* (Raleigh), *Chicago Gay Life*, and other publications, both gay and mainstream. He has also contributed to the anthologies *Gay Life, Hometowns, Lavender Lists*, and *Seduced*. Monteagudo lives in Plantation, Florida, with Michael, his lover of nine years, where he continues to be active in Congregation Etz Chaim and other community organizations.

m i c h a e l   n a v a is the author of a series of mysteries featuring gay criminal defense lawyer Henry Rios, including *HowTown* and *The Hidden Law*—for which he has won four Lambda Literary Awards. He is also the author, with Robert Dawidoff, of *Created Equal: Why Gay Rights Matter to America*. His autobiographical essays "Gardenland" and "Abuelo" were published in the anthologies *Hometowns* and *A Member of the Family*, edited by John Preston, to whose memory he dedicates "The Marriage of Michael and Bill."

j o h n   p r e s t o n was born in 1945 in Medfield, Massachusetts, and lived for many years in Portland, Maine. He was a pioneer in the early gay-rights movement, cofounding Gay House, Inc., in Minneapolis—the nation's first gay community center—and editing *The Advocate*. He was the author or editor of more than twenty-five acclaimed gay books, including the anthologies *Personal Dispatches, Hometowns, A Member of the Family, Sister and Brother*, and the *Flesh and the Word* series of gay erotic writing. He died of AIDS complications in 1994.

m i c h a e l   r o w e was born in Ottawa, Ontario, in 1962. A journalist and essayist, his work has appeared in *The James White Review, The Body Politic, Xtra!*, and numerous mainstream publications. He is a contributor to the anthologies *Sister and Brother: Lesbians and Gay Men Write About Their Lives Together* and *Flesh and the Word 3*. He is the author of a volume of poetry, *When the Town Sleeps*, and a nonfiction book, *Writing Below the Belt: Conversations with Erotic Authors*. He recently moved to Toronto from Milton, Ontario, with his life partner, Brian, and their two golden retrievers, Valentine and Ben.

s t e v e n   s a y l o r is the creator of the ancient Roman sleuth Gordianus the Finder, hero of a series of novels which began in 1991 with *Roman Blood*. Under the pen name Aaron Travis, his erotic fiction includes the novel *Slaves of the Empire* and several short story collections. He divides his time between homes in Berkeley, California, and Amethyst, Texas.

e d   s i k o v is a film historian and critic living in New York City. A graduate of Haverford College, he earned a doctorate in film studies at Columbia University. He is the author of *Laughing Hysterically: American Screen Comedies of the 1950s, Screwball*, and the *American Cinema Study Guide*, as well as articles for *Premiere, Connoisseur, The Village Voice*, the *New York Native*, the *People with AIDS Coalition Newsline*, and other publications. He has taught courses in film and gay and lesbian culture at Columbia and at Colorado College.

l a u r e n c e   t a t e has contributed to three previous anthologies edited by John Preston. He lives in Washington, D.C., and works in the nonprofit sector.

copyrights

The typeface used in this book is one of many versions of Garamond, a modern homage to—rather than, strictly speaking, a revival of— the celebrated fonts of Claude Garamond (c. 1480–1561), the first founder to produce type on a large scale. Garamond's type was in- spired by Francesco Griffo's De Ætna type (cut in the 1490s for Venetian printer Aldus Manutius and revived in the 1920s as Bembo), but its letter forms were cleaner and the fit between pieces of type improved. It therefore gave text a more harmonious overall appearance than its predecessors had, becoming the basis of all romans created on the Continent for the next two hundred years; it was itself still in use through the eighteenth century. Besides the many "Garamonds" in use today, other typefaces derived from his fonts are Granjon and Sabon (despite their being named after other printers).